THE CURSED HEIR

HEATHER ATKINSON

Boldwood

First published in Great Britain in 2022 by Boldwood Books Ltd.

Copyright © Heather Atkinson, 2022

Cover Design: Alice Moore Design

Cover Photography: Shutterstock

The moral right of Heather Atkinson to be identified as the author of this work has been asserted in accordance with the Copyright, Designs and Patents Act 1988.

All rights reserved. No part of this book may be reproduced in any form or by any electronic or mechanical means, including information storage and retrieval systems, without written permission from the author, except for the use of brief quotations in a book review.

This book is a work of fiction and, except in the case of historical fact, any resemblance to actual persons, living or dead, is purely coincidental.

Every effort has been made to obtain the necessary permissions with reference to copyright material, both illustrative and quoted. We apologise for any omissions in this respect and will be pleased to make the appropriate acknowledgements in any future edition.

A CIP catalogue record for this book is available from the British Library.

Paperback ISBN 978-1-80415-793-0

Large Print ISBN 978-1-80415-794-7

Ebook ISBN 978-1-80415-796-1

Kindle ISBN 978-1-80415-795-4

Audio CD ISBN 978-1-80415-787-9

MP3 CD ISBN 978-1-80415-788-6

Digital audio download ISBN 978-1-80415-791-6

Boldwood Books Ltd
23 Bowerdean Street
London SW6 3TN
www.boldwoodbooks.com

1

ALARDYCE HOUSE, JUST OUTSIDE EDINBURGH, SCOTLAND

Boxing Day, December 1896

Pain. It was all she knew.

Amy's hands were agony, the fingers broken, all the nails ripped from them, dripping blood onto the hard table she was tethered to. Her feet throbbed from the vicious bite of the red-hot poker.

'Amy, where's Robert?' said Matthew's cold, hard voice.

'Go to hell,' she retorted weakly.

More pain, the stench of blood filling her nostrils, but the blood was all hers.

Edward, her own cousin, grinned maniacally as he applied the poker to the soles of her feet again. As she screamed, she wasn't sure what hurt most – the physical pain or the pain of his betrayal. She'd run to him for help, thinking him her friend, one of the few she had in the world, when in fact he was a twisted psychopath, as twisted as Matthew, the father of her son. Well, she was damned if she was going to sell out her own child to this pair, even if it cost her her life.

The sound of the door opening caused Amy to jump awake. She'd dozed off in the armchair before the window in her bedroom. It had been snowing heavily for a couple of days, coating the land in a thick white blanket. Although it was only ten o'clock in the morning, the sky was almost black, blocking out what little light there was, but that was fine by Amy. The turbulence outside seemed to reflect her pain within.

'Are you all right?' said her husband Henry, concern etched on his handsome face. His hair was still so dark it was almost black but starting to speckle with grey, his eyes equally dark. In contrast, his skin was pale, almost as white as the snow outside, and his body tall and slender. Just the sight of him still made Amy's heart beat harder.

'Bad dreams,' she murmured. Even though nine years had elapsed since she'd been tortured and almost killed, the horror had never diminished and the dreams, although less frequent, still haunted her. She ran a hand down her face, as though she could wipe the nightmare away. If only it was that easy. The past was always present.

The snow started to fall again, tiny exquisite flakes landing on the glass before melting into water. The fire was roaring in the grate. Amy had been unable to get the cold out of her bones ever since she'd had her eyes opened to the horrifying truth about Robert, her eldest son, just the previous evening, ruining what had been up until then a wonderful Christmas day.

She held out one of her damaged hands to Henry and he took it. He was one of the very few people not repulsed by her hands. The fingers were twisted and bent after being badly broken by Edward, Henry's younger brother; the flesh where her nails once were was red and angry, even after all these years. When she was out in public, she always wore gloves. At least she didn't have to worry any more about Edward, who had been hanged for his sick crimes.

'Why don't you come downstairs?' said Henry. 'Everyone's asking after you.'

'I can't face them. What will I say?'

'I told them you have a headache, but if you don't come down, they'll only insist on coming up here to see you.'

'How can I look those good people in the eye? I've spawned a devil.' The memory of Robert's disturbing leer at one of the servant girls, eyes rolling back in his head and mouth stretching into a grotesque grimace, made her shudder. It had been the same look his insane, murdering biological father Matthew had pulled, and God knew she'd seen it often enough to know what it meant. She'd thought Robert was all goodness, that he'd inherited nothing from Matthew Crowle, but she'd discovered she was wrong only the previous evening, just when his engagement to a sweet, beautiful girl had been announced, and she couldn't bear it.

'This is not your fault,' said Henry. 'I will not have you blaming yourself.'

'I can't believe I never saw it before, I should have done,' she replied, feeling sick at the memory of those bruises on the wrists of Daisy, their pretty maid.

'You get ahead of yourself. We can't be sure he's even guilty. The maid never accused him, all she gave you was a look.'

'I saw him pull that same nightmarish face Matthew used to pull.' Amy shivered and it was nothing to do with the snow outside. 'There's no denying what I saw.'

'Talk to the maid first and get the whole story, please. We don't want to accuse him unjustly.'

'Very well. I'll talk to Daisy before approaching Robert.'

'Thank you. Now, why don't you come downstairs? The last thing we want is anyone asking awkward questions.'

She nodded. 'Very well, then.'

'I'm glad. It's not the same without you. Christmas is such a happy time in this house now. When I was a boy, it was so dour with Edward and my parents.'

Amy wasn't surprised. Henry's younger brother Edward had been hanged for the murder of four servant girls, as well as the imprisonment and torture of Amy herself. His mother Lenora, dead of cancer, had been cold and arrogant and had plotted to bring about Amy's downfall. His father Alfred had been murdered by Matthew to stop him from freeing Amy and Robert from him.

'Now, with you and our children, it's my favourite time of year,' continued Henry, touching her face.

Amy decided it was time to pull herself together, she didn't want to spoil this special time for him. 'Did I ever tell you how fortunate I am to have you as my husband?'

'You're not as fortunate as I am to have you as my wife,' he smiled. Henry's manner was usually so stiff and formal, it had become a habit with him since childhood after being raised by a vindictive mother to hide his emotions, but with Amy and their children, he allowed his playful side to come out. 'Now, come down for breakfast before the whole damn house ventures up here.'

Amy took his hand and allowed him to lead her to the door, feeling sick with foreboding, wondering how she was going to look upon her oldest son with love again.

* * *

'Amy, you're feeling better?' smiled Mr Buchanan. 'You rushed off very quickly last night.' He and his wife Mildred had become firm family friends. He was the family solicitor and had been a staunch supporter of Amy throughout her recovery after her imprisonment and torture at Edward's hands. The majority of society had ostracised their family in the aftermath, when all Amy's secrets had tumbled out into the public domain – that she had had an affair with a servant and produced an illegitimate child, and that the father of that child had turned out to be just as insane and evil as Edward Alardyce. But Mr Buchanan and his wife refused to bow to public pressure and had maintained their close friendship with the Alardyces. It was only now, nine years later, that society was starting to open its doors to them again, mainly thanks to Henry's wealth and influence. Not that he and Amy were concerned with society – they were happy in each other's company and the company of their family and close friends, but there were their children's futures to consider, so they were gradually building bridges.

'I am, thank you, Arthur,' she replied. 'I had an awful headache, but it's gone now. It must have been all the excitement yesterday.'

'And the surprise of your son getting engaged to Jane probably contributed.'

Amy's stomach lurched but she managed to force a smile.

'Sit down, dear, you need to eat something,' said Henry, sweeping her into a chair at the massive dining table, the footmen furnishing her with tea and toast.

Amy gripped onto her toast so hard it snapped when the door to the dining room opened, but it was only Esther.

'Morning,' said Esther sunnily, taking a seat.

Esther was always cheerful these days and Amy thought no one deserved happiness more. She had been married to Matthew, Robert's real father, when he was masquerading as Matthew Huntington, who had only cared about sweet Esther's wealth. Amy had inadvertently taken a position as governess to Esther's niece Jane after she'd fled Alardyce and, despite the difference in their supposed stations, they had become friends. Esther had freed Amy from Huntington House after Matthew had locked her up when he'd discovered he was Robert's father, only for her to be imprisoned and tortured by Edward instead. Amy loved and respected Esther. After the suffering they'd endured together, a close bond had formed between them.

'Where are the twins?' said Arthur. He adored children, but all his were grown up and he was eagerly awaiting grandchildren.

'Still fast asleep, poor darlings,' replied Esther. After Matthew had died, she'd found happiness with William, an extremely wealthy man with a gentle temperament. He was just what Esther needed after so many years of Matthew's bullying. After being unable to have children with Matthew and thinking herself barren, she'd given birth to twin boys, who were now six years old. 'Nanny will see to them when they wake.' Esther looked to Amy. 'Are you all right? You hurried up to bed last night.'

'I had a dreadful headache, but it's gone now.'

'I'm glad about that, but you missed all the celebrations. Who would have thought, all those years ago, when Robert and Jane met as children that they would end up as man and wife?'

Amy swallowed hard at the memory of those two small children – Robert with his dark hair and black eyes and Jane, the little blonde doll with the china-blue eyes.

'We have a lot of planning to do,' continued Esther, taking her seat and tucking into her food.

'We do?'

'Yes, the wedding preparations, of course,' she smiled. 'Jane has already started writing copious lists.'

'Perhaps that could wait until after the new year?' said Henry, glancing at Amy. 'There's so much going on right now.'

'You're probably right, but I don't know if you'll be able to halt Jane, she's terribly excited.'

Amy stared down at her toast, willing away the threatening

tears. She loved Jane like a daughter and couldn't bear the prospect of that lovely girl marrying a devil.

When Robert entered the dining room, Amy felt as though she'd been frozen to her seat. She regarded him with fresh eyes, trying to detect any hint of the demon she now knew dwelt inside him. But there was none, he looked so happy and handsome. The resemblance to his biological father had never seemed more pronounced and her stomach lurched. With his thick black hair and eyes, sharp cheekbones and sulky mouth, he was Matthew reborn. Amy had always been able to see past that but this morning it was suddenly difficult because she now knew him to be his father's son in more than just looks.

'Morning, all,' he said cheerily. He paused by Amy's chair to kiss her cheek, his lips ice cold. 'Good morning, Mother. I hope you're feeling better?'

Amy looked to Henry, her tongue momentarily stolen. The sight of her husband's face restored her nerves. 'Much, thank you, dear. It was just a headache. Too much wine last night.'

'Don't you mean Scotch?' said Arthur, light blue eyes twinkling. 'I saw you tucking into the single malt.'

'Mother does adore her Speysides,' said Robert, patting her shoulder, causing her to go rigid. She wanted him to sit far away from her, she couldn't bear him near her.

'Are you sure you're all right, Amy?' said Mildred. 'You've gone very pale.'

'I will be when I've eaten,' she replied, picking up her mangled toast in an attempt to distract herself from Robert's malignant presence.

'Robert, sit down and let your mother finish her breakfast,' said Henry, noting his wife's discomfort.

'We hear Jane's already planning the wedding,' Mildred told Robert as he took his seat.

'I know,' he replied. 'She's bursting with ideas.'

'You'll want to marry as soon as possible, I expect?'

'Most definitely,' he said with his charming smile.

'Surely there's no rush, Robert?' said Amy, trying to control the tremor in her voice.

'Why wait? We love each other,' he replied, puzzled by the question.

Amy took a deep breath, screwing up all her fear and hurt into a tight ball. Fortunately, her experiences at the hands of Matthew and Edward meant she had become adept at this. 'One of a lady's prime pleasures in life is her own wedding. Allow Jane to enjoy the excitement and preparation. She will only get to do it once.'

Robert relaxed. 'Oh, I see, but she's as keen to become my wife as I am to be her husband.'

Amy couldn't even think about that. What if he unleashed his darker self on that poor girl on their wedding night? Amy couldn't stand it. However, it was vital she stayed strong to protect not only Jane but all the other women Robert might hurt. 'A wedding is a precious thing,' she said, looking to Henry, the sight of him fortifying her strength. 'Enjoy it is all I'm saying.' She took a bite of toast then let it drop back onto the plate. 'I have no appetite. I'll take a walk instead.'

'In this weather?' said Arthur.

'Amy is very fond of walking in inclement weather,' said Henry disapprovingly. 'And once made herself ill.'

'That was because I wasn't prepared,' countered Amy. 'This time I will be.'

She rose, the men at the table politely getting to their feet.

'If you insist, then I'm coming with you,' said Henry.

'I'll come too,' added Robert.

'No,' Amy practically yelled at him, forcing herself to calm down when he looked shocked. 'Finish your breakfast, dear,' she said more gently.

'Mildred and I won't be joining you either,' said Arthur, looking to his wife. 'We'll be warm and cosy before the fire.'

Amy managed to give them a tight smile before hurrying from the room with Henry, Robert watching them go with a frown.

2

'Slow down, Amy, you'll make yourself ill again,' said Henry, marching along beside her. Their boots crunched through the deep snow and it was an effort to remain upright, but Amy was determined, needing to exercise off some of her worries.

'It's my mind that's in pain, not my body,' she retorted.

'And the only way to put it to rest is to speak to Daisy. You may have it all backwards.'

'Oh, no, I don't. I'm finally seeing the truth after being blind all these years. Like father like son, that's what they say, isn't it?'

'I find it difficult to believe Robert's capable of anything like that.'

She stopped and rounded on him. 'Didn't you once think Edward incapable?' Her face crumpled at his stricken expression. 'Forgive me, Henry, I don't know what I'm saying.'

He embraced her. 'It's all right, but I insist we speak to Daisy and get the whole story.'

'We will. I suppose there's no time like the present.'

With that, she suddenly veered off in another direction,

circuiting around the back of the house, leaving Henry hurrying to catch up.

They headed towards the servants' entrance that led directly into the kitchen, all the staff busy with their duties. The army of servants stopped when Henry and Amy entered, stamping snow from their boots.

'I do apologise for the intrusion at such a busy time, Mrs Clapperton,' said Amy, addressing the redoubtable cook who ran the kitchen with a rod of iron. Even their butler, Rush, was intimidated by her, but there was no denying she was a very talented cook. 'We need to speak to Daisy.'

'What's that girl done now, my lady? I can deal with her, save you the bother,' said Mrs Clapperton, determinedly hitching up her considerable bosom.

'She's done nothing, but there is something I wish to discuss with her.'

'I see,' she said in a way that indicated she thought the whole situation strange indeed. 'She's in the scullery, my lady.' Mrs Clapperton looked to the houseboy. 'Billy, tell Daisy to go to Mr Rush's room.'

Billy nodded and dashed out of the room.

'Thank you,' said Amy. 'You may carry on.'

The kitchen burst back into life as the master and mistress left, heading down the passageway towards the small room Rush used as his headquarters. The man himself was absent, attending to his duties upstairs. Amy settled herself in the comfortable armchair while Henry stationed himself against the wall, arms folded across his chest.

'Don't look so grim, Henry,' said Amy. 'You'll frighten the life out of the poor girl.'

'Sorry,' he said, attempting to look more relaxed and failing.

There was a timid knock at the door and Amy called, 'Come in.'

A small, pale girl with huge doe eyes and a tiny heart-shaped mouth tiptoed into the room. Even with her light brown hair scraped back off her face and stuffed beneath a white cap, she was still very pretty. Small and delicate, easy to overpower. Amy shook the horrid thought away.

'Please sit, Daisy,' she said as gently as she could. The girl was shaking so badly, Amy feared she might fall down. 'Don't worry, you're not in any trouble, but I assume you know what this is about?'

Daisy replied with a timid nod and took the spare chair in the corner of the room.

'You know what happened to me years ago at the hands of evil men?' continued Amy.

'Yes, my lady,' said Daisy, flushing.

'Then you'll know that I have a great deal of sympathy for any abuse you may be suffering.'

'I... I hope so,' she replied, eyes filling with tears.

'Would you mind showing Sir Henry your wrists?'

The girl unbuttoned the cuffs of her sleeves with shaking hands and rolled them back to reveal the ugly bruises. Henry couldn't help but wince as he was reminded of the state Amy's wrists had been in after she'd been tortured by his brother. He inhaled sharply and shook his head while Daisy hastily buttoned up her cuffs.

'Who did this to you?' said Amy.

'I... I thought you knew, my lady.'

'I need to hear you say it. Please, Daisy,' she pressed when the girl remained silent.

The girl shook as she took a deep breath before saying, 'Master Robert. I'm sorry,' she cried, burying her face in her hands.

Amy had known it was coming but it was still a huge blow. 'When did this happen?'

'Two days ago.'

Amy's heart broke. This poor child – and she was only a child, Daisy couldn't have been more than eighteen – had endured something no one should ever have to. 'I need you to be very brave for me, Daisy, and tell me exactly what he's been doing.'

All the colour drained from her face. 'I can't, my lady. I just can't.'

'Would it help if Sir Henry left?'

'Er, perhaps,' she said, with an apologetic look Henry's way.

'I'll wait outside,' he told Amy, throwing Daisy an encouraging smile on his way out.

'Take your time,' Amy told Daisy when he'd gone. 'But you do understand that I have to know every detail if I'm going to make him stop?'

'I won't get into trouble, will I?' she replied.

'I would never blame the woman. You are the victim, Daisy.'

The girl nodded, wiped away her tears and sat up straighter in her seat. 'Master Robert used to be so nice to me, always polite and thanking me for working so hard for his family. On my days off when I went into the village, I would always bump into him and we'd walk together. I felt safe with him, even though he was far above my station,' she hastened to add, avoiding her mistress's gaze.

'It's all right, go on,' encouraged Amy.

'On one of our walks, he kissed me. I was so surprised I didn't know what to do and he is Master Robert so I... I let him. After that, he kept giving me little presents, I thought he was so sweet even though I knew there could never be any future. But I was confused too because I knew he liked Miss Jane, who's so beautiful and rich... I didn't understand. Then he asked me to meet him in the woods, there's a pretty nook beside a stream. Suddenly he wasn't so nice. He hit me and I fell then he started beating me. He ripped open the back of my dress and I saw a knife in his hand. I thought... I...'

Daisy's voice was choked with tears and Amy grasped both her hands in her own deformed ones. 'It's all right, you're safe now.'

Daisy nodded, keeping her gaze locked on Amy's face, finding solace in this woman who understood her suffering.

'He used the knife to cut open the back of my dress and my corset, then he beat my back with a stick,' continued Daisy. 'It really hurt. I screamed, I thought that would make him stop, but he said I could scream all I liked and no one would hear me. He said he liked my screams, they excited him... Are you all right, my lady?'

Amy reeled as she was flung back in time into that cellar in Edward's London house, strapped face down to the table, his teeth sinking into her shoulder. *Keep screaming for me.*

'Shall I get you some water?' said Daisy, drawing her back to the present.

Amy shook herself out of it. 'No, thank you. Just unpleasant memories surfacing. Please continue.'

'He climbed on top of me and pressed my face into the grass.'

'Dear God,' whispered Amy, not sure she could bear listening to this girl relate how her son had raped her.

'He didn't do that to me, my lady. He...' Daisy broke off, blushing furiously, fresh tears filling her eyes. 'He touched himself. I felt his warmth on the backs of my legs, and he made this horrible groan... I'm sorry,' she wailed before bursting into tears.

Amy staggered to her feet and vomited into the small sink in the corner of the room.

Daisy hurried to her side on weak legs. 'My lady, are you all right?'

Amy couldn't reply. She was back in that cellar again, the memory so clear it could have been yesterday, hearing Edward moan as his warmth landed on the backs of her thighs.

It seems you're just too damn exciting, he'd hissed in her ear.

'Robert,' whispered Amy, before starting to cry.

'I'm so sorry,' said Daisy, forgetting protocol and rubbing a gentle hand up and down Amy's back. Right then, they were just two women, all barriers pulled down by mutual suffering.

'How do I know you're not making it up?' said Amy, rounding on the startled maid.

'I'm telling the truth, my lady. I would never lie about something like this.'

'I was tricked years ago by a maid who worked here. She made me believe Henry was a monster when in fact it was his brother. She was his lover and her lies helped destroy my life. How do I know you're not trying to do the same thing?'

'I am not lying, I wouldn't. All I want is for it to stop,' she exclaimed.

'Then show me proof. Your word is not enough to accuse my son.'

Daisy's family might have been poor, but they were honest and proud. She tilted back her head. 'Very well, my lady. If you want proof, then you shall have it.'

She practically tore open her dress to reveal her bare back. She wore no corset and when Amy saw the state her skin was in, she understood why. Daisy's creamy flesh was crisscrossed with ugly red marks, permanent reminders of what Robert had done.

'He left me alone and bleeding in the woods,' said Daisy. 'Somehow, I found the strength to get up. It took me a long time, but I managed to get back to the village. I went to my friend's house. She took me in and helped me get better. I never told her who did this to me because I wanted to protect your family. I thought you had been through enough.'

Amy felt dreadful. 'I'm very sorry, Daisy. It's just so hard listening to such awful things about my own son.' She helped the girl fasten up her dress, twisted fingers fumbling with the buttons.

'I understand,' Daisy said in a tired, weak voice.

'No, it was inexcusable of me. I encouraged you to tell your tale, assured you I wouldn't blame you, then I turned on you.'

'I think you were reliving some very disturbing memories.'

Amy nodded, exhausted. 'Have you told anyone else about this?'

'No, my lady.'

'I would appreciate it if you would keep it that way.'

'I will, but I'm afraid of him. Twice since he's cornered me upstairs. I've always been very careful to only walk into the village with one of the other maids and it's making him angry. On Christmas Eve, he found me when I was making up the fire in the library. He pinned me up against the wall and said he would do all these horrible things to me. He said next time he would be inside me and it would hurt.'

'Robert will not go near you again, but in order for that to happen, you can't continue working here. Don't look so downcast,' Amy said when Daisy's face fell. 'I have a friend in the city who requires a new maid. It will be more money for you and she's a sweet elderly lady who lives alone and won't have any young males in the house. Would you like that?'

'Oh, yes, my lady, very much,' said Daisy, starting to cry again. 'Thank you.'

'You can leave in the new year. In the meantime, would you be able to stay with your friend?'

'Yes, I think so.'

'Good. I'll pay you three months' wages, so you don't have to worry about being out of work.'

'That's not necessary, my lady. I won't say anything.'

'This isn't a bribe, it's recompense for what you've suffered at my son's hands. Do you know if he's done the same to any of the other maids?'

'I don't think so, but I didn't discuss it with anyone.'

Amy nodded. 'Now go and pack. The sooner you're away from Robert, the better. Come to Sir Henry's study and collect your wages before you leave. I'll send one of the servants to accompany you into the village.'

'Thank you... I don't know what to say. I'm so grateful.'

'I'm the one who should be grateful, Daisy. I've been so blind. Thank you for showing me the truth.'

Daisy gave her a little curtsey before leaving.

Amy took a moment to compose herself. She had spawned a demon and fear for her son vied with fury. She'd been engaged to Henry when she was seventeen, after both her parents had died and she'd been sent to live at Alardyce with family who were virtually strangers. After embarking on an affair with Matthew Crowle, who had been first footman at the time, she'd found herself pregnant and left with no option but to marry Henry, her older cousin, in order to save her reputation. It only emerged years later that her aunt Lenora, Henry's mother, had ordered Matthew to seduce her in order to shame her and force her into marrying Henry, so her sizeable fortune would be absorbed into the Alardyce estate. But Edward had tricked her into thinking Henry was a monster so, rather than marry him, she'd fled to London, abandoning the man she now loved so fiercely. She'd done all that just so she could keep her son, and this was her reward – a pervert as bad as his father. Just the thought of her son thinking he'd got away with it and that his family were blind to his true nature was enough to make her burn with rage.

She looked down at her twisted hands, deformed in defence of her son, and the rage shifted inside her. She would put Robert in his place if it was the last thing she did.

Taking a deep breath, Amy stepped into the hallway and was relieved to see Henry waiting for her, receiving respectful yet curious glances from the servants as they passed, wondering why the master of the house was skulking outside the kitchens.

Before they could discuss Daisy's revelation, the housekeeper appeared before them, seeming to emerge from the shadows. Mrs Grier had worked for them for five years, replacing the dour Mrs Adams, who had been housekeeper here for decades. She was tall and thin to the point of being spindly. Her long thin white fingers played elegantly, almost sensuously with the keys hanging from the belt of her severe black wool dress. Her face was well defined, bordering on beautiful, but her permanent scowl ruined her good looks. Her blonde hair was dusted with grey and pulled back into a bun so harsh it seemed to stretch her skin. Neither Henry nor Amy were particularly fond of her, but their house was run with ruthless efficiency and the staff thought her firm but fair, so they tolerated her.

'Sir Henry, Lady Alardyce,' she said to them in turn. 'Mrs Clapperton's just informed me that you were speaking to Daisy. If the girl has done something wrong, I will reprimand her at once.'

'She's done nothing wrong,' said Amy. 'A friend of mine requires a new maid and I thought she might like the position. It will raise her in the world.'

'That is most generous, but you're so busy with the Christmas celebrations. I would have been happy to speak to her on your behalf.'

'I'm aware of that, Mrs Grier,' said Amy with a warm smile that melted against the icy countenance of the housekeeper. 'But my friend was badly let down by her last maid and she asked me to vet any possible replacement personally.'

Mrs Grier's eyes flicked to Henry. She wasn't a stupid woman, she was aware more was going on than they were telling her. The master of the house didn't usually come downstairs to deal with maids.

'Now we need to return to our guests,' said Henry, taking Amy's hand and leading her past the suspicious Mrs Grier. 'She's a very uncomfortable woman,' he whispered to his wife as they made their way upstairs.

Amy just nodded, already forgetting about the creepy house-keeper as she recalled Daisy's words. She was grateful Henry didn't quiz her about what had been said until they were alone in his study.

'Well?' he said, the moment he closed the door behind them.

'There's no doubt. Robert assaulted Daisy very brutally.'

'And you're certain she was being truthful?'

Amy nodded sadly and sank into the armchair by the fire. 'She showed me the injuries on her back. He lured her to that special spot by the stream in the woods then he beat her, lashed her back with a stick, then he...' Amy's stomach heaved again as the memory of Edward's sickening groan returned.

'Are you all right?' said Henry, hastening to her side.

'Fine,' she replied, swallowing down the bile.

Henry poured her a Scotch and held it out to her. 'I know it's early, but these are special circumstances.'

'Thank you,' she said, feeling the trembling subside as she gulped down the warming liquid. 'Robert did to Daisy what Edward did to me in that cellar when he got overexcited.'

Henry knew all too well what she was referring to, Edward had enjoyed explaining that part to him in sickening detail. He sighed and hung his head. 'Dear God. So he didn't violate her?'

'No, although he threatened to. I'm sending her to Mrs McLynn's in the city, she needs a new maid and if Daisy stays here, Robert will hurt her again. I dread to think what he'll do when he discovers she told on him. What frightens me most is that he acted in the exact same way as Edward and Matthew – he charmed and romanced her first, made her believe she was special, and once she was under his spell, he showed his true colours.'

Henry's face was even whiter than usual. 'It's happening again, isn't it?'

She nodded and grasped his hand. 'Only this time it will be worse. Robert's father was Matthew and he's related to Edward through me. He has both of their blood in his veins. He's going to be twice as bad as either of them.'

'We don't know that. Hopefully, if we act now, we can stop it in its tracks.'

'What if this is something that starts as manhood approaches, along with all its associated urges?' said Amy. 'When did it start with Edward?'

'Hard to say,' replied Henry thoughtfully. 'He always was odd, but I think he really started to change when he was about fifteen, sixteen.'

'Robert's seventeen.'

'We need to discuss this with Robert.'

'We can't with guests in the house, we have to keep this quiet. That'll be Daisy,' she said when there was a knock at the door. 'I promised her three month's wages as compensation.'

'Let's make it four months,' he said before calling, 'Enter.'

Daisy walked in and stood before Henry's desk, shuffling with anxiety, giving the impression that she couldn't wait to leave the house.

Henry dipped into his desk drawer, took out some money, sealed it in an envelope and handed it over.

'Four months' wages,' he said.

'Thank you, sir,' she replied, taking the envelope he held out to her and staring at it in astonishment.

'Has an escort been arranged for you?' Amy asked her.

'Yes, my lady. George is waiting for me downstairs.' George was their second footman.

'Good.'

There was the sound of a door opening further down the corridor and they heard Arthur and Robert conversing in their deep basses. Daisy physically jumped at the sound of Robert's voice, dropping the envelope on the floor.

'I'm so sorry,' she said, eyes filling with tears, groping to pick it up again.

'Don't apologise,' said Henry, walking around the desk and retrieving it for her when she failed to manage it with her shaking hands. 'You've done nothing wrong. Remember that.'

'Thank you, sir. I will.'

'You're welcome. I'll walk you back to the servants' hall.'

She curtseyed and Amy remained where she was to finish her Scotch while Henry walked Daisy out. She was exhausted already, and it was only 10.30 in the morning. Soon she would have to face her son, look him in the eye and pretend everything was all right until their guests had gone. When she did finally confront him, there would be shouting, denials, insults thrown back and forth. It would be awful. Robert would deny everything, of course, but she had all the proof she needed. She'd thought Robert was different, that his shining goodness had transcended Matthew's rottenness, but it seemed it was firmly embedded in his core.

'I escorted her to the servants' hall without incident,' said Henry, returning to the room. 'Poor thing was shaking like a leaf. She almost broke into a run in her eagerness to escape the house. Mrs Grier knows something's going on, you should have seen the look she gave me when I entered the servants' hall with a maid. We might not be able to keep this entirely secret.'

'Our servants are loyal. They'll keep their mouths shut.'

Henry regarded her with concern. 'You look unwell. Why don't you go back to bed? I'll make your excuses to our guests.'

'I will not cower from this, and I have to face Robert eventually. The longer I leave it, the harder it will get.'

'I applaud your courage and I'll be right beside you.'

Amy got to her feet and kissed him. 'I must have done something right in my sinful life to have found you. I love you so very much.'

'I love you too and we will tackle this together.'

She flung her arms around his neck. 'Thank you.'

'You're welcome,' he said, hugging her. 'By the way, Nanny told me John and Stephen are awake and asking for you.' These were their younger children. John was five and Stephen was three. Their older sister, Lydia, was six. Henry was father to all three. Only Robert had a different father, although Henry went to great pains to make sure he never felt like an outsider. Now he was afraid all his efforts had been in vain.

'I'll go to them,' said Amy. 'Are they in the schoolroom?'

'I'm afraid not. They've had breakfast and they're in the drawing room with the others.'

Amy took a deep breath. 'Then it's time to face Robert. I can't cope with this without you, Henry.'

'You won't have to, I promise, and you can do this. After all you've endured, you have the strength.'

She gave him an uncertain smile as they left the study and made their way towards the drawing room. Robert's deep voice was audible as they approached the door. Her grip tightened on Henry's arm as he pushed open the door and they stepped inside.

'Mama,' cried five-year-old John, hurling himself at her skirts. 'It's Boxing Day.'

'I know, sweetheart,' she said, keeping her gaze locked on the top of his head so she wouldn't have to look at her eldest child, who occupied a chair by the window, talking with Arthur.

'I want to play in the snow,' announced John. 'Nanny says it's too cold.'

'I'll take you out later, but only for a short while,' replied Amy.

John was just like his mother. He couldn't stand being cooped up inside all day either. They both particularly suffered in the winter months. Henry was perfectly at home by the fire with a book, as were Lydia and Stephen.

'Are you all right, Mother?'

It was Robert's voice. Amy didn't want to look at him, she wasn't sure what her reaction would be, so she kept her gaze fixed on John as she replied, 'Much better, thank you.'

Fortunately, everyone's attention was taken off her when Jane entered the room. Amy couldn't help but look at Robert as he rose to greet his bride-to-be, clasping both her hands in his own and gazing at her adoringly. Amy's attention was drawn to his hands. They were large and powerful, and she was revolted by them, now she knew what they were capable of.

Robert led Jane to the couch so he could sit beside her, the happiness shining from the girl's eyes breaking Amy's heart.

William, Esther's husband, was the last to enter the room. He did enjoy a lie-in.

'I slept like a log last night,' he said. 'Your beds are so extremely comfortable, Amy.'

'Thank you,' she replied distractedly.

'Bless, look at those two,' smiled Esther, nodding at Robert and Jane, who were oblivious to the rest of the room. 'They're such a perfect match, aren't they?' Esther frowned when Amy failed to reply. 'Aren't they?'

But Amy was too busy watching Robert and Jane.

'Amy,' said Esther, patting her arm. 'Is something wrong?'

Amy knew she would have to tell her friend the truth at some point, but not today. She would let Esther enjoy the festive period before casting a huge shadow over her life.

'Sorry, I was miles away,' she said.

'Is it that headache? Do you still have it?'

'A tad, and it's wearing me down.'

'Come on, John, let your poor mother sit down,' said Esther, ushering the boy back to play with his brother and insisting Amy take a seat. Henry immediately took his place beside her. The conversation went on around Amy, everyone laughing and joking, but she was incapable of joining in. She couldn't keep her gaze off Robert and Jane. She wanted to leap up and scream at him to take his filthy hands off her.

'Amy, you must stop staring,' Henry whispered in her ear.

'Sorry,' she said, blinking back tears.

'Father,' said Robert's deep voice, cutting through all the other conversation in the room. 'Can we arrange for the banns to be read soon?'

'Er,' said Henry, glancing at Amy. 'Don't you want to decide where you're getting married first?'

'We've already decided. Here, at Alardyce Church.'

'That was quick,' said Amy, keeping her eyes on John and Stephen playing in the corner.

Robert's dark eyes flickered. 'You seem very concerned about the speed of all this, Mother?'

'I just don't see the rush. You're both so young.'

'Come on, Amy, they're in love,' said Esther. 'What's the problem?'

'No problem,' she replied, looking down at her hands.

'Your mother's just a little tired,' said Henry, patting her hand.

'Is that right, Mother?' said Robert.

She had to look him in the face. If she didn't, everyone would know something was wrong.

'Yes, dear,' she said, finally looking his way. 'So very tired.'

'You should go back to bed.'

'You know me, I'm not one to lounge about in bed until all hours. I'll have a lie-down after lunch.'

Robert stared back at her steadily and she knew he'd realised something wasn't right, but she was quite sure he didn't suspect what that was.

3

It was decided they would all go outside to enjoy the snow, which had finally stopped, a watery sun managing to penetrate the thick grey clouds. They all donned their boots, cloaks and gloves, except for Arthur and Mildred, who claimed the armchairs by the drawing room fire instead.

Robert played with the younger children, throwing snowballs before hoisting Stephen onto his shoulders, making him laugh.

'He'll make a wonderful father,' said Esther as she and Amy looked on.

'Yes,' was all Amy replied.

'Right, I've had enough of this. What's wrong? And don't deny it because I know you're unhappy about this wedding. I don't understand why, we've all been expecting it.'

'Nothing's wrong.'

'Don't give me that. I know you too well, Amy Alardyce. Is Jane suddenly not good enough to marry into your family?'

'Don't be ridiculous. Robert's not good enough for her.'

Esther was completely confused but, before she could quiz her the good man you are. We could have had so much more time together.'

'But we found each other again. I thank God for that every day.'

Amy's smile was tender. 'As do I, but what are we going to do?'

'First of all, you need to rest, you're exhausted. Hopefully, after a good night's sleep, we'll come up with a plan.'

'I need to sleep, I feel so fuzzy-headed. Could you call Hazel back?'

'No need. I can assist you to undress. I've done it often enough,' he said, stroking her cheek.

The playfulness returned to her eyes. 'If you're brave enough to tackle a corset, then feel free.'

'I've got the hang of it, and it only took me nine years. Now, turn around.'

She presented him with her back and he quickly unlaced the corset, leaving her in just her shift.

'I'm impressed,' she said.

'I know. Sit on the bed.'

She perched on the edge of the bed and he sat beside her to remove the pins from her hair. Amy closed her eyes and sighed with pleasure as he ran his fingers through it.

'You're still as lovely as the day you first came to live here,' he said, pressing his face into her hair, which was still a rich chestnut colour, the tresses thick and glossy.

Amy leaned back against him to enjoy his touch. Henry looked down and inhaled sharply at the sight of her large creamy breasts, visible through the transparent material of the shift, and his body reacted involuntarily.

'Sorry, I didn't come here for that,' he said. 'I only wanted to make sure you were all right.'

She turned to face him.

'You haven't finished helping me undress,' she said.

He removed the shift and kissed her, pressing her back onto the bed as she slid his jacket off his shoulders.

'Is this a good idea?' he said half-heartedly. 'You need some rest.'

'I've just endured one of the worst days of my life. What I need is my husband.' She pulled his shirt off over his head and cast it aside. 'Now.'

Amy clung onto Henry almost desperately as he made love to her, pressing her face into his neck, repeatedly thanking God for him.

Eventually, not even her worries about Robert could withstand the pleasure coursing through her body, so she gave in to it, letting her fears go. After insisting Henry lie on his back, she straddled him and bore down, moving frantically in an effort to rid herself of her frustration and fear until it all burst forth.

Amy flung back her head, her long hair grazing Henry's bare thighs, body convulsing, enjoying the feel of his warmth flooding inside her.

'I have an amazing wife,' exclaimed Henry, soaked with sweat, pulling her down to him for a kiss. She lay beside him and snuggled into his chest.

'I do feel better,' she murmured, already on the verge of sleep.

'Good,' he said softly.

She drifted off with a smile on her face.

* * *

Amy knew before she even opened her eyes that something was wrong. A lethargy had taken hold of her, so virulent she was unable to move, and her skin was burning.

Henry's voice sounded far away and she couldn't understand what he was saying. She'd felt like this before only twice in her life – once as a child and the second time when she was seventeen and had come to live at Alardyce. She'd got soaked to the skin after a walk in the rain and had succumbed to a fever. Amy surmised that this time, the pressure of what she had learnt about Robert had done for her.

She managed to force her eyes open, and Henry's blurred face hovered over her, his handsome features vague. He disappeared from view and she tried to turn her head, needing to see him, but she couldn't move. Then Hazel was standing over her, slipping her nightgown on over her head to hide her nakedness and brushing her hair. Why was she bothering? The penny dropped when Dr Parlow walked into the room, the young, dynamic doctor who had been so kind to her when she was pregnant with Robert. He was older now, of course, hair receding and a little plumper, but he was still the good, kind man who had permanently replaced the crotchety old doctor who had patched up the maids at Alardyce House – victims of Edward's sick desires – and said nothing to the authorities. She was glad Dr Parlow was here and not him.

'Amy, how are you?' he said, peering down at her.

She tried to reply but her tongue was thick in her mouth and instead she released an unintelligible groan. To her relief, Henry appeared beside him and her hand groped across the bed towards him.

'It's all right, darling, Dr Parlow will get you well again.' Henry's words were meant to be comforting but the worry in his eyes spoilt it. 'She had this before, years ago,' he told the doctor.

'Yes, I remember attending to her,' replied Parlow. 'Perhaps you should wait outside while I examine her, Sir Henry? Her maid can assist me if necessary.'

'I'm not leaving her,' he retorted.

Parlow nodded approvingly. This wasn't a common stance for the husbands of his wealthy patients to take, and he found Sir Henry's concern for his wife touching.

After performing a swift examination, Parlow announced, 'She has a fever and her temperature is dangerously high. I have some Warburg's Tincture in my bag, that should break her fever. Fortunately, I have it in liquid form, because she certainly can't manage the tablets,' he said, measuring out a dose before dripping it into her mouth.

'I knew we shouldn't have gone out for that walk in the snow yesterday,' said Henry.

'That wouldn't have helped. Lady Alardyce, you must stop taking walks in bad weather,' chided the doctor.

But she couldn't hear him.

'My God,' exclaimed Henry when her eyes rolled back in her head. 'Look at her. Will she recover?'

'She's a very strong woman,' replied Parlow, neatly dodging the question. 'You must keep all the other members of the family away, especially the young children, just in case it's contagious. We can't afford to take any chances.'

'I will attend to her myself.'

Parlow was unable to disguise his astonishment. 'As you wish but, as I said, this could be contagious.'

'No one in the house caught it the last time she was ill.'

'As long as you're aware of the risk.'

'I am.'

Parlow packed up his things. 'I'll visit this evening. There's nothing more I can do for now. Keep the room well aired and her head elevated. Bathe her regularly with cold water to keep her cool. If the situation changes, contact me immediately.'

After giving Henry a list of dos and don'ts, the doctor left Henry alone with his wife. Henry dragged a chair to her bedside, picked up the flannel Hazel had provided, dipped it into the bowl of cold water and used it to bathe Amy's forehead. There was nothing else he could do.

He was forced to stop a few minutes later when she started to toss and turn violently on the bed. The last time she'd been ill like this, he'd kept a similar vigil by her bedside. His mother had been hoping she'd die, his father had a morbid fear of sickness and the maid Nettie had only done the bare minimum. He was the one who'd mopped her brow, who'd dripped water onto her dry lips and held her hand during the terrifying nightmares. But she hadn't even been aware he was there. Not only had he nursed her through her sickness, he'd also protected her from Edward, who he was sure had intended to exploit her while she was helpless. Then, when she was recovered and lucid again, she'd awoken to find him in her room and had assumed he was there to hurt her thanks to Edward's lies. Now was so different, she'd been reaching out to him as the doctor had examined her. She needed him and he was damned if he was going to lose her.

It wasn't the snow that had done this to her, it was grief. The last time this had happened, she'd just lost both parents and had been forced to live in an unwelcoming house with unfeeling strangers. This time, her own son's evil had laid her low.

When she'd settled down, he started to bathe her face again, frightened by how her skin burned. She began to murmur his name.

'I'm here,' he said, clasping her hand. 'I won't leave you.'

She didn't respond.

A knock at the door had him leaping to his feet. 'Don't come in,' he cried, afraid it was one of the children.

He opened the door a crack and peered out, dismayed to see it was Robert.

'You can't come in,' he practically snarled at him.

Robert was taken aback. 'I want to see her.'

'Well, you can't.' Henry took a deep breath to calm himself. 'The doctor said it could be contagious, especially to the young and infirm.'

'There's nothing wrong with me and, if you hadn't noticed, I'm not a child any more.'

'I'm not taking any chances. Anyone who comes in here is at risk. You have to watch over the younger children. Without me or your mother, they'll need you.'

'I want to see her, she's my mother.'

'Please, Robert. You need to be the man of the house now.'

This statement pacified Robert and he lifted his head and threw back his shoulders. 'I can do that, Father, just leave everything to me.'

'Thank you, I appreciate it.'

'Arthur and Mildred are leaving. They said to pass on their apologies, they don't want to abandon Mother in her time of need, but Mildred has a weak heart and she can't risk any illness.'

'Of course she can't, I understand and so will Amy. She should leave, as should Esther and her family.'

'There's no need...'

'There's every need. They have two young children. I understand you're reluctant to release Jane, but I assume you don't want her to get sick?'

Robert nodded. 'You're right, I don't.'

'Of course not. I need you to oversee their departure. They can return when your mother's well again.'

Robert nodded again, running an anxious hand through his hair, attempting to see into the room over Henry's shoulder and failing.

'I've got to get back to your mother,' said Henry. 'Now please do as I ask.'

'I will, I promise.'

'Thank you, Robert,' he said before shutting the door. At least Jane would be protected from him for a little while.

* * *

'I don't want to leave you,' exclaimed Jane, clinging onto Robert.

'And I don't want you to leave but I am not risking you getting ill,' replied Robert. 'I will allow nothing to delay our wedding.'

'Robert's right,' said William. 'We can stay in Edinburgh, there's no need for us to return to London.'

'Yes, because I am not leaving until I know Amy is recovered,' said Esther, tears shining in her eyes.

'There,' William kindly told Jane. 'We won't be far.'

'And the twins can't stay here,' said Robert. 'It's for the best.'

'I suppose,' pouted Jane.

'We'll give you a minute to say goodbye,' said Esther, nodding at her husband.

They joined the nanny and the twins at the front door to give the young couple a little privacy, although they left the door to the room open.

'As soon as Mother's better, you can return,' said Robert, taking Jane's hand.

'I'll miss you,' she replied.

'I'll miss you too, but it won't be for long. You know my mother, tough as old boots,' he said, gazing into her blue eyes, trying to resist the urge to kiss her. 'Now I'm afraid it's time for you to leave.'

Jane nodded sadly and gave his hand a gentle squeeze.

'Please keep us updated, Robert,' said Esther as Jane finally tore herself away from her fiancé and joined them at the front door.

'I will,' he replied.

Jane looked back at him once more and he gave her an encouraging smile before she disappeared out of the door.

The younger children tore down the stairs towards him, accompanied by their nanny, a gentle, wide-hipped matron with snowy white hair.

'I'm sorry, sir,' said the nanny. 'They insisted on coming downstairs.'

'It's quite all right,' Robert replied, smiling benevolently down at his little brothers and sister as they clung onto him, looking scared.

'I want Mama,' cried Lydia.

'She's sick but she'll be better soon,' he assured her. John and Stephen looked up at him with big watery eyes. 'Why don't you go and play?' Robert suggested. 'It'll take your mind off it.'

'I want Mama,' repeated Lydia more firmly. Just like her mother, she was stubborn to a fault.

'I'll tell you what I'll do – if you go and play nicely for Nanny then I'll see how Mother is and let you know.'

'Fine,' muttered Lydia, finally releasing him.

'I'll be up to see you as soon as I know,' he called as Nanny ushered the children out of the room and back upstairs.

Robert returned to the drawing room which, for the first time in days, was empty and silent. Glancing at the clock, he saw it was ten o'clock. A wicked smile split his face and, rather than go upstairs to his mother's room, he wandered down the corridor towards the library instead. His heart leapt in his chest as he pushed open the door, excitement making his hands shake.

He stepped inside and stopped in his tracks, anger replacing the excitement. 'Who the devil are you?'

The mousy girl straightened up from stoking the fire and curtseyed, thin limbs shaking with nerves.

'Winnie, sir. I'm the new housemaid.'

He regarded her stooped, lanky frame, dull grey eyes and spotty skin with distaste.

'Where's Daisy?'

'Gone, sir.'

'Where?'

'I heard she took a position in the city.'

Her eyes widened when he advanced on her, looking murderous.

'Is something wrong, Master Robert?' said a voice behind him.

Robert spun on his heel to see Rush. 'I wasn't aware we had a new maid.'

'Winnie is a very conscientious worker,' he replied. 'We're fortunate to have her.'

'Yes, fortunate,' hissed Robert before stalking out through the door.

Rush watched him go through narrowed eyes. 'Get back to your work, girl,' he told Winnie kindly.

She nodded and returned to stoking the fire. Rush noted her hands were shaking.

4

'Thank you,' Henry told Hazel as she placed a tray of food and drink on Amy's bedside cabinet. 'But I'm not sure I can stomach it.'

'You need to keep up your strength, sir,' she replied.

'You could have left the tray by the door. It's not necessary for you to come in and put yourself at risk,' he said, without taking his eyes off Amy.

She lay prone on the bed, her skin a deep blush and beaded with sweat, her hair and gown soaking wet. Hazel had already changed her gown once that morning, but it was saturated again.

'With respect, sir, I will not abandon my mistress when she needs me the most.'

'That's very good of you, I'm very grateful. How are the children?'

'Naturally they're upset, sir. They want their parents, but Robert and the nanny are keeping them in order.'

'And how is Master Robert?'

Hazel was puzzled by the bitterness in his tone but didn't comment on it. 'Upset, sir.'

Henry slumped into his seat, staring miserably at Amy. 'It's been a full day now and she's not getting any better.'

'She will, sir, I'm sure of it.'

He shot out of his chair when Amy's breathing suddenly became more laboured.

'Amy?' he yelled. 'Amy?'

'She's struggling to breathe, sir,' exclaimed Hazel.

'Get Dr Parlow. Now.'

As Hazel dashed out of the room, Henry hauled Amy higher up the pillows in an attempt to help her breathe, her chest rattling alarmingly. His efforts made no difference so he tried dripping water into her mouth, but she couldn't swallow and it dribbled down her chin.

'Oh, God, Amy, please,' he cried, completely losing his grip on his calm. Not knowing what else to do, he climbed onto the bed beside her and held her in his arms, attempting to get her into a position that would make it easier for her to breathe, but nothing seemed to work, and the room filled with the sound of her wheezing.

Ten minutes later, Hazel burst back into the room, followed by Dr Parlow and Robert.

'Help her,' Henry yelled at him, so concerned for Amy he failed to notice the latter.

'Lie her back on the bed please, Sir Henry,' said the doctor, shrugging off his coat and placing his bag on the bed. He conducted a swift examination. 'Her throat is swollen, which is making it difficult for her to breathe.'

'Then do something.'

The doctor produced a medicine from his bag and tipped it down Amy's throat but once again most of it spilled out of her mouth, the little that did get down her throat having no effect.

'It's not working,' said Henry. 'Try something else.'

'There is nothing else, I'm afraid.'

Henry's frantic eyes finally noticed Robert, who was standing at the back of the room, staring at his mother with a frightened expression. 'Fetch Mrs Magrath from the village,' he ordered him.

'You can't bring her in,' protested Parlow. 'Her remedies are unorthodox to say the least.'

'You can't do anything for her,' Henry roared at him. 'Robert. Magda. Now.'

Robert nodded and charged out of the room while Hazel stood quietly in the corner, tears in her eyes.

'I must get some air into her,' said Parlow, worried by how blue Amy's lips had gone. Tilting back her head, he attempted to breathe into her mouth. He was still attempting this fifteen minutes later when the door opened and Robert led in Magda.

'Magda, thank God,' said Henry. 'She has a fever and she can't breathe.'

'Right,' said Magda, dumping on the bed a large carpet bag that dwarfed Parlow's Gladstone bag. She delved inside and pulled out a pestle and mortar and a bunch of herbs.

'I'm sorry, Sir Henry, but I'm a respected medical man,' said Parlow. 'I can't be party to this witchery. If you need me, I'll be waiting downstairs.'

With that, he stalked out of the room. Henry didn't even notice he'd gone as he watched Magda throw the herbs into the mortar and grind them up with the pestle before igniting the mess. Nor did he mind when she closed her eyes and chanted over it. If witchery was going to save his wife's life, then he was all for it. Besides, Amy said Magda wasn't a witch, just an immensely clever woman men were jealous of. That was all the reference he needed.

'She can't swallow, so she needs a preparation she can inhale,' explained Magda.

'Hurry, please,' said Henry, taking Amy's hand as her spine arched up off the bed, her body desperate for air.

Magda leaned over her, wafting the smoke from the mortar into Amy's face. The concoction smelled extremely odd, but Henry wasn't about to object.

'What if this doesn't work?' said Robert.

Henry glanced at him, thinking he looked like a little boy again in his fear. 'Do not say that.'

Amy's body started to relax and she was able to take in deeper breaths, although her chest still wheezed.

'Father, look, it's working,' exclaimed Robert, still maintaining his place at the back of the room.

'I know, son,' he said, allowing himself to momentarily forget the monster Robert was purported to be.

Magda added water to the mix in the mortar and trickled some of it expertly down Amy's throat. The trembling and jerking subsided, the blueness vanishing from her lips. Henry settled her back into the pillows, stroking her hair.

'My remedy should sort out her fever too,' said Magda.

'Thank you,' said Henry. 'We should have brought you in when she first fell ill. Parlow could do nothing for her.'

'People are always reluctant to turn to alternatives, even when the situation is dire. I'm glad you didn't refrain from asking for my help when it was necessary because of what people might say.'

'My wife's far too important to let that stop me. You will be very well rewarded for this.'

'I seek no reward,' she said, pouring out the remnants of the mixture into a vial. 'Give her half of this in two hours and the rest two hours after that.'

'I will. Do you seriously want no reward?'

Magda nodded regally. 'I'll return tomorrow to check on her. If you need me again, don't hesitate to ask.'

'No, that won't do. What if she takes a turn for the worst and the snow comes on again and we can't reach you? You must stay here tonight as our guest, please, until she's over the worst.'

'If you insist.'

'I do. You'll be well recompensed for the imposition. Hazel, arrange a room for Mrs Magrath,' said Henry. 'Give her our best guest room.'

Hazel gave a little dip and nodded warily at Magda. 'This way.'

As Magda picked up her bag and turned for the door, she glanced at Robert and Henry saw her eyes narrow. Clearly, so did Robert, for he frowned back at her.

Henry turned his attention back to Amy. He couldn't concern himself with any of that now. All he cared about in that moment was his wife.

'She feels cooler already,' he said, pressing his hand to her forehead.

'I heard Magda has powers, but I've never seen her use them before,' replied Robert.

'She doesn't have powers, she's just very clever, as Amy always says.'

'She'll live, won't she?' said Robert hopefully.

'Yes,' he replied. 'Would you please see if Parlow is still here and if he is, fetch him up?'

Robert left and returned with the doctor, who appeared both amazed and dubious about the transformation in his patient.

'How did Magda manage this?' he demanded.

'She gave Amy a concoction to inhale, then, when her breathing improved, she got her to drink more. Feel her, the fever's already abating.'

Parlow put the back of his hand to Amy's forehead. 'The fever certainly seems to have broken but have you any idea what was in the preparation?' he said, picking up the vial and peering at the thick brown liquid.

'Just herbs.'

'Did she chant while she made this up?'

Henry hesitated before replying, 'No.'

'Sir Henry, you must be cautious. God only knows what's in it.'

'Whatever it is saved Amy's life.'

'And what of the side effects?'

Henry tilted back his head, lip curling disdainfully. 'If it hadn't been for Magda, Amy would be dead now. What use were you? None, that's what. If that's the best modern medicine has to offer, then give me Magda and her potions every day of the week. If all you're going to contribute to my wife's recovery is criticism, then you can leave, and Magda will attend to the well-being of every member of this house from now on.'

Parlow had no wish to lose his wealthiest patients. 'I apologise, Sir Henry,' he said, trying not to choke on the words. 'I'm only concerned for Lady Alardyce's health. That is my priority.'

'Concern noted. You may leave. Amy needs peace and quiet to recover.'

'Very well. I'll be back to check on her in the morning,' said Parlow before turning for the door, gripping his bag tightly, the only sign that he was angry.

'I'll stay with her if you want to get some rest,' said Robert. 'You're exhausted.'

'I'm not leaving until she wakes up,' Henry said, running a hand down his face, feeling the stubble rasp against his palm. He'd never gone so long without shaving before.

'A couple of hours won't make a difference.'

'It will to me.'

'I can look after her just as well as you.'

Henry forced himself to be pleasant to his adopted son. 'I know you can, but I need you to be the man of the house for just a little longer.'

'Of course, Father.'

'Make sure your brothers and sister are all right. No doubt all the commotion upset them. You can tell them your mother is recovering.'

Robert took a long look at his mother before leaving. Henry sighed and flopped back into the chair by her bedside. When he touched her hair, her eyes flickered open.

'Amy?' he said, delighted.

She released a groan as she fought to keep her eyes open.

'You won't believe how pleased I am to see you awake,' he smiled, blinking back tears. She would live. A question shone in her eyes. Although she was too weak for words, he still understood. 'You were very ill with a fever, but it's broken. The doctor couldn't help, but Magda did. I've asked her to remain in the house until you've recovered. Do you approve?'

She gave a slight nod, too weak for anything else.

'You're over the worst.' He kissed her hand. 'Rest and get strong again.'

Reassured, her eyes slid shut and she seemed to fall into a deep sleep. Henry resumed his vigil, watching her until sleep claimed him too.

* * *

Amy woke to a sense of despair. The only parts of her body she could move were her eyes, everything else felt like lead had been poured into her bones. Her throat was horribly dry and she ached for water, her mouth like sandpaper while her head pounded in a slow, persistent tempo. The raging thirst encouraged her to make a monumental effort to open her eyes. She was glad she had when she saw Henry slumped in the armchair, asleep. His clothes were rumpled, he was unshaven and his hair uncombed, flopping into his pale face. She'd never seen him anything but immaculate before, but she thought he looked adorable. Amy wanted to reach out and touch him, but she couldn't even raise her hand. With some effort, she managed to open her mouth and release a raspy groan that finally got his attention. His eyes snapped open and he sat upright in his seat.

'Amy,' he cried, throwing himself onto the bed beside her and kissing her. 'How are you feeling?'

She tried to say the word *drink* but her tongue stuck to the roof of her mouth. Fortunately, he divined what she meant. He helped her sit up before holding the glass to her lips. Amy drank greedily, the tepid water the most delicious thing she had ever tasted.

'Not too much,' he said, removing the glass. 'You don't want to make yourself sick.'

After Amy had a short rest, Hazel entered, bearing a tray with Henry's breakfast, and she looked delighted.

'My lady,' she exclaimed. 'It's so good to see you awake.'

'Fetch Mrs Magrath, would you, Hazel?' said Henry.

'Of course, at once,' she replied, putting down the tray.

Hazel hurried out of the bedroom and towards the stairs, halting when Robert appeared before her.

She gave him a small curtsey. 'Master Robert.'

'Don't give me that, Hazel,' he said, taking her by the arm and pulling her into his bedroom.

Hazel released an excited gasp when he pushed her up against the wall and buried his face in her neck.

'I've hardly seen you,' he said.

'I've been busy attending to your mother,' she breathed as he kissed her. 'She's just woken up. I must fetch Mrs Magrath.'

He raised his head to look her in the eye. 'And I appreciate all the care you've shown her.'

'I'm so fond of her.' Which was why her affair with her mistress's seventeen-year-old son was the source of so much guilt for her, as well as pleasure.

'Henry's been guarding her jealously,' said Robert. 'I'm amazed he let you near her. He seems to think he's the only one in the house who cares about her.'

'Sir Henry was protecting you, he even told me I shouldn't be in the sickroom, but I insisted.'

'Because you've got such a good heart.' The tenderness in Robert's eyes vanished. 'Why didn't Henry inform me?'

'She's only just woken up.'

'Then I had better delay you no longer,' he said, releasing her.

'Oh,' she replied, disappointed.

Robert cradled her face in both hands and kissed her. 'I will try to spend some time with you once Mother is improved.'

'I cannot wait,' she breathed, face flushed. She still couldn't believe this handsome man desired her. Her husband had died six years ago and no man had looked twice at her since, until this young god started paying attention to her. He hadn't made love to her yet, but he'd done other things she'd never even considered doing with her husband and she was completely enchanted. Of course, she knew there was no future, she wasn't a fool. He was engaged to Jane Parke, a rich society beauty, but she was determined to enjoy him while it lasted.

With one last kiss, he was gone.

* * *

'I'm pleased to say, Amy, that you're much improved,' announced Magda, after completing her examination.

After Amy had married Henry, Magda had started calling her Lady Alardyce as a mark of respect, but Amy had insisted she use her first name after all the assistance she had given her earlier in her life. Magda had diagnosed her when she fell pregnant with Robert and had done her best to guide and advise her.

'I anticipate a full recovery,' continued Magda. 'But I'm afraid it will take time, your body has been through a lot.'

'No more walking in the snow,' smiled Henry.

'I quite agree,' said Magda. 'I'll leave you to get some rest. I advise you to change bedrooms for a little while. This room needs to be properly aired and the bedding and mattress burnt. I don't think it was contagious, but it's best not to take any chances.'

'She can stay in my room,' said Henry.

'May I see the room?' said Magda.

'Of course. I'll show you.' Henry smiled at Amy. 'I won't be long. Hazel will stay with you until I return.'

Amy nodded sleepily, already drifting off.

He led Magda to a room directly across the hall. 'I thought she would like this room because it gets the sun and has a very pleasant aspect,' he explained.

'Yes, it's very nice,' she said distractedly. 'I wish to ask, has Amy had a recent shock?'

Henry swallowed hard. 'Shock?'

'She's a very hardy woman. I doubt a simple walk in the snow would be enough to bring about such a violent reaction. Has there been any sudden, unexpected news?'

'No.'

'Sir Henry, I'm privy to all your family's secrets and I've kept them well. Amy came to me for help when she needed it because she trusts me.'

Henry sighed. 'Something has happened, but as yet, only myself and Amy are aware of it. It's up to her to tell you.'

'Very well, but should she require my assistance, it's always there.'

'Thank you, Magda. I owe you so much. If Amy wills it, then certainly we shall confide in you.'

Magda nodded. 'Do you wish me to stay for longer?'

'Another night, if that's convenient?'

'It is. Now, if you'll excuse me, I wish to take a walk through the garden.'

'It would be an honour if you could join us for lunch,' said Henry. 'It's time I spent some time with my children.'

'Thank you, I shall. Will Dr Parlow be there?'

'No. He's gone home to sulk.'

'He doesn't approve of my methods, even though they work. He claims they're witchcraft when in fact all my remedies come from the mother of us all, Gaia.'

'Gaia?'

'Mother Earth.'

'I see. Well, in my opinion, they're more effective than his medieval remedies.'

'I appreciate that, Sir Henry. This room will do Amy very well. Make sure to keep it cool, don't allow it to become stuffy. Give her plain, light foods and plenty of liquids.'

'Yes, I will.'

'And fill it with thistles.'

'Thistles?'

'It's one of the old ways to keep the air in the room pure to aid recovery.'

'I see.'

Magda gave him a scrutinising look and Henry wondered if she already knew about Robert. He wouldn't be surprised if she'd guessed, she had her ways.

Henry called for Hazel, who assisted Amy to wash and change while the housemaids prepared Henry's own room to receive her.

'Who are you?' he asked a skinny and very unattractive maid who timidly entered the room.

She gave him a little dip, avoiding his eyes because she was so nervous.

'Winnie, sir,' replied Rush, appearing out of nowhere. 'She's replaced Daisy. I trust that's acceptable? She's a very diligent worker.'

Henry nodded, thinking her plainness would keep her safe from Robert's attentions. 'Yes, it is.'

Rush bowed and started to walk away.

'Rush,' Henry called.

He stopped and turned. 'Yes, sir?'

There was something in the man's eyes that gave Henry pause. Did Rush know more than they'd assumed? 'Nothing. You may return to your duties.'

Rush bowed again and slowly shuffled from the room.

5

'There you go,' said Henry, gently laying Amy back on his huge four-poster bed. 'Is that more comfortable?'

She nodded wearily, still too exhausted to talk, but her eyes were brighter and more alert. He'd carried her from her bedroom himself, not trusting anyone else to do it.

'The children are desperate to see you, but I've said not until you're strong enough,' he continued. 'I'll have lunch with them, so at least they'll have seen one parent. Hopefully that will be enough to keep Robert at bay until you're stronger. He's becoming very persistent.'

Amy's eyes flared with worry and Henry sought to reassure her. 'You don't have to face him until you're ready, I promise.'

Relief replaced the fear and she nodded again.

'I will do everything in my power to protect you from him,' he said, before kissing her forehead.

Amy smiled up at him and managed to raise a weak hand to touch his face.

'I need to join the others for lunch,' he said reluctantly. 'But I will be straight back here the second it's over. Hazel will attend to your needs. Try to get some sleep.' He didn't think that would be an effort for her as her eyes slid shut. He took a moment to watch her, making sure she really was asleep before leaving.

Henry opened the door and called in Hazel. 'She's asleep but don't leave her alone, not for an instant.'

'Yes, sir,' replied Hazel, surprised by the strictness of this order.

'Good.' He took one last look at Amy before leaving and headed downstairs. He didn't think Robert would do anything to his own mother, but he refused to leave her alone when evil dwelt in their home. She'd been subjected to so much already and he couldn't stand the thought of her being exposed to its toxic touch again.

The family were already gathered in the dining room by the time Henry arrived.

'Papa,' cried Lydia, leaping off her chair to hug him. Unlike other families, Henry and Amy had always encouraged their children to display affection and if there was ever a time his children needed a cuddle, then it was now.

The two younger children followed their older sister's example and all three of them clung onto him. Henry took a moment to enjoy their warmth before facing their fourth child, although child seemed a redundant word for the dark, brooding man sitting at the table. Robert had remained seated, his eyes almost black, and Henry knew he wasn't happy about being kept away from his mother.

'Robert,' began Henry. 'I do hope your sister and brothers have been behaving themselves?'

'They've been very good, despite the circumstances,' he haughtily replied, insinuating those circumstances were entirely Henry's fault.

Henry looked down at the younger children gathered around him and smiled. 'I'm so proud of you all. You've been so brave

during this difficult time, but you only have to endure it until
tomorrow.'

'We can see Mama tomorrow?' said Lydia excitedly.

'Yes, you can. It will be safe then.'

'Did you ask Magda's opinion on that?' said Robert icily, just as
the woman herself entered the room.

'My opinion on what?' said Magda as she was shown to her seat
by a footman.

'Why we can't see Mother until tomorrow.'

'That's right, I'm afraid. It's just to protect you from possible
contagion.'

'How do we catch something that she got from being out in the
snow?' he retorted.

'I don't believe it was from being in the snow,' she said. 'There
must be an underlying sickness and the cold weather brought it
out. Better to wait one more day than have you all coming down
with it. It would be particularly bad for the younger children.
Surely you don't want them to get ill?'

The darkness fled from Robert's eyes as her words made sense
to him. 'No, of course not.'

'Good.'

Magda stared at Robert until he was forced to hang his head
beneath the force of her gaze, embarrassed by his petulant display.
Henry wondered if her gifts allowed her to see directly into men's
hearts.

The children eagerly told their father about what they'd been
doing, which mainly revolved around their lessons and making 'get
well' gifts for their mother.

'Have you seen Jane at all?' Henry asked Robert.

'No, and Aunt Esther won't permit us to exchange letters in case
the contagion is passed through them,' he said miserably.

'A wise precaution. It must be very difficult for you.'

'It is, but at least this separation should soon be over. Father, I'd like to speak to you about the wedding arrangements.'

'Let's wait until your mother's recovered. I'm sure she'd be very displeased to learn we've discussed it in her absence.'

Once again, Robert was mollified. 'All right.'

The food was brought in on silver platters, putting an end to the awkward conversation. Everyone took their places at the dining table and Henry could turn his attention to the roast beef that was placed before him, wondering how long he would be able to get away with fobbing Robert off.

* * *

Henry returned to Amy after spending a little time with the children. Hazel was ecstatic.

'She woke soon after you went downstairs, sir, and she ate the weak broth Mrs Clapperton prepared for her and she drank two entire glasses of water.'

'That is excellent news,' he replied. 'I've spoken to Rush and instructed him to give you double wages this month. You've been an absolute treasure, putting yourself at risk of possible infection. Your loyalty to your mistress is very much appreciated.'

Hazel was stunned. 'Thank you, sir. That is so kind.'

She gave him a little dip, feeling even more guilty about her affair with Robert.

'I'll sit with her now. Take the rest of the day off, you've earned it. I've already arranged things with Rush.'

Hazel left the bedroom, Henry closing the door behind her, leaving her to wonder what she should do with this unexpected time off.

As she made for the servants' staircase, she was once again

confronted by Robert. It was a constant mystery to her how he managed to suddenly appear like that.

'Where are you off to?' he said playfully.

'I'm not sure. I've been given a day off.'

'Why?'

'For my service to your mother.'

'Yes, you have been very diligent, and Sir Henry does enjoy playing the great benefactor. Who's looking after my mother while you're absent?'

'Sir Henry himself.'

'Silly question, I suppose. He wants her to himself for a little longer. Well, I find myself with some free time too if you'd...' He trailed off as he realised someone was approaching from the opposite end of the corridor. Hastily, he took a step back from Hazel.

'What are you still doing here, Hazel?' said Rush, uncharacteristically cheerful. 'You have the rest of the day off. Don't waste it indoors.'

Hazel looked to Robert regretfully. 'I was just returning to my room to change when Master Robert stopped me to ask after the health of his mother.'

'We're all relieved she's on the mend. Now go on, girl, don't hold up Master Robert. He's a very busy man.'

'Yes, Mr Rush,' she replied, throwing Robert an apologetic look as she stepped past him.

'I apologise, sir,' said Rush. 'She's a very simple girl.'

'No apology necessary,' he muttered before stalking away, forced to go in the opposite direction to Hazel.

Rush watched him disappear, just to make sure he'd really gone before returning to his duties.

* * *

The atmosphere was joyful the following morning as the children charged in to see their mother. The bedroom had been filled with thistles, vases of the prickly plants adorning every available surface, and Henry was on his guard, ready to steer the children away from them should they get too close.

Lydia threw herself onto the bed beside her mother and flung her arms around her neck. It was still an effort for Amy to move but she had enough strength to hug her daughter.

'I've missed you all so much,' she smiled as the two younger boys jumped onto the bed and joined in the hug.

Amy's stomach dropped when she saw Robert hanging back, looking lost and left out. She kept in mind the memory of him as a little boy, which made it easier for her to look at him.

'Robert,' she rasped.

He walked to her side and dipped his head to plant a kiss on her cheek, Amy only just managing to stifle the shudder that ran through her at the feel of his lips.

'I'm so glad you've recovered,' he said.

Despite his casual greeting, she saw the genuine happiness in his eyes and the strong maternal part of her allowed her to grasp his hand warmly, melting that cold exterior of his even more, and he smiled.

'I'm sorry for nagging about the wedding when you were obviously unwell,' said Robert. 'I took your lack of enthusiasm for disapproval when all the time you were sick.'

'It's all right, darling,' she croaked. 'When I'm recovered, we'll have a good long talk about it.' *And you won't enjoy it*, she thought.

'Can you come downstairs now, Mama?' said Lydia.

'Not yet, I'm still too ill,' she replied, already fighting against sleep.

'Awww,' pouted the girl.

'Your mother's strong,' said Henry. 'She'll be back to normal soon enough. Robert's done a good job of being the man of the house while I've been occupied.'

'Good,' said Amy, hoping she sounded like she meant it.

The younger children talked animatedly about their lessons and the games they'd played. Amy could only listen with one ear. Robert was a sullen shadow, and she could practically feel the tension radiating off him. Why had she never noticed before how unsettled he looked, as though he was constantly on the verge of exploding? Where did her little boy go?

Eventually Lydia, Stephen and John reached the end of their stories and the nanny ushered them back to the schoolroom.

'Now they've gone, perhaps we can discuss the wedding?' said Robert brightly, the second the door closed behind his siblings.

'Not now,' sighed Amy, annoyed. Couldn't he see she was still far too ill for all that? 'I'm so tired.'

'Wait until your mother's stronger,' said Henry.

'But there's lots to arrange and the banns need to be read.'

'That can wait until the new year,' countered Henry.

Robert forced a smile. 'Of course. Sorry, I'm just eager to be a husband. We can at least have the banns read,' he pressed.

Henry drew himself up to his full height, arching a contemptuous eyebrow. 'Stop being selfish. Your mother's health comes before anything else right now, even your wedding. Are we clear?'

'Please, Robert,' said Amy weakly when he glared at his stepfather. 'I can't do this right now.'

She watched as his eyes grew blacker, giving her a cold, creeping feeling. Then he smiled that bright, sunny smile she knew so well. Was that the illusion?

'Of course, Father's right. I'm being selfish.' Robert kissed her cheek. 'Get some rest, Mother, we all need you back on your feet.'

With that, he left, and Amy sighed. 'I feel dreadful about being relieved that my son has left the room. But I'm seeing him in such a different light.'

'His true light, you mean,' replied Henry. 'Don't think about it now. You need to sleep,' he said, tucking her in.

'Stay with me, Henry,' she said, taking his hand.

'There's nowhere else I'd rather be. Look, I came prepared,' he smiled, producing a book before sinking into the chair by her bed.

Amy settled down to sleep. Something in her son's eyes had disturbed her but she felt safe with Henry maintaining a vigil by her side.

* * *

'Are you awake yet?' said an impatient voice.

Amy rolled onto her side, away from the voice, just wanting to sleep.

'Don't ignore me.'

She buried her face deeper into the pillow, wondering why Henry was speaking to her like that, but then he wouldn't. He'd never once spoken to her crossly in all the years they'd been together.

Her body went rigid. 'Robert?'

'No.'

Amy's heart leapt into her mouth. Impossible.

'Look at me,' said the voice.

'I don't want to,' she said, refusing to turn over, eyes screwed shut.

'You have no choice,' said the voice, full of threat.

Fearing what would happen if she didn't look at him, she forced herself to turn over, which took some time as she was still so weak.

Matthew was sprawled in the armchair Henry had occupied when she'd fallen asleep. He looked as handsome as she remembered in a smart black suit, dark hair neat, mouth sulky, black eyes reflecting the small chink of daylight shining through the curtains.

'Where's my husband?' she demanded.

His lips curled into an amused smile. 'That milksop? He abandoned you hours ago, he got bored.'

'You're lying. He gave me his word and he would never break it. This is a dream, and you are nothing more than a phantom. Go away.'

'It's not that easy, Amy. We have things to discuss. Our little boy's all grown up and he's feeling the urge.'

'I've no idea what you're talking about.'

'Of course you do. Daisy, the maid. He couldn't control himself but then again, she was a very pretty piece. And what are you doing about it? Carrying on as normal, pretending nothing's wrong.'

'I'm going to tackle him about it when the time's right. We need to keep this secret.'

'I agree with you there. I won't have my son swinging from the end of a rope like that dunce Edward.'

'Your partner in crime,' she retorted.

'Don't take that tone with me. He was your kin and his blood flows through Robert's veins, as does mine, and it terrifies you.'

'Yes, it does. Ours was an unholy union.'

'As I recall, it was very pleasant. Why don't you just give in to your illness so we can be together again?'

'You want me to die?'

'Why not? You wanted me dead so much you killed me.'

'Edward killed you.'

'I could have survived that injury, but you ripped that knife right out of me, knowing full well I would bleed to death.'

'You would have hanged for your crimes anyway, you said so yourself.'

'I've had time to reflect on that. I would have made myself out to be the hero of the hour, rushing into the house of a lunatic to save the woman I loved. I could have blamed it all on Edward.'

'I would not have allowed that to happen. I would have told everyone how you imprisoned Esther and me, how you beat me and kept me from my son.'

'No, you wouldn't. You remember how things were between us in the last minutes of my life? We kissed and you held my hand until I died. In that moment, we were one, just how we were always meant to be.'

'You were a bully and a murderer.'

'Not all the time. I did have my nice moments.'

'I don't remember any.'

'Yes, you do. On the desk in my study, for one.' His smile was wolfish. 'Judging by the way your cheeks are flushing, you remember it very well.'

'Just leave me alone. I'm happy with Henry and I've no wish to talk to a memory.'

The smile dropped and his eyes flared. 'Come with me.'

'No.'

He rose and loomed over her. Amy attempted to scramble away from him but failed, her body too weak.

'You'll come with me one day, Amy, I guarantee it,' he hissed. 'No one lives forever and when it's your turn, I'll be waiting.'

'No,' she screamed.

'Amy, Amy.'

'Leave me alone,' she cried, flailing at the figure standing over her.

'Amy, it's me.'

She opened her eyes and almost burst into tears of relief to see it was Henry.

'Thank God it's you,' she said.

'Were you expecting someone else?'

'Matthew,' she blurted out before she'd thought what she was saying.

His jaw tensed. 'Matthew?'

'It was just a dream,' she hastened to add.

'Well, of course. I mean, what else could it be?'

'Nothing. It just frightened me. He wants me to die so I can be with him. When I said no, that I love you, he told me he'll be waiting for me when I die.'

'Good God,' said Henry, pulling her into his arms. 'That must have been terrible.'

Amy clung onto him, trying not to show how upset she was by the dream. 'I'd like to speak to Magda.'

'About your health or the dream?'

'Both.'

'Very well. I'll fetch her.'

'You won't be long, will you?'

'I'll be as quick as I can, or I can ring for one of the servants to fetch her?'

Amy felt ridiculous. 'No, I'll be fine.'

'Won't be long,' he said, kissing her cheek before hurrying out of the room.

Amy lay in bed, trying not to look at the armchair, expecting to see Matthew sitting there like the Grim Reaper, waiting for her to die. She didn't want to give him the satisfaction, but death was something no one could avoid.

Henry returned with Magda.

'Sir Henry tells me you had a strange dream,' said Magda.

'I did. Matthew,' she rasped.

Magda turned to Henry. 'Could you leave us alone to talk?'

He looked to Amy. 'If that's all right with Amy?'

'It is.' Seeing the hurt in his eyes, she added, 'I need to do this.'

He nodded. 'I'll pop in on the children.'

'They'll like that,' she smiled.

Magda watched him leave. 'He is such a good man.'

'I know. I'm very lucky,'

'He was fortunate to escape his mother's and brother's darkness.' Magda's eyes pierced into her own. 'But I fear someone else hasn't been so lucky.'

'You know?'

'Since I've spent some time in this house, I see the darkness gathering around Robert.'

Tears filled Amy's eyes. 'Is it too late for him?'

'Not yet. There is some light left. We must act before it's extinguished entirely. I take it you discovered this shortly before your illness?'

'Just the day before. He attacked the maid, Daisy.'

'What did he do to her? I understand it's difficult for you to discuss, but I must know everything.'

As Amy spoke, Magda's eyes remained firmly fixed on her face. It took Amy a few minutes to complete her explanation and she counted that Magda blinked only twice, which she found odd.

'It's the same as Matthew and Edward,' sighed Magda. 'I've feared this for so long.'

'As have I, but Robert's displayed nothing but sweetness his entire life, so I thought he'd escaped it. However, it was all a mask. He's rotten underneath.'

'Correction, he's *rotting*. The process isn't complete yet.'

'So he can be saved?' said Amy hopefully.

'Perhaps, but he does have a lot of bad blood inside him.'

'And don't I know it. What can be done?'

'Temptation must be kept out of his way. You're fortunate you live in this isolated position.'

'The village and city aren't far away and he's a grown man now, free to come and go as he pleases.'

'I think the knowledge that someone is aware of his activities may go a long way to curbing them and the sooner he's told he's been caught out, the better. Thinking he's got away with it will only make him cockier and more likely to repeat the behaviour. He won't dare make a move, knowing his parents are aware of his true nature, and hopefully shame will overcome.'

'I was hoping you'd have some remedy in your bag for him,' said Amy with a wry smile.

'I would love nothing more than a cure for evil. Unfortunately, such a thing doesn't exist.'

'There's something else I wish to discuss with you.'

'Oh, yes?'

'I know spirits exist after the seance at Huntington Manor with the dead maid Matthew killed. Do you sense any here?'

'It's an old house, so naturally some spirits linger.'

'There's one in particular that I'm concerned about. Matthew,' she added when Magda frowned.

'You've had a visitation?'

'I'm not sure if it was a visitation or just a dream, but it seemed very real. He wants me to die so we can be together. When I refused, he said he'll be waiting for me when I pass.' Amy's voice cracked with fear, and she cleared her throat. 'So, what do you think? Can you sense anything? He was sitting in that chair over there,' she said, gesturing to the armchair without looking at it.

'Not really. It's heavy with sickness, which is blocking any other energies.'

'Oh,' said a disappointed Amy. She had hoped Magda would give her a quick and easy remedy to the situation, but it seemed that wasn't going to happen.

6

The rest of the day passed without incident and Amy managed to sleep right through until the following morning. Now she was feeling stronger, Magda returned to her cottage in the village. With all their visitors gone, Amy decided it was the perfect time to tackle Robert.

'I'm not sure this is a good idea,' said Henry.

'I can't put it off any longer,' she replied. 'It's an endless torture and I want it over with.'

'What if it sets back your recovery? I will not have you doing anything that puts you at risk.'

'The strain is only slowing down my recovery. I need to have it out with Robert before I lose my mind. Nanny's taken the children out for a walk. It's the perfect time to tackle him.'

Henry sighed. 'I can see I'm not going to dissuade you from this.'

'No, you're not.'

'Very well, but we tackle him together.'

She was hoping he'd say that. 'Thank you, Henry.'

'My brave girl,' he said with a fond smile.

'I think the word *girl* is stretching it a bit these days,' she said wryly.

'No, never. To me, you'll always be that beautiful, fiery girl who first came to live here seventeen years ago.'

'If only we could go back in time. I would have married you in a heartbeat.'

'And I would have sent Matthew packing and had Edward locked up.'

'How different things could have been,' she said sadly.

'At least we're together.'

'I wouldn't have it any other way.'

He smiled and kissed her before getting to his feet. 'I'll call Rush.'

Henry pulled the bell and they waited in silence for the butler to arrive.

'It would have been quicker if I'd fetched Robert myself,' said Henry, just as the door opened and Rush entered.

'Yes, sir?'

'Do you know where Master Robert is?' Henry asked him.

'Yes, sir. He's playing billiards.'

'Ask him to come here. Immediately.'

Rush bowed and left, leaving Henry to wonder if Rush was watching Robert, he always seemed to know exactly where he was.

Eventually Robert strolled into the room, hands in his pockets.

'You wanted to see me?' he said.

'Yes, Robert,' said Henry. 'Rush, you may leave us.'

The butler bowed and slowly ambled out.

'Is this about the banns being read?' Robert said hopefully.

'No,' replied Amy, feeling her heart break all over again. 'We've had some very disturbing news.'

His eyes widened. 'About Jane? Is she all right?'

'She's fine, it's nothing to do with her. Actually, it is, but she doesn't know it yet.'

'Mother, what are you talking about?'

'Daisy.'

In that split second between the shock of this single word and his recovery, Amy saw everything in her son's eyes and the turbulence that seethed inside him.

Robert hastily recovered and shrugged. 'The maid? What about her?'

'You've been hurting her.'

'I have not.'

'Don't deny it. She told me everything. She also showed me the bruises you put on her wrists and the marks on her back from where you beat her with a stick. How could you?' she yelled.

'It wasn't me.'

'She said it was.'

'And you take the word of a simple, stupid housemaid over mine?'

'You sound just like Edward and Matthew. They thought women, particularly servants, didn't matter and were only there to be used and abused.'

'I don't believe this. You actually think I'm guilty.'

'I know you are.'

'You're my mother, you know I'm not capable of hurting anyone, especially a sweet young girl like Daisy.'

Amy had to own he was convincing, just like Edward and Matthew had been, it was why they'd got away with their atrocities for so long, and she resolved not to let his lies blind her to the truth.

'I admit there was something between us,' he said, hanging his head. 'I did kiss her, but I love Jane and I told Daisy that. I thought she was fine with it but obviously not. This is a cruel trick to get back at me.'

'This is no trick, Robert. I spoke to her myself and I saw her fear, and those injuries were not self-inflicted.'

Robert was outraged. 'I don't believe this. Father, will you please tell her this is madness?'

'I'm not so sure it is,' he replied.

'You've let her convince you with her insane theories. I haven't hurt anyone,' he yelled.

'Yes, you have,' Amy yelled back, her emotions overtaking the weakness the illness had left her with.

Robert ignored her, deciding to appeal to Henry for help. 'Please, Father, I couldn't hurt anyone. You know me, you know I'm not capable.'

'There was a time when I didn't think Edward or Matthew capable,' he replied.

'I am not like them.'

'Oh, yes, you are,' said Amy, drawing her son's attention back to herself. 'I saw you.'

'Saw me what?'

'Saw the way you looked at Daisy on Christmas Day. It was the same look Edward and Matthew used to pull when they were contemplating doing horrible things to a woman. I should know, I saw it often enough. That was all the proof I needed.'

Robert burst out laughing. 'So you accuse me, your own son, of something so heinous because of a single look? The fever has addled your brain. Father, will you please talk some sense into her?'

'I trust your mother's judgement implicitly,' he said.

Robert's lip curled with contempt. 'You're as mad as she is.'

'Do you remember your time at Huntington Manor, Robert?' said Amy. She smiled when he blanched. 'I see that you do. Then you'll understand why I'm so afraid.'

'Mother,' he said gently. 'I'm not like Matthew. Bring Daisy here and we'll clear up this misunderstanding.'

'That's not possible. She's already left.'

'Then how can I possibly defend myself? Although it does seem pointless, you've already made up your minds that I'm guilty, regardless of anything I might have to say.'

'Why can't you just admit it?' said Amy, feeling the headache at the back of her skull returning.

'I refuse to confess to something I didn't do. Oh, this is ridiculous,' he said, stomping to the door.

'Where do you think you're going?' said Henry.

'I'm leaving. I've had enough of this farce.'

Henry placed himself between Robert and the door. 'This conversation is not over.'

Robert's eyes filled with aggression. 'Move before I make you.'

'Robert,' exclaimed Amy. 'Do not speak to your father like that.'

'So he's my father when you want me to behave, but when you're accusing me of doing unspeakable things, then Matthew is. Make up your mind.'

'Henry is your father,' she said. 'And you are not leaving until we've sorted this out.'

'How do we sort it out? I've denied it and you don't want to believe me. Must I suffer for what Matthew did?'

'I had hoped you wouldn't, but it appears you already are.'

Robert hissed out a breath, eyes flashing. 'This is your madness, Mother, not mine. Maybe you should be locked away in an asylum.'

Both Robert and Amy were surprised when Henry grabbed him by the shirt front and slammed him up against the wall.

'Don't ever speak to your mother like that again,' he said in a cold, hard voice. 'Have you the slightest conception of what she endured for you, you ungrateful little bastard? If you ever speak to her so disrespectfully again, I will throw you out of this house with nothing.' He was so furious his grip tightened on Robert's shirt and he pressed him back harder against the wall, his voice so steely it cut through Robert like a knife. 'If you want any chance of marrying Jane, then I suggest you stop with your ridiculous denials and explain why you did what you did to Daisy.'

Robert's face turned white. 'You can't stop us marrying.'

'We can and we will if we think Jane is at risk.'

'I would never hurt her,' he cried. 'I love her.'

'Do you even know what that word means?' said Henry, his voice dripping contempt.

Robert looked to Amy, astonished. 'I can't believe you both think so badly of me.'

Tears filled Amy's eyes. 'We don't want to, please understand that, Robert.'

'There's nothing to understand and I will marry Jane.'

Amy's voice was as hard as her husband's. 'Not if you don't have our permission.'

Robert looked positively malevolent. 'Jane will be my wife. I've received a letter from her. As you're almost over your illness, she's returning with Aunt Esther the day after tomorrow, then we can all sit down together and discuss the wedding, like one big happy family,' he said sarcastically.

'Robert, think. How can you marry her when you are the way you are? If you truly love her, you will not go through with this wedding.'

'I will and I'll tell you this right now – you two aren't invited. Let me go,' he said, attempting to push Henry away.

Henry lowered his arms but still stood before him, preventing escape.

'Let him leave, Henry,' said Amy, feeling tired and sick again, although her eyes flared with challenge. 'But we will discuss this again, Robert.'

'As far as I'm concerned, the subject's closed. Ridiculous,' he yelled before storming out.

'Well, that got us nowhere,' said Henry after Robert had slammed the door shut behind him. 'We'll never get him to admit it. What we need to do is catch him in the act.'

'That may be easier said than done,' she replied. 'He's going to be on his guard now.' She hesitated before adding, 'You've no doubt he's guilty?'

'None. I saw the truth in his eyes.'

'Thank goodness. I was starting to think I was going mad.'

'Don't let him plant that seed in your head. It was cruel of him to talk of madness.'

'He probably overheard Matthew threaten me with the madhouse, he did it often enough.'

'As did my mother,' he replied.

Lenora had wanted to have Amy locked away in an asylum so she could get her claws into her fortune, but Henry's intervention had put a stop to that.

He pressed a hand to her forehead. 'You feel hot,' he said with a worried frown.

'Because my temper's up. I'm not ill again.'

'You'd better not be. I'll ask Magda to take a look at you.'

'That's not necessary.'

'Don't argue, because I won't change my mind.'

Unlike a lot of his contemporaries, Henry was a gentle husband and he didn't put his foot down often, but Amy understood this was for her own good.

'As you wish, husband,' she said, head bowed.

'Don't try to look meek, Amy. It doesn't suit you.'

She raised her head and smiled. No matter how bad she felt, he could always make her smile.

* * *

Robert slammed the door shut and started to pace angrily.

'Is something wrong?' said Mrs Grier. He'd insisted on speaking to her and had practically dragged her into one of the little-used spare bedrooms.

'My parents know,' he opened.

'Know what?'

'About Daisy,' he yelled.

'I suggest you keep your voice down. The maids are working just down the hall. What did you tell them?'

'What do you think I told them? I denied it, of course.'

'How did they find out?'

'The stupid girl told them. I thought I'd terrified her into silence.'

'Clearly not,' she sighed, shaking her head. 'Our friend isn't going to be very pleased.'

'What do I care about them? My main concern is for my parents.'

'Did they believe your denial?'

'No,' he growled. 'I think Henry might have been swayed had it not been for my mother, who is resolute that I'm guilty,' he said, pronouncing the word *mother* sardonically. 'She believed that little scrubber over me.'

'That's why she spoke to her,' she murmured, more to herself than to him.

'That's why who spoke to whom?' he demanded.

'I'm referring to the day before your mother fell ill, when the master and mistress came downstairs to the kitchens to speak to Daisy. The mistress spoke to her alone while Sir Henry waited outside in the corridor, which I thought very odd. I was informed they'd discussed a new position for Daisy as a maid in the city.'

'So that's where she's gone,' he glowered.

'Actually, she's still in Alardyce, staying in the village with her friend Violet until after the new year when the position starts.'

Robert's lips curled into a smile. 'Thank you for that, Mrs Grier. I will be paying Daisy a visit to show her how grateful I am for informing on me.'

'What are your parents going to do?'

'I don't know, but I'm certain they won't let it go. They even said they might stop me from marrying Jane.'

'Then you must be on your best behaviour and not give them any more ammunition. If you go after Daisy, it will be obvious to them who is responsible.'

'You have a point, but I so dearly want to teach her the error of her ways.'

Mrs Grier watched as Robert's eyes rolled back in his head and his mouth stretched open into a wide leer. It didn't disconcert her, as it certainly wasn't the first time she'd seen this look.

His dark, fevered eyes turned on her and he smiled predatorily. 'You're a very attractive woman, a bit long in the tooth perhaps, but I often wonder what lies beneath those dowdy dresses.'

'Don't even think of attempting to find out.'

'Why, what will you do?' he said, advancing on her.

Mrs Grier stood her ground, hatchet-faced. 'I'm not a silly young maid, whelp. I've dealt with worse than you in my time. Now stop messing about and think.'

He released an irritated sigh. 'I've no idea, except to be on my best behaviour and convince them Daisy was lying. Mother's unwell, she doesn't have the stamina for a battle. She'll soon come round to my way of thinking.'

'Lady Alardyce has mettle. She will not be easily deterred.'

'I can handle my mother,' he said, running a hand down the front of her dress, enjoying the undulation of her breasts beneath the stiff material.

'Remember what I said, whelp. Now go, before the servants realise we're in here together.'

He just smiled before leaving, closing the door behind him. Mrs Grier cleared her throat and smoothed down her dress, impassive on the surface, while inside her heart thudded. She knew the game she was playing was a dangerous one. Robert was capable of so much more evil than he realised, but it was a risk she was willing to take to get the revenge she so yearned for on this family. She was the one who had helped awaken Robert to who he really was, with the assistance of their mutual friend. If it hadn't been for her, he would still have been that sickening puppy dog, hanging off his mother's apron strings. The day would come when not a force on earth would be capable of controlling Robert Alardyce.

7

Robert hid in the bushes, watching Violet's cottage, the cold seeping into his boots. Rage seethed inside him. The stupid little bitch who had betrayed him was hiding in that house, cowering like the mouse she was. She deserved to be punished for all the trouble she'd caused him.

He gripped onto a thick, snow-laden branch with his gloved hands, vision blurring as his eyes rolled back in his head. Sometimes his body had a mind of its own and he was incapable of controlling it, just like these curious violent impulses that coursed through him. He'd no idea where they'd come from, they'd crept up on him so insidiously, beginning with tormenting him in his dreams – violent, horrific thoughts of blood and pain. He recalled his first vivid dream, which occurred when he was just fifteen, as he was blossoming into manhood. After that, the dreams had only gained in intensity until they'd spilled into his waking life too. He'd been terrified and appalled by his bloody visions at first, but then he'd become accustomed to them, even started to enjoy them.

Of course, he knew all about Matthew Crowle, his real father. His mother and Henry had broken the news to him when he was thirteen. Initially, he hadn't wanted to know any more, he'd been so appalled by what he'd heard. Then, when the bad thoughts had started, he'd rooted through old newspapers in the city library and realised just how horrific her experiences had been, the worst of it at the hands of Edward Alardyce. Matthew had died saving her from Edward and got a knife in his gut for his trouble. But the gleeful reportage of what Matthew and Edward had done not only to Amy but to so many women had really spoken to him. He wasn't alone. Those two men had the same urges as he did and doubtless other men did too. He felt part of an exclusive club that Mrs Grier and her friend had explained to him wasn't so abnormal after all. Daisy had been his second. His first had been a housemaid too, but she'd left and kept her mouth shut, unlike Daisy, who needed teaching a serious lesson, and the thought of how he would punish her almost knocked him dizzy with pleasure. It was worth standing about in the snow for hours.

He was roused from his thoughts by the crunch of footsteps from the direction of the cottage.

'At last,' he whispered as he watched Daisy's friend Violet leave, wrapped up against the cold, a basket in one hand. She was really quite pretty, but her husband was a huge brute who worked as a farmhand. The reason why Edward and Matthew had got away with it for so long was because they'd chosen their victims carefully and he'd learnt from them. Violet was safe.

Violet's husband would be out all day at work, which meant Daisy was now all alone. Finally, it was time.

He glanced around to make sure it was all clear before emerging from the bushes. Everyone was hibernating in their cottages, only a few hardy souls tough enough to brave the weather to work or fetch supplies.

The cold melted right out of his body, replaced by heat as he crept towards the cottage, the only sound the soft crunch of his boots through the snow.

Just a few yards from Violet's door, a voice called, 'Master Robert, how fortunate to see you here.'

He came slipping to a halt on the cobbles and glanced over his shoulder to see Magda Magrath, looking regal in a white floor-length cape, blending in with the snow. Combined with her silver hair, she looked more the sorceress than ever.

'I was just going to Alardyce House to check on your mother when I slipped on some ice and turned my ankle,' she explained. 'Would you be so kind as to escort me?'

Robert's rage was almost murderous. All those hours waiting, and this madwoman comes along and ruins it. If his violent emotions showed, Magda betrayed no reaction, and he forced himself to calm down. He could escort her home then come back and still have plenty of time with Daisy before Violet returned.

Robert smoothed his frown out into a charming smile. 'I'll escort you home,' he said, every inch the affable gentleman.

'I'm going to Alardyce House,' she said.

'You can't on a turned ankle.'

'It's imperative I see your mother, her health hangs in the balance.'

Robert's heart sank. What was he supposed to say to that? 'Very well,' he sighed. 'Let's go.'

'Am I keeping you from an important errand?' she said when he glanced at Violet's front door.

'No, just going for a walk.'

'It must have been a long walk, you look frozen. Your lips are almost blue.'

'I'm fine,' he said, painfully aware of the numbness in his fingers and toes. 'Take my arm,' he added, more harshly than he'd intended.

'Thank you, Robert,' she replied graciously.

Magda took his arm and Robert ground his teeth together, the sound disguised by the crunch of their boots through the snow. As they turned away from Violet's house, he could have sworn he caught movement at the window, a twitch of a curtain, but he didn't dare look back for fear of rousing Magda's suspicions.

Progress was slow because of Magda's limp and the torture was only relieved for Robert when a carriage rolled up beside them with Henry inside and he ordered them to be taken up.

'Magda, are you injured?' said Henry with concern.

'I turned my ankle,' she replied. 'The thick snow is often a mask for treacherous pockets of ice. Fortunately, Master Robert was on hand to assist me.'

Robert stared back at his father, who he had not seen or spoken to since their argument, and he saw the suspicion in his eyes.

'What were you doing out in this weather?' said Henry, voice cool. 'I thought you were back at the house.'

'I went for a walk,' he replied. 'I needed some fresh air after being cooped up inside for so long.'

Henry's look was intense, his gaze boring into Robert, who knew his stepfather didn't believe him, but Henry didn't voice his thoughts. Instead, he turned to Magda.

'You must stay at Alardyce House until you've recovered. You can't possibly manage at home alone with a turned ankle and it looks like the snow's going to come on again.'

'That's very kind, Sir Henry. How could I refuse such a generous offer?' she smiled.

As they chatted, Robert slumped into the corner of the carriage, cold, damp and miserable. He'd failed to punish Daisy and he'd got frozen for his trouble. He wouldn't be surprised if he fell ill too.

* * *

On their return to Alardyce House, Magda insisted on seeing Amy before resting. Henry assisted her upstairs, where Amy sat in the chair by the fire in her bedroom, half-dozing, a blanket covering her knees.

To Henry's astonishment, Magda's limp suddenly vanished and she purposefully strode up to her patient.

'What the...' he began.

'Forgive the deception, Sir Henry, but it was a necessary one. There is evil in this house and I think you need me here.'

Amy jumped awake and sat up straighter in her chair. 'Evil? You mean Robert?'

'Who else?'

'Please speak more delicately, Magda,' said Henry. 'You know Amy's health is fragile.'

'I'm sorry, but this is urgent,' replied Magda. 'I saw Master Robert hiding in the shrubbery outside Violet's cottage. Judging by how cold he looked, he'd been there for some time.'

'What?' exclaimed Henry.

'It's freezing out there, yet it didn't deter him from his purpose,' she continued. 'He waited until Violet and her husband had left and was approaching the cottage when I came upon him.'

'Dear God,' said Henry.

'Robert has allowed the seed of evil to germinate inside him, to spread its branches through every part of himself, and now it possesses him completely.'

It was Henry who exclaimed, 'No,' while Amy merely nodded, a tear rolling down her cheek.

'He used to be the sweetest boy,' said Amy sadly. 'It's as though the boy I have loved all these years was just a dream.'

'That's not true,' said Magda. 'Your son loves you dearly, I see it so clearly, but this compulsion is beyond his control and every day it claims another piece of him.'

'How did Robert know Daisy was staying at Violet's?' said Henry. 'We told him she'd left the village.'

'In my experience, servants are notoriously loose-lipped,' replied Magda.

'Servants,' gasped Amy. 'He's in collusion with a servant, just like Edward was with Matthew.'

'That makes sense,' said Henry. 'And George did escort Daisy to Violet's.'

'George?' said Magda.

'The second footman,' he explained.

'History's repeating itself,' said Amy.

'Now, we don't know that Robert is in collusion with anyone,' said Henry. 'He could have overheard them gossiping. I'm unwilling to accuse anyone until we know for certain.'

'Have you found a replacement for Daisy?' said Magda.

'Rush has,' replied Henry. 'A very plain, mousy thing called Winnie. I anticipate Robert will leave her alone.'

'Let's hope so. You must be very careful to only have the plainest girls work for you.'

'And what then?' said Amy. 'He'll turn his attention to the village girls.'

'You can limit his activities. Short of informing the authorities...'

'That will not happen. I will not see my son hang.'

'Of course not. Then we must do what we can to curb his activities.'

'You're right, Magda,' said Henry. 'We must watch him like a hawk.'

'For the rest of his life?' said Amy. 'He's a man now. Soon he will want to live in a house of his own. Who will watch over him then? He'll be free to do as he pleases. What if he goes too far one day and kills someone?'

'Then I shall employ someone specifically to watch him.'

'You're going to hire someone to be Robert's shadow?' said Amy with an amused smile.

'What other way is there?'

'I think it's the only way,' said Magda. 'Your only other option is to keep him at home for the rest of his life.'

'Neither can we do that,' said Amy. 'He'd only end up running away, then we'd have absolutely no control over him. He's still young and this is all new to him. If we can instil in him how wrong his actions are and how dire the consequences would be if he got caught, then we might be able to scare him out of it.'

'With all due respect,' said Magda, 'I think that's a bit naïve.'

'You're probably right, but I fear this compulsion is already slipping out of his control.'

'His youth means he lacks a man's control and he's been thwarted in his attempt to punish Daisy, which means the urge will be rapidly building within him again.'

'How do you know so much about this?' Henry asked her.

'There's something you don't know about your family's past, something that will no doubt surprise you.'

Henry swallowed hard, dreading what she was about to say.

'Your father came to see me when Edward was the age Robert is now.'

'He would never have done that,' replied Henry. 'My father was deeply religious and was very averse to your methods. Like Dr Parlow, he considered you to be a witch.'

'He was also an intelligent man who realised that modern medicine couldn't help his son. He hoped I could.'

'He wanted you to cure Edward?'

She nodded. 'Unfortunately, I had no cure. If I had, I would have rid the entire world of evil by now. All I could do was recommend he try to limit Edward's activities by keeping him under close scrutiny, which he did to the best of his ability.'

'Which is why Uncle Alfred wouldn't let him move to London like he wanted to?' said Amy.

'Precisely,' replied Magda.

'Edward should have gone to prison,' said Henry. 'I told Father that often enough.'

'Is that what you think should happen to Robert?' said Amy, eyes narrowed.

'I'm not sure. I understood what Edward was capable of, but I hope Robert can be redeemed.'

'As do I,' said Amy.

Magda pressed a hand to her forehead. 'You feel very hot again.'

'That's what I said,' interjected Henry. 'It's all the strain.'

'Amy, I know you're going to object. However, I think it's important you listen to me,' said Magda. 'I want to give you a sleeping draught.'

'I can't sleep now,' she exclaimed. 'There's so much to be decided.'

'It's vital you do. Your health is teetering on the brink, and I fear you would find it very difficult to recover from a second attack. And I want more thistles brought into this room.'

'Not thistles again,' groaned Amy. 'I used to adore them. Now I just associate them with sickness.'

'Thistles, I insist,' said Magda.

'Listen to the woman, will you?' said Henry. 'She knows what she's talking about and if you don't take her draught willingly, I will pour it down your throat myself.'

Amy and Magda both regarded him with surprise. Henry wasn't usually prone to such aggressive outbursts.

'There's no need for that,' said Amy. 'I trust Magda's judgement.'

'In that case, you'll do as she says.'

When his challenging gaze met Amy's, she smiled. 'Please help me back to bed.'

Henry tucked her in while Magda delved into her bag for her preparation.

'This will knock you out for quite a while,' she said.

Henry's heart almost broke when Amy replied, 'Good.'

Ten seconds after drinking Magda's potion, Amy was asleep.

'Will this be enough to fend off a return of the fever?' said Henry.

'I anticipate a sleep will do her a power of good,' replied Magda.

'This is all such a mess,' he sighed.

'Do you still require me to stay after my little deception?'

'Very much so. Besides, the snow's coming down heavy again,' he said, walking to the window to watch the thick flakes flurry through the air.

Usually, he could discern the boundary of the grounds in the distance, but the snow had obliterated it, caring nothing for wealth or rank. All his money and influence and he still couldn't buy what he desired most – a harmonious family life. Seven wonderful years with Amy and their children obliterated in a matter of days by Matthew and Edward's hideous legacy, all wrapped up in one boy. Now his wife was ill and his eldest son a monster and no matter how much money he threw at the situation, he couldn't get himself out of this mess.

Henry gazed down at Amy, asleep on the bed. He'd give every penny he had to make her whole again.

* * *

Robert shivered before the fire in the downstairs sitting room, wrapped in a thick blanket. His mother usually used this room to sit with her embroidery or a book. She rarely entertained friends here because she was shunned by society, and the only time she enjoyed female company was when Esther or Mildred came to visit. Not that it bothered her, she cared nothing for society or other people's opinions. Robert had always been so proud of his mother's strength and resilience. That same strength was about to be turned on him and he had the feeling he was going to have one hell of a fight on his hands. At least his mother wasn't going to be using this room any time soon, as she was still confined to bed, Henry on sentry duty, not letting anyone near except the white-caped witch. Idly he wondered if Magda knew all about him, she'd given him a strange look and she'd sneaked up on him outside Violet's cottage.

Robert pulled the blanket tighter around himself, tucked up before the fire like an old man, nursing his second brandy. It had been foolish of him to remain outside for so long, but his blood had been up. He was paying for it now, though, he couldn't stop shivering, his brow was feverish and he felt sick. If he fell ill, Daisy was going to pay for that too.

8

The snow was relentless throughout the night, so thick it was impossible to step outside the following morning. Robert was relieved when he woke to find the shivering and nausea had passed.

'What?' he growled when there was a knock at his bedroom door.

Douglas, his valet, entered the room, clothes and hair immaculate. With his severe unlined face, he was the personification of ruthless efficiency.

'It's nine o'clock, sir.'

'So?' yawned Robert, sitting up in bed and running his hands through his hair.

'You like to be woken by nine, sir.'

'Normally, yes, but I wasn't very well last night.'

'I'm sorry to hear that, sir,' replied Douglas in a voice that indicated he couldn't care less.

Robert watched suspiciously as Douglas opened the curtains to reveal nothing but a turbulent grey sky and falling whiteness. He'd grown up feeling constantly on edge, wondering whether people were thinking less of him because he was the son of a footman. It probably stuck in the servants' throats that they had to wait on someone who was from no better stock than they were. But his mother was from a good, wealthy family; he was willing to wager they conveniently forgot about that when they made their jokes.

'It's been snowing all night,' commented Douglas, straightening out the thick, heavy curtains with his long fingers.

Robert's eyes widened and he leapt up, forgetting about his aching head, and he grimaced.

'Are you all right, sir?' said Douglas in his usual snooty manner.

'Fine,' he muttered, lunging for the window. He looked out and his heart sank. All the undulations that marked out the various landmarks in the garden were gone, replaced by a thick white vastness unspoiled by a single footstep. More flakes were still coming down.

'No,' he cried. 'This cannot be.'

'I'm afraid it is,' said Douglas in a tone that made Robert want to bash his head in.

'Jane was supposed to be returning today.'

'She won't be able to get through the snow, sir. The drive's impassable, never mind the road. It will be blocked for days.'

'You mean we're trapped here?'

'I'm afraid so.'

Robert swallowed hard, thinking of his parents' disapproving faces. The prospect of being stuck inside for days with them was intolerable.

'Tea, sir?' said Douglas, breaking his train of thought.

'No. I'm going back to sleep. There's nothing to get up for now,' he said before flinging himself face down on the bed.

Douglas left, deciding to leave the sulky little sod to it.

* * *

The three younger children found the prospect of being snowed in thrilling. They rushed about the drawing room, laughing and playing, intermittently running up to the windows to admire the huge drifts.

Magda sat in an armchair with a cup of tea, her fake injured ankle bandaged and propped up on a small stool. Now she'd begun the charade, she had to maintain it. Her eyes were wide with delight as she watched the children run about.

'I adore the freedom you give your children,' she commented to Henry. 'Too many wealthy parents prefer to keep their children shut away in the schoolroom and, when they do spend rare time with their parents, they are told to sit quietly and be invisible.'

Henry had never noticed how unusual Magda's eyes were before. They were more silver than blue, almost the colour of her hair. With Amy still asleep upstairs, he was glad of her presence, otherwise Robert would have been the only other adult in the house, other than the servants. He was starting to think of Magda as an angel rather than a witch.

'We stopped caring about how our contemporaries behave a long time ago,' he said. 'Although, admittedly, I don't usually tolerate such deafening noise,' he added, having to raise his voice to be heard over the din. But he needed the children's eager smiles and bright eyes, their absolute innocence. It was like a balm and lifted his spirits.

Even the children's sunny presence wasn't enough to dispel the lead that settled in his gut when Robert prowled into the room, dark eyes flashing. Douglas had done a good job of making him look presentable, but the smartly pressed clothes and rigidly combed hair couldn't disguise the rage seething beneath the groomed surface.

'You're up late,' commented Henry in what he had hoped would

be a casual tone but came out stiff and strained. 'You missed breakfast and lunch.'

'There was nothing to get up for. We can't leave the house, and
Jane won't be coming now, not in this weather.'

'I'm afraid you're right. No one can get in or out.'

Robert sighed and started to pace. The house was huge but
already the walls were closing in.

'How's the ankle?' Robert asked Magda.

'Painful,' she replied. 'But thank you for enquiring, you're such a
polite young man.'

'I wonder why you haven't applied one of your miracle cures to
yourself? It worked well enough for my mother.'

'Your mother is still unwell. I had to give her a sleeping draught
as the fever was returning. Hopefully she'll be able to sleep it off.'

'The fever returned? Why did no one tell me?' demanded
Robert, looking hurt.

'I didn't want to worry you,' replied Henry. 'You didn't look too
well yourself yesterday.'

Robert stared back at his father, noting the mistrust in his eyes.
Henry knew full well what he'd been up to yesterday, but he
couldn't quiz him about it, thanks to the presence of Magda and the
children. 'Worry me? You haven't forgotten that we're her family too
and we love her?' he said, gesturing from himself to his siblings.

'Of course not, but I didn't want to put you at risk.'

'If it was contagious, you would have caught it by now.'

'Perhaps not,' interjected Magda. 'Some people are more
resilient than others and Sir Henry is as strong as an ox.'

'So is my mother,' he retorted.

'Who has given birth to four children. That takes its toll on a
woman's body.'

'So it's my fault now?'

'That's not what I said, Master Robert,' she replied, silver eyes boring into him. 'Did you sleep ill last night or are you feeling unwell after being out for so long yesterday?'

Robert went rigid, eyes darting to Henry, before he forced himself to relax. 'I didn't sleep well. I was concerned about the heavy snow keeping Jane away. And now it has.'

'I'm sorry for that,' she said. 'It must be very difficult for you being parted like this.'

He nodded miserably.

'You must really love her?'

Robert blushed at such a personal question.

'Of course,' he mumbled to the floor.

'When are you planning on having the wedding?' she said before taking a sip of tea.

He raised his head to meet her gaze, eyes bright with excitement. 'As soon as possible.'

'I admire your eagerness, but these things take time. There are arrangements to be made.'

'Why does everyone keep saying that?' he sighed.

'Because it's true,' replied Henry, snatching up the poker and stoking the fire for something to do. 'My God, the arrangements when Amy and I wed were unbelievable and that was only a small wedding. I assume you want to do this on a grand scale?'

'Naturally,' replied Robert, knowing full well his father was against this marriage and wondering where the conversation was going.

Henry just nodded and turned his attention back to the fire, gazing thoughtfully into the flames.

'Robert's getting married,' exclaimed Lydia, rushing up to her brother and smiling up at him.

Despite his black mood, Robert found himself smiling back. Lydia was beautiful, with the lovely blue eyes of her mother and the dark hair of her father, her nature perpetually sunny, and it was impossible not to love her. Robert was grateful for the force of his feeling for his sister. It reassured him that he hadn't become an inhuman monster.

'Yes, I am,' he replied. 'Are you excited?'

'Yes. I've never been to a wedding before.'

'Would you like to be a flower girl?'

Lydia released a tinkle of laughter. 'Silly Robert, I'm not a flower.'

'I know that, although you're as a pretty as one,' he said, making her grin. 'You're like a little rose.'

'I don't like roses, they've got thorns.'

'Well, what flower do you like?'

'Daffodils. I like yellow.'

'Then you can wear your prettiest yellow dress and carry a basket of daffodils. Would you like that?'

'Yay,' she cheered.

'A daffodil is a spring flower, is it not?' said Robert, looking to his father, who went rigid and slowly turned to face him. 'That's perfect because Jane and I wish to marry at the start of spring.'

'That's too soon,' said Henry.

'We can make all the arrangements in time, Jane and I have already discussed it,' he retorted, trying to sound as cool as his stepfather.

'And I say neither of you have a clue what you're doing, especially Jane,' he added, unable to resist.

'What is that supposed to mean?' said Robert, his temper rising.

'It means you will not be married in the spring.'

'Please, Papa,' said Lydia, pulling her famous puppy dog look that melted everyone's hearts. 'I want to be a daffodil girl.'

'Sorry, Lydia, that won't happen,' sighed Henry, returning his gaze to the fire.

Any objections Robert might have had were drowned out by the almighty wail Lydia let up.

'Lydia, enough,' said Henry. 'You'll disturb your mother.'

She ignored him, working herself up into a state, face bright red and streaked with tears, small hands screwed up into fists.

Henry closed his eyes and gritted his teeth, feeling his usually limitless patience start to slip away as Lydia's ear-splitting screech reached a crescendo. Combined with Robert's deep bass protests and Stephen and John's pleas for Lydia to be quiet, everything combined to sever Henry's last nerve.

'Enough,' he bellowed, slamming both fists down on top of the fireplace.

They all stared at him in shock, except Magda, who sympathised.

'Oh, I'm sorry, please don't cry,' he said, rushing to Stephen and John when their eyes filled with tears. They weren't used to hearing their father shout. Fortunately, a hug was enough to prevent a full-on crying fit.

Next, he turned his attention to Lydia, who had gone pale and silent at the sound of her father's raised voice. He knelt before her and took her hands.

'You'll always be my little daffodil girl,' he said, drawing a reluctant smile from her.

Pacified, she skipped back to the window and looked out. 'Papa, it's still snowing,' she commented.

Henry joined her at the window, the sight depressing him. On the bright side, they always kept a fully stocked pantry. They could easily wait it out in comfort. He glanced at Robert, who was standing in the middle of the room, body shaking with rage and eyes fixed on him.

With one last glare, Robert stormed from the room, slamming

the door shut behind him. Henry looked to Magda, whose silver eyes were troubled.

* * *

That evening, Robert prowled the house like an angry shadow. The snow had come down relentlessly the entire day, the grey sky turning prematurely black as the clouds amassed, blotting out every last bit of light. Despite all the blazing gas lights, the house was full of shadows, and he stuck to them, wanting to be left alone with his thoughts, glowering at the servants who passed him by.

His siblings had been taken back up to the schoolroom and Henry remained with Magda, chatting in the drawing room. As Robert paced, his rage grew, imagining they were discussing him. Ever since all this had started, he'd thought of Henry less as his father, gradually replacing him in his mind with Matthew.

As he roamed the halls of Alardyce House, he was very aware that he was walking in his real father's footsteps, only Matthew had been a servant here while Robert was one of the family, wearing expensive clothes, the servants his to command. There was something satisfying about that. He'd seen enough images of Matthew during the course of his research to know how much he resembled him, which only made him feel closer to him. However, when he recalled his own childhood memories of Matthew, he felt only fear, remembering how he'd kept his mother a prisoner upstairs while he'd plotted to dispose of her, then their frantic escape with Esther and Jane, Matthew in desperate pursuit...

The child in him shuddered but the man he'd become experienced a vague longing, wishing he'd taken the time to get to know his father while he'd had the chance. Instead, he'd pushed him away, shunning him in favour of his mother. Not that he blamed her. Despite what she thought of him now, he did love her deeply.

Ever since the day he was born, it had been just the two of them, and she had done everything in her power to give him the best she could provide. He so admired the way she'd given up a life of luxury here and run away to slave as a governess just for him, so her cruel aunt wouldn't take him away from her. Then Henry had come along and suddenly it wasn't just the two of them any more. Three became six after his mother gave birth to his siblings in rapid succession. Sometimes he missed the closeness they'd shared when he was a boy and he'd known that he was the only person in the world she cared about. Now he couldn't even get near her when she was ill because Henry constantly guarded her.

Robert hesitated. Henry was closeted away in the drawing room with the witch.

He turned on his heel and stole upstairs.

9

Amy was heartened to wake up without that horrible sickness in her belly or the lethargy.

She turned onto her side and settled into the pillows, determined to enjoy a bit of peace and quiet, smiling when she heard the chair by her bedside creak. Henry was still keeping his vigil.

'Are you still here?' she murmured without opening her eyes.

'I am.'

The deep, harsh voice struck a chord of fear within her that made her heart pound. She gasped with shock.

'Matthew?' she said, sitting up.

Robert sat in the chair, his dark eyes focused on her, a wicked smile on his lips. 'So you haven't forgotten about him?'

It was a relief to see a living, breathing person and not a spectre. 'How could I? He haunts my nightmares.'

'You thought I was him?'

'Your voice sounded similar.' She glanced around the room. 'Where's Henry?'

Anger shifted in Robert's belly like a slithering serpent. Why did everything always have to come back to Henry? 'Downstairs with

Magda. It's just the two of us, like it was for years. Do you remember, Mother, when it was just us two against the world?'

'Of course I do. They were good years.'

'But you wish you'd been here instead, living in luxury with Henry, without me.'

Amy was shocked. 'That's not true and you know it.'

'If you hadn't had me, you would have married Henry, then Matthew and Edward wouldn't have hurt you. You blame me and that's why you think I'm guilty of doing those things to Daisy.'

'I most certainly do not blame you. Where did you get such a ridiculous notion from?'

'I've been thinking about the past a lot lately.'

His eyes darkened and bored into her, just like Matthew's used to when he was angry with her.

'Jane isn't here,' he said. 'I'll wager you're pleased about that.'

'Actually, I am,' she said, making him scowl. 'Come now, Robert, did you expect me to say anything different?'

'I suppose it would have been too much to hope for,' he sniffed.

'Why isn't she here?' she said, dragging herself up to a sitting position.

'Because we're snowed in. Happy now?'

'That doesn't make me happy.'

'Well, I didn't hit her or beat her with a stick as you accused me of doing to Daisy. Why are you looking at me like that?' he demanded when she frowned.

'I never said you beat Daisy with a stick.'

'Then Father must have said it.'

'He didn't either, and you know there's nothing wrong with my memory. If you're as innocent as you claim, then how do you know she was beaten with a stick?'

'There you go again, thinking the worst of me.'

'Stop dodging the question and answer me,' she yelled.

Robert was surprised by her strength, he'd thought she was still weak after her illness.

'You're mistaken, Mother,' he said through a clenched jaw.

Amy stared at her beloved son as his countenance darkened, pupils narrowing into slits, lips drawing back over his teeth.

'Dear God, Robert, look at yourself. Where's my sweet boy gone? You look ready to commit...'

'Murder?'

Amy swallowed hard. 'Yes.'

'I am my father's son,' he said with a malicious smile.

'Finally, you admit it.'

Her sad look actually managed to make him feel guilty.

'Where did I go wrong, Robert?' she sighed. 'Would things have been different if we'd never gone to Huntington Manor? If you hadn't been exposed to Matthew when you were so young, you might have escaped his fate.'

'This isn't your fault,' he said when she started to cry, desperate to reassure her.

'It is. I thought you were different.'

'I am,' he exclaimed.

'It's not your fault, darling, you can't help it. Even Matthew told me he would hurt someone and then not know what had happened until it was over. But I know you, Robert, you're stronger than he was. There's hope for you. If you fight this compulsion, then you can live the nice life you want with Jane.'

Robert gazed into her bloodshot eyes that were full of tears and knew he was going to dash all her hopes. His darker half was already slipping out of his control.

'I'll try,' he replied, wanting to give her hope, for a little while at least. When she embraced him, Robert hung onto her, praying she saved him like she had before when he was a child. 'I don't want to be like this, Mama,' he said.

'I know. We'll sort it out. I will not allow what happened to Matthew and Edward to happen to you.' Amy took his face in her hands and stared into his eyes. 'Now, listen to me – you must use all your self-control to prevent another incident. If you feel yourself slipping, then come to me.'

'What can you do?' he said helplessly, dark eyes wide, the pupils reverting back to normal. 'You couldn't help Matthew and I know you tried.'

'It was too late for him, he'd dwelt in evil for too long. When he worked here, he was gentler, he seemed more... human. At Huntington Manor, he was lost inside the monster.'

'But he saved you at Edward's house. He gave his life for you. Surely those aren't the actions of a monster?'

Amy recalled Matthew's last moments. She'd lain beside him on the floor of Edward's house, both of them bleeding from their wounds, the knife protruding from Matthew's belly. 'It's all right,' he'd said. 'As long as the blade stays in, I won't bleed out.'

Amy had used the last of her strength to pull that knife out of him, ensuring he bled faster. She'd done it not just to free herself but this boy too, a boy who, it turned out, was just as bad.

'Did you ever love him, Mama?' said Robert.

Amy thought carefully before replying, 'I loved him for giving me you.'

'That's not what I meant.'

'I suppose I did in a way, but nothing like the way I love Henry. He's my soulmate and a very good man.'

'Yes,' was all he replied. 'Tell me about Matthew when he worked here.'

'Why? What would it achieve?'

'If I could understand him, it might help me understand what's happening to me now.'

'I suppose it's worth a try,' she said, attempting to hide her reluctance. She spent a lot of her time trying to escape the past, but she was willing to relive it if it helped her son. 'What exactly do you want to know?'

'What did you do together?'

A blush stole up Amy's neck and into her face. Had he asked her that to embarrass her? She studied him closely. He looked genuinely interested but what she could tell him about her time with Matthew was limited because their relationship had been purely physical.

'Please, Mama, I have to understand.'

She cleared her throat. 'All right, well...'

The door burst open, and Henry practically ran into the room.

'Amy, are you all right?' he demanded, rushing to her bedside, forcing Robert to move aside.

'I'm fine,' she told him, noting the anger in Robert's eyes, the pupils retreating again. 'Robert and I were just talking.'

Robert spied Rush lurking outside the door, which Henry had left ajar. He must have told his father he was in here. Rush gave him an odd look before lumbering away now he was reassured his mistress was unharmed.

Henry sat beside Amy, his arm wrapped protectively around her, glaring at his stepson.

'I need to speak to Robert in private,' she told Henry.

'But you're still recuperating,' he replied.

'I'm fine. Please, Henry,' she added when it became apparent he wasn't about to budge.

Henry looked back at Robert, who was doing his best not to smirk.

'Fine,' he eventually muttered. 'But I'll just be outside the door. Call me if you need me.'

He kissed Amy's cheek and left the room without a glance in Robert's direction.

'Now,' began Amy. 'Matthew was so handsome. He had a dark, sulky look that was very appealing. He was kind to me. Other than Edward and my maid, he was the only one in the house who spoke to me.'

'Didn't Henry talk to you?' he frowned.

She smiled fondly. 'No. I thought he despised me, when in fact he was just shy. Looking back, it was obvious, but I was grieving for my parents and I was so lost.'

'So, Matthew?' he said, trying to steer her off the subject of Henry.

'Yes, well, we grew closer and things... developed from there.'

'Did he always treat you gently here?'

'Yes, in fact he even defended me against a so-called gentleman who thought I was his for the taking. But he did try to control me.'

'In what way?'

'Well,' she said, shifting uncomfortably, trying to think of a time that didn't involve them having sex. 'He didn't like it when my aunt and uncle put me in the path of other men, even though he knew there was no future for us.'

'The situation was reversed when you went to work at Huntington Manor as a governess?'

'Yes, it was. I'm not sure who was more surprised by that turn of events, me or Matthew.'

'You were meant to meet up again, he was meant to find out about me.'

Amy was dismayed by the fervour in his eyes. 'I think you're reading too much into it.'

'No, I'm not. Don't you see, Mother, fate decreed we went to Huntington Manor.'

'Robert,' she said, trying to keep her voice calm. 'It was just a coincidence Matthew was there.'

'There's no such thing as coincidence,' he barked. When her

eyes widened, he paused and took in a deep breath to calm himself. 'I mean it was odd, that's all.'

'It certainly was,' she replied, giving him a searching look. 'Anyway, Matthew and I grew quite close here, we spent as much time as we could together when he wasn't working.'

'And you never had a glimpse of what he really was?'

'None. I didn't realise until we were at Huntington Manor. It was as though there were two men inside him. Does that make sense to you?'

Robert nodded thoughtfully. 'It does.'

'I knew it,' she said, almost happily, grasping his hand. 'You're still my sweet boy. Do you remember what happened at Huntington Manor?'

'Yes, I think so. I remember being happy at first, then you and Esther disappeared and the house felt big and scary. It was just Jane and me for so long. I liked Matthew, he was kind and bought me expensive things I never thought I'd own. Then he started to turn dark, like he was one big shadow and he scared me. As you said, it was like he was two men.'

'I want you to keep that in mind, Robert, it might serve you well in the future. I'd hate to see my beautiful boy consumed by the shadow. I hope you understand why I'm so afraid.'

'I would never hurt you, Mother. Never.'

'I know, sweetheart. I'm afraid *for* you because I've seen up close how this always ends, and it won't be good for you. That's what I fear the most.'

'I can control this. I want that nice life you talked about, I want to marry Jane and have children. I don't want this... curse,' he ended before burying his face in his hands.

'Come here, darling,' she said, holding her arms out to him. She rocked him and stroked his hair. 'This time, we will break the curse.'

'I'm so afraid,' he whispered.

His mother was the only person in the world he wasn't too proud to admit that to.

* * *

Henry paced outside Amy's bedroom door – three steps to the left, turn on his heel, then three steps to the right, over and over again. He couldn't hear what they were saying, but he could just make out the murmur of their voices. If Amy screamed, he'd be able to hear clearly enough.

Rush had alerted him to the fact that Robert was closeted away with Amy, making it sound like an innocent throwaway remark. *I do believe her ladyship is feeling better, she's talking with Master Robert.* Henry hadn't stopped to consider Rush's motivation before, he'd just dashed upstairs without question. Now he'd had the opportunity to think it over, perhaps Rush did know what was going on in this house; after all, he'd served here for years, seen the parade of maids who had been tortured by Edward and Matthew. He made a mental note to speak to him as soon as the opportunity arose.

Henry stopped pacing when the door swung open. He was confronted by Robert, who appeared drained. Henry was only too happy to let him go on his way, desperate to check on Amy.

'Are you all right?' he said, rushing to her side.

'Yes,' she replied. 'He admitted it.'

'Admitted hurting Daisy?'

She nodded.

'How on earth did you manage that?'

'With a little trickery.'

'You clever girl,' he smiled, kissing her. 'It must have been difficult for you to hear him finally admit it.'

'It was, but it also gave me hope. He wants to change and he's really going to fight it.'

Henry was sceptical, but he wasn't about to obliterate her hope. 'And we'll be here to support him. Perhaps this has been caught early enough and he can be redeemed.'

'I really think he can be.'

Henry smiled and kissed her forehead so she wouldn't see the doubt in his eyes.

* * *

The pressure was building inside Robert and if he didn't vent it soon, he was afraid of what might happen. Not only was the desire to take his urges out on a female rising again, but he was being followed. Wherever he went in the house, Rush seemed to be there. Robert couldn't understand how he did it, the lumbering fool took ages to get anywhere. If it wasn't Rush shadowing him then it was Henry or, once or twice, Magda, who was still staying with them.

The snow had been coming down relentlessly for two solid days now, shrouding the house in ice and gloom, making the bad thoughts return, the thoughts he'd faithfully promised his mother he would fight. She'd told him to let her know when they came back and they would fight them together, but how could he reveal to her all the horrors that lurked in his sick mind? She had faith in his strength, and he couldn't stand to see the disappointment in her eyes when she realised that he was doomed to be as bad as Edward and Matthew. What he'd done to Daisy had been the very mildest of his twisted fantasies. So he was attempting to contain it by himself. When Jane was around, the urge wasn't as strong. Then, when she was gone, it sprang back out at him with renewed vigour. It was one reason why he wanted to marry her, apart from the fact that he loved her desperately. She'd known Matthew too, lived with him for years at Huntington Manor. He'd been her uncle. Robert felt closer to Matthew through his mother, as well as Jane and Esther, as though he was just in the next room and could walk in at any moment with his customary stride, secure in the knowledge that he was master of everyone around him.

However, it wasn't just Matthew who seemed to prowl the halls of Alardyce House. Lately Robert had felt Edward here too, whose blood also ran through his veins. It was as though, now he was realising exactly who he was, they were returning, preparing to initiate him into the bloody rites.

He was roaming the lesser-used east wing of the house, which was colder than the west, subjected to the pitiless icy blasts, ensuring he was well away from the maids who were making up the beds now everyone had risen. Not that any of them particularly appealed to him, Daisy had been the prettiest by far and now she was gone.

He stopped in his tracks, every muscle tightening with the rage that swept through him at the thought of what that little bitch had done to him. The good news was she was stuck in the village until the snow melted. He still had time to punish her.

A shape appeared before him at the opposite end of the long corridor, causing him to hesitate. He didn't know where it had come from – one moment, it wasn't there, the next, it was. It just stood there, unmoving, features a vague, melded mess of shadow.

'Who's there?' called Robert.

It didn't respond, although he got the feeling it was a man, probably Rush or Henry spying on him again.

'I was only taking a walk around the house because I can't go outside,' he continued, striding towards the figure. 'Can't I get a moment's peace?'

'Robert, who are you talking to?'

He whirled around and was stunned to see Henry standing

behind him. Robert looked back the other way, heart pounding, to see the figure had gone. He'd been so sure it was Henry, the figure had looked just like him, but it was impossible.

His blood ran cold. Edward had looked just like Henry.

'I... I thought I saw someone down there,' said Robert, the cold bursting out of his bones and seeping through his skin in an icy sweat.

Henry looked to where his stepson pointed with a shaky hand. 'There's no one there, you're seeing ghosts.'

'Ghosts? Why do you say ghosts?'

Henry was shocked to see all the colour drain from Robert's face. 'No reason, it's just a saying. Being trapped inside is doing odd things to us all.'

'But...'

Henry's eyes narrowed suspiciously. 'But what?'

Robert caught his look and shook himself out of it. 'Nothing. Why are you still following me, anyway?' he said, indignant again now the fear was wearing off. 'What do you think I can get up to here?'

'I made your mother a promise to keep an eye on you and I will keep it.'

'And I made her a promise to fight this, and I will,' he retorted.

Henry's expression softened. 'Please listen to me, Robert. I understand all this has probably made you feel closer to Matthew, but I love you too. If you feel I'm being harsh, please understand that it's for your own good.'

Robert just nodded and tried to walk past him, but Henry grabbed his arm.

'I'm not the enemy here, Robert,' he said. 'Please don't shut me out.'

'Then stop suffocating me and stop coming between me and my mother. That's just what Matthew tried to do.'

Henry's grip on his arm tightened. 'I am nothing like him.'

'You'd better not be. Just bear in mind what became of him. That's what happens to men who try to separate us.'

With a haughty sniff, Robert shrugged his arm free and walked away, doing his best to mimic Matthew's self-assured stride, leaving Henry to stare after him.

10

Robert stormed through the house, seeking the one person he could really confide in. He found Mrs Grier heading up to the servants' quarters.

'I need to speak to you,' he said, pulling her towards her bedroom.

Although he hurt her, Mrs Grier didn't complain. She knew how to deal with men like him.

Robert practically pushed her inside and slammed the door shut. She waited for him to speak.

'Strange things are happening,' he eventually said after some pacing back and forth.

'Such as?'

'I... I think I'm seeing ghosts.'

'Ghosts?' she said, her tone displaying neither surprise nor scepticism.

'I could have sworn I saw Edward not ten minutes ago in the east wing.'

'It's this weather,' she said, looking to the window, all light blocked out by the swirls of snow hurling themselves against the glass. 'It plays tricks on the mind.'

'It wasn't the damned weather, you witless woman. I'm sorry,' he added when her lips pursed with disapproval. 'But this situation is really getting to me. My parents rarely let me out of their sight and Rush is becoming a severe pain in the neck.'

'Sometimes I think he knows more than he lets on. After all, he was here when Matthew and Edward were at Alardyce.'

'That old fool is the least of my concerns.'

'Your parents were going to realise something eventually, especially your mother,' she said, eyes narrowing.

Robert went to the window, gazing out with despair. If only he could go outside just for a little while, he knew he would feel so much better. 'I've got to get out of here.'

'You can't until the snow stops, unless you have a death wish.' She regarded him curiously. 'You don't, do you?'

'Of course not.' He sighed and turned away from the window. 'I need something to release the tension before I lose my mind.'

'You can't touch the maids. Your parents will know who's responsible.'

'Don't you think I know that?' he barked. 'Where's Hazel? She can be an amusing diversion.'

'She's busy with her duties,' she snapped.

Robert raised an eyebrow. 'Jealous, are we?'

'Certainly not, whelp.'

He advanced on her, forcing her to back up against the wall. His fingers played with the buttons on the front of her dress. 'I'm itching to see whether I'm right and beneath that staid, dour front lies a volcano.'

His hand slid into her hair. Mrs Grier inhaled sharply at the feel of his fingers touching the back of her neck. It had been far too long since a man had touched her, not for lack of admirers, but because she had never allowed it. This boy was weakening her resolve, but she couldn't trust hands that were capable of great pleasure and great pain.

She didn't stop him when he pulled the pins out of her hair, sending it tumbling down her back, taking years off her.

He placed his hands on the wall either side of her head and leaned into her, his lips almost brushing hers. 'I knew it. You're beautiful.'

'Stop it, whelp,' she said breathlessly.

'I'm not a whelp any more. I'm a man.' Robert kissed her aggressively, raking his hands through her hair, pressing his body against hers.

She tore herself away and turned her back on him, breathing hard.

'What's wrong, Evelyn? Don't you like men any more?'

Her eyes slid shut as the memories assailed her, body aching with want. 'Actually, I do, but I vowed never to again.'

'Why on earth would a beautiful woman like you waste herself like that?' he said, coming up behind her and kissing her neck.

'It's called love. You wouldn't understand.'

He grabbed her elbow and spun her round to face him. 'I understand love. I love Jane.'

'So why are you here, attempting to seduce me?'

'Jane is pure, unsullied and special. You, however, are a nobody, someone to fulfil a need.'

'I'm not fulfilling any need of yours,' she retorted. 'If you're seeing ghosts, then I suggest you act like the man you claim to be and deal with it instead of whining to me.'

'You're very foolish speaking to me like that. I could have you put out of this house any time I liked.'

'You need me in this house. I'm your only confidante and that's going to be especially useful during the dark days ahead.'

She shrieked when he grabbed her by the neck and pushed her sideways onto the bed. Then he was on top of her, pinning her down, laughing as she struggled beneath him.

'There's your fire,' he grinned down at her. 'I knew it was there.'

'What are you going to do now, beat me with a stick?'

'I wouldn't do that to you.' He dipped his head to kiss her, and Evelyn's thrashing stopped as she responded to the kiss. She didn't protest when he used his knee to part her legs. His hand slid up her thigh and his wolfish grin returned when she gasped, colour flooding those pale cheeks as he found the very centre of her.

'A woman as lovely as yourself shouldn't be neglected,' he said, enjoying her warmth and wetness on his fingers. 'Stop wasting yourself on some silly vow.'

'It's not silly to me. Oh, God,' she cried when he slid his fingers inside her.

'Changing your mind about that?' he grinned.

'No,' she said, eyes blazing.

When he sensed she was reaching a climax, he got to his feet.

'Where are you going?' she said, pushing herself upright.

'I'm bored,' he replied, heading for the door.

'A man never leaves a lady unsatisfied.'

He looked around the room. 'I see no lady.'

'And I don't see a man,' she screamed as he left. She picked up a shoe, which lay discarded on the floor, fallen from her foot when he'd pushed her back on the bed, and hurled it at the door. 'Whelp,' she yelled, infuriated when she heard his bark of laughter.

* * *

The house woke to a radiant morning. The snow had finally stopped falling and the sky was a clear blue.

Robert was the first to wake, somehow sensing the change, leaping out of bed to throw back the heavy curtains.

'Finally,' he breathed, eyes wide with excitement.

He rang for Douglas, who was surprised to be summoned so early.

After dressing, Robert hurtled downstairs. Bypassing the dining room, he rushed for the front door. He pulled on his boots, coat, hat, gloves and scarf and was out the door before Rush could question him.

'Master Robert,' called the butler, huffing and puffing his way to the door. It had been a very long time since he'd attempted to run.

* * *

After his walk, Robert made sure he was in the dining room before his parents descended for breakfast. However, Magda was already there, tucking into a bowl of thick, creamy porridge.

'Good morning, Robert,' she said as he seated himself opposite her.

'Morning,' he smiled.

'You look much more cheerful.'

'Because the damned snow's stopped, excuse my language. Hopefully Jane will be able to return.'

'It will take time for the roads to be cleared.'

'It will, but at least there's light at the end of the tunnel. Oh, lovely, I'm famished,' he grinned when a footman placed a plate of bacon and eggs before him. 'Are you not having bacon, Magda?'

'I don't consume the precious bodies of Gaia's children and I don't want the negativity from their brutal deaths absorbed into my body.'

'Oh,' was all Robert could think to say. 'Good morning,' he said, relieved when his parents entered the dining room.

'Amy, you're looking so much better,' said a pleased Magda.

'I feel it,' she smiled, seating herself at the table.

'I recommend you eat only light foods.'

Amy regarded Robert's plate regretfully. 'But I'm famished.'

'Your body has been through an ordeal. Eating too much is likely to result in a severe stomach ache, possibly more.'

'Listen to the woman,' Henry told Amy. He looked to the footman hovering by Amy's side, waiting to serve her. 'Lady Alardyce will have some broth, dry toast and weak tea. Nothing else, no matter what she says.'

The footman bowed and nodded before pouring out the tea.

Amy dragged her eyes off Robert's hearty breakfast and up to his face. 'And how are you this morning, dear?'

His eyes swept up to meet hers, wondering if there was an ulterior motive to her question. 'I'm very well and glad to see you looking so much better.'

'Thank you. You look very... flushed.'

Self-consciously, Robert touched his face. 'I'm hopeful. The snow's stopped. Jane will come soon.'

'Yes, perhaps.'

Robert was annoyed by her reluctance. She still didn't think he was good enough for Jane. His annoyance made him belligerent. 'When she does get here, we can discuss the wedding.'

Amy sipped her tea, giving herself time to respond. 'We'll just have to see.'

Robert looked back down at his plate, wrestling with his anger. An outburst would only be another black mark against him.

Rush entered the room. 'Ah, Master Robert. Did you enjoy your early-morning walk?'

Robert glared at his food, inwardly cursing the fool. He'd said that on purpose.

'You've been outside?' Amy asked her son.

'Yes,' he replied, knowing denial would only seem suspicious.

'Why?'

'I desperately needed some fresh air after being cooped up inside for days.'

'Where did you go?' she said, trying to keep her voice casual and failing.

'Just for a walk around the garden. It's not possible to leave the grounds, the driveway's blocked.'

'So you tried?' said Henry.

Silently, Robert called him a variety of names. 'No. I just wanted to see if the driveway was clear enough for Jane to return, which sadly it isn't.'

Henry nodded and turned his attention to his breakfast.

'I took a walk myself early this morning,' said Magda. 'While it was still dark. I do so love walking beneath the stars.'

'Wasn't that dangerous?' said Amy. 'You could have fallen.'

'I can find my way around easily in the dark. I've never had an accident yet, in all my years. Mother Earth won't let me fall.'

Amy smiled. 'I'm sure she won't.'

'Then how did you turn your ankle?' said Robert.

'That was my fault, not Mother Earth's,' replied Magda.

'How is the ankle, by the way? It seems to be healing surprisingly slowly, especially after the miracles you brought about with my mother's illness.'

'Your mother is a lot younger than me.'

'Nonsense,' said Amy. 'You've more vigour than the rest of us put together.'

Magda smiled mysteriously into her porridge.

It was a relief to Robert that his little jaunt wasn't mentioned again, and breakfast was finished in relative peace.

'I would like to take a walk,' said Amy as they wandered into the drawing room.

'Oh, no,' said Henry. 'That's what made you ill in the first place.'

'Not just that,' she murmured, glancing at Robert.

'I absolutely forbid it. Scowl at me all you like, Amy. I won't change my mind.'

'Magda, would a walk be terribly detrimental to my health?' said Amy.

'No, I don't think it would, but no longer than ten minutes and stay close to the house in case you tire.'

'But the snow's so deep out there,' exclaimed Henry.

'Amy's been inside for days. She needs fresh air.'

'Even if she sinks into a snow drift?'

'It's not that bad,' said Robert. 'Why don't I escort you, Mother?'

'I'll do it,' said Henry. 'You've already been out once today. We don't want you getting ill.'

With that, he took Amy's arm and led her away. As he watched them leave, Robert felt his resentment of his stepfather growing.

11

'It's so good to be outside,' said Amy, delighting in the crisp air. Everything had taken on a magical appearance. The garden stretched out before her into the distance, one vast, smooth blanket of pure, unsullied snow. She loved seeing the bare branches of the trees hanging low, laden with the weight of the snow, a flash of colour from a robin bobbing about, leaving small tracks in its wake.

The huge house stood behind them, their retreat from the society that had rejected them for Amy's sins. She still felt weak, her legs trembling slightly with the effort of walking through the heavy snow, but she found it a comfort knowing the house was there, waiting to receive her when she'd had enough.

'Are you all right?' Henry asked her for the sixth time.

'I'm fine,' she replied. 'Please stop fussing.'

'You're shaking.'

'It's just the exercise after so long in bed. Doesn't the old willow tree look mystical?'

'You've been spending too much time with Magda,' he said wryly.

'And look at that. A flower's survived this weather to still bloom.'

'A flower, where?'

'There. Can't you see the red?'

'That's not a flower.'

'What is it then?'

They moved closer and frowned down at the small red drop.

'Look, there's another one,' said Henry. 'And another.'

The red drops grew larger and closer together. As they rounded a large bush, foreboding grew in the pit of Amy's stomach.

'Dear God, it's blood,' said Henry.

'Help,' called a weak voice.

They both delved into the undergrowth and saw a pair of booted feet sticking out from behind a hedge. Henry gently extracted the figure, who had been thrown face down in the shrubbery.

'Look at her back,' said Amy.

The back of the unidentified woman's dress had been ripped open, the laces of her corset cut, and her skin was striped with nasty red welts, several of which were bleeding.

'Oh, no, please no,' said Amy, tears blurring her vision. She knew exactly who was responsible for this atrocity.

'It's that new maid, Winnie,' said Henry, turning the girl onto her side. 'Her lips and eyelids are blue. We need to get her into the warmth.'

Amy was appalled by the sight of the girl's swollen, bruised face, blood trickling from a cut to the back of her head.

Henry pulled off his coat, wrapped the girl up in it and gently scooped her up.

'It's all right,' he said when she whimpered. 'You're safe now.' He looked to his wife. 'Can you manage on your own back to the house?'

'Yes, I'll be fine. Get her inside before it's too late.'

Amy watched Henry run off across the garden, the maid safely held in his strong arms. She looked down at the mess of blood in the snow. A thick stick lay beside the grotesque pools, obviously the attacker's weapon of choice. Amy leaned into the bushes, bringing back up her light breakfast.

She turned and staggered back towards the house, hoping to reach it before her legs gave way. The house suddenly seemed miles away and it was getting harder to lift her feet out of the deep snow. It clawed at her, sucking at her ankles, causing her to stumble and she fell onto all fours, hands and knees sinking into the snow, which felt like quicksand, and she found she was unable to rise.

'Help,' she called, the sound weaker than the maid's cry had been.

The house swam before her eyes as she crawled towards it through the snow, which froze her hands and legs.

'Mother,' cried a voice.

It was despair and not relief that filled Amy when she saw Robert running towards her.

'How could Henry leave you out here all alone?' he demanded as he scooped her up.

All Amy could do was let him pick her up, as he failed to notice his mother was staring up at him in mute horror. Robert had hurt that poor girl. He was the reason why the beautiful, pure white snow was stained with blood.

Robert carried her into the house, calling for Magda. Once again, Rush appeared out of nowhere.

'I'm afraid she's attending to the maid in the sitting room,' he told Robert.

'So what? Mother's more important than some maid.'

Rush's lips pursed. 'She was found badly injured in the garden.'

'I don't care. Tell Magda she must attend to my mother immediately,' he snapped before carrying her into the drawing room and seating her in the armchair by the fire.

A lump formed in Amy's throat as her son tended to her, removing her sodden cloak, gloves and boots before taking her deformed hands in his own and gently rubbing them to restore the warmth. He could be so kind when he wanted to be.

'You're freezing,' he said. 'What was Father thinking?'

Amy couldn't stand the feel of his hands on her, knowing what they'd just done.

'Brandy... please,' she shivered, mainly so he would stop touching her.

'Yes, right away,' he said, leaping up.

Robert poured Amy her drink and placed the glass in her shaking hands. She drank it down in one gulp, hoping it restored her sufficiently so she could demand to know why he'd hurt Winnie. From the sitting room came the sound of the girl sobbing in pain, Magda's gentle voice coaxing her to receive whatever treatment she needed to give her.

'She's in here, sir,' said Rush's voice just outside the door.

Amy noticed Robert roll his eyes, seconds before Henry burst into the room.

'My God, what happened?' he exclaimed. 'Do you require Magda?'

'No, she's busy,' replied Amy with a weak smile. 'I'll be fine after a rest.'

Robert thrust his face into Henry's. 'You left her in the snow. I found her on her hands and knees calling for help and you weren't there.'

Amy could sense the rage building inside Henry, but he managed to contain it. His face turned to granite, only the muscle at the base of his jaw throbbing with anger.

'And why did I have to leave her? Because you are a violent little pervert who attacks women. We found Winnie bleeding in the bushes.'

Robert's face turned white. 'Winnie, the ugly maid?'

Henry grabbed him by the shirt front and yanked him towards him. 'Do not compound your disgusting crime with insults against the poor girl.'

'What crime? I haven't done anything wrong.'

'We found her abandoned in the garden to freeze to death, dress torn open, her back beaten and bloody.'

'It wasn't me,' cried Robert. 'Has she identified me?'

'No, she didn't see anyone because she was struck on the head from behind, you coward. You sneaked out of this house before anyone was even up. What happened, Robert? Could you not control your revolting impulses any longer after being stuck inside for a few days? I should fetch the constable this instant. The whole world should know what a monster you are before you hurt more innocent girls. Magda says Winnie will be scarred for life, just like Daisy.'

'No police,' said Amy.

Henry looked into his wife's eyes, which were full of determination, and he shoved Robert away from him. 'You can forget all about marrying Jane now,' he told his stepson. 'A lovely girl like that doesn't deserve to be tied to a monster for the rest of her life,' he spat before storming out.

'Robert, why?' said Amy.

He whipped round to face her. 'I didn't do it, I swear. I only went out to examine how thick the snow was on the drive to see if Jane would be able to get through in a carriage and I can prove it. There's been no snow since, so you'll see my footprints go down to the gates and then straight back to the house.'

Amy thought this over, considering her theory that he might be in league with one of the servants. If he was, then it might have been his partner who attacked Winnie, not Robert. The prospect made her heart swell with hope. 'All right, but you'll have to take Henry with you. I'm too weak to go outside again.'

He threw himself at her feet and took her disfigured hands in his own to kiss them.

'I'll prove myself to you, Mother. I haven't broken my promise.'

A nod was all she was willing to give him. 'Fetch your father, please.'

Robert exited the room and made his way across the hall to the sitting room. The door was closed, but Winnie's low moans were still audible. He paused to listen, excitement twisting in his gut at the sound of her pain.

'Can I help you, sir?'

Robert whirled round to see Rush standing there. 'Why do you keep jumping out at me?' he demanded.

'It's not intentional, sir. You just looked like you required assistance.'

'Fetch my father immediately.'

'I do believe he's upstairs with the younger children. They could hear Winnie's cries and it upset them,' he said before peering closely at Robert, as though awaiting a reaction.

'It is urgent,' said Robert when Rush continued to stand there.

'Sir,' he replied with a bow before shuffling away.

Robert glared at him, certain that bow had been sardonic.

A few seconds after Rush had ascended the stairs, Mrs Grier descended them. At first, Robert didn't notice her because he was too busy keeping his ear pressed to the door, squirming with excitement at the sound of the cries from within. It was only when she cleared her throat that he jumped for the second time that day and saw her standing there, wearing her usual black dress and a grave look.

'What's that noise?' she said.

'Winnie. She was attacked in the garden. Not by me,' he added when she frowned. They were talking in hushed tones so as not to be overheard.

'Then by who?'

'I don't know. Her back was beaten with a stick, but it wasn't me,' he repeated when her lips pursed.

'It sounds like something you'd do.'

'Not this time. I went to see if the drive was blocked, that's all.'

'You've said yourself that sometimes the urge comes upon you and you have no control over it. What if you didn't realise you were doing it?'

Robert was suddenly uncertain. 'Surely I'd remember doing something like that?'

'Consider how you've been lately – the dreams, the shadows, the ghosts. Would you really remember?'

All that horror descended upon him at once and he groaned and raked his hands through his hair. 'I don't know.'

'You must keep yourself under control or you'll find yourself swinging from the end of a rope,' she hissed at him. 'Has the girl identified you?'

'No.'

'Then there's nothing anyone can do, no matter their suspicions. Keep your head and all will be well.'

Swiftly she moved on when Henry appeared at the top of the stairs, still looking furious.

'You wanted to see me?' he said, the anger in his voice barely controlled.

'Yes.' Robert waited until Henry was standing right in front of him before continuing, not wanting anyone else to overhear. He barely recognised his stepfather. Henry was so rarely angry that it came as a shock to see his entire body shaking with it, his eyes burning. 'I've thought of a way to prove I'm innocent.'

'Oh, yes?' Henry said flatly, unconvinced.

'There's been no snow since I went outside this morning. I'll show you my tracks going down to the drive then straight back to the house.'

'How can I be certain they're your tracks?'

'Because they'll be my shoe size. Ask everyone else in the house, you'll see no one else has left.'

He sighed. 'Very well.'

After donning their coats and boots, they stepped outside, not speaking. Henry's silence annoyed Robert. He'd already decided he was guilty and now he was just humouring him, but Robert was determined to prove him wrong.

'Here, you see my footprints,' he said, almost gleefully, relieved his earlier prints were still crystal clear, heading away from the tracks left by Henry and Amy when they'd taken their walk earlier. Robert's arced to the left and they followed them, walking towards the driveway. 'See, I told you.'

'Let's just see where they end up first,' replied Henry.

Robert huffed and stomped through the snow, enjoying ruining its purity, rushing to keep up with Henry, who had already decided this was a waste of time and was eager to return to the house.

'There, that's where they end,' said a triumphant Robert. 'And look, you see them turn around and head back up the drive.'

'Not quite.' Henry pointed into the line of trees that ran off to the right, marking the boundary of the garden. 'You could have gone through there and come out just where Winnie was attacked. It's so overgrown, it would be impossible to see any tracks.'

'But I didn't,' he exclaimed.

Henry's gaze was cold. 'So let me get this clear – you admit to attacking Daisy and when another maid is attacked in exactly the same manner, you expect me to believe you're not responsible? Come now, Robert, what would you think in my position?'

'I'd take my son at his word.'

'Your word means nothing after you blatantly lied to me and your mother about Daisy.'

Robert's mouth opened then closed. He had no reply to that, but he refused to be cowed. 'I didn't do this. You have to believe me.'

'I'd love nothing more than to believe you, but unfortunately I know this estate like the back of my hand and I know you can reach the copse where Winnie was found from here.'

'In that case, you could have attacked her.'

Henry's eyes flared. 'Are you actually accusing me?'

'Why not? I might be Matthew's son, but you're Edward's brother.'

The last thing Robert was expecting from his usually placid stepfather was a fist in the face. He stumbled backwards, the soft snow cushioning his fall. All he could do was stare up at Henry in shock, a bruise forming on his cheek.

'It seems I'm not the only one capable of violence,' said Robert.

Henry glowered down at him before stomping back to the house, leaving him sprawled in the snow. The boy in Robert wanted to cry, he was so afraid for his future. Henry was the only father he'd ever known, and he needed his calm, steady assurance that everything would be all right. But the man in him rebelled. Henry had turned his back on him too easily, so Robert determined he would do the same to him.

Robert dragged himself to his feet, his fury building as he watched Henry's black-clad figure sweep back to the house without a single backwards glance. Enough was enough.

He was his father no more.

12

'How is she?' Henry asked Magda on his return to the drawing room, enjoying the roar of the fire after being out in the snow.

'I'm fine,' snapped Amy. 'I am capable of talking, you know.' She was bad-tempered, not only because of what had happened to Winnie, but because Magda was insisting she go back to bed and her hands were aching horribly from being stuck in the snow.

'She should be in bed, but she refuses to go,' said Magda.

'I'm fed up with lounging about in bed. If I have to endure it one more day, I will lose my mind.'

'It's futile, Magda,' said Henry. 'Once she's made up her mind, she's immovable.'

'How did you get on with Robert?' Amy asked him, neatly steering the conversation away from herself. 'Did you see the footprints he made?'

Once again, her eyes filled with hope and he was going to have to crush it. 'Yes. They led down to the gates then back to the house.'

'So he is innocent,' she beamed.

'I'm not so sure. You see, the tracks stopped at the tree line that marks the boundary of the garden. He could easily have cut through there to where Winnie was attacked and the tracks wouldn't show because of all the vegetation. When I pointed that out to him, he had the nerve to accuse me of attacking her.'

'But he could still be innocent,' said Amy.

'I'm sorry, Amy, but I think he's guilty. However, I have a confession to make. When he accused me, I'm afraid my temper finally snapped, and I struck him.'

'Is he all right?'

'He's fine, but I fear I've only made things worse.'

'Oh, Henry,' she sighed.

'I'm sorry, but accusing me was the final straw.' He looked to Magda. 'Has Winnie said who attacked her?'

'No. All she remembers is a pain in the back of her head, then waking up bleeding in the snow.'

'What was she doing out there anyway?' said Amy.

'She wanted to put some food out for the birds. She was worried they would find nothing to eat in all this snow.'

'Something about this doesn't make sense,' frowned Amy. 'Robert told me he enjoys the struggles and screams...' She paused as her own words made her feel sick. 'So why knock her out?'

'Perhaps he panicked, knowing we were about to wake up?' offered Henry. 'Or maybe he was worried about the sound of the screams carrying to the house?'

'Perhaps,' replied Amy. She looked to Magda. 'What do you think?'

'I think there could be more going on here than we know.'

'And Robert was very vehement that he was innocent,' said Amy.

'As he was when we quizzed him about Daisy,' retorted Henry. 'I mean, who else would do this? One of the servants? If so, Robert must know who that person is. Unfortunately, I don't think he'll confess their name to me after I struck him.'

'I'll speak to him,' said Amy. 'I got him to open up before, I can do it again.'

'Perhaps we should look at this from another angle.' said Magda. 'It may be to your advantage to keep to yourselves the fact that you know he has a partner in the house. Telling Robert will only put him and them on their guard. I believe Rush is aware of what goes on in this house. Take him into your confidence. He knows exactly where the servants are at all times. If anyone can guess who's in collusion with Robert, then it's him.'

'You may have a point,' said Henry. 'I've seen the way he looks at Robert and he came to tell me he was with you, Amy, the other day, he seemed quite concerned. Rush has been in this house since before I was born, he saw Edward grow up and he was here when Matthew came to work. He knows the signs and he's seen them in Robert, I'm sure of it.'

'If you do manage to recruit Rush into this, then you must endeavour to keep his involvement from Robert.'

'I think Robert's already suspicious of him. I overheard him shouting at Rush for following him.'

There was the slam of the front door and Amy exclaimed, 'Robert. I have to speak to him. I have to know that he's all right.'

'I'll fetch him,' said Magda, walking to the door.

When Magda had gone, Amy frowned at her husband. 'You shouldn't have hit him.'

'I know, but every man has his limit, and accusing me of attacking Winnie sent me right over the edge.'

'He will hold it against you.'

Henry nodded sadly. 'I know.'

Robert entered the room with Magda, the left side of his face bruised and puffy, expression thunderous, eyes black as they settled on his stepfather.

'I wish to apologise, Robert,' began Henry. 'It was wrong of me to strike you.'

Robert arched an eyebrow. 'Is that it?'

Henry suppressed his annoyance, keeping in mind not only Amy's feelings but the young, lost boy Robert had been when he'd first come to live here, the boy he'd gone to great pains to cultivate a close relationship with. Henry extended his hand to him. 'Let's put it behind us.'

Robert glanced disdainfully down at his hand before looking to his mother. 'You wished to see me?'

'Robert, shake your father's hand,' she told him.

'Why on earth should I shake the hand that hurt me?'

'And how many people have your hands hurt?' she retorted.

'I suppose he's told you I'm guilty of attacking Winnie.'

'He told me you accused him of attacking her. Why would you say that?'

'Because it could have been him. He shares Edward's blood.'

'Henry was with me when Winnie was attacked.' When Robert didn't reply, Amy decided to drop that particular topic. 'Do you require Magda to look at your face?'

'No, it's fine,' he mumbled to the carpet.

'All right. You may go.'

No one was more surprised by this dismissal than Robert. 'Really?'

'Yes, after you've shaken your father's hand.'

'After what he's done?' he exclaimed.

'Yes, because it's nowhere near as bad as what you did to Daisy. Don't panic, she knows,' added Amy, when his gaze jumped to Magda.

Robert sighed and kicked the rug he was standing on with the toe of his shoe before grudgingly shaking Henry's hand.

'There, that's better,' smiled Amy. 'You may go now, but don't leave the house. Don't leave yourself open to accusations by wandering off alone.'

'I won't,' he said before stalking from the room.

'He even walks like Matthew,' Amy said sadly, watching him go. 'Now we need to speak to Rush.'

The man appeared five minutes later.

'You rang, sir?' he said as he stepped into the room.

'Yes, Rush,' replied Henry. 'Please sit.'

Rush's eyebrows shot up with surprise. He'd never once been invited to sit in his master's presence before, not in Henry's time and certainly not in his father's.

'Forgive me, sir, but that wouldn't feel right.'

'You'd be more comfortable standing?' said Henry, amused.

'I would.'

'Very well. We wish to discuss something very delicate with you, Rush, but we feel you can be trusted.'

Rush's chest puffed up with pride. 'I've served your family loyally for many years, sir. You can trust me with anything.'

'And we appreciate that. It's to do with Master Robert.'

They all noticed Rush's eyes flicker.

'You know what he's been up to?' pressed Henry.

'I admit I have my suspicions, nothing more.'

'What put you onto him?'

'It was something in his eyes when he looked at the maids. It was the same way Master Edward used to look at them and, on occasion, Matthew.'

'You saw that in Matthew when he was here at Alardyce?' said Amy.

His expression was grave and a little sad. He hadn't liked Amy at all when she was younger, she'd been far too wild, but she'd grown into a strong, proud woman he couldn't help but respect, even if the rest of society didn't.

'Yes, my lady, I'm afraid I did.'

'I wish I had,' she muttered.

'So you contrived to watch Master Robert?' said Henry.

'Yes, sir,' replied Rush. 'Whenever possible. Fortunately, the majority of my duties ensure I'm upstairs, making it easier for me to keep an eye on him.'

'What did you deduce from your observations?'

'That he was romancing Daisy. I repeatedly warned her to stay away from Master Robert, but she assumed the prospect of a maid consorting with one of the family offended me.'

'And Winnie?'

'A complete surprise. I was under the impression the sight of her repelled him.'

'What exactly did you see this morning?' said Amy.

'I saw Master Robert go out early before the rest of the house had risen and he returned fifteen minutes later.'

Amy's heart sank.

'I had no idea the maid was out there,' continued Rush. 'I assumed she was making the beds.'

'Did anyone else leave the house this morning?' said Henry.

'Not that I'm aware of. I can make some discreet enquiries.'

'Please do. We require an extra service from you, Rush. We need you to help us by continuing to keep watch on Master Robert.'

He gave a low bow. 'Of course, sir.'

'We also suspect he has an accomplice in the house, most likely a servant, like Edward had in Matthew.'

'I'll watch out for that too.'

'Thank you for your loyal service. That is all.'

The man bowed again and left.

'You have a loyal ally there,' said Magda. 'You're going to need him in the days ahead. Now the snow has stopped, I must return home again.'

Both Henry and Amy were unhappy with this news, but she'd already done so much for them.

'We understand,' said Amy. 'Although you will be sorely missed.'

'You know where I am if you need me. There's a woman in the village due to give birth and I've already delivered her other eight children.'

'In that case, don't let us detain you any longer,' said Henry. 'But at least let us pay you for everything you've done for us.'

'I've spent days being waited on hand and foot in this beautiful house. That's payment enough,' she said, before striding from the room.

'I'm really going to miss her,' sighed Amy.

'She's becoming one of the family,' replied Henry. It was also one less pair of eyes to watch Robert.

* * *

Magda was in her room, packing her things into her big black bag, when the door opened.

'Robert,' she said without turning round. 'I've been expecting you.' She closed her bag and turned to face him. 'My, your eyes are black.'

'Like my heart, is that what you're going to say?' he glowered, closing the door behind him.

'I was going to say your soul, but it's not lost yet. You still have the chance to redeem yourself.'

He decided to ignore the comment. 'Your limp cleared up quickly enough.'

'As you said, I'm an expert at miracle cures.'

'I don't deny that, but I believe your ankle was never injured in the first place. I wonder what my parents would say if they knew you'd insinuated yourself into this house?'

'Not much.'

This casual comment enraged him. 'I see what you're doing.'

'And what is that?'

'You're turning my parents against me.'

'You're doing that all on your own,' said Magda. 'Turn from the darkness, Robert, while you still can.'

He threw back his head and laughed. 'You sound like something from a penny dreadful.'

'I only speak the truth. There's something dark and malevolent in this house and it's feeding off you.'

Robert thought of the shade he'd seen and swallowed hard. 'Nonsense.'

'It's not and you know it. I can help, if you'll let me.'

'You can make the thoughts go away?' he said, his voice dropping to a whisper.

'Perhaps.'

He appeared to consider her offer before chuckling and shaking his head. 'You really are a mad old bat. I wonder why Mother keeps you around?'

'Maybe the fact that I saved her life has something to do with it? Unlike you, I am entirely myself. I hide nothing.'

'We all have our secrets.' Robert's eyes slipped to her bag. 'If you've nothing to hide, then let me look in there.'

'That is private.'

'Witchcraft.'

Her lips twitched into a knowing smile. 'Perhaps.'

'I wouldn't put it past you to have attacked Winnie yourself just to set me up, you do so enjoy your solitary walks.'

'I'm a healer. I could never hurt another living creature.'

'Creature is certainly the word for that ugly bitch,' he sneered. 'Which is why I didn't attack her, but no one seems to believe me.'

'Maybe you were set up. But why? It could only be someone with something to gain and that person is not me. Think carefully, Robert. Who would fit the bill? I see you've made the connection,' she added when his eyes narrowed.

Robert got the strange sensation some sort of energy was emanating from Magda and it was trying to push him out of the room.

'It's time for you to leave me in peace,' she said, silver eyes tapering into slits.

'Fine, I'm going, but remember – I'm watching you.'

'And I'm watching you,' she replied before he slipped out the door.

* * *

Evelyn headed upstairs to check on how well the housemaids had made the beds. Since Daisy had left, their standards had slipped.

Robert appeared at the other end of the corridor, blocking her way. Just one look at his furious countenance was enough to cause her to turn and run back the way she'd come, but he was on her in seconds, one arm around her waist while his hand clamped over her mouth, and she found herself dragged into a little-used room, the furniture covered with dust sheets, staleness hanging in the air.

Robert slammed her up against the wall, fury darkening his eyes and drawing his lips back over his teeth.

'It was you, wasn't it?' he snarled. 'You attacked Winnie and tried to make it look like I did it.'

Evelyn couldn't reply because his hand was suffocating her, but she remained calm. Showing fear would bring out that side of him she had no wish to see.

He realised she couldn't speak with his hand over her mouth, so he removed it.

Evelyn took a deep breath before responding. 'I didn't intend for that to happen. How was I to know you were going to rush out into the snow so early in the morning? I intended to attack her while you were dressing, so you would have an alibi in Douglas.'

'Why?'

'To throw your parents into doubt. If you couldn't possibly have attacked her, then they'd start looking at who could, taking the pressure off you.'

'Don't you think it would have worked better if you'd told me in advance?' he exclaimed. 'You've just made everything worse.'

'That was not my intention.'

She patiently waited as he spewed a torrent of filth at her.

'Finished?' she said when he eventually ran out of steam.

'No, not by a long way,' said Robert. 'Not only have you made me look guilty, but you tried to convince me that I'd attacked that ugly bitch and not even realised. I thought I was losing my mind. You're going to suffer for what you've done.'

Evelyn reined in the fear rising in her belly when his big, powerful hands flexed and unflexed.

'You won't hurt me,' she said, relieved when her voice came out steady and strong.

'Give me one reason why not.'

'Because I'm your only ally in this house.'

'Ally?' he snorted. 'Who needs enemies with allies like you? How do I know you weren't setting me up?'

'Why on earth would I do that?' She touched his face. 'You're everything to me.'

Robert grabbed her wrist and twisted but she managed to contain her cry of pain.

'Lying bitch,' he spat.

'I'm not,' she said, her voice strangled as the pain in her wrist intensified. With her free hand, she slapped him across the face. 'Stop it, whelp.'

He released her and stared at her in surprise before his eyes blazed. 'I am not a whelp and it's time to prove it,' he growled, crushing his lips against hers and dragging up her skirts.

Evelyn welcomed him inside her, her body coming to life with thoughts and feelings she hadn't experienced in years.

She held him tenderly as his grunts filled her ears, her moans entwining with his until the pleasure culminated in a release that made her head spin, his warmth flooding inside her as his arms tightened around her waist, the strength in him both exciting and frightening her. God help them all the day he realised his own capabilities.

'I take it back,' she breathed. 'You're not a whelp.'

He pulled her head back roughly by her hair and kissed her long, elegant neck.

'I'm a man. Don't forget it.' One hand went around her throat. 'If you do, I'll snap this pretty neck.'

His grip tightened before relaxing, a hand sliding down her breasts, which were still trapped in their corset. His black eyes swept back up to meet hers and she felt her insides tighten with emotion. How she adored those eyes.

'If you betray me again, you will end up in a shallow grave,' he said. 'Do you understand?'

'Yes.'

'Good. Now you'd better get out of my sight before I get angry again.'

She straightened her clothing before hurrying from the room.

Robert sighed and went to the window, resting his forehead against the cold glass while his body cooled down. Guilt vaguely niggled at the back of his mind. He loved Jane and he knew what he'd done with Evelyn was wrong, but that had been inevitable. His ego needed that adoration. He resolved that when he and Jane married, he would drop the other women he saw casually. No one at Alardyce had any idea about those women, they were all in Edinburgh, so he only saw them when he went to visit his friends, some of whom had reputations even worse than his own. The reprobates and scoundrels were the only ones willing to associate with him. Yes, he would get rid of all the women, pay them off to ensure their silence, then he and Jane would be happy together. Forever. Just the thought of her made him smile – her golden curls, huge blue eyes full of innocence that made him want to protect her from the entire world. If he was honest with himself, that innocence excited him too, and he prayed she always stayed that way. It was a wonder to him that someone who had lived so long with Matthew could be so innocent but, then again, he'd hardly noticed her, an unwanted orphaned child who had only been given a home at Huntington Manor because of Esther's kind heart.

Feeling a little better now he'd decided to be faithful to Jane, Robert wanted to return to his room for the lie-down his mother had recommended. The blow to the face and his rage had conspired to give him a headache.

As he stepped out into the hallway, a curious impulse overtook him. Instead of returning to his own room, he headed to another room four doors down from his, a room that hadn't been used in years.

He pushed open the door and stood on the threshold, not sure this was a good idea, but something deep inside him compelled him to step inside.

This room had belonged to Edward. Although it had been transformed into a guest room, they'd never put a guest in it yet. Only the maids entered to clean it every so often and when they did, they didn't linger. The room contained a bed, a chair, a small desk beneath the window, an empty wardrobe and a washbasin and stand. None of these items had been used by Edward, but some things could never be erased. Robert now stood where Edward had once stood, no doubt dreaming the same dreams he was.

Robert walked to the window and looked out at the same view Edward himself had seen. The family vault was visible from here, the mass of grey stone surrounded by black wrought-iron railings, spiked on top to keep out intruders. A chill rippled down his spine at the thought that he would end up in there one day, decomposing. He hated the thought of dying, it terrified him. At least Edward wasn't in there. As he'd been executed as a criminal, he'd been buried in the grounds of Newgate Prison, far away in London. His mother didn't have to tolerate her tormentor resting close by.

A cold breath on the back of his neck had him whipping round to face the room, which of course was empty.

'Edward, are you here?' he whispered to the air, half-expecting a reply. He felt ridiculous when he realised one of the windows had been left open a crack to allow in some fresh air. He slammed it shut, cursing himself as a fool.

He wondered if Matthew had joined Edward in here to plot and plan, deciding which maid to attack next. How he wished he could have a confidant like that. If his father was still alive, he wouldn't feel so afraid or so alone. Instead, he was stuck with that pompous bastard Henry, who thought himself so superior. The loss of his real father suddenly hit him hard because he was only just realising what he was missing. The almost irresistible urge to tear the room apart overcame him because it had belonged to Edward and he had killed Matthew.

'If you were still alive, Edward, I would kill you myself,' he hissed to the room as a brand-new wound opened up inside him. He needed his real father, and he was never coming back.

A whisper in the corner of the room sent his heart racing but all he saw were the shadows lengthening as the sky darkened. Every nerve ending screamed at him to leave, but Robert stood his ground.

'You're nothing any more, Edward. You can watch me become more than you ever were while you whisper in the shadows.'

With that, Robert pulled open the door and stopped. 'What the devil do you think you're doing?'

'I heard strange noises,' replied Rush. 'So I came to investigate.'

Robert smiled smoothly. 'Oh, I see. Father's set you to watch me. How pathetic.'

'I'm afraid I have no idea what you're talking about, sir.'

'If you want to follow me, you'll have to keep up,' grinned Robert before running down the corridor and disappearing around a corner.

Rush didn't even attempt to follow, Robert had youth and speed on his side. Fortunately, Rush had been around longer, so he knew more tricks. He was going to enjoy employing them on the arrogant little sod.

13

Amy jumped awake, thinking it had gone prematurely dark, but it was only Mrs Grier looming over her. She'd fallen asleep in the armchair in the drawing room, exhausted after the traumatic morning.

'What time is it?' she yawned, flexing and unflexing her hands, which had fortunately stopped aching.

'Three o'clock, my lady. You slept right through lunch. Sir Henry said you weren't to be disturbed.'

As Amy had just woken up, she failed to notice how cold the housekeeper's tone was and how malevolent her eyes.

'I'm hungry, I suppose that must be a good sign. Would you ask Mrs Clapperton to prepare me some sandwiches?'

'Certainly, madam.'

'Thank you.' When Mrs Grier just stared down at her, Amy added, 'Was there something else?'

'Yes, my lady,' she replied, smoothing down her dress before clasping her hands before her. 'I've heard about what happened to Winnie and I feel there's something I must tell you.'

'Oh, yes?'

'For the past few weeks, I've had my suspicions about George.'

'The footman?'

'Yes. I've noticed him attempting to get close to the maids.'

The last clinging remnants of sleep fell away from Amy, and she sat up straighter. 'And?'

'He's been teasing Winnie in the servants' hall. Mr Rush had to reprimand him once when he went too far. Poor Winnie is a very sensitive, shy girl and it upset her. This morning, I saw him follow her out into the garden.'

'Where were you?'

'Upstairs in one of the guest bedrooms, overseeing the work of the maids. I saw it all perfectly clearly. Master Robert was walking down to the gates and George paused by the old willow tree until he'd gone.'

'So George left the house by the kitchen?'

'He must have done, my lady. He then disappeared in the direction Winnie had gone. Forgive me for not coming to you sooner, but I've been carrying out my duties upstairs and have only just been told the full story by Mrs Clapperton. As soon as I understood the relevance of what I'd seen, I came straight to you.'

'You did the right thing, Mrs Grier. Thank you.'

'My lady,' she said with a slight dip. 'I shall arrange for some sandwiches to be brought up at once.'

'Thank you, and some tea too. Could you tell Sir Henry I wish to speak with him?'

'Of course,' she replied before leaving, a sly smile playing on her lips.

* * *

Henry found Amy in a state of high excitement.

'What is it?' he said.

'Robert was telling the truth. He didn't attack Winnie and I can prove it.'

'Amy, if it's to do with those footprints...'

'It's not. Mrs Grier saw George follow Winnie into the garden and she even saw Robert go in the opposite direction. It couldn't have been him.'

'Why has she only told you this now?'

'Because she just heard what happened from Mrs Clapperton.'

'It seems very convenient,' he frowned. 'And this doesn't mean Robert's entirely innocent, it only means his partner was guilty of attacking Winnie. Robert might still have known he was going to do it.'

'Why would Mrs Grier lie? What has she got to gain? Nothing, as far as I can see.'

'Does she have some sort of grudge against George? Maybe this is her way of getting her own back.'

'She's not the pleasantest of women, but I don't think she's evil. Why don't we speak to George and see what he says?'

'I think I should do that alone.'

'Why?' she frowned.

'This is not a conversation a lady should have,' he replied, ignoring her roll of the eyes. 'And you're not well. The last thing you need is more worry.'

'This isn't worry, this is proving my son's innocence.'

'Of this crime, not of the attack on Daisy,' said Henry. 'He's still guilty of that.'

'I'm aware of that, but George might have encouraged him to attack Daisy and if we can separate them, then Robert might be saved.'

Henry wanted to weep for her. She had such faith in her oldest son, when already he could see Robert was a lost cause. 'You're right,' he said, unwilling to crush her. 'But I don't want you there when I talk to George. He might have things to say that are unpleasant.'

'All right, if you insist,' she sighed.

He raised her damaged hands to his lips to kiss them. 'We will get through this, just like we did before.'

'Only this time I have you, and that means the world to me,' she said with a tender smile.

* * *

George stood before Henry in his study, perfectly composed, while Henry shifted in his seat and cleared his throat, feeling incredibly awkward.

'Some disturbing information has come to my attention, George,' he eventually said.

The boy looked alarmed. 'Information, sir? About me?'

'Yes. Have you any idea what it could be?'

'I told Mr Rush I'd pay for that milk jug out of my wages. It was an accident. My hand was damp and it slipped from my grasp.'

'It's not about that. This is about something much more serious.'

'In that case, I've no idea, sir.'

Henry drew out the silence, studying the young man, who appeared nothing but confused. He was a stupid-looking boy who lacked the looks and charm Matthew had possessed. It was hard to see Robert pairing up with this boy, but looks could be deceiving.

'You were seen this morning sneaking out just before Winnie was attacked.'

His eyes bulged. 'I didn't do it.'

'Did you leave the house early this morning?'

'Yes, sir, but I only went outside for a smoke. Mr Rush disapproves of me starting work smelling of smoke, so I hoped a walk would get rid of the stink, that was it.'

'Did you see Winnie at all?'

'Yes, sir. She was walking through the snow to the trees, she has a thing about birds, she was going on about them not getting enough food in this weather the night before. Mrs Clapperton gave her some scraps to take out. Waste of good food, if you ask me.'

'Did you see anyone else?'

'I noticed Master Robert walking down the drive.'

'You did?' Henry said with interest. 'Did you see him return?'

'No, sir.'

'So you deny attacking Winnie?'

'Yes, sir, most vehemently,' George exclaimed, holding himself proudly.

'Apparently you've been teasing her ever since she came here.'

'It was only messing about, sir.'

'How am I expected to believe that? First you harass her, then she's found badly beaten.'

'I didn't do it,' he wailed, eyes shiny with tears. 'I'd never hurt a woman.'

Henry believed him. Robert and his real accomplice had set this boy up to take the fall, knowing he would be out in the garden for his morning smoke and that Winnie would be feeding the birds. Only a servant would have that information.

'Thank you, George. That will be all, for now.'

'What will happen to me, sir?'

'As yet, I'm not sure. You may return to your duties.'

The boy left, looking the picture of misery, leaving Henry to sink back into his leather chair, thoroughly dissatisfied. He would have liked time to mull things over, but Amy was anxiously awaiting him, so he returned to the drawing room.

'Well?' she said.

'He denied it and I believed him.'

'You did?' she said, the hope fading from her eyes.

'He hasn't the wit to commit any crime. I also learned something else – a servant is definitely helping Robert. I believe he and his accomplice set up George to make us doubt Robert was guilty of the attack on Daisy. That person has to be a servant and not someone from the village but someone who lives here. Only they would know that George enjoys a smoke before work and that Winnie wanted to feed the birds the next morning.'

'We can't rule out the possibility that George is guilty,' said Amy.

'He's just a stupid innocent boy who's being used as a scapegoat.'

'If it's not him, then it's one of the other male servants. All we can hope is that Rush comes up with something.'

'Before another girl is attacked,' ended Henry grimly.

* * *

The day grew warmer, melting the snow. By the following morning, the roads were clear enough to travel. The family were gathered together in the drawing room, Amy dozing in the chair while Henry read a book. Robert stood by the fireplace, staring into the flames. Intermittently Henry looked up to regard his stepson, noting how the flames, reflected in his eyes, made him look quite hellish.

The silence was broken by the sound of hooves. Robert rushed to the window and exclaimed, 'It's Jane.'

Amy jumped awake. 'Robert,' she called.

But he was already out the door.

'Jane,' cried Robert, rushing down the front steps of the house towards the carriage. The door was opened by a footman and Robert just managed to restrain himself from leaping forward when William descended.

Esther and the twins descended next, causing Robert to hop with impatience. Finally, his angel appeared, looking so radiant he found it hard to breathe.

'How I've missed you,' he said.

'I've missed you too,' Jane replied with a shy smile.

Robert wanted to take her in his arms and kiss her, tell her to never leave him again, but all he could do was bow to her formally.

He escorted her inside where Amy and Henry waited, the nanny just descending the stairs with the younger children after being summoned to greet their guests.

'Amy, thank God,' said Esther, embracing her. 'I've been so worried.'

'Nothing to worry about,' she smiled. 'I'm fine.'

Esther was so relieved her friend was once more in good health that she failed to notice the worry in her eyes. 'And no one else has caught it?'

'No. It seems it wasn't contagious after all.'

'Such a relief, and we're back just in time for the new year.'

As they all continued to talk and greet one another after the unexpected separation, Amy watched Jane and Robert together. There was such adoration in the young girl's eyes when she looked at her son that Amy feared it would be impossible to separate them, even if she told Jane the harsh truth about her future husband. Glancing at Henry, who was also watching them, she realised he was thinking the same thing.

The children were delighted to have the twins back and the nannies took all of them upstairs to the schoolroom to run around and play, leaving the adults to talk.

'We've started circulating the exciting news,' said William, nodding towards Jane and Robert, who were sitting together on the couch, a respectable distance between them, unable to keep their eyes off each other. Amy thought that if the situation wasn't so tragic, it would be romantic.

'Who have you told?' said Henry quickly.

'Just some friends in the city,' he replied. 'Sorry, but we couldn't wait. Jane's so thrilled.'

Amy's sharp eyes caught the smirk that passed across Robert's lips and rage twisted her insides. If he thought that was enough to ensure he married Jane, then he had a shock coming.

'Don't you think that's a bit premature?' said Henry, glancing at Amy, fearing an explosion. 'The banns haven't been read yet.'

'I know it's a bit unconventional but...' William trailed off, unable to come up with an excuse for his breach of etiquette.

'There's no harm done, surely?' said Esther.

Amy forced a smile. 'No harm done.' She looked to Henry, warning him to contain his temper, which she could see was building. It pained her that her normally placid husband was being pushed to anger so often.

14

For the rest of the day, Amy and Henry were forced to tolerate constant talk about the wedding. They managed to distract the conversation from this dangerous topic that evening with some parlour games, but they knew it was only a brief respite. The following day, they contrived to split up Jane and Robert once and for all.

While the nannies acted as chaperones to the young couple, Amy and Henry ushered Esther and William into the study.

Esther took one look at their dour faces and her heart skipped a beat. 'What's this about?' she said. 'You're starting to scare me.'

'Jane cannot marry Robert,' replied Amy.

Esther's eyes narrowed. 'I knew it. You don't think she's good enough for him. I don't know why – she's beautiful, rich and accomplished. Any man would be proud to have her as his wife.'

'Esther, shut up and listen,' snapped Amy, causing her friend's lips to purse. 'We have no objection to Jane. The problem lies with Robert. He's his father's son,' she said meaningfully.

'I don't understand,' Esther said, her eyes flicking to Henry before realisation struck. 'No.'

'He attacked a maid.'

'I can't believe it. Robert,' said Esther, sinking into a chair.

'You're absolutely certain?' said William.

Amy was annoyed. As if she'd accuse her own son of something so heinous without proof. 'Of course I am. He confessed and we found his partner in crime had attacked a second maid to try to make him look innocent.'

'How on earth would that make him look innocent?' said Esther.

'The plan went wrong. Robert was supposed to be asleep, but he took an early-morning stroll.'

'Who's the accomplice?' said William.

'We don't know, but we're certain it's one of the servants.'

'Like Matthew and Edward,' said Esther, looking frightened.

'So you understand why he can't marry Jane?' said Henry.

'I certainly do. This wedding is not happening,' said Esther, looking to her husband, who nodded in agreement.

'Jane has her heart set on this marriage,' said William. 'She won't want to give Robert up.'

'She won't have a choice. I will not have her suffer for the rest of her life,' said Esther, blazing with an uncharacteristic fire.

'We've come up with an idea,' said Henry. 'We're going to send Robert to stay with a very strict uncle of mine in the city. He'll soon whip him into shape. He's not yet reached the depravity that Matthew reached and we're going to make damn sure he never does.'

'I suppose that makes sense,' said Esther. 'He would be away from the maids and temptation.' Tears filled her eyes. 'Jane's going to be devastated.'

'My fear is even this news won't be enough to separate her from Robert,' said William. 'She worships him. Didn't he even think of that poor girl when he attacked the maid?'

'To be honest, I'm not sure he had the ability to think in that moment,' said Amy. 'It seems to be out of his control.'

'Then how will giving him free rein in Edinburgh help?' said Esther.

It was Henry who replied. 'Because he'll be kept very busy studying, reading the Bible and enjoying a Spartan lifestyle. Plus we're sending someone along to keep an eye on him.'

'Does Robert know your plans?' said William.

'No. As far as he's aware, the wedding's going ahead.'

Amy went to the window to watch Robert taking a turn about the garden with Jane, the two nannies watching over them as well as the younger children. Jane and Robert walked side by side, holding hands. They spoke animatedly, catching up after their separation.

'They won't take this well,' she commented.

'How should we do this?' said Esther. 'Separately or all four of us face them both together?'

'I think we should tackle them together,' said Henry. 'It might have more of an impact.'

'Agreed,' said Amy, turning from the window. 'No time like the present, I suppose. I am not looking forward to this.'

'Needs must and it's vital we keep in mind this is for Jane's benefit. Can you imagine the life she'd endure tied to a man like that? No offence, Amy,' William hastily added.

'None taken. I quite agree. Shall we get it over with?'

'Yes,' said Henry, ringing the bell for Rush, who he instructed to fetch Robert and Jane from the garden.

The atmosphere in the room was tense and silent, to such a degree that Robert and Jane sensed it and hesitated in the doorway.

'What's this about?' said a suspicious Robert.

'You wanted to discuss the wedding,' said Amy. 'Well, now's the time.'

Robert's black eyes locked with hers, and she stared right back at him, refusing to yield beneath the force of them. It saddened her to think that this conversation could finally sever the bond between them once and for all, but what choice did she have?

'Oh, good,' said Jane, her innocence breaking all their hearts.

'Come and sit next to me, Jane,' said Esther, sitting on the couch and patting the space beside her.

Jane happily settled herself in the allotted seat and beamed at them all.

'So, when are the banns going to be read?' said Robert, quietly confident.

It was Amy who replied. 'Never.' She found it satisfying when the cockiness was knocked out of him.

'What?' he barked.

Amy tilted her head and threw back her shoulders. 'The banns will never be read because you two aren't marrying.'

Jane's eyes filled with anguish. 'Why? What have we done wrong?'

'You've done nothing wrong, darling,' said Esther, patting her hand. 'It's him,' she added, nodding in Robert's direction.

'That's right,' said Amy. She looked to her son. 'Why don't you tell Jane why we won't allow you to marry? What's wrong, Robert?' she continued when he failed to reply. 'Ashamed?'

'What's Aunt Amy talking about?' said Jane. 'What is going on?'

'If you won't tell her, Robert, then I will,' said Amy.

Robert's glare was malevolent but still he refused to speak.

'Very well,' said Amy, turning her gaze from him to Jane. 'Robert attacked Daisy, one of the maids here. He beat her so badly, the poor girl will be scarred for life.' Amy decided not to mention what else he did to Daisy. Jane was far too delicate to cope with that.

The silence was deafening as they all awaited the inevitable explosion from Robert, but it never came. He just stood there, breathing hard, eyes growing blacker as the grandfather clock in the corner of the room ticked away the seconds.

'Robert, what is this?' said Jane.

'It's all lies,' he replied.

'Lies?' said Amy. 'You admitted it to me yourself.'

Jane shot to her feet. 'I don't believe it. Robert wouldn't hurt anyone.'

'Tell her, Robert,' said Amy. 'Tell her how you wooed Daisy, made her think she was special, just so you could lure her to a secluded place and attack her.'

Robert looked to Jane. 'I've no idea what she's talking about. I didn't attack anyone.'

'Don't lie,' exclaimed Amy.

'I'm not. Daisy is the liar but for some reason my parents choose to believe her over me and it really hurts,' he said with wide-eyed innocence.

Amy and Henry gaped at him. It was a very convincing performance.

'Have some backbone, Robert, and admit the truth,' said Amy.

Robert sighed. 'All right, I'll tell everyone exactly what's been going on around here.'

'Finally,' she said.

'I didn't want to have to tell you all this, but you've forced my hand, Mother.' He looked to the rest of the room. 'Ever since her illness, Mother's been suffering terrible nightmares about Matthew, which have been intruding on her waking days, and she's confused. Sometimes she thinks I'm him.'

Amy's voice was stolen as the hurt filled her up. She couldn't believe he would stoop so low.

'What a lot of rot,' said Henry. 'You confessed.'

'Did you hear this confession, Father? No. No one did, except her.'

'But...' Henry trailed off as he realised that Robert hadn't once confessed anything to him.

'You see, Father, it's all in her mind,' he smirked.

'Nonsense,' said Henry. 'I would never doubt my wife's word.'

'Neither would I, usually. This isn't her fault, she's just mixed up,' Robert said sympathetically.

'Oh, no, you don't,' said Amy, the force of her anger making her breathless. 'You are not pulling the same trick both my aunt and Matthew tried to pull. You will not convince everyone of your lies by trying to make me look mad.'

This statement brought back a surge of unpleasant memories to Esther, who had actually started to doubt the veracity of Amy's accusation; Robert was very convincing. At Huntington Manor, she'd allowed Matthew to convince her that Amy was mad, which had almost led to her death. She would not let her down again.

Esther jumped to her feet and cried, 'That's a low trick to play, Robert. Well, I saw through Matthew, eventually, and I see through you too. You're just as bad as he is.'

'Don't say that,' exclaimed Jane, rushing to Robert, who pulled her to him.

'Jane, come away from him,' said Esther, fear filling her at the sight of Robert's arms around her niece.

'No. I love Robert, I know him and he wouldn't do this.'

'I was married to Matthew for years and I thought I knew him too when in fact I didn't have a clue.' Esther frowned at Robert, studying him carefully. 'My God, why did I not see it before? You're as much of a devil as he was.' She rushed to place herself between Robert and Jane, forcing him to release her niece. 'Matthew used gentle words like that to dazzle me to the truth.'

'I'm being honest,' he frowned at her. 'I love Jane, and she will be my wife.'

'She most certainly will not.'

Robert stood up to his full height, glowering down at her – a big, dark hulk of a man, glaring fiercely at this diminutive woman, whose gaze was equally ferocious.

'And who's going to stop us? You?' His eyes narrowed into points. 'I'll crush you.'

'Robert,' exclaimed Amy.

'Don't you dare speak to my wife like that,' said William, gently pushing Esther aside and taking her place. 'I'll beat you silly, you little whelp.'

The use of the nickname Evelyn used caused Robert to erupt. 'Let's test that theory, shall we?' he thundered. 'I'll pull your ridiculous head from your shoulders.'

'Robert, that's enough,' yelled Amy.

When he drew back his fist to strike William, Henry slammed him back against the wall. Robert lowered his fist with some reluctance, glaring at his stepfather. But it was a lesson to them all. Robert was wary of Henry, but for how long?

'That's the man you love,' Esther told Jane. 'Do you want to marry a violent monster?'

'He is not a monster,' Jane cried, stamping her foot. 'He's just upset because you're all accusing him of doing awful things. I'm sorry, Aunt Amy, I love you, but Robert's right. What happened to you has tainted your thoughts and your illness has only made it worse. He isn't Matthew.'

Amy took a deep breath so she wouldn't shout at the silly girl. 'There's no mistake. If you marry Robert, you'll be unhappy for the rest of your life. Is that what you want?'

'The only thing that would make me unhappy is not being Robert's wife.'

'For God's sake,' sighed Esther. 'You lived with Matthew. Don't you remember what he was like? Robert has his silver tongue and you're falling for it just like I did. I will not allow you to endure what I endured. We're leaving for London. Immediately.'

'No,' wailed Jane.

'Out of sight, out of mind. It's time you were out in society anyway, and you'll soon forget all about him when you're introduced to all those eligible young men,' said Esther, throwing Robert a triumphant look.

'You can't keep us apart,' he yelled.

Henry readied himself to intervene, but Robert just slumped with defeat.

'I want to marry Jane, that's all I want,' he said before dragging his hands down his face.

Amy experienced a brief flicker of guilt. From the day he was born, all she'd ever wanted was for her son to be happy. All those difficult years working as a governess, scrimping and saving to give him the best she could afford, and now they finally had money, she had to deny him what he wanted the most. It would be so easy for her to close her eyes to the truth, to permit him to marry Jane and allow them to live their lives together, but his happiness had to be sacrificed in order to protect Jane and the other women he might hurt. One look at her own deformed hands was enough to strengthen her resolve.

'I'm sorry to say this, but the sooner you leave, the better,' said Amy.

'I'm not going,' Jane practically screamed.

'Oh, yes, you are,' said Esther, attempting to usher her to the door and failing.

'Don't you understand that you're destroying our lives with these silly accusations? I've done nothing wrong. This is all in my mother's head,' said Robert.

Henry opened his mouth to retort but Esther got there first.

'Don't you dare,' she yelled. 'Amy is the strongest, bravest woman I've ever known, and she deserves better than to be accused of being mad by her monster of a son.'

Robert's eyes filled with hurt. 'You've known me since I was a boy, Aunt Esther. How can you think so badly of me?'

'Don't look so hurt, you don't care a fig what I think. I did love that boy with all my heart, but he's gone, and I don't like what's replaced him. Jane, we're leaving. Now,' said Esther.

Everyone was shocked by the ferocious change in the usually timid Esther. She pointed Jane in the direction of the door and propelled her towards it with a strength born of fear and rage. She'd almost got her there when Jane broke free and ran back to Robert, who swept her into his arms and kissed her.

'I love you,' she said.

'I love you too and this is not the end for us,' he replied, gazing determinedly into her eyes.

Amy was slammed back into the past, to the day her aunt and uncle had discovered her affair with Matthew. They'd confronted them in this very room. They'd sacked Matthew on the spot but, before he'd left, he'd pulled her to him and given her an equally passionate kiss.

'Come on,' said Esther, as William helped usher her niece out of the room.

When Robert tried to pursue them, Henry shut the door, stopping him in his tracks.

'You will wait here until she's gone,' he told his stepson.

'This isn't right,' Robert exploded. 'You can't do this to us.'

'We can and we have,' said Henry. 'The sooner you accept it, the better. Jane will never be your wife. It would be best if you never married.'

'But I want a wife and children.'

'Perhaps one day, when you can prove that you won't become a tyrant. Until that time, you will go to my uncle in Edinburgh.'

'Not that old puritan,' Robert groaned.

'Yes, he's exactly what you need right now. Staying here, moping over Jane, will only make your condition worse.'

'I don't have a condition, but I'll do this to prove that I'm worthy of her.'

'Forget Jane, you're never marrying her, but if you behave, we might consider you marrying someone else.'

'But I want Jane!' yelled Robert.

The sound of voices outside had him racing to the window. When he saw Jane about to ascend into the carriage, he pressed his hand to the glass.

'Jane,' he murmured.

Amy went to stand by his side, guilt eating away at her, which was only compounded when Jane looked towards the house, the picture of misery as she searched the windows for Robert's face. She found him and gazed at him longingly before disappearing into the carriage, urged inside by Esther.

Robert pressed his forehead to the cold glass. 'This is so unfair.'

'I know it feels like that now,' said Amy. 'But when you've calmed down, you'll see this is the right thing to do. There's something I never told you about Matthew,' she said when the carriage had disappeared from view.

Robert turned to regard her curiously.

'He did awful things to me but, in the end, he hated himself for what he'd done and what he'd allowed to be done to me. Do you want to feel that way about Jane?'

'I wouldn't hurt her, I love her.'

'Matthew loved me.'

Her words silenced him, and he looked down at the floor.

'You said it yourself, you have no control,' she pressed. 'What if you lose control with Jane?'

Amy thought she was finally getting through to him until his head snapped up, eyes blazing. 'You don't understand, you stupid woman,' he snarled.

'Do not speak to your mother like that,' said Henry.

Robert ignored him. 'When I'm with Jane, I don't need to hurt anyone, the feeling goes away. I could have been normal with her.'

'You naïve boy,' she retorted. 'Once the first flush of excitement had worn off, things would have been very different, and adoration would have turned to contempt, just like it did between Matthew and Esther.' She rested her hand on his arm. 'Soon you'll see this is for the best.'

He shrugged her off. 'Don't touch me. You've destroyed my life. I hate you.'

'Robert, that's enough,' said Henry. 'After all the sacrifices your mother's made for you.'

'You mean dragging me away from a life of luxury to live as a governess's son? Oh, how grateful I am,' he said sarcastically.

Pain lanced through Amy. 'I did that for you, because my aunt said she'd take you away from me.'

'That's it,' said Henry, grabbing him by the back of the jacket and propelling him to the door. 'You're going to the city right now. I will not have you in this house a second longer.'

Using all of his considerable strength, Robert came to a halt in the doorway, refusing to budge another inch. He whipped round to face Henry.

'Just another year or two and I'll be bigger and stronger than you, Father.' He spat the word *father*. 'You're getting old.' He looked past Henry to Amy, who was watching him sadly from across the room. 'Then who will protect you, Mother?'

With one big shove, Henry catapulted him out into the hall-way, bellowing for the servants to pack Robert's things immediately.

Amy sank onto the couch, her son's threats ringing in her ears.

She sat in silence, listening to the scurry of footsteps and Henry's furious voice.

Eventually her husband returned, red-faced from shouting.

'He's ready to leave,' he told her.

'Already?'

'I had all the servants working on his departure.'

'Then they know something's wrong.'

'To be perfectly honest, I couldn't care less what the servants think. Do you want to say goodbye?'

'Yes, I suppose I must.' Amy got to her feet and staggered slightly as her head swam.

A few deep breaths were enough to steady Amy, and she swayed out of the room on Henry's arm, feeling light-headed but refusing to succumb to the dizziness wanting to overtake her. She needed to say goodbye to her son, to try to make things right before he left.

Robert was standing in the doorway waiting for the carriage to draw up, wearing his greatcoat, hat and boots. When he saw his mother approaching, he turned his back, but Amy walked around him so she could look up into his face.

'I didn't want it to come to this,' she said.

'It doesn't have to. I can stay and marry Jane,' he said, hoping for a last-minute reprieve.

'No. I'm sorry.'

He huffed out a breath and scowled at the ground.

'I hope one day you realise that your father and I have only done our best for you,' she continued. 'We don't want you to suffer the same fate as Matthew.'

His gaze was cold. 'Why do you keep calling him Matthew? Don't you mean Father?'

With that, he strode past her and down the steps to the carriage, leaving her to watch him go with tears in her eyes.

Henry held her to him as they watched Robert jump into the carriage. As it set off, he didn't wave or even look their way.

'He'll come round when he's had time to think things through,' said Henry.

'I'm not sure he'll ever forgive me for this. He thinks I betrayed him,' she replied, watching the carriage disappear around the bend in the drive. She could still hear it rumbling along and was reluctant to go inside until the sound had receded completely. 'It's the first time I've been apart from him. Since the day he was born, we've always been together.'

'He's a man now, old enough to strike out on his own.'

'He'll always be my baby,' she said, blinking back tears. 'I only wish he knew that.'

'As I said, give him time. Let him get settled in and we can visit him.'

'Have you sent someone to watch over him?'

'Yes, a trustworthy man named Knapp,' said Henry. 'He'll ensure Robert stays on the straight and narrow.'

'I feel better knowing someone will be watching over him. My worry is he'll fall back in with that disreputable set of so-called friends in the city. I don't know how to thank you. Sometimes I think you've been saddled with all these problems through no fault of your own.'

'I have not been saddled. I love you. You're my wife and Robert is my son. We're a family and we will get through this together,' he ended.

Amy embraced him, not caring that they were still standing on the doorstep.

'Thank you,' she rasped into his shoulder, tears stinging her eyes.

'You're shivering. Let's go inside,' he said, holding her close as they walked back into the house.

Rush was waiting to greet them. 'The fire's prepared in the sitting room and I've arranged for Mrs Clapperton to send up tea and some of her sponge cake.'

'Thank you, Rush,' said Amy. 'For everything.'

He gave her an uncharacteristically warm smile that made his blue eyes twinkle. 'You're very welcome, my lady.'

Henry joined Amy for tea and cake in the sitting room, eating in companionable silence. One of the things Amy loved about Henry was that they could enjoy peace and quiet together. There'd been precious little of that in their home recently.

Henry caught the plate when it slid from Amy's fingers as she fell asleep, the drama taking its toll on her. He stoked up the fire, kissed her forehead, then slipped out of the room and headed upstairs to see the children. What he'd decided to keep from his wife was that they'd heard all the fuss and yelling and become upset, so he'd been forced to tell them that Robert was going on a little holiday. All three of them had started to cry, they all adored their older brother.

15

'Amy, what have you done?'

She stretched and yawned, opening her eyes in dismay to see Matthew sitting in the armchair beside the roaring fire.

'I'm trying to save our son,' was her reply.

'And you think the best way to accomplish that is by sending him away?'

'He needs to grow up.'

'He will only fall back in with his notorious friends.'

'We've put measures in place. We can save him from sharing your fate.'

'You mean being murdered by you?'

'I would never do anything like that to Robert and you know it.'

'What do you think he would do if he ever found out?'

Amy's blood ran cold at the prospect. 'He won't find out.'

'How can you be so certain?'

'Because only Henry and I know, and we're certainly not going to tell him. Unless one day he conducts a seance and you tell him.'

'Very amusing.' Matthew cocked his head to one side, his eyes darkening. 'You will be with me again.'

Amy was appalled. 'What do you mean?'

'Something's coming, Amy,' he said with relish. 'Something that may throw you back into my arms.'

'You mean I'm going to die?' she whispered.

Matthew's smile was malicious. 'It's a distinct possibility.'

* * *

Evelyn stared down at Amy, who was asleep on the couch. What a waste of space she was, all she seemed to do these days was sleep. It was her fault Robert had left. What would she do if she couldn't see him every day, hear his voice, speak to him, feel his hands on her body? She closed her eyes, a tremor running through her as she relived that particular memory.

Her reminiscences were disturbed when Amy murmured in her sleep. Evelyn's sharp face honed itself into a scowl when she heard her muttering Matthew's name.

Amy gasped and sat bolt upright, sweat beading on her brow, eyes darting to the armchair by the fire. She sighed with relief and buried her face in her hands. So overcome was she by these violent emotions that she failed to realise Evelyn was even there until she spoke.

'Are you well, my lady?'

Amy visibly jumped. 'Don't sneak up on me,' she barked, harsher than she'd intended.

'I apologise, I didn't mean to scare you. I heard... noises.'

Amy's expression was suspicious. 'What sort of noises?'

'You were murmuring in your sleep.'

'It was just a nightmare. Where's Sir Henry?'

'Taking a walk with the children. They insisted on going outside.'

Amy considered joining them, but she felt too weak, so she decided to remain where she was. 'What time is it?'

'Half past three.'

'Please could you arrange for some tea to be sent up?'

'Certainly, my lady.'

'Thank you. Oh, and Mrs Grier?'

Evelyn hesitated on her way to the door. 'Yes, my lady?'

'How is Winnie?'

'As well as can be expected. She's returned to her family after vowing never to set foot in this house again.'

'Can't say I blame her. Has a replacement been arranged?'

'Mr Rush has taken it upon himself to arrange her replacement again, when the maids are my responsibility.'

'Please just indulge him, Mrs Grier,' she replied.

Evelyn's lips pursed. How she loathed her mistress. 'Yes, my lady. I shall see to the tea at once.' With that, she hurried out before she struck the stupid woman. Why had she been saying Matthew's name in her sleep?

* * *

Robert entered the Spartan hallway of his uncle's home in the city, dripping water all over the faded tiles. The heavens had decided to open just as he'd stepped out of the carriage. The entire journey, all he'd been able to think about was what his own parents had done to him, or rather his mother. His true father was dead. His mother was supposed to support him, defend him, and she'd stood by and done nothing while Henry had thrown him out of the house and that hurt.

His uncle Abel awaited him in the dimly lit hallway, all scrawny and grim, mean dark eyes set into a sallow face, sparse white hair atop his large domed skull. A most unpleasant individual, who looked as delighted to have him here as he was to be here.

'So you're Robert?' he said in a deep rasp.

'I am. And you must be Uncle Abel?'

'You're here because Sir Henry decreed it. Make no mistake, the last thing I want is an overgrown child intruding on my solitude. There are rules that you will obey unquestioningly at all times. Number one, you will be quiet, I don't like noise. Number two, you do not leave this house unaccompanied. Number three, you will avoid all women. You will not talk with them or even look at them. There are no maids here, all my servants are male. Sorry if that disappoints,' he added with a malicious smile, to reveal a mouth empty of all teeth bar two clinging to his upper front jaw. 'You will spend your time in quiet reflection and study and if you don't like it, that's tough. Any questions?'

Robert peered at Abel before waving his hand back and forth before his face. There was no reaction. The man was blind. He smiled. It would be so easy running rings around this one.

'You've probably worked out by now that I can't see,' continued Abel, wet lips contorting into a twisted smile. 'But that won't help you start up your nasty wee habits again.'

A door to Robert's right creaked open and from it emerged a vast, hulking figure. Robert had always prided himself on his height and strong build, but this man dwarfed him. His body bulged out of his expensive black suit, chest like a tombstone. His hands were the size of hams and looked just as raw, scarred from years of fighting. Robert wondered if he'd once been a bare-knuckle boxer. This theory was only enhanced by the flattened nose set into a large head surmounted by a thick mop of curly dark brown hair. His eyes were large and sea-green, but the hostility in them marred the startling colour.

'This is Mr Knapp,' continued his uncle. 'He will be your

shadow while you're in the city. Where you go, he will go, and he has licence to do as he sees fit if you misbehave.'

Robert looked at those huge hands and swallowed.

'I can sense you wilting, boy,' said Abel. 'I suppose you're big and tough when confronting innocent young maids, but Mr Knapp will be an altogether different prospect.' He waved a hand in Knapp's general direction. 'Show him to his room.'

'With pleasure,' growled Knapp.

He grabbed Robert by the scruff of the neck and dragged him towards the stairs.

'Oy, there's no need for that,' protested Robert.

'Just setting the precedent now, so you don't think about messing me around.'

'What do you think I'm going to do?'

Knapp slammed him up against the wall so hard Robert actually felt his brain shake and he glared at Knapp with all the hatred he could muster.

'Let's just get things straight right now,' said Knapp. 'Your father's told me everything about you, so if you think you can charm your way out of this, then you're wrong. From now on, your life will revolve around prayer, study and obeying the sound of my voice. Are we clear?'

'You can't do this, I'm not a prisoner.'

'You are until your father tells me otherwise.'

'Does my mother know you're treating me like this?'

'I haven't a bloody clue.'

'She'll be furious when she finds out and then you'll be for it, she'll...'

Robert crumpled in two when one of Knapp's huge fists slammed into his stomach. He curled up into a ball on the floor, trying to catch his breath, afraid he would be sick all over the threadbare carpet.

'Don't answer me back, boy.'

'Did... did my father give you licence to hit me?' he gasped.

'He authorised me to do whatever's necessary to keep you in line. It's for your own good.'

'How can this possibly be for my own good?' said Robert. 'I want to go home.'

'You're going nowhere until you prove you can be trusted not to hurt women.'

'I won't, I promise. Now let me go.'

'On your feet,' muttered Knapp, dragging him upright.

Robert was hauled upstairs and shoved into a bedroom. Before he could recover, the door was pulled shut and locked.

'Let me out,' he bellowed, pounding on the door with both fists.

When no one answered, he sighed and leaned back against the door, raining down all sorts of curses on Henry's head. Any lingering feeling he'd had for him disappeared. Sir Henry Alardyce was no longer his father. Matthew Crowle was.

His bags had already been placed in his room while his uncle and Knapp had been laying down the law. The room was austere with a basic lumpy bed, bare floorboards, a rickety old dresser in one corner with a cracked jug and ewer, an ugly wardrobe and a huge crucifix on the wall over the bed. It was cold and the windows looked out over a muddy, unkempt garden. Already he was pining for the luxury of Alardyce House. Even when his mother had been a governess, the rooms they'd been given had been better than this.

Robert slumped onto the bed, feeling wretched. Just that morning, he'd been on top of the world – heir to a considerable fortune, living in a luxurious house, about to be married to the most beautiful woman in Edinburgh. Now Jane was gone, and he was stuck in this hellhole with a religious fanatic and a violent thug, denied his freedom. Never did he think Henry would go this far. He'd underestimated his stepfather as well as the influence his mother had over him. They'd sent him away to be imprisoned and abused and he would have his revenge.

* * *

Henry watched Amy daydreaming out of the sitting room window. Since Robert had left three days ago, she'd been more distant. She was missing her son and he was desperate to take her mind off it, but nothing seemed to work.

He sat beside her on the window seat and she turned to him with a half-smile, as though she didn't have the strength for anything more. Her skin was pale, black shadows were forming beneath her eyes, and she was losing weight. She seemed unable to shake off the after-effects of her illness and that was beginning to concern him too.

'How are you feeling?' he said.

'Fine,' she replied in a faraway voice that lacked her usual vivacity.

'You don't look it,' he replied, stroking her face.

'I miss Robert. Have you had any word?'

'I've just received a letter from Knapp. Robert's behaving himself on a rigorous diet of prayer, study and plain food.'

'What sort of study?'

'Anything my uncle sees fit, he's an extremely learned man, if a little crotchety. Robert's in good hands.'

'And if he misbehaves?'

'Knapp can handle him.'

'Handle him how?' asked Amy. 'I don't want him hurt.'

'That won't happen. Don't worry, this is good for Robert. I'm more concerned about you. I want to bring Magda back. You're still not well.'

'It's just worry.'

'It's more than that, I'm certain.'

'Your foot's being put down again, isn't it?'

'Yes,' he said, responding to her smile with one of his own. 'And if you recover soon, we can go and visit Robert.'

'I would like that very much.'

'Good. Now get well. You have three other children who need you. I'll order you some tea and sandwiches, you didn't eat much at lunch again.'

'Because I feel sick all the time.'

'You don't think it could be... a child?' he said, pressing his hand to her stomach.

'I don't think so, it never felt like this the last four times. This is certainly different.'

'Well, you still need to eat,' he said, ringing the bell.

Mrs Grier herself answered the summons and fifteen minutes later, Amy was furnished with afternoon tea.

Evelyn left Amy and Henry talking in the sitting room, so engrossed in each other they failed to notice her distress. Robert's absence was really getting to her. Without him, her life was empty and meaningless. But soon he would be home again, she was going to see to that.

'Enjoy your tea, my lady,' she told Amy, forcing herself not to smile as she left the room.

* * *

Being in Abel's house was a huge learning experience for Robert. He had to admit that he'd been indulged by his mother, who had excused him most of his boyish mischief. His attack on Daisy was the first time she'd ever really challenged him over anything. Living in his uncle's house was teaching him to curb his tongue as well as his urges. Dutifully he rose each morning at six o'clock. He prayed in the small, dark chapel at the back of the house, ate a tasteless meal of porridge accompanied by a glass of water, prayed again, then joined his uncle in his ramshackle study piled high with books and manuscripts to learn about geometry, history or simply to read from the Bible. Obviously his uncle couldn't read them, but that didn't matter, Abel seemed to know every volume he possessed by heart.

Study was followed by a depressing light luncheon of stringy chicken and soup – his uncle's weak stomach couldn't tolerate rich foods – then back to study and prayer before an equally light dinner followed by more prayer and bed by nine o'clock. This strict, dull regime was boring; however, he was forced to admit he rather enjoyed studying with his uncle. The man was immensely clever and his enthusiasm for his subjects was contagious, although Robert could have done without all the Bible reading. Uncle Abel was careful to select passages about sin and all the fiery torments of hell, but he just pretended to listen with a studious expression. His uncle may have been blind, but his other senses were astonishingly acute and Robert felt sure his uncle would know if he had a derisive look on his face.

Slowly he was starting to win his uncle's trust, his ultimate goal to be allowed from the house further than the garden. Always Knapp was hovering somewhere in the background, like a huge malignant shadow that was waiting for him to slip up. But Robert made sure he never did.

It was torture to know his friends were so close, but there was no way he would be permitted to visit them. However, Robert had spotted a weak link in his prison. One of the servants – a young, hearty fellow by the name of Fry – was equally as bored in the house, the servants subjected to regular prayer and Bible readings too. The pair of them were starting to unite in the face of adversity, although Robert was careful to keep this burgeoning friendship from Knapp. He hoped that one night, when Knapp was asleep, Fry would help him sneak out of the house.

'Robert, time for your next lesson,' his uncle barked up the stairs.

He smiled to himself. 'Coming, Uncle.' He took one last longing look out of his bedroom window, able to bear returning to that dark, forbidding study in the knowledge that he would soon be free.

16

'Where's Lady Alardyce?' Henry asked George when he entered the dining room for breakfast and saw her chair was vacant.

'In her sitting room, sir. She decided to give breakfast a miss. Hazel informed me that she's feeling a little under the weather.'

'Why didn't she inform me?' he said before rushing out of the room and back down the hall to the sitting room. *Please don't let it be the fever again. Please God.*

He burst into the sitting room and sagged with relief. Amy wasn't flushed or sweating. In fact, she just looked listless, lying on the couch, gazing up at him with her black-ringed eyes. Her pale skin had overnight turned an odd red colour. Hazel was watching over her with a worried expression.

'What's wrong?' he said, sitting beside his wife.

'It's nothing. Just tired,' replied Amy in an exhausted voice.

'She almost vomited this morning,' said Hazel. When Amy scowled at her, she said, 'I'm sorry, my lady, I know you wished me to keep it a secret, but I simply can't. You're not well and I will not stand by and watch you get worse.'

'Well said, Hazel,' said Henry. 'Fetch Mrs Magrath at once.'

'There's no need to disturb her,' said Amy.

'There's every need,' he said as Hazel hurried from the room. 'Why did you keep this from me?'

'I didn't want to worry you. You've had so much to contend with recently.'

'I'd contend with the whole damn world for you, Amy Alardyce. Do not keep anything from me again.'

'I won't,' she said before turning pale. 'I feel sick again and my throat's burning.'

Dear God, what was happening now?

* * *

Unease rippled inside Evelyn when Rush opened the front door to Mrs Magrath. The white-haired witch was gripping her large black bag containing her mysterious potions.

'She's not very good at all,' she heard Rush say as they passed by.

Evelyn stood rigid in the hallway, wondering what to do. The witch would easily discover what was wrong with Amy, of that she was certain. Still, all the servants would be under suspicion, and they suspected a man of assisting Robert. But she hadn't had time to complete her plan, Amy wasn't sick enough yet. Robert might not be called home. She decided to hover by the sitting room door to see if she could discover what was going on.

* * *

'Amy, how are you?' said Magda, leaning over her with concern.

Amy's vision was hazy as she gazed up at her. 'I feel sick again.'

'She's not herself, something's really wrong,' said Henry, frantic with worry. In the short time it had taken Hazel to fetch Magda,

Amy had deteriorated even more. 'She's been feeling sick and complaining of her throat burning.'

Magda examined her with hurried, practised movements. 'Any other symptoms over the last few days?'

'Er, yes,' said Henry. 'She complained of headaches and dizziness and some numbness in her arms and legs. Her skin has slowly been turning that odd red colour too.'

Amy's eyes suddenly widened. 'Henry,' she cried.

'What is it?' he said, his voice full of panic.

Amy was deaf to their words as she clutched at her stomach, grimacing in agony.

'It really hurts,' she cried before turning on her side and vomiting all over the floor.

'What's wrong with her?' exclaimed Henry.

Magda pressed a hand to Amy's forehead then took her pulse at her wrist. 'She's been poisoned.'

'What?'

'My guess is with arsenic. I need to pump her stomach immediately. I need lots of warm water and a funnel.'

While Henry rushed to the door and yelled for the servants, Magda opened her bag and pulled out a large black case. She opened it up to reveal a red velvet-lined interior holding a shiny metal cylinder and a rubber tube.

'Will this hurt her?' said Henry, rushing back to his wife's side after ordering the servants to fetch water and a funnel.

'I'm afraid it will, but it's vital we get the poison out,' she replied, attaching the tube to the end of the metal cylinder.

'Poison?' murmured Amy, once she'd stopped being sick.

'You've swallowed some poison but it's all right,' Henry told her. 'Magda's going to get it out of you.'

The door opened and Hazel rushed in carrying a funnel, George following with a large bowl of water.

After lubricating the end of the tube with oil, Magda looked to Henry. 'You'll need to hold her down.' Her silver eyes flicked to Hazel. 'You too.'

'What's going on?' murmured Amy, the confusion overtaking her again as Henry pinned down her arms while Hazel held down her legs.

Her words were cut off by the rubber tube being forced into her mouth and down her throat. Amy's eyes bulged as she gagged on the tube, the pain and shock causing tears to stream down her face.

'It's all right, my darling, it'll be over soon,' said Henry, her distress paining him.

'Try to keep as still as you can, Amy,' said Magda. 'Funnel,' she added, holding her hand out to a stunned George.

Without a word, he handed it to her and she stuck it into the end of the tube. 'Pour the water into it. Slowly,' she told him.

The footman obeyed and Amy's body started to jump and convulse with the horror of the procedure. Once all the water had been poured, Magda removed the tube and Amy brought forth a gushing torrent of vomit and bile, covering the floor, the rug, the couch and herself. Hazel and George leapt back while Magda watched with professional concern and Henry stood on Amy's other side, stroking her hair until she'd got it all out of her system.

'You,' said Magda, pointing a taloned finger at Hazel. 'Fetch your mistress a large glass of milk. Immediately.'

'Yes, Mrs Magrath,' she replied with a small dip, glad to get out of the room and away from the stench of vomit.

'Has that got it all out?' Henry asked Magda.

'Hopefully,' she replied.

'You mean you don't know?'

'We'll have to wait and see.'

'What is the milk for?'

'It will bind to any poison still remaining in her stomach and prevent it from being absorbed by her body. Ah, finally. Don't spill it, girl,' she snapped when Hazel, in her haste, accidentally tipped some of the milk onto the floor.

'Sorry,' she replied. 'Shall I give it to her?'

'No, I'll do it,' said Magda, snatching the glass from her hand. Before giving it to Amy, she took a sip to test it.

'Isn't arsenic colourless and odourless?' said Henry.

'Yes, to other people, but if the milk was tainted, I would be able to tell. This is safe.'

'I thought arsenic had to be dyed now,' said George. 'So it couldn't be sneaked into food and drink.'

'Usually, but it's still possible to get it uncoloured,' replied Magda. She knelt by Amy's side. 'Amy, you need to drink this.'

'No, it hurts,' she rasped, indicating her throat.

'You don't want the tube down you again, do you?'

'That's too much, Magda,' said Henry.

'Not if it saves her life, it's not.'

'You're right.' Henry took the glass from her and crouched beside Amy, doing his best to ignore the stench of vomit. 'Please drink this, then you can rest.'

'Promise?' murmured Amy, huge blue eyes watery and red.

'Promise.'

She nodded, once again her determination seeing her through, and she took the glass from him. The sight of her shaky, ruined hands attempting to clutch onto the glass almost undid Henry.

'Here,' he said, steadying it for her.

It took some time for her to drink but she managed to get it all down.

'Please can I sleep now?' breathed Amy when she'd finished.

'Yes,' replied Magda. 'It will do you good.'

Henry picked Amy up off the couch, cradling her in his arms. 'Hazel, I will require your assistance,' he said.

Magda followed them upstairs to Amy's bedroom, assisting the maid to undress her, pulling off the soiled clothes and putting her into a fresh nightgown, wiping her face clean.

'Can I be of any assistance?' said Mrs Grier, appearing in the bedroom doorway.

'Yes,' said a furious Henry. 'You can round up the servants. I want to see them all one by one in my study in half an hour. Male servants first.'

'Yes, sir,' she replied, feigning confusion. 'May I enquire why?'

'You'll find out soon enough,' he retorted, unwilling to warn the person responsible so they could prepare their story.

As he settled Amy into bed, she clutched at his hand. 'Please bring Robert home. I need him.'

'Of course I will, if that's what you want.'

'It is,' she said, exhausting the last of her strength.

Evelyn turned away so they wouldn't see her smile.

Hazel set about gathering up the soiled clothes to hide her excitement. Robert would soon be home.

* * *

Robert discovered that the servant Fry was easily bribed. A gold pocket watch was enough to get him to unlock the kitchen door once the rest of the house was asleep.

'You must be back before five, otherwise Mr Knapp will know, he's a very early riser,' said the anxious, pasty-faced boy.

'I will be, have no fear.' Robert wasn't about to mess this up. If all went to plan, he could make this a regular arrangement.

Before Fry could protest further, Robert stepped out through the door and into the night. Not daring to pause, he tiptoed through the garden, and out of the back gate.

Robert was jubilant as he hurried down the cobbled street,

drinking in the sight of the moon above him in the dark, cloudless sky, the night crisp and clear. He kept glancing over his shoulder to make sure he wasn't being followed. The gaslit streets cast a multitude of shadows, but none fit Knapp's shape.

Robert managed to stop a passing hansom cab and directed it to his favourite haunt, where he thought he'd find his friends.

Robert alighted outside what appeared to be an ordinary three-storey house on a quiet street, but it was so much more than that.

After knocking three times on the door, followed by four sharper knocks, the door was opened by a man who could have rivalled Knapp in size and stature. Almost. Corrigan was an ex-prize fighter, hired by this establishment to eject any unruly clientele. The huge, scarred man gave him a nod in acknowledgement and opened the door slightly wider to allow him in.

'Good to see you, Corrigan,' commented Robert.

Finally he was among like-minded people who didn't think it a sin to indulge their desires.

'Long time no see,' said a sultry voice.

Vivienne, owner of this establishment, emerged before him. She was a very handsome woman in her late thirties with a mane of fiery red hair piled atop her head. There was so much of it that it always appeared to be on the verge of bursting free, as did her breasts from their corset. There was no modesty here.

'Viv, you've no idea how happy I am to see you,' Robert grinned, wrapping an arm around her waist and pulling her close, eliciting a growl from Corrigan. The clients weren't permitted to touch Vivienne unless they had her express permission. She'd worked hard all her life to set up this little business and now she had the luxury of choosing who she slept with. Robert was one of the privileged few to have enjoyed her favours, she'd broken him in, and it had been a night he'd never forgotten.

'It's all right, Corrigan,' smiled Vivienne. 'Robert is an honoured guest.'

'Are they here?' he asked her.

'Of course. Where else would they be?'

Men with a dubious parentage like his own, or through their own bad behaviour, developed an unwholesome reputation and weren't welcome in the best places in society, so they were forced to frequent establishments such as this, which suited them fine. Their needs and temperaments weren't suited to other places.

As he entered the salon, a loud cheer went up. Robert tried not to beam too broadly but he was delighted to see his three closest friends – Thomas McColl, Daniel Sweeney and Andrew Charteris.

'I'd no idea you were in the city,' said Andrew, getting to his feet to greet him with a hearty handshake.

'I've been sent to stay with my uncle, miserable old sod that he is,' replied Robert.

'Sent, as in exiled?' said Thomas, extending his hand for him to shake but not rising to greet him. Robert wasn't offended, it was just Thomas's way.

'You could say that. My father isn't very pleased with me.'

'Why on earth not?' said Daniel, likewise not bothering to get up, but that was more to do with the heroic amount of wine he'd consumed. He pushed out a chair for Robert with a booted foot.

'Thank you,' he said, sliding into the seat as Daniel thrust a glass of claret into his hand. 'We had an argument.'

'About what?' said Thomas.

'Something stupid, but we've been butting heads more and more recently, so he decided to send me away.'

'Did your mummy agree to that?' said Thomas with mock-horror.

Thomas was always ribbing Robert about his close relationship with his mother, but Robert let it wash over him. He knew Thomas was only jealous because his own mother couldn't stand the sight of him.

'She's been unwell, so she didn't have the strength to protest.'

'How long are you here for?' said Daniel, spilling wine down his shirt front. No one bothered to point it out to him, it was a common occurrence.

Robert shrugged. 'Until Father decides otherwise.'

'It's hardly a punishment is it, being in the city?' said Andrew. 'It's much more exciting than being stuck in the back of beyond.'

'It would be if my uncle wasn't keeping me locked up.'

'You don't look very locked up,' slurred Daniel.

'That's because I bribed a servant to let me out. Father's hired a big beast of a man to ensure I don't get up to anything, which includes meeting up with you three.'

'He's not doing a very good job,' said Daniel.

'To the Outcasts,' smiled Thomas, raising his glass in a toast. 'Every parent's worst nightmare.' This was the name they'd christened their little group, thinking it summed them up perfectly.

'Precisely. Father thinks you're all a bad influence,' said Robert, eliciting another cheer from them.

'So where's the china doll?' said Andrew. That was always how he referred to Jane.

'Back in London. The wedding's off,' he said, his mood slipping after being briefly buoyed by his friends.

'Another punishment from Sir Henry?' said Thomas.

'That's a bit harsh,' said Andrew.

Robert knew his friend wasn't convinced by his story but the other two were. Andrew had always been sharp. He was a brilliant man, the one Robert was closest to, the one he could discuss problems with and get a sensible response from, unlike Thomas and Daniel. Andrew was a very singular-looking man, tall and slender with green cat's eyes that gleamed when he was excited over some dark deed. He was immensely proud of his hands, which were long and thin and very white. Andrew said his hands were his future because he was training to be a surgeon. A scandal, involving Andrew attempting to set up a neighbour of his for fraud and then bribing him about it, had led to him being ousted from society.

'Henry's turning into a harsh man the older he gets,' commented Robert.

None of his friends knew of his secret urges, only Evelyn and their mutual friend knew about that. He'd pondered telling Andrew about it but had always lost his nerve.

'He's really preventing you from marrying Jane?' pressed Andrew, those cat-like eyes boring into him.

'Good thing if you ask me,' said Daniel. 'Women are nothing but trouble.'

'I beg your pardon?' said a husky voice.

Daniel's face cracked into a smile. 'Not you, Viv, you're not like other women.'

'Glad to hear it,' she said, topping up all their glasses with wine.

Daniel had been snubbed by society for seducing the fifteen-year-old daughter of a baronet and getting her with child. According to him, all the seducing had been done by the girl, which no one believed. With his dark, swarthy looks reminiscent of Byron himself, Daniel was popular with the ladies and his bad reputation only enhanced that attraction. Thomas was the opposite to Daniel with his ash-blond hair and soft blue eyes. His cherubic appearance hid the soul of a devil who enjoyed gambling away not only his own possessions but other people's, seducing married women, getting blind drunk and consuming vast amounts of opium.

'Jane is far too quiet and mousy for you, Robert,' said Thomas. 'You need a woman with a bit of fire, like little April here,' he said, slapping the backside of a scantily clad woman bending over to refill the glass of a man at the next table.

'Oy, you,' she said, straightening up with a smile. Her grin widened when she saw Robert. 'Robbie.'

He pulled her onto his lap and gave her a deep kiss.

'April, did you miss me?' he said with a devilish smile.

'Don't I always? You staying for a bit?'

'Hopefully.'

'And what about your china doll?' said Andrew.

Robert felt his libido deflate, so he hauled April to her feet and patted her backside. 'I'll see you later.'

'You'd better,' she replied with a smile and a wink before going to attend to another customer.

'I miss Jane,' he sighed.

'Looks like it,' said Daniel sarcastically.

'Your father will probably change his mind when he's calmed down,' added Andrew.

'I don't think so, not this time,' said Robert, gazing into his glass. 'If only I could communicate with her, but I've been banned from sending her letters.'

'What you need is a go-between,' said Andrew with a sly smile, eyes gleaming with mischief.

'Are you offering?'

'I am. I'll contact her on your behalf and ask her to send her reply to me and I'll find a way of passing it on to you.'

'Thank you, Andrew. You've no idea how much I appreciate it.'

'Jane must be heartbroken.'

'Yes, it was quite traumatic. My parents and hers confronted us together and said we couldn't marry.'

'All because of an argument between you and Henry, really?' said a dubious Andrew.

Robert inwardly kicked himself, he should have thought out his reply more, but he was just so happy to be out of his uncle's house.

'I don't want to talk about it,' he mumbled, slumping further into his seat. 'So what have you been doing with yourself, Thomas? How's that pretty little brunette you were wooing?'

'She married Gregory Misham,' he replied before taking a swig of wine. 'Stupid bitch.'

'Yes, how stupid, marrying an extremely wealthy man with good looks and a huge estate when she could have had you,' said Andrew acerbically, curling his lip with disgust when Thomas belched. 'Must you always do that?'

'You want to be a doctor, get used to disgusting noises,' he retorted.

Andrew turned his attention back to Robert. 'So, are you going to tell me what really happened?'

Robert opened his mouth to reply then went silent when the light in the room suddenly seemed to dim, as though it had been eclipsed. His friends' eyes widened and they craned their necks to look up at something huge standing behind Robert.

'Hello, Knapp,' he said without turning round.

Robert was hauled to his feet by the back of his coat and spun round.

'Thought you could sneak out behind my back, did you, boy?' growled Knapp.

Realisation struck far too late for Robert. 'Fry was in your pay, wasn't he?'

'Of course he was. Do you think anything happens in that house without my say-so?'

'Then why let me out?'

He turned his big bull head to regard Andrew, Daniel and Thomas. 'I wanted to meet your wee pals and see where you like to debauch yourself. Thanks for leading me here.' He smiled malignly, causing Robert's friends to recoil.

'Get your hands off me,' protested Robert as he was dragged to the door.

'And I thought you wanted to go home.'

'What do you mean?'

'Your mother's ill. She wants you home.'

'Ill? You mean the fever came back?'

'No. She was poisoned.'

'Poisoned?' he exclaimed.

'Aye. With arsenic.'

'Then why are we still standing around here?' he said before rushing for the door, almost falling over an unconscious Corrigan lying on the hallway floor, Vivienne beside him attempting to revive him.

'Did you do that?' Robert asked Knapp.

'He got in my way,' he growled before shoving Robert through the front door.

17

Amy lay in bed, her spirits at an all-time low. She hadn't felt this depressed since she was tortured by Edward, only this time, somehow, it was even worse. With Edward, she'd unwittingly walked into the lion's den, but this attack had been perpetrated upon her in her own home. It was one of the servants, there was no doubt about that. She wondered if this was some sort of revenge for Robert being sent away, but if that was the case, why hadn't Henry been affected too?

She shifted on the bed and grimaced. Her stomach, mouth and throat hurt from the stomach pump and she hoped she never had to endure that hideous procedure ever again. Still, it had undoubtedly saved her life, as had Magda, twice now. She was running up quite a debt to the woman and she had no idea how to repay her.

Amy gazed around the room in dismay. Vases of thistles adorned every available surface and she was starting to positively loathe the plant. The prospect of Robert returning home lifted her dull spirits. She was aware of the irony of wanting her son back when his deviant practices had indirectly led to this, but she missed him so much, and perhaps the attempt on her life would encourage him to reveal the identity of his accomplice. She also hoped the fact that she'd almost died would reconcile him to her and she despised herself for this pathetic hope.

Misery almost overwhelmed her and not even Henry's best efforts nor those of her younger children had been able to raise her spirits.

Henry had gone through the house like a dose of salts, calling in a detective from the city, and together they'd interviewed every servant, which had got them nowhere. To be on the safe side, Henry had sacked every male member of staff, except Rush, of course, who was in the process of hastily finding replacements. Only the female servants remained.

Mrs Grier entered the room bearing a tray and Amy regarded her disinterestedly.

'I brought you some weak broth, my lady, as per Mrs Magrath's instructions.'

'Thank you,' replied Amy, gazing out of the window.

'Don't touch that, Amy, until I've tested it first,' said a voice.

Magda stalked into the room and Evelyn turned to her with a frown. 'Her title is Lady Alardyce.'

'I have Amy's express permission to use her first name. *I'm* not a servant,' Magda threw back at her.

Evelyn's lips pursed into a thin line. 'If you're insinuating something has been slipped into her ladyship's broth, then you're mistaken.'

'Everyone is under suspicion,' said Magda, picking up the bowl and inhaling the vapours before dipping the tip of her little finger into the broth and sucking on it.

Evelyn looked to Amy. 'My lady, I really must protest about this woman's behaviour…'

'Oh, shut up and go away, Mrs Grier,' snapped Amy. 'You're getting on my nerves.'

Evelyn's lips pursed with surprise and indignation. Amy had always been a patient and polite mistress and this outburst was out of character. Evelyn stuck her nose in the air. 'As you wish, my lady,' she said coldly, throwing Magda a glare before striding from the room, slamming the door shut a little harder than was professional.

'What a hideous woman,' commented Magda.

'She's good at her job,' was Amy's lacklustre reply.

'She'd have to be, otherwise I can't imagine another reason to keep her around.' Magda frowned at the closed door before adding, 'How long has she worked here?'

'Five years,' replied Amy. Magda's question piqued her curiosity. 'Why?'

'She has a very strange aura.'

'What do you mean?'

'Dark.' Magda dragged her eyes back to Amy. 'How are you feeling?'

'Sore after you shoved a tube down my throat. Thank you, by the way.'

'You're welcome. Is there something you want to tell me?' she said when Amy's mouth opened and closed.

Amy sighed. 'I hate to keep whining like this.'

'I think you've every right to complain after recent events. What is it?'

'It's the way I feel inside, emotionally, I mean. It was the same after I was attacked by Edward, and no matter what Henry or my children do, I can't feel happy.'

'This will pass.'

'What if it doesn't this time?'

'You've been through so much physically and you've been forced to face some very unpleasant truths about your son. It would be enough to floor the strongest of women and you, Amy, are the strongest woman I have ever known.'

'That's very kind of you to say, but it's not cheered me up.'

'Robert will soon be home. I thought that would make you smile,' she added when Amy's lips twitched.

'Am I a terrible person for wanting my deviant son home?'

'No, you're a loving mother. Is that what's depressing your spirits, guilt?'

'Possibly. He could kill someone and I would still love him, but isn't that what a mother's supposed to do?'

'I've never had children myself, but I do know that love can never be wrong.'

'Did you never meet a man you could be happy with?'

Magda opened her mouth to reply before closing it again. Amy waited patiently. She'd never seen Magda unsure of herself before.

'When I was twenty-one, I was raped,' Magda eventually said.

'My God. I had no idea.'

'For years, it has remained a secret between myself and my attacker.'

'Who was he?'

'A man from the village, twenty years older than me. I was always the outcast, so he thought I was easy prey. I wasn't possessed of the powers or protection I have now, so I was unable to defend myself. But I bided my time, I waited until my powers came into full force. It was the one and only time I used dark magic.'

'You did?' said Amy, wide-eyed.

'Let's just say when I was done with him, he wasn't capable of penetrating a woman again.'

Amy didn't ask what she'd done to the man, she had no wish to know.

'My hair turned white the day I cast the dark magic. I learnt my lesson and everything I have done since has been in the light. From that day, I lost all interest in men. I need no one except myself.'

'As long as you're happy?'

'I'm perfectly content with my life. I look at you and Sir Henry and I'm pleased you've found such happiness together, you deserve it, but I don't seek it for myself.'

Amy grasped her hand. 'Please know, you're not alone.'

Magda patted her hand. 'I appreciate that.' With that, she swept to her feet, making it quite clear the conversation was over. 'Thank you for listening,' she smiled before stepping out into the corridor.

Magda took a moment to compose herself, dabbing at the corners of her eyes with a handkerchief, trying not to think about what that one awful experience had taken from her. She had a very important matter to attend to. Amy Alardyce was fast becoming the only true friend she'd ever had, and she would allow no one to hurt her.

She found Mrs Grier lurking downstairs, arranging a vase of flowers in the drawing room.

'I never knew a housekeeper who arranged flowers,' said Magda, watching her from the doorway. 'I thought the maids attended to that.'

Mrs Grier turned to face her, brandishing a rose as though it were a weapon.

'Those silly girls just clump all the flowers together in a mess. I like to add my own flair to the displays.'

'I hope that's all you were adding. Tell me, Mrs Grier, how often do you have access to Lady Alardyce's food?'

'Just what are you suggesting?' she demanded.

'That you poisoned her food.'

'I most certainly did not. Why would I?'

'I don't know yet, but there's something about you that I don't like.'

'You're mad.'

'No, I'm not. In fact, I'm extremely intelligent. I'll discover what you're up to. In the meantime, should anything else happen to Lady Alardyce, then guess where I shall be looking?'

'You might have her ladyship's approval, but I think you're the witch everyone claims you to be,' said Mrs Grier, eyes narrowing.

'And you're the Trojan Horse. I'm watching you,' replied Magda before striding from the room.

Enraged, Evelyn crushed the petals of the rose in her hand before casting it onto the fire. The witch had to go.

* * *

Robert sighed when he saw Henry waiting for him at the door of Alardyce House, as grim and forbidding as a marble statue. It had been an uncomfortable journey back to Alardyce, crammed into the Clarence with Knapp. The big slab of a man took up most of the room, glaring at him in silence the entire journey, forcing Robert to retreat into a corner.

A footman Robert didn't recognise opened the door of the carriage and he stepped down with great reluctance, Knapp's hand in his back propelling him forward.

'Hello, Father,' said Robert coolly. 'How is she?'

'Not good,' replied Henry. 'I wish to speak with you before you go up to see her.'

Robert didn't object, he was keen to show he'd changed, so he was careful to give no displays of childish impatience.

He followed Henry into the study, relieved when Knapp waited outside the door.

'Knapp said Mother was poisoned with arsenic,' said Robert. 'Do you know what happened?'

'I was hoping you'd be able to tell me,' replied Henry.

'It was nothing to do with me. I would never hurt my mother.'

'Do you think it's a coincidence this happens just after you're sent away in shame?'

'Father, please listen to me,' said Robert, fighting to maintain his composure. 'This was not me. I knew nothing of it and if I had, I would have done everything in my power to stop it.'

'Then tell me who your accomplice is.'

Robert chewed his lip. He had to give him a name, one that would be convincing. He couldn't give up Evelyn, their friend wouldn't be impressed, and she was one of his very few links to his real father. 'Douglas.'

'Your valet?'

He nodded, careful to look shamefaced.

Henry studied him hard before nodding. 'That makes sense.'

Robert sighed inwardly with relief.

'If you'd told us sooner, this could have been avoided.'

'I didn't think he was any danger to Mother. When I returned, I was going to give him the sack. I would have done it before I left, but you gave me no time.' He forced himself not to smile when Henry's eyes flashed with guilt. 'Can I see her now?'

'Yes,' replied Henry distractedly. 'But don't stay too long, she needs her rest. And just so you know, I called in the police when your mother was poisoned but she told me to send them away because she didn't want it coming out about you. Should anything else happen to her, I want you where I can keep an eye on you. You do not leave this estate alone. Are we clear?'

'Crystal, Father.'

'Good. You may go to your mother.'

Robert was smirking as he left the study. Henry would be so concerned with considering how different things could have been if he hadn't thrown him out of the house so quickly that hopefully he would leave him in peace.

'What are you grinning at?' growled a voice.

Robert's smile broadened as he turned to face Knapp. 'That interview with my father went better than I thought it would. And you don't scare me any more, Knapp.'

'Going to hide behind your mother's skirts like the coward I know you are?'

'You're the coward. You've bullied me for the last time. You'd better watch your back,' said Robert before sauntering upstairs.

* * *

It was a relief to Amy that Robert didn't appear to be in the slightest bit cross with her.

She sat up in bed and held her arms out to him. He ran to her, and Amy enveloped him in an embrace, tears forming in her eyes.

'My boy.'

'I'm sorry, Mama.'

'It's all right, darling,' she said, kissing the top of his head.

He regarded her with his dark eyes. 'Father said you were poisoned with arsenic.'

'I was, but once again, Magda saved me.'

'It was nothing to do with me, I swear. I would never do anything to hurt you.'

'I'm well aware of that but – and I really need you to listen to me without getting angry – we think your accomplice did it. Your father dismissed all the male servants, but we have to be sure the person who poisoned me is really gone. What if they try it again or hurt one of the children?'

'It was Douglas,' he said quickly.

'Thank you,' she replied, able to breathe easier now she knew the person responsible was gone. 'Why did you refuse to tell us before? Remember what I said – nothing will stop me loving you.'

'Henry said he wanted to take this further but you stopped him. Thank you,' he said, hanging his head.

'This must stop. Now. I pray that it does with Douglas's departure.'

'It will, Mama, I promise.'

'Good. How was it at your uncle's?'

His first instinct was to tell her how Knapp had hit him and imprisoned him, but she looked so unwell and unhappy, all thanks to him. Like Jane, his mother could still make him feel genuine emotion. 'It was fine, despite all the Bible reading.'

'Never mind, you're home now. Call your father for me, will you?'

She challenged him with a look at her use of the term *father*, but he just smiled and nodded, although he was disappointed. He'd wanted it to be just the two of them, but he also wanted to get back in her good books. 'Certainly, Mother.'

Rather than fetch Henry himself, Robert rang the bell, which was answered by Evelyn, whose eyes lit up to see him.

'Fetch my father, will you, Mrs Grier?' he said in his best authoritative voice.

'Yes, sir,' she replied, surreptitiously reaching out to touch his hand, but he slammed the door shut in her face before she could make contact.

* * *

Henry was not at all happy about Robert's return. He felt it wasn't anywhere near enough of a punishment, but he couldn't go against Amy's wishes, not when she was smiling again.

'Robert confirmed that Douglas was his accomplice,' said Amy when he entered the room.

'That's something, I suppose, but once again, he gets away with it,' he replied, nodding at Robert. 'His error almost cost you your life, Amy, and I can never forgive him for that.'

Robert listened to them discuss him as though he wasn't there, but he bit his tongue.

'I'm not too happy about it myself, but I will not allow this to tear our family apart,' said Amy.

Henry turned his attention to his stepson. 'One more slip-up, Robert, and you are out for good.' He looked back at his wife. 'Even you have to agree with that, Amy. We do have other children to consider.'

'Absolutely,' she replied, recognising she couldn't push her husband another inch without destroying their marriage. She looked to her son. 'You do understand that you're standing on quicksand, Robert?'

'I do,' he replied. 'Which is why I'm going to prove myself to you.'

'I'll believe that when I see it,' scoffed Henry before leaving the room.

'He means it,' Amy told her son when her husband had gone. 'Your father's at the end of his tether. He will throw you out of this house with nothing if you continue to push him.'

'I understand,' he said, hanging his head. His real father's reaction wouldn't be to throw him out. With every passing day, he pined for Matthew more and more.

Robert waited in Evelyn's room for her to return, his fury building by the second. The moment she came through the door, he grabbed her by the shoulders.

'You poisoned my mother,' he spat in her face.

'It wasn't enough to kill her,' she said, fighting to keep calm. 'I only wanted to make her sick enough to bring you home.'

'Liar,' he snarled.

'Honestly. I wouldn't do that to her because it would hurt you. And I missed you,' she said, running a finger down his chest.

'You're deranged.'

'I take it you haven't told your parents about me?'

'No, although I don't know why not.'

She wrapped her arms around him. 'Because you need me.'

'I need no one,' he thundered in her face.

Evelyn didn't flinch. 'Aren't you happier now you're home?'

'Yes,' was his icy reply.

'In that case, you should be thanking me.'

He pushed her away. 'You disgust me.'

'We both know that's not true.' She unfastened her dress and slid it off her shoulders. 'Look at me, Robert.'

'I don't want to. You make me sick.'

She grasped his face between both hands. 'Look at me.'

He raised his head, his dark eyes turbulent. 'If I do, then I might just kill you.'

'You won't,' she whispered, touching his face. 'You're my beautiful Matthew.'

Her eyes widened when she realised what she'd said. Infuriated, he grabbed her wrist and twisted, Evelyn fighting not to cry out.

'I am not him,' he snarled. 'But you wish I was, don't you?'

'No. I know you're Robert, your own man.'

'Give me one good reason why I shouldn't tell my parents about you?'

'Because then you'd have no one to understand what you're going through. You'd feel even more alone than you do already.'

He sighed and released her.

'I'm right, aren't I?' she purred, thinking it safe to slide her arms around his waist.

Robert shoved her away. The touch of her hands revolted him. 'If you ever hurt my mother again, I will kill you.'

Evelyn's lips pursed. 'Why does everyone run around after Amy Alardyce? I don't understand.'

'Because she's a unique, strong woman. I see it and so did Matthew, which is what makes you so furious.'

With a smirk, he left the room, slamming the door shut behind him. Evelyn started to pace, wrestling with her hurt, fury and her hatred for Amy.

She unhooked her corset, and turned to look over her shoulder in the mirror at the scars licking their way up her back and onto her shoulders. They were all she had left of Matthew, except for the gold ring she wore hidden beneath her dress, hanging from a chain around her neck. Just the sight of the scars soothed her, and she breathed a little easier.

'You really loved me, I know you did,' she said, running her fingers lovingly over the scars. 'Your feelings for *her* were nothing but sentiment and I'll prove it to the whole world. I'll finish the job Edward couldn't and then I'll be the only woman you loved, my darling Matthew.'

* * *

Over the next couple of days, Robert went out of his way to avoid Evelyn, ruing the day she came to work at Alardyce House. A number of years ago, he had found out it was part of an insidious plan to get near him, and when she'd first approached him with the truth, he'd been flattered. Now he'd realised she'd also come for his mother and he feared what else she might do. He'd contacted their mutual friend, but they were being slow about responding. They were the only one who could make Evelyn go quietly.

These were the thoughts that troubled him as he paced the gardens. Henry had said he wasn't permitted to leave the estate alone and from now on he would be the perfect son until he'd regained his parents' trust. But he couldn't shake the sense of foreboding.

* * *

Amy jumped awake, the hairs on the back of her neck rising. She'd drifted off in her armchair in the sitting room. Four days had passed since she'd been poisoned, and she was feeling much stronger.

She woke to find the housekeeper staring down at her, unblinking. Her lips were so pinched they'd practically disappeared and her long thin hands were curled into fists. She was so still Amy couldn't even detect her breathing.

'Mrs Grier, is something wrong?' said Amy.

'Yes, my lady, there is.'

'What is it?'

'I just want to say that... that...' She paused to take a deep breath, steadying herself before continuing. 'I hate you.'

Amy thought she'd misheard. 'Excuse me?'

'You heard. Just the mere sight of you makes me want to vomit.'

'Are you ill?'

'Yes, because I'm looking at you. I never had him completely, it was always you.'

'What on earth are you talking about?'

Evelyn drew in a deep breath, drawing back her head before bellowing, 'Matthew.'

Amy jumped, not because she'd shouted but because she'd mentioned *his* name. 'You knew Matthew?'

'Knew him? You truly are a stupid woman. It baffles me why everyone thinks differently.'

'How did you know him?' demanded Amy, slowly rising from the chair and backing away, attempting to sidle to the door.

'I was his wife,' she cried.

Amy was so stunned she forgot about the desperate need to escape the room.

'When he was dismissed for his affair with you, he went into the city, seeking work. He found me working in a grand house, we fell in love and married. But I was never enough. I knew he missed you, he thought about you when I should have had all his attention. What's so special about you?' she sneered.

Amy ignored the question. 'Why are you only telling me this now, Mrs Grier?' she demanded. 'Why did you come to this house?'

She sighed and shook her head. 'You're Robert's real accomplice, aren't you?'

The look on Evelyn's face said it all. 'I know what you did to Matthew. I know you killed him.'

Amy's stomach dropped. 'You're insane.'

'Don't try and lie your way out of this. I was informed by a very reliable source.'

'There were only two people who knew about that and one of them is dead.'

'Your little secret's out, Amy.'

'Have you told Robert?'

Evelyn's maniacal smile flipped into a scowl. 'Not yet.'

Amy was relieved. 'I want you out of this house right now.'

'I bet you do. Afraid I'll tell your precious boy who you really are? Saint Amy, who's suffered so much, is as bad as the men she condemns.'

'I am nothing like Matthew or Edward. I acted in self-defence. Matthew himself said it was the right thing to do.'

'If you don't feel guilty, then why do you dream about him? I've heard you say his name while you've been having one of your many naps. Longing for a real man after years of being stuck with Sir Henry?'

'My husband is far more of a man than Matthew ever was. He's honourable, strong and decent. If you'd married a man with similar qualities, you might not be the evil bitch you are now.' Amy's temper was up and when that happened, she found it extremely difficult to curb her tongue. 'And anyway, if you and Matthew were so perfect together, why did he end up marrying Esther? Was that marriage even legal?'

'Of course not. We never divorced because he couldn't bear the thought.'

'Oh, yes? He told me his deepest, darkest secrets, but he never once spoke about you and you know why? Because he'd forgotten all about you.'

'Rubbish. He was doing it for us. He wed that insipid stick insect so we could live a life of luxury together.'

'Then why weren't you at Huntington Manor? He could have sneaked you in as a servant or governess, but he didn't because you were nothing more than a vague memory. I was the one he wanted, me and the son we had together, and that's what's tearing you apart. Jealousy.'

Evelyn's eyes seemed to protrude from her face, her rage was so intense. From inside her sleeve, she drew a long, thin, silver letter opener Henry kept on his desk in the library.

'Matthew said that big mouth of yours would get you into trouble and now it has,' Evelyn told her.

'Think twice before you do anything drastic. Remember what happened to Matthew and Edward when they tried to kill me,' said Amy as she continued to back up towards the door behind her.

'Unlike them, I don't want to inflict various tortures on you. I just want you dead. Dead and gone, like my Matthew,' she hissed, advancing on Amy, gripping the letter opener in one hand. 'Then I can finally be at peace, knowing I'm the only woman on the face of the earth he cared for.'

'Sorry, Mrs Grier, I'm afraid I can't oblige,' said Amy before racing for the other door that led to the rear of the house.

Evelyn just watched as she frantically wrenched at the handle.

'I took the liberty of locking it from the other side earlier,' she said with a chilling smile.

Amy snatched up a vase sitting on the fireplace, smashed it against the wall and retrieved one of the jagged shards.

'Call for the servants as much as you like, no one's coming,' said Evelyn before lunging at Amy.

* * *

As Robert returned to the house after his stroll around the garden, he heard raised voices from the direction of his mother's sitting room. His guts twisting with panic, he raced towards the house, almost falling in his haste.

He charged up the steps and burst into the house, the sound of yelling and things being thrown even louder.

Bellowing for the servants, he charged at the door and was infuriated when it refused to open. He was relieved to hear his mother's voice calling for help. At least she was still alive.

The door gave way and he stumbled inside just in time to see his mother, clothing torn, a bruise on her cheek and hair in disarray, whack Evelyn around the side of the head with a poker. She dropped with a thud.

'Are you all right?' he exclaimed, rushing to his mother's side.

Amy nodded and lowered her arm, the poker falling from her hand. 'I am. I can't say the same about Mrs Grier,' she coolly replied.

Robert was both astonished by and proud of his mother in that moment. There was that famous strength of hers that had seen her through so much trauma and made her determined to survive both Matthew and Edward. She was magnificent.

He hugged her, feeling her shake in his arms. Rush appeared in the doorway, astonished to see the lady of the house in disarray and the housekeeper bleeding on the floor.

'Mrs Grier attacked my mother,' Robert told him. 'Fetch the constable at once.'

'Yes, sir,' replied Rush before ambling away to carry out his orders.

Robert steered his mother out of the room, across the hall and into the drawing room.

'Leave everything to me,' he told her. 'You rest and recover.'

'Yes, thank you, Robert,' she replied in a vague voice, shock starting to overtake her.

He hurried back into the sitting room, picking his way through the debris of the violent fight to reach Evelyn.

'Wake up,' he whispered, gently tapping her face.

Her eyes rolled open and she groaned. 'My head hurts.'

'You need to get out of here right now. Henry will insist on calling the police this time.'

'I don't think I can walk.'

'I'll help you. Come on, we need to go,' he said, indicating the door Amy had tried to get through and failed.

'I locked it. Here's the key,' said Evelyn, scrabbling at her dress pocket.

Impatiently, Robert retrieved the key, unlocked the door and pushed it open.

Gathering Evelyn up into his arms, he hurried through the door and towards the back of the house, aiming for the conservatory. The door leading out into the garden was unlocked and he stepped outside, making for the trees.

'I'm cold,' murmured Evelyn, pressing her face into his chest.

'You'll be all right,' he replied, racing across the garden, her weight nothing to him.

'What will I do?' she said, eyes closed, blood seeping from the cut to the side of her head and dripping onto his shirt.

'We'll sort something out,' he said as he pelted through the trees and out the other side. When the frozen pond that lay beyond the gardens appeared before him, he slowed down to catch his breath.

'Why are you stopping?' demanded Evelyn.

'I need a rest,' he replied, taking in the majesty of the pond of ice.

The landscape was white and barren, everything covered in a

film of ice. The absolute silence was so strange after the scene inside the house, the fact that he cradled a bleeding woman in his arms just making it seem even more surreal.

'You must get me away from here, Robert, please,' said Evelyn, her voice soft. 'We can leave together.'

'Sorry, you're on your own.'

With that, he tossed her into the pond. Evelyn screamed as she spun through the air, landing on the ice, which gave way beneath her with a loud crack and she sank into the freezing water, horror contorting her delicate features.

'Help me, Robert,' she cried, desperately clawing at the ice, which continued to break around her.

Every time she tried to gain purchase on a piece of ice, it disintegrated into a dozen more. Her heavy wool dress began to drag her under as it became saturated.

'Robert,' she screamed as she sank, the grey water closing over her head. Spookily, a white hand managed to break the surface, clawing at the ice before sinking beneath the water.

'The Lady of the Pond. Doesn't have quite the same ring to it,' he murmured to himself before chuckling.

He'd just killed someone, for the first time in his life. All he could do was stare at the spot where she'd sunk, his body turning numb.

Then it hit him – fire flooding his veins, making his heart hammer in his chest. He felt powerful, even more powerful than when he'd attacked Daisy. This fire spurred him into action.

Taking a deep breath, he plunged his hands into the icy water, ensuring it splashed up the arms of his jacket and onto his shirt front, ignoring the stinging cold as well as the uncomfortable thought that Evelyn's claw-like hand might reach out of the water and pull him under. He was in control now.

Robert turned and raced back to the house, running faster than he'd ever run before, rejoicing in the power in his muscles, understanding for the first time in his life what he was truly capable of.

When he arrived back at the house, he found his mother already recovered from her shock and calling for him.

'Robert, where have you been and where's Mrs Grier?' she demanded, hands on hips.

'She's in the pond.'

'What is she doing in the pond and why are you all wet?' Her eyes widened. 'My God, is she...'

'Yes, I'm afraid so. You see, she wasn't really unconscious, she was just faking. After I took you into the drawing room, I returned to the sitting room to find the door leading towards the back of the house was standing open and Mrs Grier gone. I spied her staggering through the garden. I made chase but I wasn't quick enough to prevent her from falling into the pond. The ice gave way beneath her, and she went under. I tried to reach her, but the ice just kept breaking... I'm sorry.'

Amy clasped him to her, frightened by how cold he was and attempting to warm him up.

'I'm just glad you're safe,' she said. 'You're so cold. Go upstairs and change before you catch your death.'

She spotted the blood on his shirt from Evelyn's head wound, which he'd failed to consider when concocting his story. But he didn't panic. Steadily he met her gaze.

'Change,' she told him. 'Immediately.'

Robert nodded and ran towards the stairs. He paused to look back and saw his mother watching him with suspicion in her eyes.

19

'What in the name of God is going on?' Henry demanded of Rush
the moment he was through the front door.

'It's all right, Rush, I'll explain,' said Amy, appearing in the hallway. She took Henry's hand and led him into the library, well away
from the servants, closing the door behind them. 'Mrs Grier
attacked me,' she began. 'It turns out she was Matthew's first wife as
well as the one who poisoned me. She hated me because she knew
what I did to Matthew at Edward's house.'

Henry stared at her with his mouth hanging open, attempting
to process this shocking information.

'Are you all right?' Henry asked her.

'I'm fine. She really wasn't a fighter.'

'That's a relief. Why do you keep referring to Mrs Grier in the
past tense?'

'Because she's dead. She escaped and ran from the house and
straight into the pond. She must have been confused. I did bash her
on the head with a poker.'

'You said she was Matthew's wife?'

'Yes. When he left here, he went to the city and met her. She was a maid and they never divorced, which means his marriage to Esther was bigamous.'

'And how did she know about what happened with you and Matthew?'

'Hobbs must have told her.'

'Or Mrs Crowle.'

'She spoke as though the person who told her was still alive and that old hag died years ago.'

'So Robert doesn't know about what you did?'

'No, and I'm afraid of what he'll do if he finds out.'

'He lied to us. He told us Douglas was his accomplice. Even after Mrs Grier poisoned you, he still protected her. Then she tried to kill you. Again.'

'I think he regretted that.'

'How can you continue to defend him after this?'

'Because I think he killed her.'

'My God,' he sighed, dragging his hands down his face.

She related to him Robert's tenuous explanation about Mrs Grier's fate, as well as the blood that had been on his clothes.

'Did he admit anything to you?' said Henry when she'd finished.

'Of course not. His own weak lie gave him away. You should have seen his eyes as he spoke, he was enjoying reliving it.'

'This has got to stop right now. We must tell the authorities.'

'If we tell anyone, he will hang for it.'

'How many more will die at his hands if we don't?'

'Do you really want to see the boy you raised for nine years swing at the end of a rope, just like your brother?' She hung her head when he winced.

'You're right, I don't want to see that, but I don't know what else we can do.'

'We don't know for sure that he did kill her. Let me talk to him first.'

'We'll tackle him together. I don't want you alone with him.'

'He would never hurt me.'

'We do this together or not at all. If you prefer, I can fetch the constable and explain everything to him.'

'No,' she exclaimed.

'Amy, he's a man now. Stop protecting him.'

'He's my son and he always will be.'

Tears formed in her eyes at the memory of her sweet little boy.

'I'm sorry,' Henry said, pulling her to him. 'You just need to understand that your son is now a dangerous man who quite possibly sent a woman to a horrible death.'

'I can't stand the thought that all these years I've been raising a monster, one just as bad as Edward and Matthew.'

* * *

After making Amy promise not to discuss things with Robert alone, Henry headed down to the pond.

'Have you managed to retrieve her?' he asked the constable, who had brought two of his men with him, all three staring into the still waters of the pond.

'I'm afraid it's impossible, Sir Henry, with all the ice and the temperature of the water,' he replied. 'We'll have to leave it until spring.'

'We've got to get through the rest of winter knowing a dead body lies at the bottom of our pond?'

'I'm sorry, sir, there's no way of getting her out without risking someone else's life. The moment the ice thaws, we'll fish her out.'

Henry gazed into the water, feeling sick. The pond had always been one of his favourite places to sit and think or to enjoy a picnic in the summer. Now it was ruined, not only because of what had happened to Mrs Grier but because Robert was responsible. It marked the scene of his descent into true evil.

* * *

Amy was sitting in her bedroom wringing her hands, trying to keep her promise to Henry not to talk to Robert.

There was a tap at the door and it was slowly pushed open to reveal Robert.

'Can I come in?' he said.

'Of course, dear,' replied Amy.

She wasn't breaking her promise, Henry hadn't said she couldn't see him at all, he'd just said they couldn't discuss Mrs Grier's death. Normally being told what to do infuriated Amy, but she knew Henry was genuinely afraid for her safety. But Robert would never hurt her, of that she was certain, no matter how much she ranted and railed at him.

'Have they found Mrs Grier yet?' he said.

'I don't know. That's what Henry's gone to find out,' Amy said, studying him carefully.

Robert's black eyes met hers and narrowed. 'What?'

'Do you feel warmer now you've changed clothes?'

'Yes, I'm fine. I wasn't in contact with the water for long.'

She longed to ask him more about what had happened, but instead, she indicated for her son to sit beside her and she took his hand.

Robert was suspicious. He'd expected an inquisition, but that hadn't happened and he didn't like it. What was going on?

'I expect you want to talk about what happened?' he said.

'Not yet.'

His mother's forced serenity was making him nervous. She was a volcano, her emotions erupting in a fiery torrent, so why was she keeping it all in?

'Why not?' he said.

'We're waiting for Henry.'

Robert sighed and hung his head, staring at her deformed hand holding onto his. Her hands had never repulsed him before, but they did now, and he had to fight the urge to tear his hand away. He'd seen her in hospital after Edward had torn her to shreds, seen her struggle to get well again, not just outside but inside too. Her mangled hands had simply become a part of her. So what was different now? Then it struck him.

'Henry,' he sighed. This strange new longing for his real father meant he was starting to resent the love his mother shared with her husband, and he was finally seeing her flaws.

Amy opened her mouth to reply but knew if she did everything else would come tumbling out, all the hurt, fear and anger, and she would end up breaking a promise to her husband for the first time. The love they shared was pure and she would not sully it, so she bit her tongue, feeling Robert's hot, sweaty hand squirm in her own.

They sat in silence until Henry appeared twenty minutes later. He halted in the doorway, looking from Amy to Robert.

'I haven't said a word to him,' she told her husband, releasing Robert's hand.

'Apparently we've to wait for you,' scowled Robert.

Henry closed the door. 'Good, because we've a lot to discuss.' He remained standing, staring sternly down at Robert. 'I want to hear exactly what happened with Mrs Grier.'

Robert related what he'd told his mother, with added embellishments about his heroism because he'd had time to think about his story and improve upon it. Unbeknownst to him, he was only digging a deeper hole for himself.

'Have they found her yet?' Robert ended, the picture of innocence.

'No,' replied Henry. 'It's much too dangerous, so we'll have to tolerate a dead body in our pond until the weather thaws.' Henry's gaze was granite. 'I'm going to ask you this once Robert and I want an honest answer – did you kill Mrs Grier?'

Robert shot to his feet, bristling with outrage. 'Why are you so determined to believe the worst of me?'

'Let's just run through the reasons why, shall we? And believe me, Robert, when I say you're amassing quite a list. Number one, you attacked Daisy and lied about it. Number two, you knew Mrs Grier attacked Winnie and you said nothing. Number three, when we asked you who your accomplice was, you lied. Number four, you allowed Douglas to take the blame and you let us sack our entire male staff. Number five, and this is the worst for me, you knew Mrs Grier poisoned your mother and still you protected her. Is there anything you disagree with there?'

Robert pouted, making him look more like Matthew than ever. 'There was a reason why I didn't tell you about Mrs Grier.'

'Please do enlighten us,' said Henry, folding his arms across his chest, expression stormy.

'It was because I was afraid she would tell you everything,' he blurted out. 'And I couldn't stand for you to think any worse of me.'

'Well, we do, so it seems your little plan didn't work. Your mother could have been killed,' he yelled.

'I didn't want that. I'd already told her she had to leave.'

'That was probably what prompted her to attack Amy in the first place, you stupid boy. You killed her, didn't you?'

Robert went white, his Adam's apple bobbing up and down in his throat.

'Admit it,' pressed Henry.

Robert looked to his mother for assistance. 'I didn't, I tried to save her.'

'Please do not compound this mess with more lies,' said Amy.

'Mama, I didn't...'

Amy shot to her feet and slapped him across the face. Robert gaped at her. Never, in all his life, had she struck him.

'I could have died today,' cried Amy. 'Or what if Mrs Grier had decided to take her displeasure out on Henry or your siblings? Did you consider any of us in your attempts to protect yourself?'

Robert grunted with frustration and started to pace. Henry placed himself between his stepson and the door, just in case he tried to bolt, but he made no attempt.

'We are not leaving this room until we get the truth,' said Amy.

Robert stopped pacing and hung his head. 'I didn't know who she was when she came to work here and that is the truth.'

It was Henry who replied. 'The problem is, Robert, that when you tell so many lies, it becomes very difficult to take you at your word.'

'This is the truth,' he barked back, head snapping up. 'When she did finally say she was Matthew's wife, I didn't believe her at first, until she gave me proof – *cartes de visite* of her and Matthew together. It was nice to see him as a normal person, not some monster created by the newspapers.'

'The newspapers didn't create that particular monster,' said Amy. 'He was made a long time ago.'

'Anyway,' said Robert, deciding not to reply to that. 'She started to tell me about him, she was a woman obsessed, she couldn't come to terms with the fact that he was dead. She said I should live up to what my real father would have wanted.'

'The sly, manipulative witch. Why didn't you tell us?'

'Because she was telling me things about Matthew, normal things, his likes and dislikes.'

'You lived with Matthew,' said Henry.

'But I had no idea who he was back then, and I had so little time with him. I wanted to learn about him, and you always refused to talk about him, unless it was to say something bad.'

'Why should your mother say anything nice about that man? He locked her up, abused her and tried to separate her from you.'

'Are you also forgetting that he sacrificed his own life to save hers?'

'It was Matthew's fault she was in that house in the first place. She ran to Edward because she thought he would protect her from him. Matthew had ample time to inform her about Edward's evil, but he didn't.'

'Neither did you,' glowered Robert. 'One word from you would have saved her.'

'No, it wouldn't, because I wouldn't have believed him,' said Amy. 'I thought Henry was the monster back then and if he'd tried to tell me any different, I would have thought he was trying to slander Edward.'

'Exactly,' said Henry. 'And stop turning this on us. Yes, we've both made mistakes, which is why we're so desperately trying to stop you from making your own. I wish you'd realise that we're on your side.'

'It doesn't feel like it,' muttered Robert. 'Mrs Grier kept trying to entice me into attacking a woman and once the seed was planted, it grew. I dreamed about attacking someone, until one day I couldn't take it any longer. She purposefully hired pretty maids in an attempt to lure me in and it worked with Daisy. I couldn't resist her.'

'So this is Mrs Grier's fault,' said Amy.

'No,' replied Henry. 'Robert has to take responsibility for his actions.' He looked to his stepson. 'Why didn't you come to us when you realised what she was doing?'

'I was ashamed.'

'So you should be.'

'Tell us what happened today down at the pond,' said Amy.

'She ran,' said Robert. 'I tried to catch her...'

'No. More. Lies,' hissed Amy. 'Stop treating us like we're fools.'

Robert groaned and buried his face in his hands.

'I don't know why you're so concerned with Mrs Grier anyway,' said Robert casually. 'It's a good thing she's dead. If she'd lived, she would have blabbed, and another scandal would have hit our family.'

'What on earth do you think is going to happen now?' said Henry. 'We have a dead body in our pond.'

'We can tell everyone she lost her mind. She's not alive to tell a different story, this won't be linked to Matthew, she was living under an assumed name. I didn't kill her, but I bet you're relieved that she's dead. Go on, admit it.'

'I have to own that part of me is.'

'Henry,' exclaimed Amy. 'What a thing to say.'

'I will not lie about my feelings. Mrs Grier's absence does mean our family is safe from her. But that doesn't excuse the fact that you killed someone, Robert.'

'For Christ's sake,' he retorted. 'I didn't kill her but anyone who hurts my mother deserves to die, I don't care who they are,' he said with a look that told Henry that applied to him too.

Henry opened his mouth to reply but was interrupted by a knock at the door.

'What is it?' he called impatiently.

The door was opened by Rush. 'Forgive the intrusion, sir, but there's a gentleman here to see Master Robert. A Mr Andrew Charteris, sir.'

'One of his friends from the city. Send him packing.'

'You can't do that,' said Robert. 'He's come to see me. He's my friend.'

'One of your unsavoury cronies,' countered Henry.

'Andrew isn't unsavoury. He's going to medical school, he's training to be a surgeon and it's started snowing heavily again. You can't send him away, it will look suspicious. He knows nothing about recent events if that's what you're worried about.'

Henry wavered. 'Very well, he may stay but as soon as the snow stops, he leaves. You tell him there was an accident and a servant fell in the pond. That's the official version. Nothing else.'

'Thank you,' said Robert, rushing off before either of them could say another word. Rush left too, closing the door behind him.

Henry thought it was the first sincere thing his stepson had said to him in weeks. 'Once again, he's rewarded with his friend coming to stay,' he sighed. 'Anyway, you seem a lot calmer,' he said, keen to change the subject. 'Should we tell Esther that her marriage to Matthew was bigamous?'

'No. She's suffered enough at that man's hands, and we only have Mrs Grier's word.'

'Agreed. Get some rest after your ordeal. I'm going downstairs to keep an eye on that pair. I don't trust them an inch.'

'Neither do I,' she replied, feeling troubled. 'Henry,' she said when he made for the door.

'Yes?' he said, turning to face her.

'You said you would throw Robert out if he set another foot wrong. Are you going to?'

'I feel I should, but I know it would break your heart. I also fear what Robert would do if we let him loose. But he must be punished somehow.'

'I agree, but how?'

'Leave it with me. I'll come up with something,' he said with a wily smile.

'Andrew, what are you doing here?' said Robert, vigorously shaking his best friend's hand.

'You left the city so abruptly, I had to make sure you were all right,' he replied.

Robert was pleased. 'Well, you are most welcome. Things have been really dull around here. Rush, arrange a room for Mr Charteris,' he ordered.

'I shall have to attend to it personally, sir, as we no longer have a housekeeper,' he retorted before ambling away.

Robert glared at his retreating back.

'What happened to your housekeeper?' said Andrew.

Robert inwardly sighed, but there was no point lying. If Andrew ever heard from one of the servants – especially that damned Rush – about what had become of Evelyn, it would only make him suspicious.

'She drowned,' he said.

Andrew arched an eyebrow. 'Where?'

'In the pond on the estate. The madwoman was about to lose her position. She attacked my mother and ran away. In the panic of her escape, she tried to flee across the frozen pond, but the ice wouldn't support her weight and it cracked beneath her.' Robert was a little breathless as he spoke, enjoying reliving the memory.

'My God.'

'She's still out there,' added Robert, unable to resist.

Andrew turned to the window, even though the pond wasn't visible from the house. 'How macabre. Is your mother all right?'

'Fine, she's as tough as old boots. She bashed Mrs Grier around the head with a poker, which was what probably led to her disorientation in the first place.'

'She sounds like an impressive woman.'

'Who, Mrs Grier?'

'God, no. Your mother. Can I meet her?'

'Certainly, but she's having a lie-down upstairs. She'll be down for dinner.'

'I look forward to it.' Andrew spotted Henry frowning at him from the bottom of the staircase and bowed. 'Sir Henry.'

Henry didn't like the look of this one at all, but he stepped forward to shake his hand.

'Father,' said Robert. 'This is my friend, Mr Andrew Charteris.'

'Pleasure to meet you,' said Henry, although the coldness in his eyes indicated otherwise.

'And you, sir,' replied Andrew. 'Robert's told me so much about Alardyce, so it's tremendous to finally be here.'

'Yes, well, we'll talk more at dinner,' was all Henry said before marching into the library and closing the door.

'Sorry about that,' said Robert. 'All this business with Mrs Grier has hit the family hard.'

'No need to apologise.' Andrew looked around to make sure no one was listening before adding, 'Is there somewhere we can talk? I have news for you.'

Robert was thrilled. It must be to do with Jane. 'In here,' he said, leading him into the drawing room. The second they were closeted away together, Robert turned to face his friend. 'Have you been in contact with Jane?'

'I have,' replied Andrew, producing a letter from his inner jacket pocket with his dexterous fingers.

Robert snatched it from him and tore it open, joy filling him at the sight of Jane's elegant script.

'Can I ring for some tea?' said Andrew. 'I'm chilled to the bone after that journey, and it doesn't seem I'm going to be offered any.'

'Go ahead,' said Robert, eyes glued to his letter.

With a smile, Andrew rang for the servants. A footman appeared, took his order for tea and cake, then Andrew sank into an armchair to enjoy the fire.

Robert read the letter through three times before staring thoughtfully out of the window.

'Well?' said Andrew in his deep baritone, gazing into the flames.

'It seems she's missing me as much as I miss her.' He sighed miserably. 'But my parents won't budge.'

'Why, exactly?'

'I told you, it's Henry. Because we've had a few arguments, he's got it into his head that I'll make a terrible husband.'

'He's right, you would.'

'I beg your pardon?' scowled Robert.

'How many women have you been with since you became romantically entangled with your china doll? Dozens.'

'But they don't matter.'

'They would to Jane if she found out.'

'She's not going to find out, is she?' hissed Robert. 'And I would reform my ways if I married her.'

'Maybe you would, for a little while, anyway. Then, when the routine of marriage had replaced the excitement of first love, you would soon sink back into degradation.'

'Why do you have such a low opinion of me?'

'Because I know you,' Andrew replied with a wry smile. 'Oh, don't bluster,' he added when Robert puffed up, ready to argue back. 'You're my best friend but I know what you're like. It's not a criticism. In my opinion, it makes you much more interesting, but I doubt Jane would see it that way.'

'All right, I admit I do love pleasure, but I love Jane more and it's torture being separated from her.'

'Well, if your parents won't budge, there might be a way.'

Robert's interest was piqued. 'How?'

'There is a place one can flee to when one doesn't have permission from parents to marry.'

'Are you referring to Gretna Green?'

'I am.'

'You're suggesting Jane and I marry in secret?'

Andrew nodded, enjoying watching his friend's face turn from disbelief to thoughtfulness.

'Would it work?' said Robert.

'Of course it would and, once you're married, there's nothing your parents can do about it. A marriage in Gretna Green is perfectly legal.'

'You're right. Why did I not think of it before?'

'Because you were too busy thinking of ways to persuade your parents to let you marry. Where is that tea? I'm wasting away here.'

'You'll survive,' said Robert dismissively. 'How did you get this letter anyway? Aunt Esther's watching Jane like a hawk.'

'I procured the assistance of a servant in her household who appreciated the supplement I made to his wage. This is a way you can regularly communicate with her. I wanted to deliver your first letter by hand, but I won't be able to fetch them all personally. We'll have to set up some sort of system. Would a servant here be willing to assist?'

'I'll arrange that before you leave, which I hope won't be for a few days yet. It's been deathly boring here.'

'I'll stay. This is all far too thrilling. You know how I enjoy secrets. Ah, at last,' he said when the door opened. 'I'm warning you now, you'd better have brought tea and cake.'

'Aye, just like you asked,' the young trainee footman drawled back rudely.

Andrew and Robert looked at each other and smiled. They might just have found their helper.

* * *

Robert rushed upstairs to change for dinner, after ensuring Andrew was comfortable in his room. As he changed – with the assistance of the reinstated Douglas, who had been enticed back into service with a pay rise – he wondered how he could engineer it so he could marry Jane at Gretna Green. Granted, it wouldn't be her idea of a dream wedding but, judging by her letter, all that mattered was marrying him. However, she was down in London. How could he get her to come up to Scotland without arousing Aunt Esther's suspicions? He was so glad Andrew was here because Robert was certain that between them, they could come up with a solution.

He headed downstairs for dinner, feeling much more upbeat. His mother noticed the difference immediately when he entered the drawing room for a pre-dinner drink.

'Is something wrong?' she asked him.

'No. Why?'

'You look... flushed.'

'I'm just happy. It's so good having Andrew here.'

'Has he settled in comfortably?'

'He has. Thank you,' he said to the footman as he handed him a glass of port.

'What prompted his visit?' Amy asked him.

'He was concerned when I left the city so abruptly.'

'What did you tell him?'

'That you were ill.'

'And as to the reason why you were in the city in the first place?'

'That Henry and I had a falling out.' When Henry entered the room looking dark and dour, Robert added, 'I didn't think it would be a difficult lie to perpetuate.'

'What wouldn't?' said Henry, nodding at the footman to leave the room. The footman nodded back and obeyed.

'Robert told his friend that you and he had a falling out, which is why he was sent to the city,' replied Amy.

'And he would be right,' said Henry. He studied Robert thoughtfully. 'Are you sure he knows nothing about your... urges?'

'Of course not. I told you, no one outside this house knows.'

They were forced to cease their conversation when Andrew entered the room. Sensing he was interrupting something, he stopped in the doorway. 'Am I intruding?'

'Not at all,' said Robert. 'Come on in.'

'Thank you,' he replied, stepping into the room.

'Andrew, you've already met my father,' said Robert.

The two men gave each other a nod.

'And this is my mother, Lady Alardyce.'

Andrew stepped forward to greet her, gently taking her hand. Most people, meeting Amy for the first time, winced when they saw the state of her hands and did their best to avoid taking them. But Andrew clasped her hand warmly and stared in wonder. Robert shuffled awkwardly. He was well aware of Andrew's fascination with medical oddities and deformities.

'It's a pleasure to meet you, Lady Alardyce,' he said.

'Please, call me Amy. It's wonderful to finally meet one of Robert's friends from the city. He's spoken so much about you.'

'And you, Amy,' he said, his gaze intense.

Henry didn't like the way their guest was staring at his wife, so he intervened. 'Drink, Andrew?'

'Er, please,' he replied, as though waking from a dream. 'Port would be wonderful.'

Henry called the footman, who poured Andrew his drink and handed it to him. Henry then led him away to admire a painting on the wall.

'He seemed fascinated by my hands,' Amy quietly told Robert.

'I noticed,' he replied. 'He's studying to be a surgeon. Anything remotely medical interests him.' Robert hadn't liked the look in Andrew's eyes at all, it had been downright creepy. Was that how his parents felt when they looked at him?

The gong was sounded for dinner and the four of them filed into the dining room. As he was a guest, Andrew was seated to Amy's right.

'Robert tells me you're a medical student,' Amy said to Andrew.

'I am,' he replied. 'It's been a lifelong ambition of mine.'

'Is your father a surgeon?'

'No, I'm the first in our family. He's in the church, as is my younger brother.'

'I think anyone who can be a surgeon is wonderful.'

'Or a butcher,' commented Henry from the other end of the table.

'A surgeon saved my life,' said Amy, as a plate of meat was placed before her. 'It's a calling. How do you progress in your studies, Andrew?'

'Very well. Top of my class, especially in dissection.'

'How gruesome. Do you know any body snatchers?'

'No, I'm glad to say. Burke and Hare are long dead. However, one of the professors at the university might,' he replied, mischief in his eyes.

'I do so admire Sophia Jex-Blake,' said Amy, always eager to discuss a woman doing well in a man's world. 'It's thanks to her that an Act of Parliament was passed sanctioning degrees for women. I do believe she studied at Edinburgh University?'

'She did, although I've never had the honour of meeting her.'

'And what is your opinion of women studying medicine?'

'It's a good thing. They are much more nurturing, which makes them the perfect doctors.'

Amy was delighted. 'How refreshing to hear from a man. One day, women will be permitted to study right alongside men, although I fear I may never live to see that day.'

'Nonsense, Lady Alardyce, you're in the first flush of youth with many happy years ahead. Why, you could be Robert's sister.'

Amy smiled. 'You flatterer.'

Henry and Robert were briefly united in their astonishment that Andrew was blatantly flirting with Amy and she was responding. His eyes also kept flicking to her hands, but if Amy noticed, she didn't mention it.

'You must come to the university,' said an eager Andrew. 'I'll give you a guided tour and you can walk in the footsteps of the famous Sophia Jex-Blake.'

'Sounds thrilling,' she smiled. 'Shall we go, Henry?'

Amy looked excited at the prospect, but he wanted her to have as little to do with Andrew Charteris as possible. 'We'll see,' was all he was willing to reply.

21

To Robert, the post-dinner drinks seemed to take forever to conclude. The younger children came down to say goodnight and, after meeting their guest, they too joined the party. To Robert's surprise, Andrew was very good with children, entertaining them with magic tricks. All he wanted to do was speak with his friend in private so they could discuss the plan to elope to Gretna Green, but it seemed the party was far from over. At least his mother was looking happier and, for that reason, Henry was too.

Finally, the nanny managed to gather the children together and usher them upstairs to bed, but only after Andrew promised more magic tricks in the morning.

'Right, I'm off to bed too,' announced Robert once they'd gone, trying to flash Andrew a meaningful look as he stood and stretched.

His friend caught the look. 'Yes, me too. I'd better turn in. Goodnight.'

'Goodnight, Andrew,' said Amy. 'Robert,' she added when her son kissed her cheek.

'I thought we'd never get a chance to talk,' whispered Robert as he and Andrew headed upstairs together.

But his friend wasn't listening. 'Your mother really is the most remarkable woman. I'd no idea she was so enchanting.'

Robert stopped to glare at his friend. 'Enchanting?'

'Yes. So intelligent and witty, such sparkling company. I really had an excellent evening.'

'Please don't tell me you're attracted to my mother.'

'She's a very handsome woman.'

'And old enough to be your mother.'

'Don't look so stormy, Robert, you should take it as a compliment.'

'Well, I don't. Compliment her by all means but in a more gentleman-like manner.'

'Fine,' he replied, holding up his hands. 'I've no wish to get bruised.'

As they walked, Robert tried to get his mind off his friend's comments and back on the matter at hand. He needed Andrew on his side.

* * *

Henry entered Amy's bedroom just as Hazel finished brushing out her hair. He took a moment to admire the cascade spilling down her back, the glow of the candlelight on her creamy skin.

Amy caught his gaze in the reflection in the mirror and smiled. The way the light twinkled in her eyes took his breath away.

'You seemed to have a good evening,' he said as they climbed beneath the bedclothes together once Hazel had gone.

'I did, to my surprise,' she replied. 'Robert's friend is very charming.'

'He did seem rather taken with you.'

Her smile was mischievous. 'He was good with the children too. They loved his tricks.'

'I can't stand magic tricks,' he sighed.

'I thought it was entertaining. Jealous, were you?' she said, lips twitching.

'Hardly. I know I have a loyal wife.'

She leaned in to kiss him. 'Aren't you going to reward your loyal wife?'

Henry rolled her onto her back and kissed her. 'I most certainly am,' he said, pushing up her nightgown while sliding down her body.

Outside the door, Andrew crouched with his eye pressed to the keyhole, attempting to control his accelerating heart rate and heavy breathing as he watched Amy moaning and writhing on the bed, legs splayed, her husband's face between her thighs, the sight of her deformed hands sliding through his hair only making him breathe even harder.

* * *

The next morning at breakfast, Robert was attempting to contain himself. He and Andrew had come up with a foolproof plan and, with the assistance of the surly footman, he would soon be wed to Jane.

'Has Mr Charteris risen yet?' he enquired of Rush.

'He's still in bed, sir. Apparently he's not feeling very well.'

'What's wrong with him?'

'A cold, sir. Mr Charteris believes he caught it after travelling through the snow yesterday.'

'Have you called a doctor?'

'I did offer, but he declined. He said there was no need for a trifling cold.'

'What's this? Who's got a cold?' said Amy, walking into the room with Henry.

'Andrew,' replied Robert.

'Oh, dear. Colds can turn into something much worse. It's this awful weather,' she sighed, staring out of the window at the falling snow. She frowned. 'There's a carriage coming up the drive. Who would be mad enough to venture out in this weather?'

'Apart from you?' smiled Henry, taking a seat at the table.

'Yes,' she smiled back. She returned her attention to the window. 'It's Magda.'

Robert seethed inside. He and Andrew had not factored the witch into their plans. She had a way of knowing things without being told. It was vital he warn his friend.

'I'm going to see Andrew,' he said.

'What about breakfast?' replied Amy, but he'd already shot out of the room.

* * *

Robert stared at the lump beneath the bedclothes. 'You're not ill.'

Andrew sat up and smiled. 'What gave me away?'

'I know you too well. You want a few days lying about being waited on hand and foot.'

'Your logic is irrefutable and it's much better than my draughty lodgings at the university. Where's my breakfast?'

'Do I look like a footman?'

Andrew briefly considered making some crack about his real father, then decided it wouldn't be wise. 'In that case, could you please kick one up the backside and send him up here with my breakfast?'

'First, we have more pressing matters to attend to.'

'More pressing than my breakfast?'

'Will you please forget about your stomach? Magda Magrath is here.'

'Who?'

'The witch I told you about.'

'How thrilling. I'd like to meet her.'

'Out of the question. She'll spot you're not ill immediately.'

'Then I'll just say I was mistaken. It's not a cold, just a weakness.'

'Can't you come up with something better? You're training to be a doctor, for God's sake.'

'It'll be fine, don't worry. I don't know why you think this house is dull, it's a never-ending source of entertainment. A witch, indeed. Fascinating.'

'Magda will know we're up to something, she could scupper all our carefully laid plans.'

He waved a dismissive hand. 'Stop fretting. If you go around looking anxious, everyone will know something's going on. Nonchalance is the key to a good lie.'

'I'll do my best, but it's not easy,' sighed Robert. 'If my parents get wind of this, they'll probably lock me up for life.'

'Really, that harsh? In that case, we must endeavour not to get caught.'

'What are you doing?' he said when Andrew lithely jumped out of bed.

'I must make an appearance. We don't want Old Mother Hubbard coming up here to examine me and finding me to be the perfect specimen of manhood that I am.'

'It will look even more suspicious if you suddenly make a full recovery.'

'Please credit me with some sense. Where are my trousers?' he said, looking around the room. 'Your man put them away somewhere last night. Honestly, does someone undress you every night? You're old enough to dress yourself.' Andrew's family were well off but not rich, certainly not rich enough to employ a valet, so it had come as a shock the previous night when a strange man had entered his room, asking if he could remove his clothes for him. He'd almost struck the fool, until the cringing man had hastily explained that it was normal practice here.

'Why do something when someone else can do it for you?' replied Robert.

Andrew shook his head. 'How idle. Where are my trousers?' he exclaimed for the second time.

'Here they are,' said Robert, fishing them out of the wardrobe and holding them out to him. 'This is for storing clothes, you know.'

'Did I ever tell you how amusing you are?' said Andrew sarcastically. 'Did you write to your china doll?' he asked as he dressed.

'I was up half the night, but I eventually got it just right. I made sure to direct her to disguise her handwriting and send her letters through Wyles, the new second footman. She's clever, she'll follow my instructions to the letter.'

'Excellent. Did you ask her to elope with you?'

'Naturally. If she replies no, then I know where I stand, but she'll say yes. She's as desperate to marry as I am.'

'Let's hope Wyles doesn't let us down. Do I get to be best man?'

'I'd like that very much.'

'Excellent. Now please can I have some privacy to finish dressing, or would you like me to instruct you on how to do it?'

Robert rolled his eyes as he left the room. Andrew's wit had always been dry and sometimes it could be scathing, but Robert took it with a pinch of salt.

He returned to the dining room to find Magda sitting at the table, eating porridge. Could that woman smell food cooking?

She raised her head when he entered, sharp eyes boring into him. 'Hello, Robert.'

'Magda. To what do we owe this pleasure?' he said, trying to sound sincere because his parents were in the room.

'I wanted to check up on your mother.'

'As you can see, she is perfectly healthy,' he replied, taking his seat at the table. 'Is something wrong?' he added when Magda continued to stare at him.

'You look... different.'

Robert's stomach flipped over when his mother's head snapped up to look at him, panic in her eyes. Silently he willed her to relax, she would give everything away looking like that.

'I assure you I am quite unchanged,' he replied, his voice sounding darker and deeper than usual.

'Hmmm,' was all Magda said, giving him another searching look before turning her attention back to her porridge.

Robert looked to his mother, who regarded him with puzzlement.

They ate in silence, the atmosphere now awkward, and Robert desperately prayed for something to interrupt the uncomfortable moment. Once again, his friend came to the rescue and Andrew entered the room looking much worse than he had ten minutes ago, skin pale, eyes red-rimmed.

'Good morning,' he croaked.

'Oh dear, Andrew,' said a sympathetic Amy. 'We hear you're feeling unwell.'

'It's nothing, just a chill.'

'Magda can look you over. I can vouch for her skills, she's saved my life more than once.'

'There's no need, really. I've examined myself. There is nothing to be done but rest.'

'Andrew's training to be a surgeon at Edinburgh University,' Amy explained to Magda.

'How can a butcher know if he is unwell?' she countered.

Andrew's green eyes flared. 'Not a fan of modern medicine then, Magda? May I call you Magda?'

'Yes, you may,' she graciously replied. 'And I have remedies your professors at the university have never even dreamed of. I can have that chill shifted in minutes.'

'It's really not necessary. If Lady Alardyce would be so kind as to permit me to rest here for a day or two, I will be quite recovered. I don't want to cause a fuss.'

'It's not a fuss, I have all my remedies right here,' said Magda, indicating her large black bag, which she'd placed beside her chair, not liking it to leave her sight.

'Then I promise to call on you the moment I feel any worse.'

'Do you think you can manage something to eat?' Amy asked Andrew with concern.

'I'm certain I can force something down.'

'Maybe you shouldn't be here,' said Henry. 'Amy's just recovered from a fever and I will not risk her getting sick again. Will you consent to Magda examining you?'

Andrew glanced at Robert, both divining this was some sort of test. Henry was doubtful about Andrew's sudden illness.

'Very well, Sir Henry, if you insist.'

'I do.' Henry's eyes flicked to Robert, who did his best to look impassive, before flicking back to Andrew. 'No offence, I just don't take any chances with Lady Alardyce's health.'

'I quite understand,' he replied, remembering to put on his croaky voice.

Henry nodded sternly before turning his attention back to his breakfast, leaving Andrew and Robert to cast each other uncertain looks.

* * *

'I'm happy to say that you're as strong as the proverbial ox, Amy,' announced Magda once she'd completed her examination.

'I didn't think otherwise,' Amy replied. She was sitting on her bed. 'It puzzles me why you felt the need to do this now.'

'I admit I do have an ulterior motive for coming.'

'What do you mean?' said Henry.

'I sensed something malevolent here, a dark presence that shadows your house.'

'You're referring to Robert?' said Amy sadly.

'No. He is something entirely different.'

'Do you mean some sort of ghost then?' said Amy, thinking of Matthew's persistent presence.

'Oh, no. This being is living flesh and bone.'

'You're not referring to Andrew, are you?'

'I most certainly am. I felt his dark energy the moment he entered the village.'

'But he seems so nice.'

'I don't wish to sound callous, but didn't Edward seem nice once, and Matthew?'

'You have a point.'

'I knew it,' said Henry. 'I didn't like the way he looked at Amy.'

'And how was that?' said Magda.

'He was flirting with her and he kept looking at her hands.'

'He did? Interesting.'

'What does it mean?'

'I'm not sure yet. He's a friend of Robert's?'

'Yes,' said Amy. 'One of the disreputable set from the city.'

'Why is he disreputable? Wait, don't answer that. I feel it's something to do with a crime, probably involving money.'

'I have absolutely no doubt about it,' replied Henry.

'So, is he a danger?' said Amy. 'What if he has the same

impulses as Robert? We can't have the two of them in the house. Look what happened the last time with Mrs Grier.'

'And the time before that,' added Henry, thinking of Matthew and Edward.

'No,' said Magda. 'I don't get that from him, but his intentions definitely aren't good. He reminds me of a snake, sneaky and insidious. He slithered back upstairs to his room before I could examine him because his illness is a bit of fakery. You need to be careful.'

'I'll do more than that,' said Henry. 'I'll throw him out of the house right now.'

'No, don't,' said Amy. 'Robert's already pulling away from us. This might sever our bond with him permanently. Please Henry, don't drive him away. Right now, we are the only restraints on his violent behaviour.'

'All right,' he sighed. 'But we'll watch him very closely. I want to know where he is every minute of every day.'

'I'm sure the servants can help us with that.'

'Why does this house attract all these malevolent souls?' said Henry.

'They're not attracted to the house,' said Magda. 'They're attracted to the occupants.'

A shiver ran down Amy's spine. 'I understand this is a huge imposition, Magda, but would you mind staying a night or two? Your presence will make me feel infinitely better, you see things we can't.'

'It's no imposition. I would like to keep an eye on the pair of them.'

'You had something to say about Robert too?' said Henry.

'Yes. I heard about what happened to Mrs Grier at the pond. Was Robert responsible?'

Amy glanced at Henry before replying, 'We think it's a distinct possibility, although he's admitted nothing. It turned out Mrs Grier was Matthew's first wife and, from what we can gather, she was keen to get close to Robert for that reason.'

'His soul has grown darker,' said Magda. 'To the extent that I barely see the light in him any more. Soon, I fear, it will disappear altogether.'

Amy closed her eyes and took in a few deep breaths, trying to push away the pain Magda's words were causing her. 'And Andrew Charteris? Does he have any light?'

'More than Robert, but I shudder to think what they'll get up to together.'

22

Henry's solution to Robert and Andrew's malign influence on one another arrived at the house when the family were gathered together before the drawing room fire. The children were saying goodnight and Magda was knitting. Andrew was upstairs in his room to maintain his charade of being ill.

Rush went to answer the doorbell and returned to the room to announce, 'Mr Knapp to see you, sir.'

Robert jumped up, startling his siblings. 'What's he doing here?'

'I'll see him in my study, Rush,' said Henry, without bothering to reply to Robert or even look his way.

'What's he doing here?' Robert demanded of his mother when Henry had gone.

'I've no idea,' she replied. 'Who is he?'

'The tormentor Father sent to watch over me in the city. Please don't tell me he's brought him here to guard me.' He frowned when Amy looked embarrassed. 'Mother?'

'I really have no idea. You'll have to wait for Henry to return.'

Amy's eyes flicked to Magda, who was studying Robert intently. He noticed this close scrutiny and turned his back on them both to gaze out of the window, although there was nothing to see except blackness. Amy finished saying goodnight to the younger children and indicated for the nanny to take them upstairs.

It didn't take long for Henry to return with Knapp.

'So, this is the famous Mr Knapp,' said Amy, getting to her feet to greet him.

It was almost comical when the big man bowed, his jacket threatening to burst open at the chest. 'Lady Alardyce.'

'Knapp's here to assist us with the aftermath of recent events,' said Henry.

'I take it I'm the recent event?' said Robert, turning to face the room with defiance in his eyes.

'You are,' replied Henry.

'So you bring back my babysitter. Do you know, Mother, that this brute punched me in the stomach then dragged me around?'

'Is this true?' Amy demanded.

'An exaggeration, madam,' said Knapp. 'When he arrived at Abel's house, he was foolish enough to backchat me.'

'So you struck him?'

'I disciplined him, as Sir Henry gave me leave to.'

Robert was very satisfied when she turned her furious gaze from Knapp to her husband.

'Did you give him leave to hurt Robert?' she demanded.

'I gave him leave to keep him in line,' replied Henry. 'Which was exactly what he needed.'

'I want to make this clear right now – I will not tolerate violence against my son. Do you understand?'

Both men nodded.

'Good,' she said, cheeks flushed with anger. 'So what exactly will your role be here, Mr Knapp?'

'I'll make sure Robert doesn't get himself into any more trouble.'

'You're a guardian?'

'More like a jailer,' muttered Robert.

'You brought this on yourself with your recent antics,' Henry told his stepson.

'You mean after I tried to save a woman from drowning?' It was his turn to flush with anger when they all regarded him doubtfully. 'You still think I killed her?'

'That's what happens when you tell so many lies,' said Henry. 'Your room's ready, Knapp, right next door to Robert's.'

'What?' Robert said, even louder.

'Thank you,' said Knapp before ambling out of the room, Henry following him.

'Mother, aren't you going to stop this?' exclaimed Robert.

'I think it's a good idea.'

'Good? How can it possibly be good?'

'Because, if anything else does happen, you'll have proof that it wasn't you.'

How was he supposed to argue with that logic without making himself look guilty?

'Fine,' he pouted. 'I'm going to see Andrew,' he said before stomping from the room.

'Every time I think things are finally settling down in this house, something else happens,' sighed Amy.

'If it helps, no one's life is peaceful,' said Magda. 'Now, if you'll excuse me, I'm going to bed.'

'Already? It's still quite early.'

'I'm not as young as I used to be,' she smiled, getting to her feet with the agility of a twenty-year-old.

Amy had no idea how old Magda was, although she'd estimated anything from mid-forties to early sixties. Her silver hair and eyes and lined hands, combined with her energy and vigour, made it impossible to judge. 'All right, goodnight then, Magda.'

'Goodnight, Amy.' She paused to give her arm a gentle squeeze. 'Mr Knapp is an excellent idea.'

'I agree.'

Magda smiled and nodded before exiting the room, leaving Amy alone with her thoughts.

* * *

Robert burst into Andrew's bedroom, slammed the door shut and started to pace.

'Something wrong?' said Andrew, who was stretched out on his bed, reading a book.

'Father's only gone and brought Knapp to the house to keep an eye on me.'

'Who?'

'The brute who dragged me out of Vivienne's,' thundered Robert. He stopped pacing to glare at his friend. 'Will you put that book down?'

Andrew sighed and cast it aside. 'I was enjoying that.'

'With Knapp here, all our plans are scuppered. He'll make sure I never leave the house again.'

'Do calm down, Robert. Nothing is scuppered. All we have to do is adapt our plan.'

'You don't know what Knapp's like. He has this sixth sense, just like Magda. We won't stand a chance with both of them here.'

'Stop being so dramatic. We stick to what we agreed. When the time comes, Knapp will be distracted like everyone else.'

'Distracted?'

'Just leave it to me,' said Andrew, picking his book back up.

Andrew smiled to himself when Robert stormed out, slamming the door shut behind him.

When there was another knock at his door two minutes later, he sighed and called, 'What is it now?' Assuming it was Robert returning, he added, 'Has Knapp spanked your little bottom?'

'He wouldn't dare,' said Magda, walking inside and closing the door behind her.

Andrew was so surprised, the book fell from his hand. 'What are you doing in my room?'

'I wish to talk to you,' she said, standing over him, making him feel inferior. 'I want to know exactly what you and Robert are up to.'

'We're up to nothing,' he coolly replied.

'Then what did Robert want?'

'He was complaining about that fellow Knapp. Apparently, he's been brought in to keep an eye on him.' When Magda just stared at him with her icy eyes, he coughed and shifted about on the bed, reaching for his book before retracting his hand in a rare moment of confusion. 'Was there anything else?'

'Yes. I want you to tell me what else you and Robert were discussing. You're plotting something.'

'I can assure you we're not,' he replied with a smooth smile.

'You are a liar and a snake. There's nothing wrong with you. The illness was a ruse to ensure you weren't thrown out the door. You and Robert are plotting and I'm going to discover your little scheme.'

Andrew tried to make his mind go blank, he wouldn't be surprised if she was capable of reading thoughts, but it was impossible to clear his mind completely. There was always some treacherous thought rushing to the surface.

Magda just continued to stare at him until he finally broke.

'What are you going to do, curse me?'

'I don't do that. Curses always rebound threefold onto the person doing the cursing, but I do have other weapons in my arsenal, weapons you've never even considered, boy.'

'You'll soon discover, old woman, that I am no boy,' he said, green eyes glimmering with danger.

'And you will discover that I'm no old woman. I'm keeping my eye on you,' she said before quietly slipping out through the door.

'Ridiculous woman,' said Andrew when she'd gone.

He picked his book back up and attempted to concentrate on the words but his mind kept drifting back to Magda and her threats, so much so that he decided to forgo his nocturnal wanderings that evening.

* * *

The atmosphere at breakfast the following morning was tense. Robert spent the entire time glaring at Henry and Knapp, who both ignored him, talking quietly together. Andrew was busy contemplating what Magda had said to him, glancing at her when he thought she wasn't looking. More than once, she caught him, and when she did, he forced himself to stare back at her. Amy was quiet, anxiously watching her son, despairing of the way he kept throwing daggers at his father.

Magda was the only one who appeared perfectly poised as she ate her porridge, raising the spoon to her lips in a regular beat, a fact that drove Andrew up the wall.

'I wish to go into the village today,' Robert suddenly announced.

'But the weather's so inclement,' replied Amy.

'It's inclement in here too,' he said, scowling at an amused Knapp.

'Remember what happened to your friend here when he ventured out into the snow?' said Magda sardonically, nodding in Andrew's direction. 'He fell ill with a cold'.

'If I don't get some fresh air, I will go mad,' said Robert.

'Then take a turn about the garden,' countered Amy.

'I don't want to go into the garden, I want to go into the village.'

'Why?'

'I don't want to hurt any girls if that's what you're worried about,' he barked before recalling Andrew was at the table.

Andrew's head snapped up, a questioning look in his eyes. When it became apparent no one was going to enlighten him, he remained quiet, ears pricked up for more information.

'Excuse me, Lady Alardyce, but I could accompany him,' said Knapp.

'What a good idea,' said Henry with a malicious smile. 'You have two choices, Robert. You can either go into the garden with Andrew or into the village with Knapp.'

Robert flung himself back in his chair and folded his arms across his chest. 'Fine, I'll go into the garden. I'm going nowhere with him,' he muttered, nodding at Knapp.

'I'm glad that's settled,' smiled Henry.

Robert looked to his mother for support, who was feeling increasingly caught between her husband and her eldest son.

'Your father's right,' she said.

Robert shot to his feet and stormed out of the room.

'I'll go and see if he's all right,' said Andrew, relieved to escape Magda's silver eyes.

Henry's amused chuckle irritated Amy. She rose majestically, shaking with anger.

'This isn't funny,' she yelled.

Henry was shocked. She'd never shouted at him since they were married. When she'd first come to live at Alardyce, she'd shouted at him frequently.

'Sorry,' he replied, wiping the smile from his face. 'I just feel he's finally getting what he deserves.'

She glared at him before storming out.

'Amy,' he called.

When he made to go after her, Magda said, 'Leave her be. She won't listen until she's calmed down.'

'Perhaps you're right,' he said, retaking his seat.

Once, when they were younger, Amy had struck him in a temper. Her fire had been exciting, but Henry had no wish to endure another stinging cheek.

* * *

'Can you believe that damn Henry?' said Robert as he and Andrew took a turn about the garden. 'He loves humiliating me and treating me like a child.'

Andrew let him ramble on, waiting for his moment to ask the burning question.

'What did you mean about hurting a girl?' he said when Robert finally paused for breath. He watched his friend's reaction carefully.

'Oh, nothing,' muttered Robert. 'We had a maid who worked here called Daisy. Pretty thing. I had a little indiscretion with her.'

'Another one?' said Andrew in a bored tone.

'When I broke it off, she took it rather badly and claimed I attacked her.'

'Did you?'

'Of course not.'

'I just can't help but recall Missy.' He smiled when Robert's jaw throbbed. 'I take it you remember her?'

'Maybe,' he mumbled to the ground.

'Then let me refresh your memory – Daniel, Thomas and I got the fright of our lives one evening at Vivienne's. You were upstairs with the delectable Missy when we heard her screaming. I recall the blood, her back whipped to shreds...'

'Ssshh,' he hissed. 'No doubt Knapp's lurking somewhere in the undergrowth.'

'That man is far too big to lurk anywhere. Don't tell me you've forgotten about poor little Missy. Did you do the same to Daisy? Robert?' he pressed.

Robert sighed and nodded. 'I did,' he whispered, still fearing someone overhearing. At least he wasn't feeling murderous towards Daisy any more. Now his wedding to Jane had been called off, he'd lost the compulsion to punish her.

'What is going on in that head of yours?'

Robert nodded at Andrew, indicating for him to move further from the house. When he felt they were a safe enough distance, Robert stopped, eyes troubled.

'There's something inside me, something I can't control.' He ran a shaky hand down his face. 'I don't know what's happening to me. I'm scared.'

Andrew knew it had taken his friend a lot to admit he was afraid. He clapped him on the shoulder. 'What does it feel like when this compulsion overcomes you?'

'I don't know... like someone else takes control.'

'Like a possession?'

'I wouldn't go that far. I'm aware of what I'm doing, I know it's wrong, but there's nothing I can do to stop it.'

'Does it... feel good?' Andrew almost scared himself asking that question, but he simply had to know.

Robert nodded, eyes darkening.

'I'm not sure what to say to that. Is your china doll aware of any of this?'

'Mother, Father and Aunt Esther tried to convince her of the truth, but she refused to believe it.'

'So that's why they don't want you going to the village unaccompanied? Now everything's starting to make sense. What does your mother make of it all?'

'Naturally she's scared for me, she's afraid I'll hang like Edward.

She said she'd love me no matter what.'

'You're a lucky man. Most mothers would have packed you off by now. I know mine would.'

Robert was starting to wonder whether he was actually fortunate to still be at Alardyce House.

'So your parents said you're not allowed to marry your china doll because of your unpredictable impulses?'

'Yes.'

'Why didn't you tell me all this in the first place? I've never lied to you.'

'Oh... I don't know. I just thought the fewer people who knew, the better.'

'Robert, we're best friends. Afraid I was going to turn you in?'

'The thought never crossed my mind.'

'Good, because if our plan is to work, it's vital you trust me.'

'I do.'

'Then we should have nothing to worry about.'

'Except Knapp.'

'Leave him to me. Now, will you be able to control yourself when you're a married man?'

'Why are you so concerned about Jane?'

'Because I know it would destroy you if you hurt her.'

'You're right, it would. But I wouldn't hurt Jane. When she's around, those feelings go away.'

'How can you be sure if you're not always in control of them?'

'Jane's my one chance at a normal life. If I lose her, I'm finished. I'll end up either dangling from the end of a rope or with a knife in my gut. You have to help me, Andrew, you simply have to,' said Robert, gripping onto his sleeve.

'I said I would and I will. I'm not one to go back on my word. We'll soon see you wed,' he replied, gently prising Robert's hand from his arm.

Robert relaxed. 'Thank you. I want to step up our plans, this needs to be done as soon as possible, before my freedom is restricted even more. Things are going to be difficult enough with Knapp here.'

'It all depends on how quickly we can communicate with Jane. There'll be no wedding if she doesn't know about it.' Andrew smiled. 'You look like you're about to burst with impatience.'

'I can't wait for my life to change. Being kept prisoner here is driving me insane.'

'I don't know why, it's a very pleasant place, almost mystical,' Andrew said, admiring the grounds. 'Where did the housekeeper drown?'

'You really want to see it?'

'Yes, I rather think I do. Which direction is the pond in?'

'This way,' said Robert, leading him through the gardens, finding he was keen to see it again too.

They walked in silence, the snow crunching beneath their boots. Andrew's eyes were riveted on the glimmer of water just visible as they headed down the hill.

'Here it is,' said Robert.

Andrew stared in fascination, which Robert was glad about because it gave him the opportunity to relive the moment he'd tossed that mad hag into the water, the fear in her eyes.

'So she's still down there?' Andrew eventually said.

'Yes, until the weather warms up.'

'When she will most likely come floating to the surface.'

Robert hadn't considered that might happen and he didn't like it, it would be as though Evelyn had come back from the dead, unwilling to let him go even in death. 'How gruesome.'

'Did you kill her, Robert?'

'Yes,' he replied. He'd said he wouldn't lie to his friend again and he intended to keep his word. He got the feeling Andrew would understand.

'Why?'

'Because she tried to kill my mother. First she poisoned her with arsenic, then she attacked her with a letter opener. She underestimated her. The arsenic failed to do its job and then mother bashed her around the head with a poker.'

'Why on earth would a housekeeper do that?'

'She was Matthew's first wife and she couldn't stand it that he loved my mother and not her.'

Andrew's eyes widened before he turned his gaze back to the pond. 'Do your parents know about what you did?'

'They suspect, but I denied it and I will continue to do so. I dread to think what Henry would do if I admitted the truth.'

'Yet you trust me with your secret.' Andrew's pink tongue darted out to wet his lips. 'How did you do it? The water would have been too cold to hold her under.'

'I threw her in. The ice cracked and she sank.'

'Clever. No trace. It would look like a simple accident. What did it feel like?'

'Extremely satisfying, especially after what she'd done to my mother.'

'I'll bet.'

Robert glanced from Andrew to the water and back again, puzzled by the strange look in his friend's eyes.

23

'What are they doing?' said Henry when Knapp returned to the house, shaking the snow from his boots. The man amazed Henry, he'd watched Knapp run across the garden with the agility of a man half his size.

'Just talking,' replied Knapp. 'It seemed intense, although I was too far away to hear what they were saying. Then Robert led Andrew down to the pond.'

'The pond? I would love to know whose idea that was.'

'Perhaps Mr Charteris has heard all about what happened. There's something wrong with that man. I wouldn't be at all surprised if it was his suggestion.'

'Magda said the same about him.'

'A most astute woman. My recommendation is you get him out of the house as soon as possible. He's up to something.'

'Nothing would give me greater pleasure, but if I do, I risk upsetting Robert, which in turn will upset my wife. She's already angry with me.'

'The atmosphere in this house is getting very dark, it's affecting us all. In that case, I recommend you make things up with Lady Alardyce and get her onside.'

'That's easier said than done. You've never seen her in a rage before, but I will try. If you hear screaming, it'll be me,' Henry added wryly before heading into the sitting room.

Amy was in the armchair by the fire, stabbing at her embroidery, the shining needle in her hand looking lethal.

'May I speak with you?' Henry said politely.

She looked up and frowned, her blue eyes sparkling with suppressed rage. 'About what?' Her voice was icy, but nothing about Amy was cold, she was as hot and explosive as a volcano.

'I think you know.'

She sighed and put aside the embroidery and needle, to his relief. 'Robert?'

'Yes.'

'I'm tired of discussing him.'

'How about we discuss Andrew Charteris instead? He must leave, both Magda and Knapp say so.'

'We can't just throw him out, he's a guest, and if we do throw him out, Robert will be even more furious with us than he already is. I want to build bridges with him, not push him further away.'

'I completely understand, but please remember what happened when Matthew and Edward got together.'

'Robert's accomplice is dead and gone.'

'What if someone else takes her place?'

Amy appeared thoughtful, gazing out of the window.

'I think I've come up with a way to get round this,' continued Henry. 'If we were to suddenly leave, then Andrew would be forced to part from Robert.'

Amy turned back to him and smiled. 'That's an excellent idea. We could say for the sake of my health we need to get away from this snow, perhaps journey further south?'

'We're both very fond of the Lake District.'

'True, although I doubt it will be any warmer there.'

'It doesn't matter, just as long as we separate Robert from Andrew.'

'I'm just so afraid of losing my boy by telling Andrew to leave.'

When tears filled Amy's eyes, he rushed to her, kneeling before her chair and taking her face in his hands. 'I would do anything to lift this burden from you.'

'But you can't. I must face it. I'm sorry, I shouldn't have shouted at you at breakfast but this situation is crushing me. Something needs to be done and I think getting away might just be the solution. We're all still feeling Mrs Grier's hateful presence and I'm constantly conscious of the fact that her body is at the bottom of our pond.'

'Then we're agreed. I'll make the arrangements immediately.'

'Thank you, and I promise not to shout at you again. It's vital we stick together and let nothing come between us.'

'I would never allow that to happen,' he said before kissing her.

'I thought you had arrangements to make,' she smiled when his lips moved to her neck.

'You're a cruel woman,' smiled Henry, getting to his feet.

Amy picked her embroidery back up with a smile. 'And you always know how to cheer me up. Thank you.'

'Glad I could be of service,' he replied with a grin and an over-exaggerated bow.

He left Amy with a smile so broad it almost hurt. Henry didn't used to be so playful. When they'd first met, he'd been a very serious young man, but age had mellowed him, as had the birth of their children.

'Back so soon?' called Amy when there was a knock at the door. 'You just can't stay away.'

'I confess I can't,' said Andrew, walking into the room.

'I thought you were taking a walk with Robert?' she replied, spine rippling with unease.

'It was too cold to stay out for long. May I?' he said, indicating the chair on the opposite side of the fire.

Male guests traditionally didn't join the lady of the house in her sitting room, but Amy's heart was generous and she told herself he hadn't been raised in this environment, so he might not even be aware he was breaching protocol.

'Please do,' she replied.

He smiled, slumped into the chair and crossed his ankles, gazing into the flames.

'Would you like some tea?' she said.

'No, thank you,' he replied, eyes fixed on the fire.

When he remained silent, Amy relaxed a little, picked her embroidery back up and continued to work.

Amy didn't want to seem like she was prying but this was the perfect opportunity to find out what Andrew and Robert had got up to on their walk. 'Did you enjoy the gardens?' she said, keeping her eyes on her embroidery.

'Yes, thank you, it was very refreshing. Although everything was concealed beneath the snow, I expect they're spectacular in summer.'

'They are.' She placed her embroidery on her knee and made a show of wrestling with herself before saying, 'May I speak to you in confidence, Andrew?'

He regarded her with surprise. 'Of course.'

'I'm very worried about Robert, he's been so sullen lately. Did he confide anything in you?'

'With all due respect, he's my best friend and I gave my word...'

'I understand, but if you could help him, I would be ever so grateful.'

'Well… all right,' he said reluctantly. 'If it will help Robert. He's missing his china doll.'

'China doll? You mean Jane?'

'Yes. Forgive me, I'm used to calling her that, she's so fragile.'

'What has he told you about the break-up of his engagement?'

'Not much. Whenever I ask, he's very vague. He said it was something to do with a row with his father, and apparently his Aunt Esther objected, for a reason that wasn't too clear. He seems to think the world is against him.'

Amy studied Andrew carefully. He did appear to be being honest with her, but she was aware that men like him were adept liars. However, it was hard to imagine Robert confessing his crimes to anyone, he was still in denial about them himself.

'And what do you make of it all?' she said.

'If I may be frank?'

'Please.'

'I think it all a bit strange. I got the feeling there was something he wasn't telling me.' Andrew's eyes searched hers, but she was giving nothing away.

'Did Robert mention the pond?' said Amy.

His eyes flared with interest. 'He did, as a matter of fact,' he replied, leaning forward in his seat.

'Was it his idea to go down there?'

'Ah,' he smiled. 'Spying on us, were you?'

'Whose idea was it?' she repeated.

'Mine. I've always had an interest in the macabre,' he said, eyes flicking to her hands before returning to her face.

'So I see.'

'I don't wish to offend you, but please don't be ashamed of your hands.'

'I'm not,' she retorted.

'I know. You're far too strong, but I have noticed that sometimes you hide them.'

'What business is that of yours?'

'Absolutely none, I apologise. What else would you like to know?'

'What did he say about Mrs Grier?'

'The dead housekeeper? Not much. Just that she attacked you then ran out of the house and attempted to make her escape across a frozen pond, which didn't turn out too well for her. He also said he tried to stop her and failed. That was about it.'

Amy nodded, feeling a little better. In her wildest dreams, she couldn't imagine Robert confessing the truth.

'May I ask why you're so interested in what he said about the housekeeper?' enquired Andrew.

'I would appreciate it if you didn't.'

'As you wish. Anything else I can help you with?'

'Yes. What would make Robert happy?'

'If you're hoping I'll come up with something that will distract him from his problems, I'm afraid you're going to be disappointed. He misses Jane and only she can make him whole again.'

'What would distract you from worrying about a woman?'

'I wouldn't know, I've never worried about one before.'

'I find that surprising after hearing you frequent a brothel.' Amy smiled at the surprise on his face. 'You are shocked that I can be brutally honest.'

'No, I admire that quality about you, my lady, it's such a refreshing change. If only more people were, the world would be a happier place. The truth is, I visit the brothel because I can indulge in all the pleasure I want with none of the emotional strings. I have no wish to marry and have children, that's for ordinary people. I'm on my way up in this world and nothing will stop me from achieving my goals. I will tread on anyone who tries.'

'So cold.'

'So I've been told.' He smiled. 'I've shocked you, I can see, but please don't fret, Robert's not like me. On the contrary, he feels too much. He has the traits of a volcano, like your excellent self. He's twisting the Jane issue over and over in his mind, until it's something else entirely, something that's quite far from what it originally was.'

'What do you mean?' she said, intrigued by the way this man spoke.

'It's not just about how unsuitable he and Jane may be together and the fact that both families have intervened before they made each other miserable. He sees Jane as his Juliet and he is Romeo, fighting for his true love against a heartless family and, as the hero of the piece, he intends to be the victor.'

'Interesting. You're a very astute man. How do we take his mind off it?'

'You could let him marry Jane.'

'Out of the question.'

'Or you could distract him with another female, a more suitable one.'

'That is out of the question too.'

'In that case, I have only one idea left – send him away somewhere he can forget about her, somewhere new and exciting that will take his mind off his lost love and open up a whole new range of possibilities to him.'

'That is a most interesting idea,' said Amy, although she didn't think the Lake District would quite fit the bill, as beautiful as it was. 'Thank you, Andrew. Our conversation has been most insightful.'

'Glad I could be of assistance.' His eyes flicked back to her hands. 'Do they hurt?'

Amy considered telling him to mind his own business, but she wanted to keep things civil, for Robert's sake. 'Sometimes they ache in the cold weather and occasionally the skin itches.'

'It must be torture for you this time of year. I have an ointment that could do wonders for your skin.'

'Thank you, but I get my treatments from Magda.'

'Ah, the witch, as Robert refers to her.'

'She isn't a witch,' snapped Amy. 'She's an extremely intelligent woman who men are jealous of.' She recalled her desire to keep this man onside and cursed her sharp tongue. 'Excuse me, I didn't mean to sound so brusque.'

'You need never apologise to me.' He leaned forward in his seat, green eyes bright. 'You look enchanting in the firelight.'

'Please don't speak to me like that.'

'Is it wrong for a gentleman to compliment a lady?'

'It is when the gentleman in question is two decades younger than the lady. The only compliments that please me are the ones from my husband.'

'Sir Henry is a fortunate man indeed. I do hope he appreciates you.'

'He does,' she said before rising. 'Now, if you'll excuse me...'

He leapt up and placed himself between her and the door. 'I've insulted you. I'm sorry, I didn't mean to.'

'Get out of my way, Mr Charteris,' she said, hoping she didn't sound as afraid as she felt. There was something in those green eyes that she really didn't like.

'Don't leave on a bad note. Please sit and we can talk some more. I was so enjoying our chat.'

As she couldn't escape the room, Amy decided to retake her seat. Fortunately Andrew sat too, which stilled her thudding heart. It was almost lunchtime, so he would soon be forced to relinquish her.

'Was there anything in particular you wished to discuss?' she said, glad her voice didn't tremble.

'No, I just enjoy your company.'

When they'd sat in silence for a couple of minutes, Amy grew impatient. 'It's almost lunchtime, I really must go and change.'

'Oh, yes, of course. So must I after walking through the garden. I'll walk with you.'

Silently cursing to herself, they left the room together, heading for the stairs. At the top of the stairs, they parted ways, Amy heading to the left while Andrew had to go right, towards the guest bedrooms. As she walked, she felt his eyes on her back and, glancing over her shoulder, she saw him standing there, watching her, making no move to go to his own room. Amy grew increasingly uncomfortable, and she rushed into her room, slammed the door shut and locked it, leaning back against it to catch her breath. She rang for Hazel, needing the comfort of a trusted individual.

The sound of approaching footsteps had her holding her breath, pressing her ear to the door as she strained to hear. It wasn't Hazel, the tread was too heavy. Hazel walked with the speed and lightness of a bird.

The footsteps stopped right outside her door and were replaced by a heavy, ragged breathing that caused Amy to stagger backwards. Glancing around the room, she snatched up a heavy silver candlestick from the fireplace, ready to use as a weapon. She stared at the doorknob, expecting it to turn, but it didn't. After what seemed like an age, the footsteps started up again, only this time they were heading away in the direction of the guest bedrooms.

Amy exhaled and replaced the candlestick on the fireplace. She let out a cry when the doorknob rattled.

'My lady, are you all right?' called Hazel.

Amy breathed a sigh of relief. Her arrival must have scared

Andrew off. She flung open the door to reveal her startled maid and struggled not to hug her.

'I heard a cry,' said Hazel.

'I thought I saw a spider, but it was nothing.'

Doubt shone in Hazel's eyes. She knew her mistress wouldn't have cried out at the sight of an insect. 'Shall I fetch one of the footmen to remove it?'

'That won't be necessary, thank you. It's gone now. Anyway, I need to discuss something with you. The family will be going away.'

Hazel's thoughts immediately flicked to Robert, who had only just returned and who she had barely seen. 'You are? Mr Rush never mentioned it.'

'We've only just decided. I need to get away for the sake of my health and after recent awful events.'

'I see. Do you wish me to accompany you?'

'Of course. How could I ever manage without you?' said Amy with a fond smile.

Hazel felt even more guilty when her mind filled with thoughts of intimate encounters with Robert in new and exotic places.

* * *

24

Amy decided not to tell Henry about her uncomfortable encounter
with Andrew Charteris. The last thing she wanted was for him to
throw him out and upset Robert. It was vital they stick to their plan,
it was the only way they could get rid of their unwanted houseguest
without making the present volatile situation even worse. While
they were in the Lake District, she planned on talking to Henry
about sending Robert on his grand tour, hoping Andrew's idea
about new places and fresh adventures would drag him from the
edge of the abyss.

In order to put up even more of a buffer between herself and
Andrew, Amy instructed the nanny to bring the children downstairs
for lunch and their cheerful, innocent chatter lifted all their spirits,
even Robert's.

Once lunch was over, they all retired to the drawing room. Amy
was heartened by the sight of the sun breaking through the heavy
grey clouds, the snow-laden tree branches dripping as their burden
began to melt. Soon they would be able to leave on their trip.

She turned her gaze from the window and back to the room and
saw Andrew watching her. She couldn't wait to get rid of him too.

Amy smiled inwardly as he sipped his claret. With Rush's assistance, she would ensure he was no more trouble during the rest of his stay here.

* * *

Hazel couldn't keep still. Robert had said he would visit her in her room. As maid to the mistress of the house, Hazel didn't have to share with another servant, meaning they would have privacy.

For the seventh time, Hazel patted her hair, ensuring it was still tightly coiled in its neat bun, then smoothed down her dull black dress. It was fortunate Robert was able to see past her plainness to the warm, loving woman beneath. That's what she told herself, anyway. The thought that she was being used had occurred to her more than once. She was privy to a lot of secrets, some of which she passed on to Robert, some of which she kept to herself. Keeping back information made her feel like she wasn't a complete traitor to her mistress. But Robert was the light of her extremely dull life, so she kept feeding him titbits to keep him coming back.

A knock at the door made her jump. She was smiling as she rushed to open it. Robert entered the room, closing the door behind him, his smile making her heart thump.

'I missed you,' he said, pulling her to him and kissing her.

'And I missed you,' she replied breathlessly.

'I'm sorry I haven't been up to see you sooner, but it's been difficult with Andrew around.'

'I understand.' Hazel was even more delighted to be back with him knowing he wasn't going to marry Miss Parke. She didn't need to feel as guilty any more. 'How long can you stay?'

'Not long, I'm afraid, but I have enough time to make my absence up to you,' he said before kissing her again while walking her back to the bed.

Robert knew he could get anything out of Hazel if he gave her enough physical pleasure, which he was very adept at, thanks to Vivienne and her girls – they really were excellent teachers – and a minute later, Hazel came. He retracted his hand from between her thighs and wiped it on her bedclothes. She wasn't attractive to look at and he had to use his imagination to pleasure her, but he maintained their relationship because she told him secrets. He knew she had something to tell him now, he could see it in her dull eyes as they slowly rolled open, her ugly frog mouth stretching into a smile.

'Thank you,' she breathed.

Robert inwardly cringed at how pathetic she sounded. 'You're welcome,' he replied, forcing a smile. He missed Jane. Yes, she was sweet, but she had dignity too, like his mother. This stupid scrap of a woman didn't come close to either of them. He reclined back on the bed beside her, waiting until her breathing slowed, her heavy panting annoying him.

'It's going to be such fun for us in the Lake District,' she eventually said.

He rolled onto his side to face her. 'Excuse me?'

'The family's going away to the Lake District. Her ladyship asked me to make the arrangements. I'm to accompany you.'

Robert sat bolt upright, confused and angry. 'This is the first I've heard of it. Am I going too?'

'Yes,' she said, sitting up with him. 'You didn't know?'

'No. When are we supposed to be leaving?'

'As soon as the snow clears enough to travel.'

Robert brightened up. England. It was the north of England, but it was still a significant step closer to Jane. Neither was it too far from Gretna Green. It was perfect.

'So they really didn't tell you?' she said when it appeared he'd drifted off into his own world.

'No, but if that's what my parents wish me to do, then do it I must.' He forced a smile. 'As you said, we may even get to enjoy some time together.' Dammit, why had his mother invited the frog-faced bitch too? Still, the good thing about Hazel was that she was quiet and compliant, she might even be of some assistance. 'That would be most satisfactory,' he said, kissing her. He got to his feet and straightened his collar.

'You're leaving already?' she said, disappointed.

'I'm afraid I must. I said I'd look in on Andrew, he's not feeling well again. I'll see you again soon,' he said, giving her one last kiss.

Robert left, wiping her off his lips the moment he was out the door.

* * *

'Andrew, wake up, there's nothing wrong with you,' said Robert, bursting into his room.

'What is it?' he groaned, flopping onto his side. 'I was asleep.'

'Pretending to be ill, more like.'

'I think I might actually be unwell this time. I feel rotten. What time is it?'

Robert glanced at his pocket watch. 'Half past five.'

'I've been asleep for four hours. How did that happen?'

'Never mind all that. We're all going to the Lake District.'

'Lake District? What's that?'

'For God's sake, Andrew, shake the fuzz out of your head. My parents are planning a surprise trip, probably in an attempt to get my mind off Jane. They don't know that I know yet.'

This puzzled Andrew's fuddled brain. 'Then how do you know?'

'My mother's maid told me.'

His green eyes, normally so vibrant, were dull but they still narrowed suspiciously. 'And why would she tell you that?'

'She's a dim-witted woman. It's easy to trick her into revealing things.'

'Nonsense.' Andrew's smile was sly. 'Robert, are you romancing one of the maids? I know you like the maids. What did you give her to get her to talk? Pleasure or pain?'

'Oh... fine. I give her a bit of pleasure now and then, and in return she tells me things. She's an ugly old spinster, so it's not much fun.'

'Not like pretty little Daisy, then?'

'Unfortunately not, but she does come in useful.'

'Now we've finally got that straight, let's consider this new development.' Andrew attempted to rise and sank back onto the bed with a groan. 'My head. Something's really wrong with me.' His eyes widened. 'The witch.'

'Magda? What about her?'

'She came into my room and said she knew what I was up to and that she was going to stop it. She's trying to make me sleep myself to death.'

'That's the stupidest thing I've ever heard. You probably drank too much claret.'

'I've drunk a lot more in the past and never felt a thing. Maybe I should see the doctor.'

'Stop being a little girl, it'll wear off. Now help me think about how I can turn this Lake District trip to my advantage.'

'I'm overwhelmed with sympathy,' said Andrew dryly. 'But the most obvious thing is to telegram Jane immediately and let her know, so she can perhaps prepare something.'

'Prepare what?'

'I don't know, I'm dying here,' he said, falling back onto the bed.

'Oh, go back to sleep. Hopefully you'll be more use when you wake up.'

With that, Robert left Andrew's bedroom and set out in search of Wyles, the grumpy footman. He discovered him setting the dining table for dinner and instructed him as to what to put in the telegram to Jane before slipping him some money. The man solemnly promised to send the telegram the following morning on his day off.

Feeling happier than he had in weeks, Robert strolled into the lounge and poured himself a Scotch, rocking back and forth on his heels as he imagined his reunion with Jane, and their wedding, followed by their wedding night. He tingled all over at the prospect of finally bedding her after years of wondering what it would be like to see those huge blue eyes staring up at him, blonde curls splayed across the pillow, cheeks flushed with desire...

He knocked back the last of the Scotch, excitement coursing through his body. If he didn't see her again soon, he'd lose his mind.

'Hello, sweetheart,' said a gentle voice.

Robert wiped the lascivious look off his face before turning round.

'Hello, Mother. You're looking much better.'

There was colour to Amy's cheeks and her eyes sparkled but she definitely moved more slowly than she had before the illness, as though age was finally starting to catch up with her.

'I feel it,' she replied.

'Scotch?'

'I really shouldn't.'

'Go on, I won't tell Magda.'

'All right, then,' she smiled.

With a grin, he poured her a Scotch and refilled his own glass. This was how he liked it – just the two of them, how it was before he had to share her.

'Thank you,' said Amy, accepting the glass and taking a sip.

He enjoyed watching his mother drink whisky. She was so different to any other woman he'd ever known, even Jane, and he adored her for it. He knew he'd let her down, frightened her even, and he didn't want that, he couldn't stand the thought of anything coming between them. He really loved her and she loved him and he didn't want that to change.

'What?' she smiled when she realised he was watching her.

'Are we all right?'

Her heart went out to him when anxiety shone from his eyes. 'Just as long as you continue to control yourself and stop lying to me.'

'I am. I haven't hurt anyone since Daisy.'

She studied him closely, drawing out the silence, probably in the hope that he would break down and admit to killing Evelyn, but he casually sipped his whisky as she continued to stare.

'Good,' she eventually said. 'Keep it up.'

Robert nodded, purposefully remaining silent in the hope that she would tell him about the trip to the Lake District, but she didn't and he couldn't understand why. What was the point in keeping it a secret?

His good mood slipped when Henry entered the room. He ignored Robert, went straight to Amy, wrapped his arm around her waist and kissed her cheek.

'How are you feeling?' he said.

'Fine,' she smiled.

Robert frowned. The adoration that always shone out of her eyes when she looked at Henry never failed to annoy him. It felt like he was stealing his mother from him.

Henry deigned to turn his attention to his stepson. 'And have you been behaving yourself, Robert?'

'No. There's a pile of injured maids in the garden.'

'There's no need to take that attitude,' frowned Henry. 'If I were you, I'd be going out of my way to become a paragon of goodness.'

Robert sighed in irritation but one pleading look from his mother was enough to make him bite his tongue. 'Yes... Father.'

'Good boy,' said Henry, infuriating him even more.

Robert's spirits rose when Andrew entered the room. Finally, things were evened up a bit. His friend looked dreadful, pale and exhausted.

'What happened to you?' Henry asked him.

'I had a nap this afternoon and I don't think it did me any good.' Andrew sank into an armchair, slender body limp. 'I never nap and I don't think I'll be doing it again.'

'Have a drink, it'll perk you up,' said Robert. He picked up a decanter and brandished it maliciously. 'Claret?'

'No, thank you,' he mumbled, sinking further into the chair.

Robert hovered nearby, expecting an announcement about the Lake District trip now they were all together, but still nothing.

By the time they were seated around the dining table, he still hadn't been enlightened and he was starting to feel uneasy. It was beginning to feel like a plot. What were his parents up to now? Was it worse than the loathed Knapp? Would the brute be coming with them to the Lakes? The prospect was appalling, he was looking forward to getting away from his jailer for a while. Speaking of which, where was he? Knapp's absence made him even more nervous.

'Andrew, you do look dreadful,' said Amy. 'Would you like Magda to take a look at you? She's gone home to tend to her animals, but I'm sure she wouldn't mind coming back.'

'No need for that, thank you,' he replied, slumped at the table, looking glum. 'I'm just overtired. I'll be right as rain tomorrow.'

'In that case, have some claret. It's good for the blood.'

Taking his cue, Rush picked up the decanter and made to fill up his glass.

'No,' cried Andrew, putting his hand over the top of the glass.

Rush glanced at his mistress, who appeared perturbed.

'It will help you feel better,' pressed Amy.

'I appreciate your concern, my lady, but I really couldn't stomach a drop.'

Left with no choice, Rush replaced the decanter on the sideboard and retook his position by the door.

Dinner passed uneventfully, although for Robert it was torture. He kept expecting his parents to announce the trip to England, but they never did. Andrew retired to bed early and Robert decided he would go up too as there was nothing else to stay up for. An evening alone with his parents was not his idea of fun.

* * *

Before following Henry to bed that night, Amy hung back to speak to Rush in private.

'I'm sorry, my lady,' he began before she could speak. 'I tried to get him to take the claret, but he refused.'

'It's all right, you did your best. I do, however, have another idea,' she said with a wicked smile.

* * *

'Oh, what is it?' exclaimed Andrew.

He'd been on the verge of sleep. After sleeping away the entire afternoon, it had been difficult for him to drift off, despite how tired he felt. Now, just when he'd finally been about to accomplish his goal, some fool had disturbed him.

He'd expected Robert to walk in but instead it was Rush, bearing a cup on a tray.

'I'm sorry to disturb, sir,' he said.

'Then why did you?' sighed Andrew.

'Her ladyship recommended I bring you a cup of hot chocolate. She swears by it when she's ill.'

'Fine, just leave it there,' said Andrew, waving his hand at the nightstand, intending to turn over and go to sleep the second the stupid old man left.

'She gave me explicit instructions to see that you drink it all down,' he pressed, hovering by his bedside.

Warning bells started ringing in Andrew's head. Why was Lady Alardyce so concerned with his drinking habits? The fuzziness in his head, the thickness of his tongue and the nausea suddenly made sense. But why would she drug him?

'I'm not a child. If I promise to drink it right down like a good little boy, will you leave me alone?'

'Yes, sir.'

'In that case, I promise. Now please leave.'

'Very well, sir,' he said before shuffling from the room.

When he'd gone, Andrew grabbed the cup and sniffed it. It was impossible for him to detect anything beneath the sweet smell of the chocolate and sugar, but he threw the contents onto the fire then stared into the cup, the foamy brown remnants clinging to the sides infuriating him.

'Oh, Lady Alardyce, you have been very naughty,' said Andrew, eyes gleaming.

25

Amy got a shock the next morning at breakfast when Andrew came downstairs, bright-eyed and whistling cheerfully. Robert and Henry still hadn't risen.

'Good morning, Lady Alardyce,' smiled Andrew, taking his seat at the table.

'Good morning, Andrew,' she replied, hiding how disconcerted she was. 'You appear to be much recovered.'

'I am after a wonderful sleep. I always shake these things off quick enough. Are you quite all right? You look a trifle pale.'

'I'm absolutely fine,' she replied, eyes flicking to the footman gathering up some empty plates, wondering if it would look strange if she ordered him to stay, but she knew it would. She returned her attention to her breakfast, but her appetite had gone. She was quite certain Andrew had caught her out.

'You've been very naughty, Lady Alardyce,' he said.

'I beg your pardon?'

'You drugged me.'

'I most certainly did not.'

'Denial is useless. I know the truth. With my medical knowledge, I should have spotted it sooner, it's why you were so keen for me to drink the claret last night and why Rush was so desperate for me to have my hot chocolate. But I got wise to your game which is why I'm sitting here all bright-eyed and bushy-tailed. The only thing I can't work out is why? I assume you don't drug all your guests, but I would appreciate being told exactly what I've done wrong.'

'Nothing.'

'Please don't lie on top of everything else. If you insist on playing this charade, then I will have no option but to tell Robert what you've done.'

'He'd never believe you.'

'He's ready to believe anything confirming his theory that everyone is against him and you know it.'

Amy sighed and put down her spoon. 'Very well. You made me extremely uncomfortable the other day.'

'The other day?' he frowned before realisation dawned. 'Are you referring to our very pleasant chat in the sitting room?'

'I am. You wouldn't let me leave. Then you came to my bedroom door.'

'I did nothing of the sort.'

'Yes, you did, I heard you.'

'How can you possibly know it was me? It was most likely Sir Henry.'

'My husband does not lurk outside people's bedrooms.' Her eyes narrowed. 'It was you.'

'So you drugged me on a suspicion?'

When he suddenly rose from his chair, she did the same, backing away as he advanced on her.

'Stop or I'll scream and dozens of servants will come running,' she said breathlessly.

'I was merely going to inspect the kedgeree,' he said, walking over to the silver dish and lifting the lid. He gave her a sideways look and smiled. 'I make you nervous, don't I?'

'I've faced much worse than you in my time.'

'So I believe, but I still make you nervous. Interesting.'

There was something in Andrew's eyes that told Amy he was going to get her back for what she'd done, which only made it even more urgent that she get him out of the house.

* * *

That afternoon, Robert stalked Alardyce House, searching for Hazel in the hope of getting more out of her about the trip to the Lake District, but the stupid woman was nowhere to be found. As he descended the stairs after searching the servants' quarters, he heard a voice calling his name but he ignored it, not in the mood to be pestered.

'Master Robert,' called Wyles. 'Master Robert,' he repeated louder when he ignored him.

Robert stopped and spun on his heel. 'What?'

Wyles rushed up to him, brandishing a piece of paper. 'You really need to read this. It's from your lady.'

Robert snatched it from him and scanned the telegram eagerly. 'She's here, in Edinburgh,' he said with wonder.

'Aye, sir. What would you like me to do?'

'Where's Knapp?'

'In the billiard room with your father.'

'Ensure they both stay there.'

'How?'

Robert sighed. Wyles was not an imaginative man. 'Oh, never mind. Just keep an eye on them and let me know if either of them leave.'

'Where will I find you if they do?' he called when Robert rushed away.

'In Mr Charteris's room.'

* * *

Andrew sighed and cast aside his book when his door erupted open again. He thought he'd get some peace and quiet at Alardyce House, but he'd have got more rest staying in the city. 'What's happened now?' he said in a bored tone.

'Jane's here, in Edinburgh.'

Now he had his attention. 'You're certain?'

'Absolutely. She sent Wyles this telegram,' he said, thrusting it under his nose.

'The china doll has more grit than I thought. It says she came here alone.'

'And she wants to marry me. I have to reach her before Aunt Esther realises she's missing and alerts my parents.'

'Then we must act immediately. Do you have a bag packed?'

'I do, but my father and Knapp are downstairs. I need to sneak out without them noticing.'

'Can't you use the servants' entrance?'

'Not without my parents being informed. I need to go out the back way so I can get my horse from the stables. Then I can leave through the woods at the rear of the house, so I won't be seen going down the drive.'

'Get your bag. I'll cause a distraction. Stop gawking at me and go.'

Robert shook his hand. 'Thank you, Andrew.'

'That's what friends are for. I only hope you'll remember this if I ever need you.'

'Of course,' he said with a devilish smile. Then he was gone.

'Distraction, distraction,' Andrew muttered to himself as he hurried downstairs. Briefly he considered setting fire to something but thought Robert wouldn't appreciate him vandalising his inheritance. There was nothing for it. He had to pull his dying swan act.

At the bottom of the stairs, Andrew paused by a large vase of flowers, dipped his hand inside and splashed some of the droplets on his face then tugged at his shirt, opening the top button and skewing the collar. He then staggered towards the billiard room. He saw Wyles on sentry duty outside the door, making sure no one left. The footman regarded Andrew with surprise, as he put his finger to his lips.

'Sssh,' he told Wyles, before pushing open the door. 'Help,' he called weakly as he fell into the room.

'My God, what's happened?' said Henry, rushing to his side as he sprawled on the floor.

'I don't know... I suddenly fell ill, my head's spinning.'

'Knapp, ring the bell for the servants,' ordered Henry.

Knapp replaced his billiard cue in the rack and wandered over to the bell with exaggerated slowness. Ten seconds later, Wyles entered.

'Yes, sir?'

'Fetch Dr Parlow at once. Mr Charteris is unwell.'

'That's not necessary,' said Andrew, feigning weakness, relieved he hadn't asked the boy to fetch Magda.

'Yes, it is. Immediately,' Henry told the footman.

'Yes, sir,' he nodded before running off.

'Can you rise?' Henry asked.

'I... I'm not sure.'

'Knapp, help me,' he said.

Knapp hoisted Andrew up by one arm and practically dragged him to a chair.

Andrew was surprised to find Sir Henry was being sympathetic towards him. Perhaps he was unaware Lady Alardyce had drugged him and thought he'd been genuinely ill.

'That's right... took me completely by surprise coming down the stairs,' panted Andrew. 'Thought I was going to fall.'

'But you didn't,' said Knapp.

'No, although I did fall into the door.'

'Hmmm,' said Knapp, folding his arms across his chest, which was quite a feat because his chest was so huge. His beady eyes remained fixed on Andrew as Henry poured him a brandy, his cure in any emergency.

Knapp's head snapped up so suddenly it startled them. He lumbered over to the window and peered out.

'What is it?' said Henry.

'Where's Robert?'

'I've no idea. Do you know, Andrew?'

'No, sorry. Haven't seen him since breakfast.'

'Nonsense,' snarled Knapp. 'You two are as thick as thieves.' He clamped his huge hand down on Andrew's brow, knocking him back in his chair.

'What are you doing?' exclaimed Andrew.

'There's nothing wrong with you. Feel him, Sir Henry, he's cold, like the reptile he is. It's a distraction. We need to find Robert. Now.'

Knapp and Henry raced out of the room, leaving Andrew alone with his brandy and a smile on his face.

* * *

Henry almost crashed into Amy as she came out of her sitting room.

'What's going on?' she said.

'Have you seen Robert?'

'Not for a couple of hours. Why?'

'Andrew suddenly fell ill. We think it was a distraction.'

She visibly paled. 'Rush,' she called, racing along the corridor, hunting for the butler, knowing it would be quicker than waiting for him to come to her.

'Yes, my lady?' said a polite voice.

The butler emerged from the staircase that led down to the kitchens.

'Have you seen Robert?'

'I did see him go upstairs about forty minutes ago, then I was asked to attend to something downstairs.'

Henry and Knapp raced past them and upstairs to Robert's bedroom, but he wasn't there.

Knapp looked out of the window. 'His room overlooks the stables.'

'Robert has his own horse,' replied Henry.

They ran back downstairs, past Amy and Rush.

'What's going on?' she called after them.

'Stables,' Henry breathlessly called back, amazed by Knapp's speed. It was an effort to keep up with him.

They raced outside, Henry's slippers sliding on the patches of ice, but Knapp's sensible shoes gripped remorselessly to the cobbles as they rushed into the stables.

'Have you seen Master Robert?' demanded Henry, breathing hard.

'Yes, sir,' said the young stable-hand, surprised to see Sir Henry Alardyce standing in hay and horse excrement in his slippers and indoor clothes. 'He left on his horse about ten minutes ago.'

'Did he have anything with him?'

'Yes, sir. A bag.'

'Did he say where he was going?'

'No, sir. Did I do wrong?'

'No, Sam, it's not your fault,' said Henry before marching back to the house with Knapp. 'What can this mean?'

'There's only one person who can tell us,' replied Knapp, face like thunder.

Henry nodded. He would get it out of Andrew Charteris if he had to beat it out of him.

'Have you found Robert?' said Amy, who was waiting for them at the door.

'Sam said he left on his horse about ten minutes ago,' replied Henry.

'Where for?' she said, following as they strode back towards the billiard room.

'We don't know but Charteris will.' He flung open the door and stopped. 'Where is he? You didn't see him leave?'

'No.'

'Knapp, check his room. I want to know if his things are still there.'

Knapp nodded and ran upstairs.

'What is going on?' said Amy.

'We might know if we could find Charteris,' said Henry. 'He fell down in here claiming he was ill, but it was all a distraction to allow Robert to leave.'

'He's run away, hasn't he? I'll never see him again.'

'Robert wouldn't give up his comfortable life here for anything less than...' He trailed off as realisation struck.

'Jane,' she ended for him. 'But he can't go all the way to London on his horse.'

'We need to contact Esther. There's a good chance Jane isn't in London.'

* * *

Robert descended from the carriage, clutching his bag, and looked up at the hotel with breathless excitement. He hadn't had the chance to stop and think since he'd received that telegram. After the frantic horseback ride into the city, he'd left his horse at Thomas's house and borrowed his carriage to bring him here. This was the first chance he'd had to stop and consider what he was doing. Not that he regretted it for a moment.

He rushed inside the hotel and up the stairs. Jane had given him the room number in the telegram. His hand shook as he knocked on the door, which opened to reveal that dear little face.

'Jane,' was all he said as he stepped inside, took her face in his hands and kissed her.

They staggered back into the room together, Robert kicking the door shut.

'God, I can't describe how much I've missed you,' he said.

Tears shone in her eyes as she gazed up at him. 'I've missed you too, it feels like I've been buried alive these past few weeks.'

'I will allow no one to part us again.'

'Good, because I couldn't bear it.'

'Does anyone know you're here?'

'No. Aunt Esther sent an old cousin of hers to watch over me. It was easy giving her the slip and I went straight to the train station. I didn't even think twice, it just felt like the most natural thing in the world to come to you.'

He beamed at her, stroking her soft skin. 'And so it is. Do you still want to marry me?'

'More than anything.'

'Then will you come with me to Gretna Green?'

'Yes, but I am worried about upsetting our families.'

'I think it might be a bit late for that. They've left us no choice. They've driven us to this.'

'What they said about you... it was horrible.'

'You don't believe it, do you?'

'Of course not. I know you, Robert, you have a good heart, you could never do those awful things they accused you of.'

'Good,' he said, deciding it would be best to let that subject drop. 'But if we want to marry, we must leave as soon as possible. We can't stay in Edinburgh, they'll be looking for us.'

'I'm ready to go,' she said, indicating a carpetbag on the bed.

'I love you,' he smiled.

'I love you too, Robert.'

'So we're really going to Gretna Green to get married?'

She nodded determinedly. 'Yes.'

He kissed her, unable to stop himself from glancing at the large bed right behind them. For the first time in their relationship, they were truly alone, and it was tempting to take advantage of the moment, but he was so close to finally getting everything he'd ever wanted and he could not afford to delay.

'Then what are we waiting for?' he smiled.

They both laughed nervously. Robert picked up their bags and they left the hotel together, Jane holding onto his arm. Thomas's carriage was still waiting for them outside the hotel. Robert hesitated before climbing in, thinking of his mother and how hurt she was going to be.

'Are you having second thoughts?' said Jane.

Robert gazed into that face he loved so much and his mother's image melted away.

'Not at all. Let's go and get married.'

26

Andrew skulked at the bottom of the garden of the cottage belonging to the witch. It looked like a witch's house too with its patches of weird and wonderful plants and crooked chimney. The house appeared to be in darkness but that didn't mean she wasn't in, so he decided to be quick.

Gleefully he began ripping up the plants, which seemed to be thriving despite the weather, more proof of witchery. He knew it would have been wiser to bypass this vengeance and just run to Gretna Green to meet up with Robert and Jane, but he had to do this to show her he wasn't a man to be mocked.

Putting all thoughts of curses out of his mind, Andrew continued with the vandalism, soon growing bored of attacking the plants and turning his attention to the cottage instead. He picked up a rock and brandished it, deciding which window to throw it at, when he heard a growl behind him.

He went rigid and slowly turned to see a wolf standing there, blocking his exit out of the garden, its hackles rising. Its coat was a glowing silver, one eye green, the other blue.

Andrew took in all the silver fur and frowned. 'Magda?'

'My powers don't extend to shape shifting,' said a voice.

He stared at the wolf, attempting to process whether it had spoken before realising someone was standing behind him. He turned and found himself pinned by those silver eyes.

'What on earth do you think you're doing in my garden?' said Magda, voice colder than her eyes.

'Me? Er, I saw some children in here pulling up plants as I was passing, so I scared them off. Little scamps must be around here somewhere.' He trailed off as he realised how ridiculous he sounded. Magda continued to stare at him while the wolf growled.

'Well,' said Andrew. 'I won't keep you and I do have somewhere to be...'

'The children in this village are far too sensible to come into my garden,' she said. 'I know what you're up to. You came here thinking you were capable of hurting me.' She threw back her head, eyes flaring. 'But I have protection you can't even conceive of. I knew you were here the moment you set foot in the village, I sensed the evil in your heart. Fenrir does so loathe evil,' she said, indicating the wolf. 'Do you know what he does to it?'

'What?' he rasped.

'He consumes it.'

Andrew looked back at the wolf, who was positively snarling now, drool dripping from his fangs. 'Now let's not get carried away,' he said, holding up his hands.

When he attempted to back away, the wolf only growled louder.

'You're the one who came onto my property and began destroying things,' said Magda. 'You put yourself in this position, so why should I deny Fenrir his fun?'

'That's a bit uneven, don't you think?' he said, feeling his throat constrict. 'Taking a chunk out of me for spoiling a few plants?'

'Ah, so you admit it?'

'What, I... no.'

'Fenrir, it's supper time.'

'Wait,' cried Andrew when the wolf readied itself to spring.

'You shouldn't have come here tonight. I was content to let you be, but you've gone too far.'

Andrew was appalled when her eyes rolled back in her head and she started to chant.

'Are... are you cursing me?' he stammered.

She ignored him, continuing with her bizarre chanting as the wolf circled him.

'My God, you're cursing me, aren't you?' he shrieked.

Not even the threat of the wolf could stop him as he ran out of the garden, hurdling the fence, and raced down the road out of the village.

Magda opened her eyes and laughed, patting the wolf's head.

'Well, that was amusing, wasn't it, Fenrir? At least he's done some of the weeding for me,' she said, looking down at the plants he'd uprooted. 'Oh dear, he touched the Cotton Bush. He's going to feel that when he's calmed down.' She stroked Fenrir's soft fur. 'Let's have our supper. It looks like you're stuck with rabbit tonight. Snake is off the menu.'

* * *

'Douglas has gone through Robert's things and he said some of his clothes are missing as well as a bag,' Amy told Henry.

'There was a sighting of Charteris in the village,' said a furious Knapp. 'He paid one of the men to take him back to the city. He asked to be dropped off at Waverley Station.'

'Which means he's not going back to the university,' said Henry. 'But where could he be going?'

'To meet up with Robert, no doubt,' said Knapp, his huge face bright purple. Never, in all his life, had anyone got the better of him, let alone two men who were young enough to be his sons. When he found them, he would crush their windpipes.

'So how do we find them?' said Amy, wringing her hands.

'This has to do with Jane, I'm certain of it,' said Henry. 'They could be on their way to London.'

'But what would be the point? He can't marry her, he has no licence, no witnesses, nothing.'

'There is one place where you don't need all that to get married,' said Knapp.

'Gretna Green?' replied Henry.

'That's it,' said Amy. 'They're going to elope. Once they're married, there's nothing we can do, not without causing a huge scandal, and they both know we'd do anything to avoid that.'

'This elopement will still cause a scandal,' said Henry. 'They must be stopped.' He looked to Knapp. 'If we hurry, we might still beat them to it.'

'I'm coming with you,' said Amy.

'We won't be able to stop for you to rest.'

'I'm well aware of that.' She hurried to the door, pausing to look back at the two men. 'Well, what are you waiting for, gentlemen?'

* * *

'This is so pretty,' said Jane as the carriage rolled to a halt outside Gretna Hall, a pleasant white two-storey manor house.

'It is,' replied Robert, afraid the modesty of it all would cause her to change her mind. Jane had grown up with only the best, so it was reasonable to expect that she would want the best wedding.

'I like it,' she smiled, to his relief.

The sun was just rising, making her tired eyes sparkle, and he took a moment to admire her in the gathering dawn. Her dress was rumpled after the journey and her curls were springing out from the side of her head, but she still looked lovely. They'd travelled through the night, stopping only to change horses, and they'd barely managed to snatch brief naps in the rattling carriage. Not daring to delay, Robert had ordered food and drink be brought out to the carriage so they wouldn't have to stop, and it had been exhausting. But finally they were close to their goal.

The landlord of the hall came out to greet them. He was a thick-set, bald-headed man who looked unnervingly like Knapp. However, his smile was friendly.

'Where's the parson?' said Robert as he stepped out of the carriage, turning to assist Jane down. 'We need to be married immediately.'

'It takes half an hour to summon the parson, sir,' replied the landlord respectfully. 'Maybe even longer this early, but you're welcome to enjoy some refreshments inside while you wait.'

Robert was tempted to bark at the man for the delay, but he didn't want to appear unreasonable and perhaps risk delaying things even further. And Jane did seem to be on the verge of fainting.

'Yes, please,' he said as he wrapped an arm around her waist to support her.

The landlord led them inside to a pleasant sitting room where a fire had been lit. Jane sat beside it, shivering in her travelling cloak.

'Are you all right?' said Robert, taking her cold hand and attempting to warm it up.

'I'll be fine after some tea and a rest by the fire.' She looked to the landlord. 'Is there a room where I can change? I can't possibly get married in these clothes and I will need a maid to assist me.'

'Of course. There's a room already waiting. As soon as you've finished here, my wife will show you up.'

'Thank you,' she smiled, the colour returning to her cheeks with the warmth of the fire. 'Oh, lovely,' she smiled when a young maid brought in a tray laden with tea, bread and cakes.

When the girl leaned over their table, Robert's heart started to pound and as the landlord walked away and Jane was occupied with selecting a cake, he was free to admire the curve of the maid's body beneath her dress, the pale creaminess of her skin. He pictured what that soft skin would look like red and striped, bleeding...

'Thank you,' Jane said to the maid.

Her voice jerked him out of it and he jumped, banging his knee on the underside of the table. 'Ouch.'

'Are you all right?' said Jane.

'Fine,' he grimaced, rubbing his leg.

Fortunately, the pain had doused his ardour. He gazed at his bride-to-be, wondering how he could possibly look at a simple maid when he was about to make this beauty his wife. Not only was she the loveliest creature he'd ever seen, she'd been his friend since they were small children. When he'd feared he would never see his mother again, Jane had been there, comforting him. He would never forget that.

* * *

After they'd finished their meal, Jane was escorted upstairs by Frances, the landlord's wife, while Robert hastily changed his suit then kept lookout for the parson. Finally, a white-haired old man doddered up the steps of the hall, still shaking off the remnants of sleep. He sank into an armchair and yawned.

To Robert's frustration, Jane took her time changing. He was aware that at any moment his parents could tear into the village. They weren't stupid, they'd work out where he'd gone, eventually. And where was Andrew? He should have been here by now.

The old parson appeared to drift off in the chair while Robert continued to pace back and forth. 'What is she doing?' he huffed.

Just as he was considering going upstairs and dragging her down, Jane walked into the room, a vision in white silk trimmed with lace, a white flower sitting at her breast.

'Well, what do you think?' she asked nervously. 'I didn't have the opportunity to purchase a real wedding dress, but I saw this in a shop and thought it would do.'

'I think you're the loveliest woman who ever walked the face of the earth,' he breathed. Dear God, he had tears in his eyes. He simply couldn't grasp the fact that this divine creature was going to be his wife. He held his arm out to her. 'Ready?'

She smiled and accepted his arm. 'Ready.'

Robert looked to the parson and his smile dropped. 'We're ready,' he said loudly.

The old man jumped awake with a snort. 'What did you say?'

'We're ready to get married,' said an exasperated Robert.

'All right, no need to shout.'

Slowly the parson got to his feet, stretched and yawned, plucking at Robert's taut nerves even further.

'There may be someone on their way to stop us,' Robert told the landlord.

'It wouldn't be the first time,' he replied. 'We have something that will stop them in their tracks. Meet Garraghan.'

Robert smiled when a man mountain emerged from a back room. He would keep Knapp busy.

* * *

'We're here, finally,' exclaimed Henry as they reached Gretna Green, the village still asleep.

'Where should we start looking?' said Amy.

Despite Henry's insistence that she sleep on the journey, she hadn't so much as closed her eyes. How could she rest until she knew her son wasn't going to destroy one of the people he loved the most and, in turn, destroy himself? As they'd left Alardyce, they'd instructed Rush to contact Esther and inform her of what was going on. No doubt she was already on her way up to Scotland, but it would take her a while to arrive.

'Gretna Hall is where most people go to get wed,' said Knapp.

'Then that's where we'll go,' said Henry before shouting instructions up to the driver. The hall was obviously a popular place because there were signs all over the village for it.

It was a relief to Amy that the hall was very pretty and respectable-looking, romantic, even. Not what she'd imagined.

The driver opened the carriage door and Henry hopped out first then turned to assist Amy. A maid came scurrying out of the hall to greet them, assuming they were another eloping couple.

'Good morning,' said the mousy girl with a sweet smile.

'Have a couple arrived, the man tall and dark, the woman pretty and blonde?' said Henry.

The girl's smile dropped as she was put on her guard. It wasn't the first time she'd encountered irate parents. 'Dunno.'

'Oh, yes, you do. Speak up, girl.'

The maid backed away, looking hostile. She glanced over her shoulder at the hall and a massive figure appeared in the doorway.

'Trouble, Mags?' called the giant.

'Yes, Garraghan,' she called back before turning to Henry with a smirk.

The huge man lumbered his way towards them, the muscles in his thick arms twitching in anticipation of ejecting someone from the property.

'This is private property,' he told them. 'You have to leave.'

'We're going nowhere until we stop this sham of a wedding,' retorted Henry.

As the leviathan continued to advance on him and Amy, behind them the carriage rocked from side to side as Knapp dismounted. Garraghan came to a halt, not so sure of himself now he was confronted by someone of equal stature.

'You can't come in, a wedding's in progress,' added the giant in a quieter voice. He cleared his throat and shuffled when Knapp just glared at him.

'There won't be for much longer,' said Henry, making his way towards the door of the hall, Amy following.

When the giant tried to block their path, Knapp's fist shot out and knocked him flat on his back.

'Oy, you can't do that,' cried the maid, rushing to tend to her fallen colleague, who was out cold.

'Says who?' smiled Knapp.

Amy and Henry raced up the steps into the hall. Following the sound of voices, they burst into a room to find Robert and Jane holding hands and kissing before a parson, two strangers looking on, the only witnesses to their son's wedding.

'No,' said Amy, the sight of the gold band on Jane's finger making her feel sick. 'We're too late.'

27

The newlyweds looked to Henry and Amy. Robert was grinning from ear to ear, but Jane had the grace to look ashamed.

'Mother, Father,' said Robert. 'I'm sorry, you just missed it.'

'You mean... you're married?' rasped Amy.

'We are,' he said, taking Jane's hand.

'Dear God,' said Amy, pressing a hand to her forehead.

'I'll have this marriage torn apart in days,' thundered Henry. 'It's a ridiculous sham.'

'Actually, sir,' said the landlord, stepping forward, 'marriages here are perfectly legal.'

'He's right,' interjected the hook-nosed parson. 'I've been doing this for forty years and not one of the marriages I've performed has ever been found to be invalid in a court of law, no matter how hard people have tried.'

'We've done nothing wrong,' said Robert. 'We're in love.'

Amy didn't reply but her expression was sad.

'Why don't you join us for a celebratory meal?' said Robert jovially. Not only was he married to the love of his life, but he'd got one over on his parents. 'Frances here is a wonderful cook,' he said, gesturing to the landlord's wife.

'You're more than welcome,' said Frances respectfully.

Henry was about to tell them where they could stick their meal, but Amy took his arm. 'I could use something to eat.'

Noting how pale and weak she was after the journey, he nodded.

'You just need to sign the register,' Frances told Robert and Jane.

Leaving them to it, Amy turned and walked back outside, breathing in the fresh air, trying to prevent the hot tears from spilling down her face.

'The stupid, stupid boy,' she said. 'He has no idea what he's done. He will destroy that girl.'

'Let's not discuss it now,' said Henry, sliding an arm around her waist. 'You need to sit down before you fall down.'

The giant had woken and was picking himself up, Knapp watching with an amused smile. He wiped the grin off his face when he saw his employer.

'Did we get here in time?'

Henry shook his head. 'No, they're already married.'

'Damn,' he hissed, glaring down at Garraghan as though it was his fault. 'So what now?'

'We eat and rest. After that, I have absolutely no idea.'

Leaving Garraghan on the ground with the maid fussing over him, Knapp followed Amy and Henry inside. The landlord and his wife were waiting for them, eager to please.

'This way, sir,' said the landlord, pointing them towards the sitting room. 'I've ordered some tea to be brought up while you wait for breakfast.'

Without a word, they strode past him and into the sitting room, unable to bring themselves to be pleasant to the man who had facilitated their son's downfall.

They sat in silence. The maid entered the room and began pouring the tea in hostile silence, casting glares at Knapp, who didn't even notice.

Amy felt sick at the sound of Robert's happy voice approaching as he talked with Jane. When the door opened and she saw them standing there arm-in-arm, she had to restrain herself from slapping the silly smiles off their faces.

'Is no one going to say congratulations?' said Jane, looking hurt.

'Congratulations is a word for a happy occasion,' said Henry coldly.

Jane turned her huge pleading eyes on Amy. 'Aunt Amy, you at least must be happy for us. You know we've been in love for years, that this is all either of us wants.'

Before replying, Amy glanced at her son, who was bursting with smugness. 'You expect us to be happy about you going behind our backs like this?'

'No, of course not,' replied Jane. 'But we saw no other way.'

'There was the option of not marrying.'

'That wasn't an option for us,' she said before bursting into tears.

'Do not upset my wife,' said Robert, revelling in the words, wrapping an arm around Jane's shoulders.

'We don't need to,' said Henry. 'You'll do that all on your own.'

'You can't talk to me like that any more, Father,' he hissed back. 'I'm a married man now and I will not be treated like a child.'

'Very well. If you want to be a man, then I assume you'll be moving into your own house, one you'll pay for with your own money and you'll provide for your new wife.'

Robert's jaw clenched. 'You have my money.'

'I do?' Henry said, feigning confusion. 'I was under the impression I was entirely in possession of my own fortune.'

'I'm your son.'

'Oh, I see. You're my son when it suits you. Well, let me tell you something, Robert – men don't go grovelling to their parents for money. They provide for themselves. It looks like you'll have to get a job.'

Robert looked to his mother. 'I know you have money set aside for me, a considerable sum. I can use that.'

'It won't last forever,' she replied.

'I'll invest it, I'll do something. I can manage.'

'Very well, if that's what you want,' she sighed. 'But Henry's right. You brought this on yourself. When that money runs out, you're on your own.'

'Don't worry,' said Jane, lifting her head proudly. 'I have my own money too. We'll be fine.' She grasped Robert's hand. 'Now we're married, we need no one else.'

Amy just sighed and shook her head, knowing Jane would soon be disabused of that stupid notion.

'I'm your daughter now,' said Jane, deciding to have one last try to appeal to her new mother-in-law. 'Doesn't that please you in the slightest?'

Amy felt herself starting to waver. This poor girl, whom she did love dearly, was completely head-over-heels. She wasn't the first woman to do something stupid for a man and she certainly wouldn't be the last. She rose to embrace her.

'Of course I am, you know how much I love you, but this elopement was the wrong thing to do.'

'I had to marry him,' she croaked. 'I don't mean like that,' she hastily added when Amy's eyes blazed and she glanced down at her stomach. 'I mean I had to do it because being parted from him has been torture.'

'I see.' Amy glanced over her shoulder at Henry, who was barely containing his rage. She completely sympathised with him but there was only one thing she could do.

When she embraced Jane, the girl started to cry.

'Welcome to the family,' said Amy, the words almost choking her.

She took Jane's lovely face in her hands. Robert would drain that beauty and vivacity right out of her, just like Matthew had almost done to Esther, only Jane didn't have her aunt's strength.

Amy released her and looked to Robert.

'Aren't you going to hug me too, Mother?' he said.

His smirk infuriated her. 'I would like to speak to you.'

He followed her out of the room, almost running into Frances, who was about to enter the room carrying plates of food.

'I wish to speak with my son in private,' Amy imperiously told her.

'You can talk in there,' replied Frances, nodding at a door across the hall.

'Thank you,' she sniffed before stalking past the woman.

Robert followed her into a small parlour. 'Surely you must be pleased on some level, Mother? I've given you a lovely daughter-in-law.'

Amy slapped him hard across the face, bristling with fury. Now she'd started, she couldn't stop, and she kept hitting him.

'Stop it,' he said, holding out his arms to ward her off.

But she kept going, all the anger, fear and worry he'd put her through pouring out of her and she continued to strike at his hands and arms, managing to catch his face twice more.

'Enough,' barked Robert, grabbing her wrists and forcing her arms to her sides. He kept her pinned as they glared into each other's furious faces.

'It's the least you deserve,' she spat back. 'How could you do this to someone you claim to love?'

'I love her, so I want her to be my wife. Why do you find that so difficult to understand?'

'Because you will dismantle her, piece by piece. I saw Matthew do the same thing to Esther. She will love you with her whole heart and you will take that love and use it as a weapon against her. Why can't you see that?'

'I could never hurt Jane.'

'Oh, yes, you will and guess who'll be picking up the pieces when you do?' she exclaimed, shaking him off.

'You're being ridiculous. How can you even know that?'

'Because I knew Matthew and I know you.'

His smile was wicked. 'I'll take that as a compliment.'

When she tried to slap him again, he grabbed her wrist. 'You got away with that once, Mother, not a second time.'

He squeezed a little harder, her grimace broadening his smile and accelerating his heartbeat.

'Stop it, Robert,' she said.

His grip tightened even more in his desire to see her pain.

'I said stop it,' she snarled, wrenching her arm free. She cradled her throbbing wrist to her chest, appalled by the wild look in her son's eyes. 'Already it's getting out of your control.'

'Nonsense,' he said, shaking himself out of it. 'You just made me angry.'

'I've seen that look before. I'm your mother, for God's sake.'

'Then why don't you start acting like one and support me?'

'I've done nothing but support you. I could have turned you over to the authorities for what you did to Daisy, but I protected you. When you didn't tell us about Mrs Grier being Matthew's first wife, I defended you, and when you threw her into the pond, I still supported you.'

His face turned white. 'I didn't.'

'I'm not a fool, Robert, of course you did. Even though you're a murderer, I still protected you because I love you,' she said, voice cracking. 'But what you've done to Jane is a step too far. She does not deserve the future you will inflict on her.'

'Fine, just leave us to it. But just so you know, if you do decide to cut us off without a penny, then you will not see me again, nor will you see Jane or any of your grandchildren.' Just as he knew it would, the mention of grandchildren caused her eyes to flicker with uncertainty. 'Is that what you want?' he pressed.

'No,' she sighed. 'Of course not.'

'Then support me one last time. Please,' he said more gently.

'It seems you leave me no choice. Very well, Robert, I'll support you, but I swear to God if you hurt that girl then I'm done with you.'

'And I've told you that won't happen. Have some faith.' He decided to ignore her doubtful look. 'Now, if we're finished here, and you've finished hitting me, I would like to return to my bride.'

Reluctantly she followed him back into the sitting room.

'Wonderful news,' Robert announced to the room. 'Mother's given us her blessing.'

Amy avoided Henry's gaze when he regarded her with outrage.

'Oh, that's wonderful news,' said Jane, getting to her feet to embrace her. 'Thank you, Aunty Amy.'

'Don't you mean Mother?' smiled Robert.

'Of course, Mother.' Jane grasped Amy's hands in her own.

Amy forced a smile. 'Let's eat, shall we?'

She took the vacant seat on Henry's right, giving him a look that pleaded with him to wait until she'd explained.

'Oh, no, am I too late?' said a voice as the door was pushed open. Andrew Charteris stood there caked in mud, hair in disarray. 'Uh-oh,' he added when he saw Amy, Henry and Knapp.

'Come here, you devil,' roared Knapp, flying out of his chair and lunging for him.

Andrew tried to back out into the hall, but the landlord had come up behind him with more trays of food, so he was penned in.

'Now take it easy, Knapp,' said Andrew, holding up his hands in a feeble attempt to ward him off. 'It was just a joke, no need to take it seriously.'

'Don't give me that nonsense. It was part of a plot no doubt masterminded by you, you snake.'

'Now that's a bit strong. Just relax,' he exclaimed as Knapp's huge hands bunched into fists. Andrew looked to the rest of the room. 'Is no one going to assist me?'

'Personally, I'd take great pleasure in watching him dismantle you bit by bit,' smiled Henry.

'Please don't spoil our wedding breakfast with violence,' exclaimed Jane, to Andrew's relief.

'She's right,' said Henry, surprising everyone. 'Knapp, let Mr Charteris sit down.'

Knapp stood aside to allow Andrew into the room, glaring at him as he scurried into a chair between Robert and Amy.

'Congratulations,' said Andrew, shaking Robert's hand then kissing Jane's cheek.

'It would have been better if I'd had my best man,' frowned Robert. 'What kept you?'

'Well, I managed to hitch a lift into the city from some brute of a farmer in Alardyce village and the train journey was absolutely no problem. It was when I arrived here that the trouble started. The carriage I hired to transport me from the train station to the hotel fell into a ditch, so I had to start walking. Some fool sped past me in their carriage and showered me with mud, then I saw Sir Henry's carriage approach, so I flung myself behind a wall, not knowing there was a pig pen there, which I fell into.'

'You were going to be best man?' said Henry. 'Isn't that a contradiction in terms?'

'I understand you're upset, Sir Henry, but these two beautiful young things are happy. Surely that's the most important thing?'

Henry's lip curled with contempt. 'You stupid, stupid man.'

'Excuse me?' retorted Andrew, scratching at his hands, wondering why they were so itchy and fearing it was part of the witch's curse.

'Do not speak to my friend like that, Father,' said Robert.

'If he was any friend of yours, he would have talked you out of this madness.' Henry sighed and got to his feet, throwing down his napkin. 'I refuse to be part of this ridiculous charade any longer,' he yelled before storming out.

'I'll go and talk to him,' said Amy, unable to bear the sound of Jane's snivelling and Robert's nauseating attempts to comfort her.

When she'd gone, Knapp took the chair she'd vacated right beside Andrew and stared at him while Andrew did his best to ignore his massive presence, still scratching his itchy hands.

28

'Henry,' called Amy as he hurried upstairs to the room they'd taken.

'I'm sorry, Amy, but I couldn't sit there and look into Robert's smug face,' he said as he walked. 'How can you condone what he's done?'

'If you'd give me a chance to explain,' she said breathlessly, struggling to keep up.

Henry stalked into their room, which was small but clean and pretty with a nice view of the gardens at the rear of the house.

'Robert left me no choice,' said Amy. 'He said if I didn't then he'd cut himself and Jane off from us and we'd never see our grand-children.'

His expression softened. 'Grandchildren. He really knows how to hurt you, doesn't he?'

'I couldn't risk it.'

'I hate how he's backed us into a corner. We can do nothing.'

'Yes, we can. If he wants to be a man, then let him. I'll give him his money just like he asked, then he's on his own. Robert's about to get a taste of the real world for the first time in his life.'

Henry smiled. 'I look forward to seeing him flail about.'

'That's better,' she said, wrapping her arms around his neck. 'You haven't smiled in so long.'

'Perhaps this is for the best. Now he's out of our hair and Jane can deal with him.'

'You're right.'

'You look exhausted, you should rest.'

'Later. I want you to make love to me, right now in this wild, romantic place,' said Amy. 'With everything that's been going on, it feels as though we're pulling away from each other.'

'Nothing will ever come between us, I promise.'

'Good,' she smiled, kissing him, sliding his jacket off his shoulders.

Henry's eyes widened when she pushed him back onto the bed and leapt on top of him.

* * *

Jane sat up in bed, anxiously awaiting her bridegroom. The maid had assisted her to change into her nightgown and brushed out her hair. She knew she looked beautiful, but would that be enough for her new husband? She had absolutely no idea what she had to do. She was the first of her friends to marry and her Aunt Esther had never once explained to her about the birds and the bees. A lump formed in her throat. She would give anything to have her here right now.

Jane shook away all thoughts of the aunt who had raised her from girlhood. She had to concentrate on her new husband and the last thing she wanted was to be a disappointment to him. Fear of the unknown and fear of letting Robert down appalled her. She wasn't a fool, she was aware that gentlemen of Robert's class ensured they were educated in the carnal arts before marriage, while women were forced to remain ignorant until their wedding night. It seemed so unfair.

To soothe her nerves, she smoothed down the bedclothes that were neatly tucked around her waist. The room was pretty, the bedclothes a light pink, in keeping with the romance of the place, the bed itself a walnut half-tester with a canopy overhead. In one corner of the room was a mahogany washstand, opposite this a pair of carved oak chairs, a small wardrobe and a mirror. Every available surface was adorned with vases of fresh flowers and Jane wondered where they'd found them in the middle of winter.

Her heart leapt into her throat when the door slowly opened and Robert walked in. He looked so handsome, she still couldn't believe he was all hers. Her stomach fluttered with butterflies, the prospect of finally lying with him after years of wondering what it would be like both scary and exciting.

'How's my beautiful bride?' he said, removing his jacket and tossing it onto a chair.

'Nervous,' she squeaked.

Robert smiled. Her blue eyes were bright with anxiety, and he found himself enjoying her vulnerability. Many of the women he'd been with had been professionals or a lot more experienced than him. With Jane, he was the one in control.

'Don't be,' he said, kicking off his shoes then sitting beside her on the bed and taking her hands. 'This is our time and it's going to be wonderful.'

His certainty soothed her a little. 'It is, isn't it?'

'We've waited so long for this. Now let's enjoy it.'

He kissed her, running his fingers through her blonde curls. He felt the tension flood her body when he kissed her neck, his fingers playing with the ribbon that laced up the front of her nightgown.

'Wait,' she said when he started to untie it.

'What's wrong?' he said softly.

'Nothing... I just... I'm nervous about you seeing me.'

'Why?'

'I don't want to be a disappointment.'

He smiled and cradled her face in his hands. 'You could never be that.'

'I don't know what to do, Robert,' she whispered, ashamed.

'Don't worry, I'll show you. Why don't I undress first?'

'All right,' she said eagerly, having pictured many times what he looked like beneath the clothes.

He stood and started to remove his waistcoat, which joined the jacket on the chair. Next was the shirt, which was peeled off to reveal a body honed to perfection. The closest Jane had ever got to the naked male form before was the statues in museums. Robert's pale muscular body looked like it had been carved from marble. She longed to reach out and touch him but lacked the courage.

He sat back down beside her, took her hand and pressed it to his chest. She'd half-expected his skin to be cold and hard, like a statue, but instead it was warm and vital.

'There,' he said. 'Is that better?'

She nodded in wonder, letting her fingers trail through the patch of black hair in the centre of his chest. Her hand slid further down to his stomach, hastily retracting when his eyes closed and he inhaled sharply.

'Sorry,' she said. 'Did I do something wrong?'

He took her hand and replaced it on his stomach. 'Not at all. It feels really nice.'

'Oh, good,' she said, continuing to caress those taut muscles, her eyes widening when she saw the large bulge in his trousers. Was that good or not?

He kissed her, this time managing to unfasten the front of her gown. She gazed at him, her lips pink and puffy from his kisses, blue eyes wide and bright, cheeks flushed as he gently slid the gown off her shoulders and pulled it down her body. Her breasts were smaller than he'd expected. Thanks to corsets, it was often difficult to accurately judge size, but the perfection of those creamy orbs offset their size.

'Oh, my,' she gasped when he started to kiss them.

Her head fell back and she moaned while allowing him to press her back into the bed.

'Lift your hips,' he told her.

She obliged and he whipped the nightgown down her body.

'You're so beautiful,' he said when she was finally naked before him, returning to her stomach, feathering her bellybutton with kisses. 'Perfection.'

Jane could relax a bit more now she knew she didn't repulse him. Emboldened, she allowed herself to explore his muscular back with her hands.

Her body tensed again when his hand went between her thighs and started to rub. At first, she felt awkward, unable to believe he was actually touching the most secret part of her. Then a strange thing happened. Delicious feelings began to radiate out of her most private place and she felt a curious dampness between her thighs. Was that supposed to happen? Her head snapped up with worry, but Robert appeared relaxed, sliding back up her body to kiss her mouth while his hand continued its delightful work.

'What is that wetness between my legs?' she said.

'It means you're ready.'

'Ready? Oh,' she said when realisation struck.

'It's nothing to be afraid of.'

Her eyes flicked down to that bulge in his trousers, which looked even bigger.

Jane watched as he sat back on his haunches to unfasten his trousers. Her jaw dropped when that demanding male part sprang free. It had never looked like that on the statues, she'd no idea it could even turn into a hard, rigid length that both thrilled and scared her.

'Does it hurt?' she rasped.

'A little bit your first time, but after that it won't.'

Jane was unable to take her eyes off it, even though she desperately wanted to look away. It didn't seem fair that her wedding day should include a fair amount of pain and fear.

'I'll go slowly,' he said, hoping he could keep that promise, he was so desperate to plunge himself inside her, eager to feel what it was like with a virgin. 'Try to relax,' he said as he pushed against her and met a barrier of resistance.

'I can't,' she cried.

'We want our baby, don't we?'

She smiled up at him and nodded. 'I want nothing more than to carry your child.'

'Then this is the only way we can achieve that.'

'You're right,' she said determinedly. 'I think it would help if you could do that thing with your hand again.'

'Like this?' he said, smiling when she gasped and dug her nails into his shoulders.

Her moans grew louder when he kissed her breasts. This time when he pressed against her, he actually managed to penetrate. Jane bit her lip as he filled her up. When he reached a certain point, she released a small cry.

'It hurts, Robert.'

'It's all right, it'll pass,' he said before pushing his hips harder and breaking through that barrier, feeling sweat bead on his forehead. By God, she felt like a vice. One more push and he was all the way inside her. He forced himself to go still, allowing her body to adjust.

'Are you... all right?' he panted, hardly able to talk.

'That hurt,' she whispered, tears shining in her eyes.

Oh, wonderful, this was the last thing he needed, her showing him she was in pain. Now he was looking at her differently, wondering how he could prolong that look. He could flip her onto her front and give her a damn good spanking, which would have her shrieking in seconds, or he could put a hand about her throat... No, he would never do that to Jane. She was his wife, the woman he loved, and he refused to injure her in any way.

Instead, he decided it would be best to forge ahead. If they stopped now, she wouldn't let him near her again. Gently he moved his hips, kissing her to try to distract her, sliding his hand down to that warm, wet mound of hers. As he continued to move, her muscles unwound themselves slightly, her hands moving from his shoulders to his buttocks and pulling him tighter against her.

'Better?' he said.

'Yes... better,' she said, eyes screwed shut, as though deep in concentration.

He allowed himself to move a little faster. His orgasm was rapidly approaching and he wanted to fend it off, having the grand idea of bringing her to a climax on her first time, but it was becoming apparent that wasn't going to happen. She appeared to be enjoying his attentions more, but she just wasn't where he was. With three last thrusts, he groaned and spilled himself inside her.

Jane's eyes flew open and she gazed up at him in wonder and confusion as his eyes shut and jaw gritted, moaning in a way she'd never heard before while she felt him flood inside her. Was this how a baby was made, by the man depositing his seed inside the woman? She decided it must be.

'Are you all right?' she said when he collapsed on top of her. All those lovely new sensations that had been building inside her began to ebb away, to her disappointment. Was that the most a woman could expect or were there more delights to come?

He raised his head and his playful grin reassured her that everything had gone to plan. 'I'm wonderful. How are you feeling?'

'A bit sore, but I enjoyed it. Did you?'

'Oh, yes,' he said, grin widening. 'You were wonderful.'

'I was? But I didn't do anything except lie there.'

'It was your first time. With practice, we'll be able to do so much more.'

Gently he pulled out of her, lay beside her and took her in his arms, both already on the verge of sleep after their busy day.

* * *

Henry removed the pillow from his head and listened. 'They've stopped.'

'Thank God for that,' said Amy, unwrapping the bedclothes from her ears. 'That's something no mother should have to hear.'

'We should have asked for a room further from the honeymoon suite,' he said wryly.

'At least we know he treated her gently.'

'There is that.'

He rolled her onto her back and whipped back the bedclothes to reveal her naked body.

'Do you mind?' she said. 'I'm cold.'

'No, you're not, your skin still burns,' he smiled, kissing her breasts. 'We're much better than they are.'

'Henry,' she exclaimed, slapping his shoulder. 'What a thing to say.'

'It's true.'

'That's because we've had more practice.' Kissing him, she forced him onto his back and climbed on top of him. Now Robert and Jane had finally done what they'd all feared, a weight had been lifted from them both. Amy was enjoying reconnecting with her husband after all the recent tension.

'I think they're asleep,' said Henry, gripping onto her thighs and pulling her tighter against him. 'Time for round two?'

'Absolutely. The last thing I want to do now is sleep.'

'Jane,' screeched a voice from downstairs.

They both paused to listen.

'What was that?' said Henry.

'I think it was Esther,' said Amy. 'A very angry Esther.'

'Jane,' repeated the voice.

There came the sound of footsteps charging up the stairs, more than one set, accompanied by a cacophony of voices.

'Jane.'

Henry and Amy just managed to pull the bedclothes back over themselves before their door burst open and in charged Esther, followed by the landlord and his wife.

'Amy?' said Esther. 'What are you doing? Oh,' she said, blushing and scurrying out.

'I do apologise about that,' the landlord told Henry and Amy before closing the door.

* * *

Robert could hear the noise, something persistent and annoying, like a buzzing fly, but he was too content to bother finding out what it was. He was curled up in a warm bed with a naked Jane, his wife. Paradise.

He could no longer ignore the noise when it burst into the room and started shouting in his ear.

'Aunt Esther,' gasped Jane, sitting upright, clutching the covers to herself.

'Get out of that bed right now, young lady,' yelled Esther. 'You're coming back to London with me.'

'I am not,' she retorted. 'Robert and I are married, and you can't tell me what to do any more.'

'Don't be ridiculous. This is all a sham. You're no more married than that chair,' she exclaimed, indicating the chair over which Robert had draped his clothes.

'I'm afraid that's not possible,' calmly interjected the landlord, who was experienced at dealing with irate relatives. 'Every marriage conducted here is entirely legal.'

'What rot,' she spat. 'Get out of that bed, Jane.'

'No, I'm not leaving Robert.'

'You can't split us up any more,' said Robert. 'We're man and wife in every sense of the word.'

His smug look infuriated her so much she slapped him across the face. 'How dare you abduct my niece?'

'He didn't abduct me, I came willingly,' said Jane while Robert scowled at Esther.

At that moment, Henry and Amy rushed into the room, both wearing robes, their hair dishevelled.

Esther turned her anger on them. 'How could you permit this to happen?' she demanded of them.

'That's not fair, Esther,' said Amy. 'We did try to stop them, but we arrived too late, we travelled through the night to get here.'

'Yelling the house down isn't going to help,' said Henry. 'Why don't you calm down, Esther, go and get something to eat and we can discuss this civilly.'

'I don't want to discuss this civilly,' she exclaimed, cheeks bright pink with anger. 'All I want is to get my niece away from that monster.'

'Robert is not a monster,' said Jane passionately. 'He's gentle and kind and loving. How can you think these bad things about him?'

'You're a silly, naïve girl, Jane,' Esther told her.

When Jane's eyes filled with tears, Robert wrapped an arm around her naked shoulders and kissed the top of her head. 'Say what you like about me, Aunt Esther, but I will not have you upsetting my wife. Now, if you don't leave, I will climb out of this bed and make you and I don't care that I'm naked.'

'You dirty beast,' hissed Esther.

'I mean it,' he said, moving to draw back the covers.

With an indignant huff, Esther stalked from the room, Henry following.

'Happy now?' Amy asked her son.

'I will be once Jane and I are alone again,' he retorted.

Amy left too, slamming the door shut, almost colliding with Andrew.

'My lady,' he said, bowing low. 'I heard a commotion. Can I be of any assistance?'

'Yes. You can go away.' Amy frowned. 'Why is it that everywhere I turn, you're there?'

'Because I worship you, Amy,' he said passionately, penning her in against the wall. His eyes slid down to the front of her gown, which was gaping slightly, revealing some cleavage. 'You're a real woman, not a silly skinny doll like Jane.'

'Andrew, after the men I've encountered in my time, foolish little boys fail to intimidate me.'

'I'm no ordinary boy, if only you'd allow me to prove it to you,' he whispered, leaning in for a kiss. His eyes bulged and he dropped to the floor when her knee connected sharply with his crotch.

'I'm no ordinary woman. You'd do well to remember that,' she said before stalking back to her room, leaving him groaning on the floor.

'What kept you?' said Henry when she entered their room, in the process of pulling on his clothes.

'Just chastising a naughty boy,' she smiled sweetly.

'Good. Robert needs a bloody good chastising.'

'Not him. Andrew. He claimed he worships me. When he became too ardent, my knee cooled his passion.'

Henry wasn't sure whether to be furious or laugh. 'I'll kill him.'

'No need,' she said, planting a kiss on his lips. 'I've dealt with it. We've more pressing matters to attend to.'

'An angry Esther. I can't believe I used to think her timid.'

'She can be ferocious in defence of Jane. Although she's turning her anger on us, she'll really be mad at herself for letting her out of her sight. Let's get downstairs before she levels the building.' The sound of Esther shouting at the landlord and his wife for being irresponsible enablers carried up the stairs.

Esther was surrounded by a veritable feast in the parlour, the landlord thinking he could appease her with his wife's excellent food. Knapp occupied an armchair in the corner of the room, watching Esther's fury with admiration.

'I'm very disappointed in you both,' she snapped at Amy and Henry as they took their places at the table. 'I thought I could trust you to stop this outrage.'

'We did our best,' said Amy. 'If we'd pushed the horses any faster, there was a good chance we'd have been killed.'

'I appreciate that, but you allowed them to lie together. Now it will be impossible to have the marriage annulled.'

'Robert swore if we tried to part them then he wouldn't allow us to see Jane or any grandchildren they may produce.'

'If you hadn't allowed them to lie together, then grandchildren wouldn't be an issue.'

'What should we have done, Esther, abduct them?'

'Yes, if it put a stop to all this nonsense.'

'They were intent on marrying each other. We would have had to keep them prisoners for the rest of their lives.'

'Better that than this.'

'Where's William?' said Henry.

'He was away on business when I received the telegram about the elopement. I didn't have time to wait for him to return, but I did order the servants to send him a message.'

'You travelled all this way alone?' said Henry, surprised.

'Of course not. I brought a maid with me. There was no time for the niceties,' she said icily.

'There was nothing we could do,' Amy told her. 'They're married now, and we have to accept it. If we don't, we could lose them both.'

'I can't stand the thought of my sweet little Jane being married to that monster,' said Esther, eyes filling with tears.

'I know, we feel the same way, but the deed is done. We must make sure we're there for her when he inevitably reveals his true self.'

All the colour drained from Esther's face. 'You don't think he'd hurt her?'

'No. I think he'll treat her like Matthew treated you – once the first flush of marriage has worn off and his eye starts to stray, he'll grow cold and distant, and she'll be heartbroken. By that time, they may even have children. We must think of our grandchildren and do all in our power to keep them close to us.'

Amy's logic started to calm Esther's rage. 'You have a point,' she said grudgingly. 'But there will be a scandal over this.'

'All the more reason to mark this out as a happy occasion,' said Henry, hoping this fresh scandal wouldn't adversely affect their younger children. He sighed and shook his head. 'Robert would have to do this just as we were being welcomed back into society. Not that I'm bothered for myself, it's our other children's futures I'm concerned for.'

'You're right. What this requires is damage limitation,' said Esther, both Amy and Henry glad that she was starting to see sense.

'To the outside world, this is a good marriage,' said Amy. 'It's vital we keep up that charade.'

'Everyone will discover they eloped,' said Esther. 'No banns have been read, no lavish church ceremony.'

'We'll place a discreet announcement in the papers about the marriage,' said Henry. 'We won't give any details and everyone will assume the service was performed at Alardyce. We'll say the ceremony was kept small due to Amy's ill health, it's common knowledge she's been unwell recently. Then we pay the landlord here a good sum of money to keep his mouth shut.'

'It's a good plan,' said Esther. 'I can't bear the thought of my little Jane being hurt, but it's inevitable now.' She sighed sadly. 'I'm sorry for blaming you two. It's not your fault, you did your best.'

'We warned Jane,' said Amy. 'Unfortunately, she chose not to listen. There comes a time when our children have to be responsible for their actions.'

'Men like Robert don't understand responsibility. It's always someone else's fault. When the day inevitably comes that he hurts Jane, he'll blame her.'

'I have every expectation that you're right,' said Amy.

* * *

Matthew visited Amy again that night. She'd been half-expecting it after recent events.

'Well, our little boy's married,' he smiled as she sat up in bed, rubbing her eyes.

He was sprawled sideways in the armchair, one long leg dangling over the arm. She looked to Henry, who was fast asleep beside her.

'Give Jane her due,' continued Matthew. 'She has grown into a beauty, even if she is scrawny like Esther.'

'If I'd had my way, he never would have married.'

'I'll wager you wish I was alive now. I would have been able to keep him under control.'

'No, you wouldn't, you would have encouraged him to act badly. At least part of him is still good. He's not entirely a monster, like you.'

Matthew looked to Henry's prone form. 'What do you see in him? Look at all that pale skin. It hurts my eyes just looking at him.'

'Then don't look. What can I do about Robert?'

'Nothing. He isn't a child any more. He's a man with a man's urges and strength. You knew the day would come when he would slip out of your control and go his own way. This is his first step on that path.'

'So it's only going to get worse?'

'Hold onto your hat, my darling. It's about to get even rougher,' he winked.

Amy woke with a start, Henry's hand on her arm.

'You were talking in your sleep,' he said.

'What was I saying?' she replied.

'Something about Robert. It was Matthew, wasn't it?'

She sat up and glanced at the armchair. 'Yes,' she said shakily.

'Have you mentioned him to Magda yet?'

'Yes, but she couldn't sense anything. I'm sure it's just my imagination.'

'So what did he have to say this time?'

'That Robert's going to get even worse.'

'I'm forced to agree. What?' he smiled when she stared at him.

'You're such a wonderful husband. Anyone else would have me locked up for talking to ghosts.'

'That's because I absolutely adore you,' he said, kissing her.

She nestled into him, enjoying the feel of his warm arms around her. When they were together like this, she felt nothing could touch them.

'If I knew Robert and Jane's marriage was going to be as good as ours, I would be a very happy woman,' said Amy. 'She will never get to feel what I feel every day with you.'

'You never know, they might surprise us.'

'I do hope so, but I doubt it.'

29

The happy couple appeared at breakfast the following morning and gazed at each other adoringly. Henry regarded them with an expression that indicated he might be sick at any moment.

'Jane and I have been discussing our honeymoon,' said Robert. 'We'd like to go to Italy.'

'Have a safe trip,' said Henry before biting into his toast.

Robert frowned at him. 'Isn't it the duty of the parents to pay for that?'

Henry almost choked on his toast. 'What did you say?'

'Well, you've not paid for any other part of the wedding.'

Henry looked to an equally astonished Amy before turning his attention back to his stepson.

'So let me get this right – you go against our wishes and elope, drive us frantic with worry, have us tearing across the country in the middle of the night, put us under considerable strain when you know your mother's been unwell, then you expect us to fund your trip to Italy?'

'Yes,' Robert replied, while Jane's cheeks grew pinker by the second.

'Then you're in for a nasty shock,' Henry bawled at him across the table. 'Like you said, you're a man now. If you want to take your bride to Italy, then you fund it.'

'Fine, I will,' he said before turning to his mother. 'You said I could have my money?'

'Yes, but it's going to take some time,' she replied. 'There are documents to be drawn up and signed.'

'Then we'll go once that's been done,' said Robert cheerfully, pouring himself out some coffee.

'Where will you go from here?'

'I thought we'd come back to Alardyce.'

'But you're the man now,' said Henry icily. 'It's up to you to put a roof over your bride's head, not us.'

'Once again, I will do that when I get my money. Unless you'd like to lend me some and I'll pay you back when it comes through? Then we can be out of your hair sooner.'

'No, you can come back to Alardyce until then,' said Amy, wanting them where she could keep an eye on them. 'Stay until you get on your feet.'

'Thank you, Mother,' said Robert, giving Henry a hard look before turning his attention to the plates of food Frances carried in. 'Mmmm, smells delicious,' he smiled, clapping his hands together.

Jane sat awkwardly beside him, a lot more attuned to her family's ill feelings. She looked even more uncomfortable when Esther walked in, followed by a tired-looking William.

'When did you arrive?' said Henry, getting to his feet to shake his hand.

'About five hours ago,' replied William before slumping into a chair. 'I travelled here non-stop when I got the message about the wedding.' He regarded the happy couple with disapproval. 'I bet you two are pretty pleased with yourselves?'

'We didn't want it to come to this,' said Jane. 'If you'd just let us marry like we'd wanted to...'

'We had our reasons,' he countered. 'An elopement, how ridiculous.'

Jane looked down at her lap while Robert leaned forward in his chair, black eyes turbulent. Amy had noticed a change in her son since his marriage – he was more sure of himself, finally in control of his own destiny, or so he would be when he inherited his money. Already Amy was thinking of ways she could delay that.

* * *

The journey back to Alardyce was a tense one. Amy, Henry and Knapp sat on one side of the carriage while Robert and Jane sat opposite them in awkward silence. Esther and William had decided to return to London, realising there was nothing else they could do. Amy felt sorry for Jane, the girl should have been thrilled – after all, she'd married the man she loved – but instead she looked miserable, knowing the happiest day of her life had hurt so many people. It didn't seem to bother Robert, who was just pleased he'd got his own way.

Fortunately, their homecoming was much warmer, the children eagerly gathering in the hall to greet them.

'What a lovely welcome,' smiled Jane when Lydia flung her arms around her waist.

'Is it true you're married to Robert now?' said the girl, gazing up at her.

'It is, sweetheart.'

'You promised I could be a flower girl.' Her eyes filled with tears. 'Now I'll never get to be a flower girl.'

'I'm sorry, darling, but it all happened so fast there was no time for a flower girl or bridesmaids or anyone else.' Jane's gaze flickered as she experienced a moment of sadness. 'I tell you what, why don't we have another wedding here so everyone who missed it the first time can see it?' Jane looked for approval to Robert, who nodded.

'I think that's a wonderful idea,' he said, kneeling before Lydia and taking her hand. 'You'll be a beautiful flower girl.'

'I will, won't I?' she smiled, her tears drying up in an instant.

Robert turned his attention to his brothers. 'And we have to find something for these handsome boys to do.'

They both cheered and took turns hugging him.

'So are you my sister now, Jane?' Lydia asked her.

'Yes, I think so,' she smiled.

'Are you going to live here?'

'For a little while, until Robert and I find our own house.'

'I don't want you to find your own house, I want you to stay here. Why do you have to leave? We've got lots of bedrooms.'

'That's what people do when they marry, they find their own home and raise a family.'

'Are you going to have a baby?'

'I do hope so.'

'Please, Lydia,' said Amy. 'Let them rest and get something to eat. We're all very tired.'

'There are refreshments in the drawing room, my lady,' said Rush.

'Aren't you going to offer us your congratulations, Rush?' smirked Robert.

'Congratulations, sir,' he said dourly.

* * *

A small service was arranged in the vast conservatory at Alardyce House, primarily so the younger children could feel a part of things. Lydia finally got to be a flower girl to Jane, who sported the white dress she'd worn at Gretna Green. John acted as best man, while Stephen was a very proud page boy. The local vicar blessed the marriage, Amy and Henry looking on in stony silence, the sham sickening them both. Knapp, no longer required, had been released from his duties and returned to the city.

Now Robert was a married man, Henry and Amy had no say over what he did any more and Robert was well aware of this, the perpetual smirk he wore stretching Henry's nerves to the limit. Every morning at breakfast, he would ask his mother whether Arthur, who managed her fortune, had drawn up the documents for the funds she'd set aside for him to be transferred into his control and every morning, she would come up with another excuse as to why it hadn't been done. When Robert announced he would journey to London to see Arthur personally, Amy was left with no choice but to order the documents be drawn up.

Robert and Jane, impatient to be a real married couple, found a beautiful townhouse in the city to rent, paid for with Jane's money until Robert's finally came through and they could purchase their own. To their mutual surprise, Amy and Henry didn't object when they broke the news that they were leaving Alardyce House. In fact, they seemed rather relieved.

When they left Alardyce House for the last time, Amy and Henry standing in the doorway to wave them off, Robert was sure his parents were wearing their first genuine smiles in weeks.

* * *

Robert loved being master of his own house. He left the hiring of the household staff to Jane, delighted when she employed a couple of very pretty maids. He could come and go as he pleased without being interrogated and there was no one to question him or give him disapproving looks.

For the first couple of days in their new home, he and Jane barely left their bedroom, working hard to produce their first baby. Robert wanted his child growing in her belly as soon as possible to show the world how virile he was. He opened up a whole new world of sexual pleasure to Jane and she eagerly received his expert tuition. He even got her to do things no respectable gentleman would ever consider asking his wife to do. But Jane, in her innocence, didn't know this and thought all married couples indulged in these exotic practices.

The excitement of his new home and bride staved off all violent thoughts. Not even the pretty maids could tempt Robert. Neither did he visit Vivienne's establishment, turning his friends away at the door when they came to call. He was pleased, he knew Jane would keep him on the straight and narrow.

His idyll was marred by a letter written in a familiar hand that he suddenly had no wish to see now he had his new life. The letter was from the mutual friend Evelyn had spoken of. He decided it would be best to meet them at the suggested time and place; he couldn't have them causing trouble, not now.

* * *

The assigned meeting place was in the woods behind Alardyce House, well out of sight of any of the occupants. Robert left his horse tied to a tree and delved deeper into the undergrowth on foot to find two figures waiting for him.

'Hello, Grandmother,' said Robert, addressing the smaller figure.

Mrs Crowle smiled, revealing just a couple of crooked teeth. She was an unpleasant character, all wrinkles and sagging skin in a dowdy, stained black dress. On occasion, Robert slipped her some money, it made him feel magnanimous. Despite what his parents thought, Matthew's mother was very much alive.

'You're taking a risk coming onto the estate,' he added.

'I heard about your wedding. I wanted to offer my congratulations. I brought you a present.'

'That wasn't necessary,' he said, knowing it wouldn't be much.

'I couldn't let my only grandchild's wedding day pass unmarked. Here you go,' she said, holding a box out to him.

Robert opened it and his eyes widened. 'Is this genuine gold?'

'It is. It used to belong to your father. Your real father.'

He lifted the gold pocket watch out of the box by the chain and stared at it in wonder. This was the first thing he'd been given that Matthew had possessed or even touched, and he found it thrilling.

'There's an inscription inside,' said Mrs Crowle.

He opened it up and inside the lid was the inscription: *Happy birthday from A. 1880.*

'It was a gift from your mother,' she added.

'This is expensive. She must have cared for him once.'

'I believe she did, but then she grew selfish and didn't want to share what they created together. You.' When he didn't reply, she continued, 'If she'd agreed to what he wanted, you'd be with both your parents now. Amy wouldn't have been tortured by Edward. Matthew would have had no objection to you marrying Jane, he would have understood what you were going through, he would have been able to help. And my only child would still be alive.'

'That's a nice picture you paint.'

'I know you would have been a good son to him. How he would have loved to watch you grow into a man. He would be so proud of you.'

'How did you get hold of this? I thought Aunt Esther inherited everything of his.'

'She did and she got rid of it all,' Mrs Crowle replied with disgust. 'But Matthew carried this everywhere with him from the day Amy gave it to him, that's how much she meant to him.'

'She dreams about him. I've heard her asleep in her sitting room saying his name. But if he loved her so much, then why did he keep her locked up at Huntington Manor and why did he hurt her?'

'Because they were in a battle over you, a battle your mother started. Anyway, Mr Hobbs managed to salvage the pocket watch. It fell from Matthew's pocket during the fight with Edward, so he rescued it.'

'Hobbs was there?' he said, eyes flicking to the man hovering at Mrs Crowle's shoulder.

'He was. He went back to the house just as the fight ended. He saw my son fall to the ground with a knife in his belly, put there by Edward.'

Robert frowned. Something about her story wasn't right. He knew every detail of what had happened in that house after repeatedly reading over the court reports. 'But the knife wasn't in his stomach. It was found beside his body.'

'True. Do you know how it got from his belly to the floor?'

Robert's heart started to thump as he got the feeling he was about to learn something momentous. 'How?'

'Your mother.'

'My mother? Was she trying to help him?'

Mrs Crowle's smile was vicious. 'Help him? Bah. She took hold of that blade with her bloodied hands and she dragged it out of him.'

'Why?' croaked Robert when he was eventually able to speak.

'Matthew told her that if the knife was left in place, there was a chance he could survive the wound, it was stopping him from bleeding out. But she didn't want him to live, so she ripped it out of him, and he bled all over the floor.'

'No, this isn't true,' he said, appalled.

'It is,' said Hobbs's deep voice. 'I saw the whole thing.'

'Why didn't you try to help him?'

'No one could help him with a hole like that in his stomach, not even the best surgeon in the country. Besides, Matthew charged me with going to his mother if anything happened to him. I was to become her protector, which is what I did. I had to lie low for a couple of years after Matthew's death because the police were searching for me, but they never got close.'

'Amy caused your father's death, not Edward, and he was hanged for it,' said Mrs Crowle. 'That's who your mother is, a killer who allowed someone else to take the blame for her crime.'

'She wouldn't. I mean, why would she? He saved her life.'

'Because she didn't want to share you with him. If he'd lived, she would have been forced to let him be a father to you after what he'd done for her. She's a cold, cruel creature.'

'I don't believe you,' Robert said, furiously shaking his head. 'My mother is not like that.'

'Why don't you go and ask her? Only then will you see the truth in her eyes.'

'I will,' he hissed, pocketing the watch before stomping back to his horse.

'When you're ready to talk again, I'll be waiting,' she called after him as he stormed away.

Rage pulsated inside Robert as he raced to Alardyce House, a thick, black rage that threatened to swallow him whole. His mother had sat him down and explained everything when he was thirteen years old, swearing she'd told him the God's honest truth when it had all been a lie to hide her horrible crime. He couldn't stop imagining how hurt Matthew would have been. He'd sacrificed everything for her and that was how she repaid him.

After leaving his horse at the stable, Robert stormed into the house.

'Where's my mother?' he demanded of Wyles, who was there to greet him.

'In the sitting room, sir.'

'And my father?'

'Gone into the city on business.'

'Perfect,' he said before striding across the hall and throwing open the sitting room door.

Amy was sitting in her armchair by the window with her embroidery. She looked up at him and smiled. 'Hello, darling. I wasn't expecting you.'

Robert closed the door behind him and stood over her. 'I'll bet.'

'You look upset. Have you had a fall-out with Jane?' she said, putting the embroidery aside.

It had always amazed him that she could manage such intricate work with her deformed hands. Now he knew why they were so ugly – because there was blood on them.

'I met someone today,' he said.

'Who?' she replied, growing increasingly concerned with his odd behaviour. It seemed to be an effort for him to speak.

'My grandmother.'

She looked puzzled. 'Your grandmother's dead, she died before you were born...' All the colour drained from her face. 'Impossible, she's dead too.'

'She wasn't ten minutes ago. In fact, she's very sprightly for her age.'

'Mrs Crowle is dead,' Amy hissed through her teeth.

'I know you'd like to believe that, but she's not. Someone of similar age and appearance died and she just allowed everyone to think it was her.'

'Why?'

'Because she knew you were keeping an eye on her.'

'This is nonsense, someone's playing a trick on you.'

'If it's a trick, then how did I get hold of this?' he said, producing the watch. 'I take it you recognise it?' he added when her eyes widened.

'That's Matthew's watch.'

'The watch you gave him. He kept it all those years.'

'I know. He showed it to me at Huntington Manor.'

'Hobbs salvaged it when he was dying.'

'Hobbs? Have you seen him?'

'Oh, yes.'

'That man is a criminal. He kept Esther and me prisoner and he killed my uncle,' Amy said, leaping to her feet. 'When did you first see him?'

He shrugged. 'A year ago.'

'A year? You've been in contact with them all this time?'

He nodded.

'She's the reason you started attacking women, she pushed you into it because she wants a replacement for her son.'

'And why's that? Because you killed him.'

Amy physically recoiled, clutching her hands to her chest. 'Edward killed him.'

'No,' he said, shaking his head. 'He could have survived the wound.' Robert's countenance darkened. 'You knew exactly what you were doing and don't make your crime worse by perpetuating your pathetic lie.'

Amy knew further denial would only push him further away. 'I had to, he left me no choice.'

'Finally, some honesty,' he exclaimed.

'I did it for you because he would never have let you go. He would have moulded you into a younger version of himself.'

'You did it for yourself too.'

'I didn't, because I thought I was dying. I never expected to leave that house alive with the injuries I had. Even Matthew said it was the right thing to do, that I'd saved him from a hanging, those were his exact words. Mrs Crowle has filled your head with nonsense. Do you really think that if he'd survived, you would be living happily ever after with Matthew? He'd done some truly horrible things. He would have dangled from a rope right beside Edward and he knew it.'

'Matthew was clever, he would have found a way.'

'Stop being so naïve,' said Amy. 'He was a cruel murderer.'

'Why did he save you if he was so cruel?'

'I don't know,' she sighed.

'Grandmother told me all about it. He would have given you the world if you'd let him, but you couldn't bear to share me with him.'

'Is that what she told you?' she laughed. 'The woman is quite mad. I turned him down for many reasons. Firstly, I didn't love him. Secondly, he wanted to get rid of Esther and Jane and I would not do that to them. Thirdly, I would not allow us to live in shame as his mistress and bastard child.'

'That didn't seem to bother you when you bedded him here. You were quite happy to wallow in shame then.'

She ignored the vicious comment. 'And finally, he would have wanted me out of the way when he'd tired of me so he could have you all to himself. I would have joined Sally, buried in the grounds of Huntington Manor with my throat cut. If things had gone differently, then yes, you would have had Matthew as a father, but I guarantee you would have had no mother.'

'That wouldn't have happened. You meant more to him than any other woman in his life, including his own wife. Evelyn knew it and it drove her insane.'

'What rot. If he truly loved me, then why did he keep me a prisoner?'

'Because he was terrified of losing you again.'

'You mean he was terrified of losing you.'

'No, both of us.'

'He beat me and strapped me with his belt,' said Amy. 'You saw the injuries I had.'

'I did and that was terribly wrong of him, but he was desperate.'

'So it's my fault he beat me?' she exclaimed.

'You could have handled it better.'

A crack filled the room and Robert put a hand to his reddening cheek. 'Violence is becoming a habit with you, Mother.'

'Because I'm tired of you making Matthew out to be a misunderstood hero. He was a rapist, murderer and bully and Mrs Crowle has put a pair of rose-tinted spectacles on you. I did what I had to do in order to protect us both and Matthew didn't love me enough to stop Edward from torturing me. He stood there and watched Edward rip out my nails and burn me with a poker and he did nothing.'

'He died for you,' he yelled, shaking with rage. 'He could have left you to Edward, got on a train and gone back to Derbyshire but he didn't, and I hear absolutely no gratitude for his sacrifice.'

'Of course I'm grateful,' she yelled back. 'But I will not have you turning him into a saint.'

'You and he were well suited, both murderers,' he spat back at her.

'What I did was very different to his crimes. Matthew killed for pleasure.'

'And you killed for necessity.'

She took a step closer and lowered her voice. 'When you killed Mrs Grier, was that a necessity, or pleasure? You forget I've encountered men like you before. I can see the satisfaction in your eyes whenever it's mentioned. Do you enjoy reminiscing about it when you're alone?' Amy's eyes narrowed when he shuffled from foot to foot. 'Look at you, Robert. And you have the nerve to stand there and lecture me for protecting my son. You've no idea what it is to be a parent. Maybe one day soon you will, then you will understand that desperate need to protect your child from every possible danger, even if that danger comes from another parent. Maybe I should have stayed my hand, you've turned out like him anyway.'

'Who else knows about what you did to Matthew?'

'Only Henry.'

'I might have known.'

'I had to tell someone. It was eating me alive.'

'When did you tell him?'

'Shortly before Edward's trial. He told me not to say anything. Edward killed Matthew, end of story.' Amy took his hands in her own. 'Please believe me when I say I will be eternally grateful to Matthew. If it wasn't for him, I wouldn't have had all these years with you and Henry, nor would Lydia, John and Stephen be in the world. But neither do I regret what I did, it was the right thing for us all, Matthew included. As he saved me from Edward, I saved him from the hangman, and you've had a wonderful father all these years.'

He snatched his hands from hers. 'Henry, a weak fop in comparison to my real father.'

'Don't you dare talk about him like that. He took you in, treated you like his own son and this is how you repay him. When did you become so ungrateful?'

'I'm not ungrateful. I appreciate the fine house and clothes, the luxuries, but it's a poor substitute for a real parent.'

With that, Robert turned on his heel and walked to the door, shoulders slumped.

'Wait,' she said. 'We haven't finished discussing this.'

He stopped and turned to face her. Amy's instinct warned her of danger. Before she could react, he lunged at her, grabbed her by the shoulders and pinned her up against the wall.

'Robert, what are you doing?' she exclaimed.

'Grandmother was right, you are cold and cruel. You couldn't
are less that you killed my father, all you cared about was covering
our tracks. You also kept from me the fact that he was my father
when we were at Huntington Manor. If only you'd told me, I could
have appreciated him more.'

'Matthew could have told you, but he didn't. Did you ever
consider why?'

'Because you wouldn't let him.'

'As if I could have stopped him from doing what he wanted. It
was because he wanted me out of the way first and he was enjoying
the power he held over me, taunting me, making me wonder
whether he was going to tell you or not.'

'You've taken so much from me, and I will never forgive you for
t.' His fingers dug into her shoulders, eyes darkening with rage. 'I
hate you.'

'You don't mean that, you can't,' said Amy, a tear sliding down
her cheek. 'You're my son, my firstborn, the reason I ran away from
my family and slaved as a governess for years.'

'You're nothing to me.'

When his eyes flicked to her throat, Amy flashed a macabre
smile. 'I know what you're thinking. Matthew looked at me the
exact same way so many times, wondering whether he should kill
me. Well, go on then and get it over with, because I don't have the
stamina for a fight any more.'

Robert wrapped his hand around her neck and thought of all
the happy times they'd shared, of how loving and protective he'd
felt towards her when she was recovering in hospital after Edward's
vicious attack, how he'd prayed for her, telling God he'd never do
anything wrong again if He let her live. He'd been a different person
then, an innocent boy whose entire world had revolved around his
mother. Sometimes he wished he could go back to being that little
boy, but now she was forever tainted in his eyes.

'You know something, Amy,' he said, enjoying the hurt in her eyes at his use of her first name. 'You're not worth the effort.'

With that, he released her and walked away.

'Robert,' she called but he ignored her.

Amy ran after him with tears streaming down her face but by the time she reached the front door, he was already galloping away on his horse.

As she stepped back into the house, she realised Rush was standing in the hallway, his eyes full of concern.

'Not now, Rush, please,' she breathed when he opened his mouth to speak.

He nodded and closed his mouth, although he looked stricken, desperate to help his mistress.

Amy returned to the sitting room, feeling wretched. She slumped onto the couch, buried her face in her hands and sobbed. She would never win Robert back now he knew the truth.

Anger coursed through her, so unexpected it made her physically jump. She leapt up and paced the room, going over Robert's words. How dare he speak to her like that after what she'd suffered? Everything she'd done had been for him – fleeing from Alardyce, giving up Henry and a life of wealth, toiling as a governess, scrimping and saving to make ends meet, culminating in almost being murdered. All of it had been so she could keep her boy, and this was how he repaid her. Well, she'd had enough. If he wanted nothing to do with her and to stand on his own two feet, then so be it. She would let him, and *he* could deal with the consequences.

30

Mrs Crowle and Hobbs were waiting for Robert where he'd left them.

'Well?' said his grandmother, her eyes gleaming as he dismounted his horse.

'She admitted it, eventually,' he spat. 'But she doesn't regret murdering my father.'

'What reason did she give?'

'That she was protecting me. She never expected to get out of that house alive. Apparently, it was all for me.' He was so furious he snarled more than spoke, pacing back and forth as he attempted to contain his rage.

'She did it for herself, which is typical of that selfish woman.'

'I told her I hate her and that she's nothing to me any more.'

Mrs Crowle hesitated before replying, 'You confronted her and you got the truth after years of lies. You did well. What will you do now?'

'I'm going into the city to get blind drunk.'

'You're not going home to your pretty new wife?'

'I can't face her. She wouldn't understand this.'

Robert kissed her cheek before climbing onto his horse and riding away.

Mrs Crowle watched him go with a smile. 'He's a fine rider, just like his father,' she commented, Hobbs nodding in agreement. 'You've kept your promise faithfully all these years, Hobbs, and I appreciate that. Amy knows her son is aware of the truth. Now you can enjoy the revenge you've been waiting for.'

'Finally,' he said, lips cracking into a rare smile.

'And however you do it, just ensure that what Edward did to her pales into insignificance.'

'It will, have no fear. And what about the boy? He'll know it was us.'

'You heard him, she's nothing to him any more. Nothing now stands in the way of justice for my son.'

* * *

Henry was greeted by an uncharacteristically anxious Rush.

'What on earth is wrong?' he demanded as the butler took his coat.

'It's Lady Alardyce, sir. She had words earlier with Master Robert and now she refuses to come out of her sitting room or allow anyone inside.'

'Robert, what have you done now?' muttered Henry as he stalked to the sitting room door. He entered without knocking to find Amy slumped on the couch, looking wretched.

'What's happened?' he said, sitting beside her.

She looked to the door to ensure it was closed before replying, 'Robert knows I killed Matthew.'

His eyes widened. 'How?'

'Matthew's mother.'

'She's dead.'

'Apparently not. A woman of similar age and appearance died, and Mrs Crowle pretended it was her because she knew you were watching her. Hobbs is with her too.'

'He's still wanted by the police, which Robert knows full well. How long has he been in contact with them?'

'A year.'

'And he never thought to inform us?' he exploded.

'She told him all about Matthew. To Robert, he's some sort of god who I ruthlessly cut down.'

'To protect him.'

'Robert doesn't see it that way. To him, I'm incredibly ungrateful for doing what I did after he rescued me from that cellar. Now he hates me and wants nothing more to do with me.'

'Did he hurt you?'

'He pushed me up against the wall and wrapped his hand around my throat.'

'What?' Henry exclaimed, shooting to his feet, quivering with rage.

She took his hand. 'Please sit.'

Henry obeyed, sensing she needed him close.

'We've feared this for so long and finally it's out. He wants nothing more to do with me and that's fine by me. I'm so tired of it, Henry. All I want is to live quietly here with you and our children. Is that so much to ask?'

He wrapped an arm around her. 'Of course not. Robert will come round when he's thought things through, although I'm not sure I want him to after he attacked you.'

'He didn't really hurt me.'

'But he could have done.'

'Perhaps,' she said thoughtfully. 'He's never looked more like his father.'

'If he's decided to go and sulk, he'll be out of our hair for a while. Now we have to consider damage limitation. Is he likely to tell anyone else?'

'I don't think so.'

'What about Jane?'

She shrugged. 'Even if he does, so what? There's no proof except the word of a man wanted by the police.'

'Now we know Hobbs is still around, I think I'll bring Knapp back.'

'You don't think he'll try anything, do you?'

'Mrs Crowle's secret meetings with Robert feel very insidious. I don't like it.'

'Me neither.'

'Why don't you go for a lie-down while I contact Knapp?'

She sighed and nodded. 'All right.'

Henry was becoming concerned by how vague and faraway she seemed. 'You're not feeling unwell again, are you?'

'No, not this time. That boy's broken my heart so many times, he can't possibly do it again.'

Black rage bubbled up inside Henry against Robert. It seemed that boy had been put on this earth just to hurt Amy.

* * *

'My God, what's happened now? You look awful,' said Andrew as Robert slumped into a chair at their usual table at Vivienne's establishment. Daniel was also at the table, but he was fast asleep, head lolling over the back of the chair.

'Just Mother,' he muttered.

'That wonderful woman,' he smiled. 'What's the minx done now?'

'You wouldn't think she was so wonderful if you knew.'

'Let me guess – she wants to rip off my clothes and devour me whole. Sorry,' he added when Robert glared at him.

'It doesn't matter what she's done. The fact is that she's no longer my mother and no, that doesn't mean you can seduce her,' he added when Andrew smiled.

'Oh, well, never mind. Plenty more fish in the sea. Aren't you being a bit harsh?'

'No.'

'Then enlighten me.'

Robert was on the verge of confessing all to this man who already knew his worst secret when Daniel woke from his slumber with a loud snort. He peered at Robert through bloodshot eyes and broke into a dopey grin. 'Congratulations. It's the groom,' he slurred before laughing.

'Shut up,' Robert spat, giving him a vicious kick under the table.

'Ow,' he groaned, too drunk to feel any real physical pain. 'What was that for?'

'Nothing. Go back to sleep. Where's Thomas?'

'Debtors' prison, again,' said Andrew.

'Has anyone done anything about getting him out?'

'His brother's going to, after he's spent a few days inside. He's hoping it will teach him a lesson.'

Robert's impatience only increased when April draped herself across his knee and smiled up at him sultrily.

'Miss me?' she said.

'Sorry, April, I'm a happily married man now.'

'So are most of the men who come in here,' she grinned.

Robert took in her large breasts spilling over the top of her corset, a pleasing contrast to Jane's tiny chest. Her grin widened when she felt him stiffen beneath her.

'See,' she chirruped. 'A wedding changes nothing.'

He thrust his tongue into her mouth, taking the opportunity to run a hand over those creamy orbs before tipping her back onto her feet. 'As I said, I'm happily married.'

April wasn't used to being rejected and it hurt coming from her most handsome client. 'Then why did you come here tonight?' she demanded, hands on hips.

'To see my friends.'

Her pout only increased.

'Don't worry, April,' winked Daniel. 'I'll pay you a visit later.'

'Why, so you can vomit all over my bedroom floor then fall asleep, like last night?' she snapped before stomping off.

Daniel shrugged, settled back in his chair and closed his eyes, Andrew stifling a laugh while Robert just looked troubled.

'It must be love if you're turning down little April,' said Andrew.

'It is,' replied Robert. 'Jane is everything I've ever wanted.' *Apart from the tiny breasts*, he thought.

'We'll see how long it lasts.'

Robert scowled and got to his feet. 'I don't know why I bothered coming here.'

'Don't be so hasty,' said Andrew, attempting to pull him back into his seat, but Robert shook him off.

'Where are you going?' Andrew called after him as he made for the door.

'Where I should have gone in the first place. Home.'

* * *

Robert was so relieved to see Jane that he pulled her to him and clung onto her.

'What's wrong?' she said.

He ushered her into the drawing room, shut the door then opened it to make sure a servant wasn't listening before closing it

gain. He wouldn't put it past Henry to have installed a spy in his
house.

'Will you please tell me what's going on?' said Jane. 'You're
scaring me.'

'I didn't want to drag you into this, but I have to confide in you
before I go mad.'

'Robert, I'm your wife. You can tell me anything.'

As she stared up at him with her innocent blue eyes, he
wondered if he could put this on her shoulders. But if he didn't
unburden himself, he knew the dark thoughts would return to
torment him. 'My mother killed Matthew.'

She blinked at him as she attempted to process this information. 'Edward killed him.'

'That's what she'd like everyone to think,' he said, starting to
pace again. 'Edward stabbed him, and she pulled the knife out.'

'Maybe she was trying to help him?'

'He told her if the knife stayed in then he might survive, so she
pulled it out, and he bled to death.'

Jane turned ashen. 'Why?'

'To protect me.'

'And you think she was wrong?'

'Of course I do,' he exclaimed. 'Are you telling me you don't?'

'I'm sorry, Robert, I know he was your father, but I recall the
man I lived with for years. He was cruel and very frightening.'

'He also saved my mother's life and that was how she repaid
him.'

'Obviously she wasn't thinking about Matthew when she did it,
she was thinking of you.'

'How could killing my father possibly help me?'

'Have you forgotten the Matthew we knew?'

'You mean the man who took us in, bought us nice things and
expensive clothes?'

'I'm talking about the man who locked away your mother and my aunt, who chained them up and treated them like animals,' said Jane.

'She stabbed him in the arm.'

'In self-defence because he attacked her first. Your mother is a strong woman who would do anything to protect her son.'

'Don't you see, Jane, everything that happened could have been avoided if she'd only been honest with him from the beginning.'

He was surprised when she defiantly shook her head. He'd thought he would get sympathy from Jane, but she was actually disagreeing with him.

'You don't understand how desperate he was for a child. Every moment I lived in that house, I was made to feel inferior because I wasn't his blood. I was a permanent reminder that he was childless and he made Aunt Esther and me suffer for it. If your mother had told him the truth, there was a good chance he would have got rid of her because he would have wanted you all to himself.'

'He wouldn't. He truly loved her.'

'I rather think he did, in his own way, but Matthew didn't feel things like normal people, you must remember that. That love would have quickly faded had he lived and the consequences for your mother could have been dire.'

'So she didn't really do it for me, she did it for herself.'

'In a way, but I believe her primary motivation was you.'

'I can't believe you're defending her.'

'That's because I know your mother and she's a good woman. It surprises me that you doubt her.'

'She's a killer.'

Jane sighed and shook her head. 'I don't know what it's like to be a mother, although I do hope to find out soon. But I can imagine the instinct to protect your child at all costs, which is what she did. Why can't you just be happy that you have a mother who would ight the world for you rather than think about a father who only exists in your imagination?'

Robert was stuck for words. He'd no idea his wife could be so eloquent, and it was so at odds with what he'd expected that he didn't know how to respond.

'How did you find this out, anyway?' said Jane. 'I doubt Aunt Amy confessed after all this time.'

'She didn't tell me, my grandmother did.'

'Grandmother. I don't understand.'

'Mrs Crowle, Matthew's mother.'

'She's dead.'

'She's not. It was all a trick so Henry would stop keeping his beady eye on her.'

'How long have you known she's alive?'

'A year.'

Jane looked furious. 'That hideous, evil old crone? You let her drip poison in your ear? Are you mad?'

'She's the closest I'll ever get to Matthew.'

'You can't trust a word she says.'

'She was right about what my mother did.'

'Don't you remember what she was like at Huntington Manor? We hated her.'

'Only because she was our governess.'

'Aunt Amy was governess to us both and we adored her. Can't you see what she's doing? She wants revenge for her son and she's using you to get it.'

'Nonsense. She only wants to get to know me, I'm all she has left of Matthew.'

'Perhaps, but I can guarantee her primary motive is hurting your mother. She's an old, frail woman, so the only way she can do it is by getting at her through you.'

Robert thought of Hobbs, still tall and strong despite the

passage of so many years, and suddenly he felt uneasy. 'Perhaps not.'

'What do you mean?'

'Hobbs is with her.'

'Matthew's henchman who killed Sir Alfred? My God, Robert, what have you done?'

'Nothing. He won't do anything to her.'

'Don't be ridiculous, of course he will. You have to warn her. Well, don't just stand there,' exclaimed Jane when he failed to move.

Robert smiled at his wife. He'd no idea she possessed such fire. He grabbed her and kissed her hard.

'I'll be back soon,' he told her, leaving her breathless as he sped outside, calling for his horse.

my lay on her bed, continually mulling over her argument with Robert, finding her vow to cut herself off from him easier said than done. Her memory tormented her, raking over the past, going all the way back to her time with Matthew, falling pregnant, wondering, if she could change one single decision, whether things would be different now, for the better. If she hadn't had her affair with Matthew, she wouldn't have Robert and, despite everything he'd done, that was still unthinkable. But if she'd remained at Alardyce and married Henry, this wouldn't be happening now because she would never have encountered Matthew again. He would still be alive at Huntington Manor with Esther and Jane, making their lives miserable and murdering maids, and Robert wouldn't hate her for killing him.

'What if?' she murmured to the ceiling. Such thoughts were useless. For all she knew, things could have turned out even worse. That was a horrifying prospect.

In an attempt to quiet her turbulent mind, she listened to the sounds around her. There wasn't much to hear, just the occasional door opening and closing as the servants quietly attended to their duties. It was late, close to bedtime. Henry was still out but would be back soon, the children were asleep, and Robert had flown the nest. A lump formed in her throat. It seemed nothing that boy did could kill her love for him, not even threatening to strangle her.

She tried to find the will to rise and ring for Hazel to help her change into her nightgown, but she couldn't find the impetus, she just wanted to be alone and lose herself in the past. Normally she did her best to avoid thinking about it but now she felt she must in the hope of forming an argument that would bring Robert round to her way of thinking. It hurt that all the sacrifices she'd made for him meant nothing, but she hoped that one day, perhaps when he became a father himself, he would understand why she'd done what she had. She felt uneasy at the prospect of Robert having a child. What if he had a son who turned out like him and Matthew?

No, she must think positively about the future.

Eventually she fell into a fitful sleep, while outside the sky darkened and rain started to spatter against the glass. Below her, the sounds of the house faded away as the servants completed their upstairs duties and returned below stairs. Amy slept on, dreaming of Matthew.

She was appalled to find herself writhing with him on his desk at Huntington Manor, clawing at his naked back, his face buried between her bare breasts. He raised his head and smiled, revealing a row of small, sharp white teeth.

'I knew you loved me,' he said, that disturbing grin broadening.

'I do not,' she retorted.

He moved inside her, making her moan.

'As much fun as this is,' he breathed, 'you need to wake up.'

'I don't want to,' she said, letting her fingers trail across his chest.

His eyes burned with fire, mouth stretching wide open.

'Wake up,' he roared in her face.

Amy jumped awake, her body tingling, forehead beaded with sweat, ashamed to find she was moist between the thighs. Something was wrong.

She tried to scream when a hand clamped down over her mouth and a face she'd hoped never to see again loomed over her.

'You have to be quiet,' whispered Robert. 'He's here.'

'Robert,' she breathed when he removed his hand, thinking it had been Matthew. 'Who's here?'

'Hobbs.'

'He's come to kill me, hasn't he?'

'Well, I certainly don't think he's here to give you a belated Christmas present.'

'Amusing,' she said, slowly sitting up. 'What?' she added when Robert stared at her knowingly.

'You were saying Matthew's name in your sleep and you seemed to be rather enjoying yourself.'

'Don't be ridiculous. Are you certain Hobbs is here?'

'I entered by the conservatory door. There was a broken pane of glass.'

'He's taking a risk with all the servants about.'

'The majority of whom are below. Henry's out and the children are asleep. It's the perfect time.'

'What do we do?' asked Amy.

'Try not to get killed. He's a trained soldier, adept at killing. I'm hoping we don't have to physically tackle him.'

'Why are you here? I thought you hated me.'

'I don't hate you, I was just angry. Besides, I don't think Matthew would want you to die after everything he went through to save you. Now come on,' he said, taking her hand and leading her to the door. He opened it a crack to peer out. 'All clear.'

'Wait, do you have any weapons?'

'None,' he replied, wishing he'd considered that before setting out. 'We could just wait in here and lock the door.'

'What about when Henry comes home? Hobbs might attack him, or he might hurt the children.'

'You're right, hiding isn't an option.'

Robert led the way, holding his mother's hand, which made her smile, despite the perilous situation they were in.

They managed to get downstairs without incident. The house seemed to be deserted. The servants were all enjoying their supper before retiring to bed.

'We must go to the servants,' said Amy. 'Safety in numbers and we could send one of them to fetch help.'

'Good idea,' replied Robert, leading her towards the staircase that would take them downstairs to the kitchens.

When a huge dark figure lunged at them, Amy squealed with surprise and Robert dragged her down the corridor, away from the pursuing shadow. They raced through the conservatory towards the back door that would take them out into the garden, coming to a halt when a second figure confronted them, blocking their exit.

'Grandmother?' said Robert. 'What are you doing here?'

'I wanted to confront this bitch,' she hissed, pointing at Amy. 'I had to hear it from her why she killed my boy.'

Amy's gaze was cold. 'You know why – so Robert and I could be free. You've been using my son, your own grandchild, just to get back at me, to encourage Robert to do horrible things that don't come naturally to him.'

There was the thud of footsteps behind them and Hobbs stalked into the room. He closed the door behind him and turned the key in the lock.

'But the bad things do come naturally, don't they, Robert?' smiled Mrs Crowle, her eyes blazing in a way that reminded Amy of the way Matthew's had burned in her dream. 'He couldn't talk to

ou about it, he needs someone who understands him, who has
lready raised a child with the same primal urges. Who better to
uide him through this difficult time than me?'

'He doesn't need you dripping your venom in his ear, twisting
is thoughts,' said Amy. 'Did it ever occur to you that Matthew
might have been a normal, decent man if he hadn't had you as a
mother?' Even as she spoke these thoughts that had never occurred
o her before, she knew them to be true. 'He could have been so
much more. The goodness in him that had been buried beneath all
he madness would have come forth and he would still be alive
ow. I didn't kill him, you did, and I will not let you drive Robert to
he same fate.'

'Why, are you going to rip a knife out of his belly too?'

'Don't be ridiculous. Now, I want you out of his life for good.'

'Robert's a man now, aren't you, dear?' said Mrs Crowle, turning
er attention to her grandson. 'And I think it's his decision.'

Robert looked from one to the other as both women stared at
im, demanding an answer.

'You can't listen to this woman, darling,' said Amy. 'She's pure
vil. If you want someone to blame for what happened to Matthew,
hen blame her.'

'Nonsense,' countered Mrs Crowle. 'Matthew was a man in
very sense of the word. He knew exactly who he was and what he
wanted. Do you think I could have ever controlled anything he did?
She was the one who brought about his downfall,' she said,
odding at Amy.

Robert turned to his mother with a frown.

'You don't know what it's like to raise a child,' she told Robert,
eeping an eye on Mrs Crowle, thinking it would be wise not to let
er out of her sight. 'It's so easy to mould someone into what you
want them to be when they're young, that's why it's vital they're
aised decently, to know right from wrong. Think about it, Robert –

I wasn't just your mother, I was your teacher, and so was Mrs Crowle. Who did you prefer as a governess?'

'You,' he said without having to think about it.

'Exactly, and why was that? Because I treated you fairly, taught you that life is a combination of pleasure and responsibility. What did she do? Put you down, shouted at you, told you all the things you enjoyed were frivolous wastes of time. Do you remember how she hurt Jane?'

'I do,' he said, turning his scowl on his grandmother.

'Imagine having that every day of your life, imagine how different you would be now if you'd had her as a mother,' said Amy passionately, realising she was fighting for her son's very soul. Yes, he'd already killed, but she felt sure she could pull him back from the brink.

'Robert had your supposedly divine mothering his entire life,' said Mrs Crowle with a malicious smile. 'It didn't stop him from throwing Evelyn into the pond, did it?'

'He didn't,' said Amy, her instinct being to protect her son in any way possible.

'Of course he did, I'm not stupid, and why did he do that? Because he thought it would be fun. Actually, it was a relief, she was a nuisance. Everything was a drama with that one.'

'I was protecting my mother,' said Robert. 'Evelyn tried to kill her.'

Mrs Crowle patted his cheek. 'You keep telling yourself that if it makes you feel better.'

'It's the truth,' he retorted.

'Do you know how old Matthew was when he first killed?'

'Let me guess,' said Amy. 'Seventeen?'

'No, eighteen, actually, but close enough. It was an old man who lived in the next cottage to ours. We didn't have anywhere as grand as this,' she said, gesturing to the room. 'Anyway, this man was a onstant thorn in my side, always complaining about something, I'd ut up with it for years. Then one day he disappeared. His body as found floating face down in a loch half a mile from where we ved. Everyone said it was an accident, he was a keen fisherman, he ust have fallen in, his little boat was found bobbing about on the vater. No one thought twice about it, but I knew, I saw the look in Matthew's eyes when he came home that afternoon soaked to the kin, shivering with cold. He said he'd done it because the old man vas driving me mad, but I saw the pleasure in his eyes. It was the ame for you, wasn't it, boy? The power of having control over vhether someone lives or dies. It's a drug to you already.'

Robert stared back at her, feeling her words connect with something deep and dark inside himself.

Amy placed herself before him, breaking the spell. 'There you o again, putting thoughts inside his head that didn't exist there before, just like you did to Matthew. Do you know why your son oved me?'

'He didn't,' she spat back at her.

'Yes, he did, because when he was with me, he saw the life he could have had. If he hadn't been a monster, he could have had what he'd always dreamed of with me and Robert. I made him realise in the last hour of his life that what he'd done was wrong. You can't stand the fact that he finally knew you for what you really are – a monster.'

Mrs Crowle's face contorted with fury. She grabbed Robert's arm and tried to pull him away. Panicking, Amy grabbed his other arm, but Robert was so strong he just stood there, immobile, looking from one to the other in confusion.

'Don't listen to her, son,' said Mrs Crowle. 'If it wasn't for her, you'd be with your father now.'

'This is her fault,' countered Amy. 'She twisted Matthew into a killer. Listen to me, darling, you've known me your entire life.'

'And you've lied to him your entire life,' Mrs Crowle hissed a
her. 'Come with me, Robert, and you can be the man you truly wan
to be, the man your father would have been proud of.'

Finally, his decision was made. Robert turned to his mother, hi
eyes sad.

'Grandmother's right. This will never work because I can't b
who you want me to be. I'll only let you down.'

Amy shook her head. 'You could never do that.'

'I already have,' he whispered. With that, he snatched his arm
from her grip, took his grandmother's hand and walked with her to
the door leading into the garden.

'Robert, don't go, please,' cried Amy, running after them.

'It's for the best,' said Robert sadly before leaving.

Amy was left standing alone in the conservatory, chest heaving,
knowing she'd permanently lost her son to darkness. She was also
attempting to deal with surprising new thoughts about Matthew,
but she forced those to the back of her mind.

It was then she recalled Hobbs was still standing behind her,
blocking the door leading back into the house. Slowly she turned to
face him, the murderous look in his eyes causing her to retreat a
few steps.

'Time to pay for your sins, Amy,' he said, advancing on her as
she backed up to the door.

She took a deep breath. 'You're going to kill me?'

'Yes. I've been looking forward to it for a long time,' he said,
cracking his knuckles. 'I saw you pull that blade out of him, I saw
the hurt in his eyes.'

'I didn't have you down as the sentimental type. Why does it
matter to you so much?'

'I'll tell you why, you bitch. When I left the army, I had nothing.
All my family were dead, I couldn't get any work, life was bleak.
Then Matthew found me, recognised my skills, gave me a job and

with it my self-respect. He gave me everything and you took it all away again. After his death, I found myself on the run, forced to hide like a dog with nothing but the clothes on my back.'

'Do you expect me to feel sorry for you? You killed my uncle and you helped keep me and Esther prisoner. I'm glad you lost everything and you've suffered all these years. It's nothing less than you deserve.'

'Who are you to judge after what you've done?' said Hobbs. 'You're a murderer like me.'

'I was trying to protect my son. You just enjoy taking life.'

'You're right, I do, but nothing is going to give me greater pleasure than killing you.'

'Do you think Matthew would want me dead after he gave his life for me?' she said, continuing to back up towards the door leading out to the garden.

'Matthew doesn't think anything because he's dead, and whose fault is that?'

'His mother's.'

'Nothing's ever your fault, is it?' he snarled. 'Even your own son rejected you and you blame her. Well, these things have a habit of catching up with you and now it's time to pay for the life you took.'

'Robert,' she screamed, hoping he was still within earshot.

Amy ran for the back door but Hobbs reached it first and slammed it shut with one hand while the other went around her mouth and dragged her backwards, silencing her screams.

He grunted with pain when she bit down on his hand so hard blood filled her mouth. Enraged, he threw her against the wall, jarring her back, but he'd underestimated the strength of her steel corset, which absorbed most of the impact. Consequently, she didn't feel much of anything, so when she sprang back to her feet and ran for the door again, she had the element of surprise on her side and almost reached her goal before he grabbed her.

Amy brought back her elbow and was astonished when it connected with his eye. In his surprise, Hobbs released her and she ran for the vase on the windowsill, smashed it and picked up a jagged shard, ready to use as a weapon, giving her a flashback to the time she'd physically fought Matthew. She'd succeeded in injuring his arm but had come off much worse, which she had the feeling was going to happen here.

'Help,' she screamed, but the house was vast, and all the servants were downstairs in the kitchen at the opposite end of the house. Henry was out and her son had abandoned her. She was on her own. She was going to die.

Hobbs glared at his injured hand in outrage. 'You fucking harridan,' he yelled.

'If you think I'm going to go meekly, then you're in for a shock,' she yelled back.

Hobbs stalked her, his eyes never leaving the weapon she held. When he lunged at her, she made the mistake of lashing out. He dodged the shard, grabbed her wrist and twisted, forcing her to relinquish it. Before he could grasp her other arm, she poked him in the eye then raked her nails down his face, causing him to bellow with pain, but still he refused to release her. A smack to the face sent her staggering back against the wall, then his hands were around her throat. When she opened her mouth in an attempt to breathe, he grasped her tongue.

'I'm going to rip this right out of your head,' he said, eyes wild. 'Payback for all the lies you've told.'

Amy's eyes bulged, breath coming out in frantic gasps, fists uselessly pounding against his chest as he started to pull, panic gripping her as pain swelled inside her mouth.

The door erupted open and Robert charged in.

'Get off her,' he yelled before throwing himself at Hobbs.

The pressure was released on Amy and she dropped to the floor, asping for air while bangs and crashes echoed around her. Robert truggled valiantly with Hobbs; however, he didn't have the older nan's experience and he was starting to succumb. She had to do omething or they were both dead.

Spotting the shard she'd dropped lying on the floor, she neaked up behind the two men, Hobbs attempting to get Robert in headlock while he furiously fought against being pinned down. Ieart hammering, she drew back her arm, ready to strike. Hobbs ttempted to move but Amy's aim was true and the shard sank into is left shoulder, making him roar with pain.

Robert took the opportunity to drive his elbow into his ribs and ush him away with such force that Hobbs fell onto his back, ushing the shard even deeper into his shoulder. Robert leapt on im, pinned down his arms with his knees, put his hands about his hroat and started to squeeze. Robert had large, powerful hands just ike his father and he put them to good use around Hobbs's neck.

Hobbs knocked Robert's hands away from his throat, threw him ff and drew a knife from his boot. But Robert went in low and unched him in the knee. Amy surmised Hobbs must have had an ld injury, possibly from his time in the army, because he threw ack his head and howled. Robert took the opportunity to punch im hard in the face, knocking him onto his back. He snatched the nife from Hobbs's hand and raised it above his head, ready to lunge it into his opponent's chest.

'Robert, stop,' cried Amy.

'I can't, he knows too much about you.'

'You can't just kill him.'

'What if he tells everyone about what you did?'

'So what if he does? There's no proof. It'll be his word against nine, and who do you think the authorities would believe?'

'If he lives, you'll always be in danger.'

'He'll be locked up.'

HEATHER ATKINSON

'But for how long?' Robert's gaze softened. 'You did this once for me, now let me do it for you.'

While Robert's attention was diverted, Hobbs grabbed a large rock lying off to one side, which had rolled out of the base of a large pot plant that had been knocked over during the fight, and bashed Robert in the side of the head with it, sending him crashing to the floor, the knife falling from his hand.

'No,' screamed Amy when he loomed over her son, raising the rock to deliver the death blow.

Robert was sprawled on the floor, dazed, blood trickling from his temple. Snatching up the knife Robert had dropped, she plunged it into Hobbs's belly.

He looked down at his stomach, stunned, before his expression filled with resolve and he raised the rock even higher, a roar leaving his lips.

In sheer panic, Amy yanked the knife out of his stomach and stuck it into his chest, withdrawing it for a third time and plunging it into him again.

Hobbs slumped to his knees, the rock falling from his hands, staring down at his wounds.

Amy looked down at her twisted hands, which were covered in blood, then to her son, flailing about on the floor, injured in his defence of her.

Hobbs forced his head up, his ferocious gaze locking with hers as his hand groped for the rock again, determined to finish Robert off while he still had the strength.

'Don't,' she warned him.

But he ignored her. When his hand closed around the rock, she stabbed him in his belly again, recalling where the knife had struck Matthew and doing her best to replicate that. She assumed she'd hit the mark when he started to gurgle, all the colour draining from is face, body jumping as she twisted the blade, opening up a wide, ugged hole that steadily pumped out blood.

'No one hurts my son,' she hissed before violently tearing it om the wound.

Hobbs released a groan and finally toppled backwards, a hand ressed to his bleeding stomach.

Amy threw herself down by her son's side. 'Robert?' she cried.

His eyes flickered open and widened. 'You're covered in blood.'

'It's not mine. Are you all right?'

'Yes, I think so,' he groaned, pressing a hand to the side of his ead and slowly sitting up. 'Dear God,' he said when he saw Hobbs iddled with holes, lying on the floor. 'Did you do that?'

'He was going to kill you. I had no choice.' Amy couldn't bear to ook at her handiwork. With Matthew, she'd been able to use the xcuse that Edward had put the blade in him, but this time, she had io such recourse. 'When I said I'd do anything for you, I meant it.'

Robert threw his arms around her and hugged her.

'I thought I'd lost you when you left,' she whispered, tears queezing from the corners of her eyes.

'You never lost me. I just wanted to get her out of the house.'

'Where is she?'

'Outside.'

'She's going to raise holy hell for this,' sighed Amy, looking lown at Hobbs's body. She still couldn't quite believe what she'd lone, and shock was keeping all emotion at bay, her body numb, apart from the relief that both she and Robert were all right. She had no doubt that it would hit her hard later.

32

Amy and Robert jumped when there was a terrific hammering at the door that Hobbs had locked.

'It's Henry, thank God,' said Amy when she heard her husband's voice demanding to be let in.

She leapt up and staggered towards the door to unlock it.

Henry charged in. 'Rush said he heard screams... dear God,' he exclaimed when he saw the carnage. 'Is that Hobbs?'

'It was,' replied Robert.

'He attacked us,' said Amy.

Henry's eyes flicked down to the blood on his wife's hands before placing himself in the doorway to prevent Rush, who was slowly following, from seeing anything.

'It's all right, Rush, Master Robert slipped and fell.'

'Shall I fetch the doctor, sir?'

'No need, thank you.'

The butler nodded and started to lumber back the way he'd come. Henry hastily closed the door to block out the sight of the body.

'Are you hurt?' he asked Amy.

'No, just a bit bruised.'

'The blood's his?' he said, nodding at Hobbs.

She nodded, lips pursed.

'Robert?'

'I'll be fine,' he replied. 'Although I'll have a headache for a while.'

'I had no choice,' said Amy, eyes filling with tears. 'He would have killed us both.'

'I don't doubt it,' Henry said, pulling out his handkerchief and wiping her hands. 'Now we must think how we're going to explain this.'

'Why must we come up with a story? Why not just tell the truth?'

'Because you've just killed a man and I will not allow you to be punished for it.'

'I won't be. I was defending myself and my son.'

'Questions will be asked, and I won't have you put through that.'

'What else can we say? We just found him lying here like this? No one will believe it.'

'I don't know, but I'll think of something.'

'There's something else you need to see,' said Robert.

'Steady,' said Amy when he swayed on his feet.

'I'll be all right... just a bit dizzy.' Gritting his teeth, Robert talked to the door, opened it and stepped out into the garden.

Puzzled, they followed him around the side of the house.

'Oh, hell,' sighed Henry.

In the bushes lay Mrs Crowle, her mean dark eyes glassy and staring up at the night sky, her head lying at an odd angle.

'Her neck's been broken,' added Henry.

'I know, I broke it,' said Robert casually. 'She was saying all these awful things about Mother. When she told me Hobbs would make her pay for taking my real father from me, I knew she had to go or this would never stop. Finally, I understood what you meant, Mother, why Matthew had to die. There was no other way.'

'I'm glad you realised,' she said gently. 'But I wish this hadn't been the price you had to pay for understanding.'

'It's done now,' he said, looking down at the body of his grand-mother dispassionately.

They returned to the conservatory in silence.

'No one will miss these two,' said Henry. He looked to Robert. 'Does anyone else know they're here?'

'No,' he replied.

'Then we hide the bodies and mention this to no one.'

'We can't do that,' said Amy. 'It's wrong.'

'Then what do you suggest? If we call the authorities, everyone will know what happened here today, there will be an investigation, our family will be dragged through the courts and newspapers again. It will be the final nail in the coffin for Lydia, John and Stephen ever being accepted into society.'

'I can't believe you're suggesting we cover this up.'

'He's right,' said Robert. 'If this comes out, then our family might not survive the scandal. What future will Lydia have? She'd never find anyone to marry her. It might not be so bad for the boys, things never are, but she'd be left an old maid, shunned by society. Is that the future you want for her?'

'Oh... what am I supposed to say to that? There's no choice, I suppose.' *God forgive me*, she thought to herself.

'And we have the perfect hiding place right here on the estate,' said Henry. 'The crypt.'

'Good idea,' said Robert, feeling his respect for his adopted father returning.

'You can't put them in there with our family,' said Amy.

'We have little choice. Most of the servants have already retired to bed and it's dark outside. Robert and I will put them in the crypt.'

'I don't like this, it feels wrong.'

'Neither do I, but I can't see what else we can do.'

'The alternative won't go well for any of us,' said Robert. 'Don't let this pair destroy our family.'

Just as he knew it would, this touched something deep inside his mother.

'All right,' said Amy. 'But for heaven's sake, don't get caught.'

'We won't,' replied Henry. 'Now why don't you go upstairs and wash and change? Burn those clothes, we don't want to arouse Hazel's suspicions.'

'I won't sit upstairs like the little woman,' she retorted. 'I clean up my own mess.'

'This is going to be unpleasant work.'

'Not as unpleasant as it was stabbing him,' she said sadly, gazing down at Hobbs's body. 'Why couldn't he just let it go? He could have left the country, started a new life.'

'Because that man loved to hate and you were the perfect focus. It gave him an excuse to commit another murder. Save your pity for someone who deserves it.'

Robert frowned and knelt beside the body. 'He's still alive.'

'Impossible,' gasped Amy. 'Look at all the blood he's lost.'

He pressed two fingers to the pulse in his neck. 'He is.'

Henry tested the pulse at Hobbs's wrist then placed a hand on his chest. 'Robert's right.'

'Dear God,' exclaimed Amy. 'We must get him to a hospital.'

'He wouldn't survive the journey,' said Robert. 'The kindest thing is to put him out of his misery.'

'You're talking about murdering someone who's injured and defenceless. That's very different to killing them in self-defence.'

'Amy, go upstairs. Leave this to me and Robert,' said Henry with a dark look she'd never seen before.

'I won't let you do this. It's beyond all limits of decency.'

'If he lives, he could denounce you to the authorities for what you did to Matthew and he certainly wouldn't hesitate to denounce us all for what happened here this night.'

'You should be pleased, Mother,' said Robert. 'It means you didn't kill him.'

'I cannot countenance cold-blooded murder,' she retorted.

'He's dead anyway, look at the state of him. Do you think those butchers at the hospital can help him now? He'll linger in agony for hours, maybe even days before finally succumbing anyway. If he was a horse, you wouldn't hesitate to shoot him.'

'But he's not a horse, he's a human being.'

'Who's murdered God knows how many people,' said Henry. 'This creature killed my father.'

'Don't think I've forgotten that, but this will make us no better than him.'

'Sometimes we have to do bad things to survive. Now go upstairs and leave this to us.'

Tears filled Amy's eyes. 'Please don't do this, Henry. You'll never be the same again.'

'I'll be fine.'

'You won't. I know you, it will torment you for the rest of your life.'

'Ridding the world of the man who not only killed my father but was complicit in the imprisonment and attempted murder of my wife won't trouble my conscience one bit.'

'It will, and I will not sit back and watch it slowly destroy you.'

'I'll do anything to protect my family.'

'You're not capable of murder, Henry. Oh, my God, Robert,' she cried when he snatched up the knife and plunged it straight into Hobbs's heart.

Robert shrugged, leaving the knife in situ. 'I had blood on my hands anyway. A bit more won't make any difference.'

Amy stared at him in horror. First Mrs Grier, then Mrs Crowle and now Hobbs. Her son had killed three people.

'The deed is done,' said Henry quietly. 'Now let's get this mess tidied up.'

Amy couldn't believe how cold her usually warm and loving husband sounded. She shook her head and backed away from them both before turning and running from the nightmarish scene.

'She'll be all right,' said Robert, locking the door behind her. 'She's tough.'

'She shouldn't have to be tough. We should be protecting her from all this.'

'Sir, can I be of assistance?' said a voice through the closed door.

'It's Rush,' said Henry.

'Send him away,' replied Robert.

'He's not a fool, he knows something's wrong.'

'We can't let him see this.'

But Henry was already opening the door, relieved to see the butler was alone.

'Come in, Rush.'

'Sir,' he bowed, stepping inside, freezing when he saw the mess on the floor, his face paling.

'Let me explain,' said Henry. 'This is Hobbs, he worked for Matthew. He was the man who murdered my father.'

'Yes, I remember, sir,' he replied, gaping at the corpse.

'He came here with the express purpose of killing Lady Jardyce. Fortunately, Robert was here to stop him.'

Rush's pale face appeared to glow in the darkness. 'He was there at the museum the day your father was killed, sir. I met Lady Jardyce and escorted her upstairs where your father waited. This man was there that day, I particularly noticed because he was so tall and he was staring at us. At the time, I thought he was there to see the exhibits and I never thought any more of it. It was only after her

ladyship had been rescued from Master Edward's house and
Hobbs's description was printed in the newspapers that I connected
him with your father's death.'

'Why have you never mentioned this before?'

'Forgive me, sir, but I couldn't bring myself to. I blamed myself.'

'Why?'

'If I'd mentioned the man to either her ladyship or your father
then Sir Alfred's death might have been avoided.'

Henry felt sorry for him, he looked so stricken. He placed his
hand on his shoulder. 'Don't blame yourself. It's Matthew's fault my
father's dead, not yours.'

'But if I'd only said something,' Rush exclaimed.

'It would have made no difference.'

'You're too kind, sir, kinder than I deserve.'

Now Henry understood Rush's unwavering loyalty to his family,
a loyalty that had never really existed before his father's death.

'Rush, you do understand that we can't have our family going
through another scandal? It would destroy her ladyship, and the
younger children would be very adversely affected, so I propose we
place his body in the crypt and never mention it again.' Henry
decided not to mention Mrs Crowle lying just outside, feeling that
might be a step too far.

They waited in silence for Rush's reply, Henry and Robert
staring intently at the old man as rain gently spattered against the
glass of the conservatory, the breeze whispering around the house.

'A most sensible move, sir,' Rush eventually said.

'I'm relieved you concur,' said Henry, glancing at Robert, who
was equally relieved. 'Robert and I will see to it.'

'And I'll clean up this room. It's such a mess,' sighed Rush. 'I'll
tell the servants who are still up to go to bed, so there's no risk of us
being caught in the act.'

'Thank you, Rush. We are in your debt.'

'Not at all, sir. If I'd been more vigilant, then all this might have been avoided, so it's the least I can do.'

'I doubt it,' said Henry, thinking how tired and old he looked. Soon it would be time for him to retire and he wondered what they'd do without him. He appeared to move even slower as he shuffled out of the room, leaving Henry and Robert with the body.

'I'll fetch the gardener's wheelbarrow,' said Robert, looking down at Hobbs. 'He's so big, we'll need help moving him.'

'Good idea. Just, for heaven's sake, make sure it doesn't squeak.'

'I will,' he said before rushing out.

It was an uncomfortable few minutes for Henry, alone in the dark with a dead body. The lengthening shadows reached across the corpse, making it seem to come alive. Relief filled him when Rush returned, armed with various cleaning apparatus.

'The rest of the servants were delighted to have an early night,' said the butler. 'We won't be disturbed.'

'Excellent,' said Henry, feeling a little better now there was a second living person in the room with him. 'About time,' he added when Robert returned too.

'I greased the wheels so it moves silently,' said Robert, manoeuvring the wheelbarrow into the room.

'Good. Now let's hope we can get him into it.'

It took them several attempts, wrestling with the large, limp slab of flesh until they'd manoeuvred Hobbs into the capacious wheelbarrow, one leg hanging out and an arm stuck up at an awkward angle, as though he was waving.

'That wasn't easy,' panted Robert, sweat dripping off him.

'The hard part isn't over yet. Rush, do you have the key for the crypt?'

'Yes, sir,' he replied, producing it from his pocket and handing it over before returning to the task of cleaning up the blood.

'Thank you. Let's go, Robert. The sooner this night is over, the better.'

Robert was the one who wheeled the barrow out of the door, Henry guiding the way as the darkness closed in around them, swallowing them whole.

Henry continually looked back at the house, afraid of being seen with their macabre delivery, eyes narrowed against the cold wind. Thankfully the rain had stopped. He only lit the lamp once they were a safe distance from the house, which was in darkness, except for a discreet light in the conservatory so Rush could work and another in Amy's bedroom. He gazed longingly at that light, wishing he was tucked up in there with her instead of out here with a murderer and the body of his victim. At least Amy had the comfort of knowing she hadn't killed Hobbs, although she would have to cope with having seen her son murder a man.

The massive wrought-iron gate marking the crypt loomed out at them, the lamplight dancing up and down the metal bars.

Henry unlocked the gate, cringing as it opened with a creak.

'Wait here while I get the door open,' he told Robert, who took the opportunity to put the wheelbarrow down and rest.

Henry cringed again as he unlocked the crypt and dragged open the heavy wooden door, startling a bird in the tree beside him, which rose into the air, screeching in protest.

'Bloody owl,' muttered Robert, a hand to his heart in a futile attempt to calm the frantic thudding.

The air that assailed Henry's nostrils was dank and unpleasant and he was painfully aware that he was inhaling the decomposing vapours of generations of his family. His stomach rolled over and he had to take a moment to steel himself to go inside.

'Are we going to stand here all night?' said an impatient Robert.

Henry stared into the dark pit that he knew he must delve into.

We can't get the wheelbarrow through this doorway, so we'll have to carry him in.'

'How wonderful,' sighed Robert.

Henry turned his back on the door into the crypt and grabbed Hobbs's legs while Robert slid his arms under his shoulders, both groaning beneath the strain as they lifted him out of the wheelbarrow.

Cold, clammy air closed in around Henry as he walked backwards into the crypt, the lamp dangling from his arm throwing fearsome shadows against the walls, highlighting the coffins surrounding them. The wood of some of the oldest coffins had split open to reveal dry, brown skin and the odd wisp of hair. Henry wasn't sure which was more unpleasant – the dusty old corpses or the freshly butchered body he carried covered in congealed blood. The air got danker and thicker the deeper they progressed, the ground sloping downward slightly. Fifty years ago, the crypt had had to be extended as the family grew, so the newer burials had been placed at the back, which Henry thought ridiculous because it meant when a new family member had to be interred, everyone had to disturb those already slumbering down here, but his grandfather hadn't wanted to disturb the dead by moving their coffins, so that's the way it was.

'This is really creepy,' commented Robert. 'Especially knowing we're all going to end up down here one day.'

'I'm trying not to think about it,' replied Henry. His hands were sweating with the strain and at one point, he almost dropped Hobbs's left leg.

They rounded a corner, coming to the most recent section of the crypt. Neat ledges had been set into the walls, each ledge holding a coffin.

'All right, let him go,' said Henry.

Robert dropped Hobbs before wiping his hands on his trousers.

'Isn't there something we can put him in? It's going to look suspicious when the next Alardyce is placed in here and they find a rotting corpse on the floor.'

'I'm hoping that won't happen for a long time but yes, there is. This coffin is mine,' he said, indicating one lying on a ledge to his left.

'You've already got your coffin?' said Robert, thinking this very morbid.

'The traditional ones used in the service are too wide to be stored down here. When my time comes, the plan is for me to be transferred into this. It's also lighter and easier to move. Then the original coffin will be disposed of.'

'Looks like you'll have to order yourself another,' commented Robert.

They hoisted the coffin down off the ledge and loaded Hobbs into it, having to stuff his limbs awkwardly into the narrow box. Then they replaced the lid and heaved it back onto the ledge.

'I need to catch my breath,' said Henry, sitting on the dusty floor, soaked in sweat.

Robert, younger and sprightlier, decided to study the brass plaques on the coffins, finding the ones that belonged to Henry's parents first. 'Would my mother's parents have been placed in here if they hadn't been lost at sea?'

'No. Her father had his own vault in London.'

'Whose coffin is this?' said Robert, indicating the plainest of the lot. 'There's no plaque.'

'No one's,' said Henry.

'There's a body in it,' said Robert, heaving the coffin from side to side.

'I said it's no one,' repeated Henry through gritted teeth, willing him to drop the subject.

'You haven't bumped off someone else and hidden them down here, have you?' said Robert mischievously.

'Don't be ridiculous.'

'It's not Matthew, is it?'

'Why on earth would I have him placed down here?'

'Then who?' He gasped. 'My God. It's Edward, isn't it?'

Henry shot to his feet, bristling with anger. 'Yes, it is, but you will keep that to yourself.'

'So my mother doesn't know? Well, of course she doesn't, she wouldn't countenance the man who did all those horrible things to her resting so close. How could you do this?'

'Because he was my brother and it's what my father would have wanted. How could I have let him be buried in a stinking prison pit with no marker?'

'I'll tell you how – because he was the bastard who nearly killed the woman you claim to love.'

'Don't you dare question my feelings for your mother. She's the centre of my world.'

'In that case, take that outside and burn it,' yelled Robert, jabbing a finger at Edward's coffin.

'I will not commit such an indecent act. Now we need to finish cleaning up the mess you made. Go and get Mrs Crowle and bring her down here.'

'Stop changing the subject.'

'We can discuss it later. Right now, we need to hide the body of the woman you killed before someone stumbles across it.'

Robert left, grumbling to himself, leaving Henry alone with the decaying remnants of his family.

Henry stood before Edward's coffin, wondering if his stepson was right, but he knew he could never bring himself to commit such a desecration. He'd broken most of the morals he held dear just in this one night and he would not break any more.

'I hate you for what you did to Amy,' he told the coffin. 'It wil never leave her. All this stems from your evil,' he said, gesturing to Hobbs's body. 'If it hadn't been for you, we wouldn't be in this posi tion now and Amy wouldn't have been shattered into a thousand pieces again. I bet you're looking up from the hell you're no doub in and revelling in all this, but we'll get through it, and with Hobb and Mrs Crowle finally gone, there's no one left to spoil our little slice of heaven.'

Approaching footsteps made his heart sink. There was still one person.

Henry turned to face Robert, carrying the limp body of his own grandmother, and was startled to realise that he was in a dark lonely place with a man who had murdered three people. He'd always thought he could control Robert but now he realised how ridiculous that assumption was. He had a fully-fledged killer for a stepson but, unlike Edward, he didn't seem possessed of the same frenzied madness. Robert was more like his father – cold and in control, which made him much more dangerous.

'Have you got a spare coffin for her?' said Robert nastily. 'Maybe one that you've set aside for my mother?'

'Actually, I have,' he coolly replied, indicating the ledge below which Hobbs now lay.

Robert dropped Mrs Crowle to the ground and assisted Henry to take the coffin down. Together, they placed her inside, Robert releasing some of his anger by stamping on her wrist, the sound of snapping bone cracking through the crypt.

'Despite what she's done, she was your grandmother,' said Henry. 'Does that mean nothing to you?'

'Not after what she did. Mother was right, she was evil. She wasn't interested in forming a relationship with me. She just wanted to use me to get to Mother and mould me into another version of my father.'

'It seems she was successful in doing both. If only you'd warned s she was in your life, all this could have been avoided.'

Robert's expression was positively malevolent in the shadowy ght cast by the lamp.

'You don't get to preach to me any more, not after this,' he said, esturing to Edward's coffin. 'Mother would never forgive you if she ound out that you'd kept her tormentor here all these years. It's an sult.'

'Nothing changes the fact that your actions almost cost your other her life and it frightens me how easily you disposed of your wn grandmother.'

'I would do the same to anyone who tried to kill my mother, as I now would you.'

'On that we're agreed, but if you think you can use this as a lackmail opportunity, then you're sadly mistaken.'

'Blackmail? The thought never crossed my mind,' Robert said ith a sly smile.

'Of course it did. You're becoming more like Matthew every day.'

'And just like him, I'll go to extreme lengths for her. Where were ou when Edward was torturing her and where were you tonight? lways too late, aren't you? If it had been left to you, she would have een brutally murdered.'

'And if it hadn't been for you, she wouldn't have been put in anger in the first place.'

Robert glared at him, knowing he was right, but his pride revented him from admitting it. 'From now on, you stay out of my fe. At the first sign of interference from you, I'll tell Mother about our little brother here,' he said, gesturing to Edward's coffin. 'And ou will lose her.'

'You underestimate the strength of our relationship.'

'I understand it perfectly, I have Jane.'

'That's not love, it's about possession. You need Jane because she's beautiful and sweet and you think that sweetness will help keep your darker half in check, but it won't, and you'll end up despising her for her goodness, just like Matthew did Esther.'

'Our love is nothing like that. How dare you sully it,' Robert yelled. 'I'm so sick of you preaching at me. I'm tempted to go back to the house right now and tell Mother about Edward just to wipe that sanctimonious look off your face.'

'You won't do that because she's been through enough and you don't want to see her hurt again.'

'Maybe you're right, for now, but one day, she will get over what happened tonight and then I might just let something slip.'

'Do you think she'll ever recover from seeing her firstborn murder someone right in front of her?' He smiled when Robert's gloating grin fell. 'Of course she won't, that will torment her until the day she dies and that is your fault too. Blame me all you like, but this mess is on your shoulders.' When Robert squared up to him, Henry thrust his face into his. 'What are you going to do, snap my neck too?'

'Tempting. I wonder if there's another spare coffin in here?'

'There is. Yours.'

A shiver raced down Robert's spine at the sight of the pine box Henry indicated, knowing his stepson hated to think of his own mortality.

'Are we finished, because I want to return to my wife?' said Henry. 'She needs me.'

'I want to talk to her first,' replied Robert, blocking his way.

'About what?'

'Not your little secret, I'm going to savour that one. I just want to speak to her in private.'

'You want to know if she can look you in the face after seeing you kill a man?'

'You know what? I've really had enough of you for one night.'

With that, Robert walked away, leaving Henry to close the lid of the coffin and attempt to manoeuvre it back onto the ledge alone. Mrs Crowle weighed nothing, but the box did, and he found he was unable to manage it. Instead, he left it on the floor and slid it to one side. No one would question it. At least, he hoped they wouldn't. With any luck, they wouldn't have to return here for a good number of years, although with Robert on the loose, this crypt might quickly fill with bodies.

33

Amy perched on the end of her bed in her nightgown, staring down at her hands. It had taken a long time to wash the blood away, the remnants of Hobbs being extremely stubborn and refusing to go. They looked even rawer than usual after the rough scrubbing with carbolic soap she'd subjected them to, and the skin felt tight and sore.

'Come in,' she said when there was a knock at the door, her voice filled with sadness. She'd assumed it was Henry and was looking forward to feeling his comforting arms around her, but Robert walked in instead.

He stopped in the doorway, noting how she clutched her hands closer to her, which were an awful shade of red, and how her eyes widened.

'Do you want me to go?' he said.

She shook herself out of it. 'No, darling. Come, sit.'

He sat beside her on the bed and gently took one of her hands. 'They look painful,' he commented.

'They are, but they'll be fine again in a couple of days.'

'How are you feeling?'

'Not very good, to be honest, Robert.'

He noted she avoided his eyes. 'Look at me, Mother. Look at me,' he repeated, harder.

Amy had to force her gaze to meet his, not actually seeing her son but seeing the moment he'd plunged that knife into Hobbs's chest.

'I had to do it,' he said, reading her thoughts. 'You know that.'

'I understand why, but seeing you do it...' She closed her eyes and took a deep breath, fearing she would be sick.

'I did it for you, just as you pulled that blade out of Matthew for me.'

She found it hard to argue with that. 'What made you realise?'

'Listening to what you were saying when you were asleep. You truly cared for Matthew and, in a way, I think you loved him.'

She shook her head. 'I love Henry.'

'Of course you do,' he said, swallowing down his annoyance. 'But Matthew was before Henry. I know you loved him, which meant you made the ultimate sacrifice for me. I never abandoned you. When I left the house with Mrs Crowle, I intended to convince her to leave you alone. I thought I could get her to call off Hobbs.'

'You snapped her neck.'

'It was quick and painless and she didn't know anything about it, her back was turned to me at the time.'

'You've killed three people – Mrs Grier, Mrs Crowle and Hobbs.'

'Mrs Grier ran into the pond.' His lips pursed at her ferocious look. 'All right, I admit that one,' he sighed.

'Finally. Three murders, Robert, that's going to take its toll on you. If you think you can go back to how you were before, then you're wrong.'

'I'll be fine.'

'You don't understand what it's like, unless it simply won't bother you like it bothers me.'

'It doesn't. They all tried to kill you, so why should I give them
second thought?' His eyes darkened. 'I would kill anyone who hur
you, I don't care who they are.'

Amy understood that threat was directed against Henry. 'Tha
won't be necessary, thank you.'

'Let's hope so,' he said with a gentle smile. 'It's always been you
and me against the world and it still is. Wasn't it wonderful going
up against them together?'

Amy thought her son was quite deranged, but she didn't allow
him to see that. 'I only hope we don't have to do it again,' she said
wryly.

'It brought it home how similar we are,' he continued eagerly
'Both willing to commit the ultimate act for each other. I saw your
face when you thought Hobbs was going to kill me. You were a
lioness and I was your cub, and I was so proud that you were my
mother.'

'I'd do anything for any of my children.'

'Yes, but with us it's special. All those years together with only
each other for company. Sometimes I miss those days. Don't you?'

'We did have good times,' she tactfully replied, thinking how he
was romanticising the past. He'd just been a child with no idea how
frightening life had been for her, especially at first, until she'd
established an excellent reputation as a governess, fearing where
the money would come from to keep them both fed and clothed,
crying with loneliness when he was asleep because she was
desperate for some grown-up company. All the families she'd
worked for had been kind, but they certainly hadn't sought her
friendship, and nor had the servants because a governess was above
the level of a servant but below the family, caught in a limbo of
isolation, the children her only outlet for conversation. Robert had
seen none of that.

'Are the bodies in the crypt?' she said, wanting to change the subject.

'Yes, have no worries about that, and Rush is cleaning up the conservatory.'

'Rush knows?' she exclaimed.

'It's all right, he's on our side. He saw Hobbs at the museum the day you met your uncle. He thought nothing of it and mentioned it no one; consequently he blames himself for your uncle's death.'

'That explains his loyalty.'

'And why he was following me about the house.'

'Only because he could see the path you were going down long before anyone else, but he has been in this house a long time. He saw Edward grow into...'

'A monster?' he said when she hesitated.

'I wasn't going to say that.'

'But you thought it,' he said darkly.

'Please don't start your word games. I'm extremely tired.'

'Sorry,' he said, kissing her cheek. 'And don't worry about me, I'll be fine. The danger's gone. Now I'm going home to see my beautiful bride.'

'Be kind to her, for my sake if not hers.'

'I've told you I could never hurt her. You think my heart is cold and hard, but not when it comes to Jane – and you. The two people love most in the world.' He raised her hands to his lips to kiss them, detecting the faint scent of blood that still clung to them, and his spine shuddered.

'Are you all right?' she said, a little alarmed by his reaction.

'Fine, just cold and tired.'

'Why don't you spend the night here? I don't like the thought of you returning to the city so late.'

'I need to go home, or Jane will worry.'

'Then take the carriage. Damn, all the servants are in bed.'

'I'll be fine, don't worry.'

'All right. Safe journey,' she said as he kissed her cheek.

'Please try to get a good night's sleep, for me.'

'I'll do my best, but I can't promise anything. I think I'll have some disturbing dreams tonight.'

As Robert left, Amy glimpsed a shadow in the corner, a smirking shadow, but the moment her eyes made contact, i vanished. Cold fear crept up her spine. She wasn't asleep so she couldn't call Matthew's visitations a dream any more.

Amy wondered what sort of man Matthew would have been i he'd had a decent mother. Would he have been a man she could have loved? In those last moments of his life, when they'd collapsed to the floor together from their injuries, their spilled blood mingling, and held each other's hands, she had felt something for him. She used to think that emotion stemmed from the fact that he'd given his life to save hers but, recalling the dream she'd been enjoying before Robert had woken her, she wondered if her son might be right. In the last minutes of Matthew's life, she had genuinely loved him, and that was a bitter pill to swallow. That one heroic act had wiped the slate clean and she'd forgiven him every wrong he'd done her. This epiphany was definitely something she was going to keep from her husband, despite the promise she'd made him. Some secrets weren't meant to be shared.

Amy looked to that shadowy corner of the room, getting the uncomfortable feeling Matthew was still there, keeping vigil waiting for the day she died.

* * *

Henry waited in his bedroom until Robert had gone, unable to bear the sight of that smug face. To think he'd once loved the boy like he was his own son. Now he loathed him, which was going to make life

ery difficult because no matter what Robert did; Amy would
rotect him. Not that he blamed her, she was an excellent and loyal
other. But he'd seen the consequences of his own father being too
nder-hearted towards Edward, which had led to Amy being
reparably scarred and the deaths of at least four women. Henry
as convinced Edward's body count had been much higher.

After Robert's footsteps had faded away, he crossed the hall into
my's room.

'Can I come in?' he said, poking his head around the door.

'Of course you can,' she replied. 'You don't normally ask.'

Her welcoming smile assured him that Robert had kept his
outh shut about Edward's body resting in the crypt.

'I'm sorry for what you had to go through tonight,' he said,
tting beside her. 'But at least you know you didn't kill a man.'

'I wish I had. It would have been preferable to watching Robert
o it. He finally admitted to killing Mrs Grier. My seventeen-year-
ld son has murdered three people. What will that do to him?'

'I wish I could provide you with words of comfort, but it would
e futile. We both know it won't be good. Now Robert is buoyed up
ith self-confidence, thinking he can get away with anything, and
ve got the feeling things are going to get a lot worse.'

Now this arrogant, over-confident and very lethal boy had some
otentially damaging knowledge about him that he would go out of
is way to keep from his wife. Guilt ate at Henry. He and Amy had
romised not to keep any secrets from each other, and he'd been
eeping this from her all these years. Should he tell her now and
eg her forgiveness? But she looked so miserable he couldn't bring
imself to make her feel any worse. He would tell her when she'd
ecovered from this fresh shock. Perhaps.

* * *

'What took you so long?' said Jane, flying into Robert's arms the second he came through the door. 'I've been so worried.'

'It's all right, don't panic,' he smiled.

'You have a cut on your head. I knew it, Hobbs attacked you didn't he?'

'We did have a bit of a scuffle, but that was it.'

Jane looked doubtful. 'A scuffle?'

'Yes, but my grandmother stepped in and calmed everything down. The pair of them have gone.'

'What do you mean, gone?'

'Left, gone on to pastures new. They realised what they were doing was no good for anyone. I think they mentioned France.'

Robert stared into her eyes, willing her to believe his rather pathetic lie. He saw Jane waver, part of her wanting to know the truth, part of her recoiling from it.

'Are Aunt Amy and Uncle Henry all right?'

'Absolutely fine.'

'In that case, I'm glad they've gone,' she eventually said, deciding ignorance was bliss. There was something feverish in her husband's eyes that she didn't like. 'And they won't be back?'

'Absolutely not.'

Another look she didn't like that sent a shiver down her spine. 'Well, that's all right then.'

He kissed her hard, his blood still pumping lava. 'Let's go to bed.'

'To sleep. I'm exhausted, Robert.'

'But...'

'No buts. I've been up the half the night worrying, with no word from anyone at Alardyce House. I need to sleep.'

'Fine. I'll see you in the morning,' he pouted, stomping for the stairs.

'You're still welcome to join me in my bed.'

He bit back the insult that almost flew from his lips and smiled, ot wanting to give her a reason to probe deeper about what had ally happened.

'That's all right, darling, I don't want to disturb you. Get a good ght's sleep and I'll see you in the morning.'

This pleased her and she kissed his cheek on her way past him o the stairs to her bedroom.

Knowing he wouldn't sleep at all that night, Robert prowled e lower level of the house until he felt certain Jane and the rvants were asleep. Then he sneaked out. One reason why he'd osen this house was because it was an easy journey to vienne's.

'Hello, Robert,' beamed Viv when he entered.

He grabbed her, pushed her up against the wall and kissed her.

'It's all right, Corrigan,' she said when he made a move to tervene.

'Is April here?' said Robert.

'Upstairs. She's just finished with another guest.'

'Thanks, Viv,' he said, slapping her on the backside before cing upstairs. He ran to April's room, threw open the door and inned.

'Robbie,' she smiled.

'Don't bother putting your clothes back on.' He looked to the iddle-aged man who sat on the end of the bed, pulling on his ousers. 'Get out.'

'I beg your pardon?' frowned the man.

Robert's gaze darkened. 'Out. Now.'

Nodding, the man gathered up the rest of his clothes and rried out, avoiding Robert's malevolent eyes as he squeezed past m through the doorway. When he'd gone, Robert slammed the or shut and admired April lying naked on the bed. 'I hope he's ot worn you out?'

'Nah, I didn't have to do anything. He just likes to look at m[...] while he makes himself happy. Easy money.'

'In that case, brace yourself,' he grinned before hurling himsel[...] at her, knocking her back onto the bed, thrusting his tongue int[...] her mouth while opening his trousers.

'Someone's keen tonight,' she groaned as he started to poun[...] into her.

'I've had a hard evening,' he panted, delighted when sh[...] groaned with pleasure.

For April, sex was nothing more than a chore, a routine part o[...] daily life, but now she appeared to be revelling in it, clutching at th[...] bedclothes as she moaned and threw back her head, pressing he[...] breasts into his face. In response, he drove into her harder, feelin[...] the sweat bead on his back.

'Robbie,' she cried as she came, saturating him.

With one last powerful thrust, he grunted and spilled himsel[...] inside her.

Spent, he collapsed on top of her, breathing hard, enjoying th[...] exhilaration. Jane didn't like it fast and frantic like that, she[...] expected it to be slow and tender, every time they made love a[...] repeat of their wedding night, when sometimes all he wanted was a[...] good hard fuck and then to get on with his life. April was perfect fo[...] that.

'Robbie... Robbie,' she gasped.

His head snapped up and he was shocked to see his hand[...] wrapped around April's slender white throat.

'God, sorry,' he said, moving his hand.

'You were strangling me,' she cried, slithering out from[...] under him.

'Calm down,' he said gently. 'I wasn't strangling you, I was just[...] resting my hand and I didn't realise I'd put it down on your neck.'

e flashed his most charming smile. 'Come on, you know me. I've
ever hurt you before.'

She relented a little. 'I suppose,' she said in a quiet, scared voice.

He kissed her to distract her. 'It was an accident, that's all.'

'I've been hurt by clients before. I didn't expect it from you,' she
id with a hurt sniff.

'I would never hurt my little April shower, you know that,' he
id, running a hand through her hair, drawing from her a reluctant
mile.

'All right, it was an accident,' she said before kissing him.

Robert dressed, paid his money and left her room, walking on
r. He'd got away with it *again*. He'd been blatantly throttling the
rl and his charm had convinced her she was mistaken, just like
'd got away with killing three people. He could do anything he
ed and he would never pay the consequences. It was a heady
ought, filling him with power as he strutted downstairs.

'I take it you enjoyed yourself?' grinned Vivienne, who was
aiting for him at the bottom of the stairs.

'Don't I always when I come here?'

'You're the first to make April cry out like that. My girls will be
ueuing up for you next time you're in.'

'What a shame I only have eyes for you,' he smiled. 'Andrew
ere?'

'No. He said he wouldn't be in for a couple of weeks. Exams or
omething.'

'Shame. Goodbye, Viv,' he said, bestowing upon her another
ss before flashing the frowning Corrigan a smile on his way out.

As he stalked the streets, the blood continued to thunder
rough his veins. His pleasant encounter with April hadn't done
uch to ease the tension inside him. Footsteps ahead caught his
tention. He saw it was a young woman of his own age, walking at

a brisk pace. Judging by her shabby clothes, she wasn't quality, mos
likely a servant, probably a maid.

His blood surged. Finally, an outlet.

The woman, sensing she was being watched, turned to lool
over her shoulder. When he flashed her a smile, she smiled back
looking less afraid. It really was amazing the effect good looks hac
on people, it made them think you were harmless. Ridiculous
really.

He glanced around to make sure no one was watching befor
pulling his hat down lower, quickening his pace, feeling his mouth
stretch open into a leer as he followed her down a dark, quiet street

MORE FROM HEATHER ATKINSON

We hope you enjoyed reading *The Cursed Heir*. If you did, please leave a review.

If you'd like to gift a copy, this book is also available as an ebook, digital audio download and audiobook CD.

Sign up to Heather Atkinson's mailing list for news, competitions and updates on future books.

http://bit.ly/HeatherAtkinsonNewsletter

ABOUT THE AUTHOR

Heather Atkinson is the author of over fifty books - predominantly in the crime fiction genre. Although Lancashire born and bred she now lives with her family, including twin teenage daughters, on the beautiful west coast of Scotland.

Visit Heather's website: https://www.heatheratkinsonbooks.com/

Follow Heather on social media:

twitter.com/HeatherAtkinso1
instagram.com/heathercrimeauthor
bookbub.com/authors/heather-atkinson
facebook.com/booksofheatheratkinson

Boldwood

Boldwood Books is an award-winning fiction publishing company seeking out the best stories from around the world.

Find out more at www.boldwoodbooks.com

Join our reader community for brilliant books, competitions and offers!

Follow us
@BoldwoodBooks
@BookandTonic

Sign up to our weekly deals newsletter

https://bit.ly/BoldwoodBNewsletter

Milton Keynes UK
Ingram Content Group UK Ltd.
UKHW020646290924
1900UKWH00028B/101